The Ore and the Dross

THE
ORE
AND THE
DROSS

A Novel About Priests

FRED
MERTZ

RICKSHAW PUBLICATIONS

Rickshaw Publications
391 Laurel Avenue
St. Paul, Minnesota 55102

ISBN: 0-9633092-0-X

These are fictional characters. I suspect that local readers may say "This is so and so." He or she is not there. I have sometimes used a pattern of speech, a mannerism or an incident from life, but there are no consistent characters. They are invented persons, including the interlocutor, George Schwartz.

My thanks go to those who read parts of this and encouraged me: Sisters Anne Redmond, Mary Virginia Micka, and Margery Smith; to John and Maggie Murphy, Shirley Donovan, John Malone, and especially to Frances Rand, who endured either reading or having read to her a good portion of the book. Thanks also to Ellen Foos who edited this volume.

ONE

✖

The Retreat

It was a rainy night in June, the year, 1947; what came to be known in later years as THEE retreat. There we sat in choir stalls; in imitation of the monastery arrangement. In point of fact, much of seminary life had been shaped by monastic life going way back to the sixteenth century, to the counter-Reformation, the Catholic Church's response to Martin Luther. Choir stalls faced toward each other, so that one had to turn to the side in order to see the altar, or on this night to see the rather short, sixty-year-old man with a slightly owlish face who sat rather than stood, as he delivered his conferences, as his five daily sermons were called.

From my present distance, a full forty-five years, the whole scene seems enormously funny; 350 of us, dressed in cassocks, black dresses in effect, and little three-corner hats (birettas), on our heads, sitting on a Sunday evening listening intently to an old and unhappy priest. Here we were, young Americans, dressed in these medieval costumes, because some people in faraway Rome had decided it was important. It was as if, like Alice, we'd wandered through the looking glass into the sixteenth century. As I say, it's funny now, but it seemed very obviously sane and right to every one of us at the time. Since then, I've seen the same sort of easy acceptance of strange dress and manners with fraternal orders like the Knights of Columbus or I imagine, the Shriners, or any similar fraternities. Such is the marvelous human capacity for compliance.

The chapel was almost devoid of human noise; the usual shuffling of garments reduced to a minimum; no coughs could be heard. The human silence seemed to amplify the distant thunder. Retreats lasted six days and occurred in September as the school year began, and this one in June, which marked the end of the school year and was the week which led to the ordination of deacons and priests. The silence was partially fueled by anxiety. The retreat master had us in his grasp for most of a week. If he was boring or caustic, it could add up to a long week. Even Frank Cody, who usually made staccato wisecracks, was quiet.

The retreat master, Father Jonquill Adams of the Redemptorist Order looked out at us from his chair. His expression seemed to convey that he was not very pleased with what he saw.

"This," he said, "is a silent retreat. There is to be no, I repeat, no conversation among you during these six days. Monsignor Slovene tells me that last fall, some of you, while preserving silence, engaged in what is called 'touch football' with considerable signalling." He said "touch football" with a disdain that suggested something both erotic and evil. "There will be none of that in this retreat."

Frank Cody groaned aloud, which caused the good priest to look toward the disturbance. Cody turned and looked at me. I turned red, and Father Jonquill decided that I was the culprit.

"If you disturb this assembly once more, I will have the rector place you in a chair next to me. Do you understand?" Since he was looking directly at me, I had little choice but to shake my head affirmatively. He went on. "Beginning tomorrow, the conferences will be promptly at nine a.m., eleven, two-thirty and four p.m., and at this hour, seven-thirty." He paused then as if to shift into another gear.

"I knew a priest once who was the most promising seminarian in his class. The bishop appointed him to the chancery. Everyone assumed that he was destined for higher things. Each morning as he offered Mass for the nuns, they marveled at his pious sermons. After a year he began to give instructions to a very handsome woman of the parish in which he lived. She would accept no one else as instructor, even though he was only supposed to live in the rectory, and had no parochial duties. At about this time, he enrolled in night classes at the secular university, classes in modern philosophy." As Father Jonquill pronounced the words "modern philosophy", it was clear that it ranked right up there with "touch football."

"He continued to instruct the young lady, and behind closed doors."

Cody, his face well hidden, whispered, "Yeah. Abelard!" It brought a few guarded chuckles, not loud enough to disturb the preacher.

"In that very year, with his mind corrupted by atheistic philosophy, and his body inflamed by this temptress, he left the priesthood and then died three years later, a disgrace to the Church and his aged mother as well."

There was a great silence in the chapel as this grisly lesson sunk in. He played the dramatic pause well, letting us feel, as it were, the fires of hell licking at our ankles. This sort of thing was expected in retreats. There was the idea that the beginning of wisdom was fear of the Lord. After a well established dread of hell and its horrors, the soul could deal with the milder motivations of love of Jesus. Tomorrow, no doubt, the retreat master would inspire us with the love of God. But not that night! Jonquill managed to fill the rest of the hour with tales of more and more Judases. When the conference mercifully ended and Benediction began, I found that I was more than a little relieved, and walked back to the red-brick dormitory, shaken but still optimistic about the morrow. The rain had stopped, but the great elm and oak trees still dripped on our stiff birettas. The twilight gave no promise of a sunnier Monday.

Back in my room (or rooms, because as a fourth year man I had both a bedroom and a study in the ancient dormitory), I read some of the spiritual book I had selected for retreat, Chesterton's *Thomas Aquinas*. I felt mildly guilty for selecting such a gay and literary work. Possibly, I should have picked out a more dolorous book. Or at least a work serious about sin and virtue. At nine-thirty, I went dutifully to the can, which would shortly be the only lighted area, since the individual rooms were all darkened at ten p.m. Frank Cody was in the washroom smoking, which was forbidden, as was talking during the "grand silence" which began at nine p.m. and ended after breakfast in non-retreat times.

Frank routinely ignored both the smoking ban and the grand silence, but was not talking then, solely because the only other occupant, Gerald Fox, was a rigid rule keeper, and would not respond to any conversation after the grand silence began. Fox was quietly brushing his teeth. As soon as Frank saw me, he asked, "From under what rock did old Adolph find this sourpuss?" Adolph was Monsignor Slovene, the rector. "This is going to be a God-awful long week."

I said, "Thanks, jerk, for setting me up." Frank laughed, "Why didn't you look at someone else as the disturber?"

"Because I was already blushing."

"George, that's your trouble. You're more of a worry wart than ol' Jerry here. Ain't that right, Jer?"

Gerald Fox ignored us both, his stiff backside able somehow to convey his disapproval of our immoral trampling of the sacredness of the grand silence. Frank, now sitting on one of the sinks, blew out a cloud of forbidden smoke. I said, "Maybe tomorrow, he'll strike a more positive note."

"Oh, he'll be positive, all right, positive that we're all going to hell in a handcart." The conversation stopped there

4

because someone on the second floor, two floors down, banged the wake-up bell just loud enough to indicate that the dean was on the way up. We both ran back to our rooms, leaving Fox to explain why the washroom was full of smoke. Rigid though he was, we knew he'd never tattle.

I remember that I had trouble getting to sleep that night, which was a rarity, because we were up very early every day, and in addition to studies, usually engaged in athletics for an hour or two. What kept me awake was not what the gloomy retreat master had said. I had confidence in those days that I'd never sell out like those fallen away priests. The priests I knew weren't like that: old Father Walsh from the home parish; the priests from Dowling Hall, the minor seminary; and the guys I'd known as seminarians. No, what bothered me was a passing remark of Frank Cody's about me being full of guilt. Cody probably made one hundred remarks like that every day, but sometimes he hit the mark as he had this time. I was a man full of guilt and fear. It was guilt that brought me to the seminary.

I remember sitting with my parents, Father Michael Walsh, the home town pastor, and Monsignor Thomas O'Brien on registration day at Dowling Hall. O'Brien, the rector was a patrician looking man. He was later a bishop in the east. He had the easy look of a man born to command. He asked me, "Mr. Schwartz," (I'd never been called 'Mr.' in all my fifteen years) "Mr. Schwartz, have you a religious vocation?" I wasn't prepared for the question, but it seemed to me the kind of question you'd better not hem and haw about. "Yes." I said, and immediately felt guilty. Guilty on two levels. First, that probably nobody could know if he had a vocation, and therefore the rector had caught me in a kind of lie. Right off the bat, too, before I was even registered. But the second level was more serious and more complex. How could I, George Schwartz, sitting in the rector's high-ceilinged, white-painted, almost bare room, with the huge, uncluttered desk, possibly explain how I ended up here? And in the presence of these people, my parents, my pastor and this aristocratic monsignor? How could I explain the web of fear that brought me into this spare room with the gigantic clock making large noises every two minutes as it moved ahead? The truth was that I thought God, not I, had decided that I was to be a priest. I thought the whole life looked gloomy; dealing with whispered sins in the horrid little room called the confessional; dealing too, with sick folks and death and burial, and all that seven days a week. And then going into the red-brick house where old Father Walsh lived alone, although an old lady came in each day to cook his meals.

But God wanted me to do this. Worse, at age twelve in some kind of a fix, maybe with parents or teachers or classmates; I'd forgotten what the thing was that prompted me to do it, but I'd said to God, "O.K., You get me out of this and I'll do it. I'll go be a priest." A promise almost forgotten a day later, but it sat there, stored in some dim, murky part of my brain where it grew like a cancer and finally one night, I blurted out to my parents. "I want to be a priest." They looked a little surprised. And this was what brought me into Dowling Hall before a future bishop, the then rector, who asked me an unanswerable question: "Do you have a vocation?" Later on, two years down the pike, a senior in high school, I'd learned that a twelve-year-old's promise to God can be annulled by a single word from a confessor and it probably wouldn't be valid in the first place. By then though, I'd fallen in love with the place. First of all, the setting was a pleasant surprise. Whenever I'd heard the name, Dowling Hall, for some reason, I'd pictured a dull looking building, like a jail or the old folks home in my town of Sioux Lake. Dowling was in fact a beautiful brick building with magnificent twin towers, stone floors, long bright hallways and large well-lighted study halls, and a gym, a theater, and a magnificent library full of books which were much more interesting than my textbooks. All this was located on Brown's Lake, with gracious large grounds which led into 200 acres of woods. Well, the place was not what kept me there for those two years of high school and two of college. No, it was the entire wholesome enterprise; the day begun with prayer and Mass; the sense of preparing for a useful life. It was great to live with guys who lived by conscience, by high moral standards and who wanted to serve people. So, even though I felt free of those promises to God, I stayed because I really wanted to be a priest. Since I'd come in the third year of highschool, and most of the class had been together for two years and had established friendships, it was a little hard breaking in, but I'll tell about that later. So what had begun in fear had evolved into love. Still there were funny old tapes running in my head; like did I mostly love God or fear him? That was the tape running through my head that night.

I don't remember each and every day of that week, or every moment, but it did rain every day. I do remember laying awake for a while that night, so that I suppose the five-forty a.m. bell that next morning might have been particularly cruel, but then it always was. The routine was always the same. We all rushed to the washroom, and after relieving ourselves, tried to get a sink. There were not quite enough because those were the days of many seminarians. Forty-five years later, as I write this, there are less than a third of the number we had in those days. If you couldn't get a sink, you gathered around a big basin where four or five guys would be sort of communally brushing their teeth, and you had to be careful not to spit at the same time that another would be extending his brush to the water tap.

No one spoke. The grand silence was still on, but it was easier to keep at that early hour, because nobody wanted to speak in the first place. Eventually you got to have a sink. Then, back to the room; put on the cassock and down to the oratory for morning prayer. That was over in about five minutes, and then meditation. Meditation was a well-meant exercise, but from the hindsight of forty-five years, it strikes me as self-defeating. First of all, the hour was ill-conceived. There would be a voice, the man assigned to lead that week, saying, "First prelude, Jesus in the garden of Gethsemane." The idea was that then you were supposed to picture Jesus in the bloody sweat. I'd try, and I suppose that everybody did. After about five minutes, the same voice would shatter you out of sleep to announce, "Second pre-lude, Jesus takes all of the guilt of our sins upon himself." Then, I'd really try to get into that. My sins causing him all that suffering. But then, out of some faraway place, the voice would say, "Third prelude, Jesus accepts the chalice of suffering." And, for a brief time, we'd all be awakened. But there was a greater problem than our sleepiness. It was a little like a force-fed friendship, like a mother who might say to her eight-year-old, "Why don't you go play with Ronald, the boy next door?" So you'd go and try to play with him, but neither child would want to play, so it would come to nothing. It might have worked better if the adults had stayed out of it. What was wanted, of course, was a good personal relationship with Jesus, but like all relation-ships, it needed space to grow. Most friendships do not spring up formally, like having to cultivate Ronald. Instead, they grow informally. You might be sitting in a classroom, smiling at something the teacher said, something she didn't mean to be funny, but the guy across the aisle sees you smile and has had the same reaction. So, at recess, you talk about it, and before you really know why, you are together a lot and become fast friends. Well, I know that a relationship with the Lord is different, but somehow the meditation books in the oratory were soporific. At six-thirty, medita-tion was over and the 200 yard walk to the main chapel woke us up, so that we could take part in the Mass more at-tentively. Monsignor Slovene said the Mass in mournful tones, but he was honestly mournful, so I was not turned

8

off by him. Around the chapel were eight small altars at which the faculty said separate-but-equal Masses. They muttered the Latin quietly, so as not to disturb the main Mass. Well, most of the time. Monsignor Baker had been known, when irritated, to say the whole canon of the Mass out loud, precisely *to* disturb the main Mass. He could be easily irritated; if the sacristan, a seminarian, forgot to put out his vestments, or, worst of all, gave out his altar to a visiting priest. The fact that the canon was to be said silently, and some ruled that it was a mortal sin not to do so, did not deter him. After the Vatican Council, the idea of priests saying Mass in this separate fashion was thought to be liturgically and theologically fallacious and the practice became pretty much abandoned.

Mass over, we went, in silence, to the refectory for breakfast. After all these years, that simple daily silent march of 350 young men sticks in my memory warmly, and I don't understand why. Perhaps it is an unacknowledged nod to the value of that kind of discipline. At breakfast, most times, we could talk; the "grand silence" over. Not during retreat, though, for one of the students would read from a "spiritual" book amid the clatter of plates. So it must have been that morning, like so many more mornings of our seemingly endless journey toward priesthood.

I do remember the first conference that morning, because, unlike my classmate, Cody, I really expected the retreat master to get away from the gloom of ex-priests into something more optimistic and happy. He began, as the night before, "I knew a priest once . . . " This priest, he told us, took off with his housekeeper late on a Saturday night or early Sunday morning, so that when the parishioners came for Sunday Mass, there was no Mass. The scandal was seen by all of them, and, when they went to the rectory, they discovered that the two had stripped the rectory of the silverware, the china and much furniture. The people of the parish were so stunned, that they never took legal action.

Cody, hand covering his mouth, sniggered, "Now these are role models that I can identify with."

But Jonquill didn't stop there; he managed two more priestly defections in the next half-hour. When the good Father Jonquill mercifully finished his list of clerical miscreants, he announced that there would be no conference at eleven a.m., so that if anyone wished to go to confession or consult him for spiritual advice, he'd be in his room. I couldn't imagine the waiting line would be very long.

Outside the chapel the heavy rain had stopped, and only a very soft drizzle, scarcely more than a heavy dew, was falling. Since there was a full two hours before I had to be anywhere, I decided to take a walk. St. Anselm's Seminary in St. Paul, on the banks of the Mississippi, consists of forty acres of beautiful grounds, with magnificent elms and oaks. The grounds were well-kept in those days, and a favorite pastime was to "walk the perimeter." I say "favorite pastime" because we weren't allowed off the campus except for brief times on Wednesday and Saturday afternoons. The idea, I guess, was to protect us from the corruptions of the world, the flesh and the devil, more or less in that order. And so, in free time, we walked endlessly around the "perimeter," discussing studies, sometimes personal problems, but, most often, the real and imaginary peculiarities of our profs. At the time, we accepted the restriction to the campus without much demur, but years later, it struck me as a poor form of discipline. In one of the parishes I later served, a family had trained their German Shepherd to halt at the boundaries of their property. They were very proud that the dog, even in pursuit of a cat or squirrel, would stop at the edge of their yard, almost as if there was a fence. Possibly I overstate the comparison, but the training seems more Pavlovian than human maturing.

The campus, while lovely, had various moods; in winter, the great trees, bare and stark against the white snow had an elegance different from the brilliance of the reds and yellows of fall. On a dark and rainy June day, the trees, abundantly leaved, seemed to increase the darkness and had a gloomy and almost forbidding quality like a landscape out of Poe. Yet, as I walked the perimeter, alone and silent, the large and somber trees gave me a kind of comfort and relief from the dolorous messages of the good Father Jonquill. Still, he'd gotten to me. I felt confident of my own self-mastery and loyalty, but then, did those other men as seminarians, have a similar conviction of virtue? Ought I to look for Judas-like tendencies in my own soul? Despite these dark thoughts and the dark and dreary day, I came back to my room less despondent, perhaps buoyed up by the exercise. I had a kind of detachment from the retreat and the retreat master, even the beginning of rebellion against him. Father Jonquill continued his litany of fallen priests that day and on the next day and still the next. He must have done formidable research. The cloudy, dark, drizzly days were a match for the good Father. And we, poor and doomed souls, continued to go to his lugubrious sermons. Although, I noticed Cody's place in chapel vacant at times. On Wednesday night Father Jonquill gave us, at long last, a change of pace. He lectured us on holy obedience. How we must as fledgling priests, obey our pastors. I remember one sentence, almost word for word. He said, "If your pastor tells you to go out and cut the front lawn with a tweezers, that is what you do." There was a rather large sigh across the chapel. It was a compound of ennui and pent up laughter. It did not deter the preacher. He continued to harangue us on absolute obedience. There was one other notable response. Gerald Fox, who had been faithfully taking notes, stopped. Nor did he take one more note the rest of the retreat. By this time I had devised a theory about the retreat master, perhaps, in order to preserve my sanity. I decided that other priests, seeing his penchant for scandal, made up stories, stories he could use to add to his repertoire.

It was, however, on Thursday morning that he outdid

himself. He told us a story about a seminarian in an eastern minor seminary. He had met with some old friends who regaled him with dirty stories. In fact, he walked away so as not to hear more. That night, however, he though about those smutty tales and committed the solitary sin (masturbation). That night he died, and he appeared to the rector of that minor seminary, and explained that he was sent to hell because of that solitary sin. "It is," said Jonquill, "plainly recorded in the history of that seminary." That did it. The smoldering rebellion which had been growing within me exploded. I did indeed believe, as had been taught, that masturbation was a mortal sin. I had never done it. I had read psych books which contended that 96% of boys had masturbated; others 93% and still others 100%. I didn't believe them. I knew that they were wrong; at least the man was who contended the 100%, if he meant a full 100%. At any rate the penalty in Jonquill's story was way out of proportion. And what kind of old wive's tale was this anyway? This had been the nine a.m. conference and I stewed over it all day. Seminarians in those days seldom confronted or even questioned priests. In addition, I was quite shy and almost never challenged my elders. As I look out now at the present time, such confrontations of authority are expected, routine. At that period of my life, I can hardly understand what prompted me to upbraid this figure of authority, to beard this lion in his den.

Perhaps my anger needed relief; perhaps free of sexual sin, I felt that I was not being defensive, but appropriately confrontative.

"Come in."

I walked into the sparsely furnished "visitors room" in the faculty residence. He glowered his welcome. "Did you want to go to confession?"

"No."

"Did you want some spiritual counsel?

"No."

"Then what?"

"I want to talk about the retreat. What are you trying to do?"

"I'm trying to warn you of the dangers of infidelity."

"That story today; that God would send him to hell for one miscue. Especially when he took himself away from the lewd stories."

"It is recorded in the seminary files."

"Do you think people routinely visit others on their way to hell?"

"Young man, I've given hundreds of retreats. I don't need any advice from a hotheaded novice like you."

"It's the most negative, least grace-filled retreat I've ever attended."

"Young man, if you want to go to confession or want spiritual advice, I'll accommodate you. Otherwise, I'll ask you to leave."

"Gladly." I said. And that was the end of the retreat for me. I took a walk that night, and though the light rain was still falling, the weather was no longer oppressive for me. I had bearded the old lion in his den and had, at least in my mind, beat him. I had a feeling of lightness as I walked through the gloom.

That night the gang was gathered in the "can" and were talking and smoking, the retreat over for them as well. Gerald Fox was the only silent one. He was quietly brushing his teeth. As I came in, Frank Cody pretended not to see me since he was facing away from me, but I knew he'd picked up my image in the mirror. Every class had at least one mimic, and Frank was ours. In a perfect imitation of the mournful retreat master, he began, "I knew a priest once, let's call him by the fictional name of Schwartz. Well, this Schwartz was a holy man; he was as pure as an angel; sometimes purer. But on his twenty-fifth anniversary as a priest, an old highschool flame came back to see him, and one thing led to another, and they ended up in bed. But, you see his equipment was so rusty and unused that he wore himself out in the effort and he died, and, of course, went directly to hell—well, not directly, because he stopped off to say goodbye to his old rector who was in a rest home and didn't know what day it was, but he gave him a blessing which, of course, did no good, since he was already judged. He said 'goodbye' to his former pastors, but they weren't surprised. He said 'goodbye' to his assistant priests and they weren't surprised either when he told them he was on the way to hell. Then he said 'goodbye' to the trustees of the parish and they were glad, because now they could get a replacement, then he went to the archivist so they would take a record, and then he went to the bishop and told him where he was going and the bishop said, 'I told you to go to hell a long time ago.' Last of all he went to his old classmates and everyone of them said, 'Frankly, we don't give a damn.' Oh, excuse me, George, I didn't see you come in."

Cody was funny and he had captured both the dolorous tone of Jonquill as well as the content. We all laughed hilariously and I even thought that I caught a grin on the face of the scrupulous rule keeper, Gerald Fox. Cody was genuinely funny, but I suspect that the heartiness of our laughter came from a deep substratum of our collective guilt-feelings, where both anger and fear were stored. I had, at that moment, no thought of sharing my confrontation with the good Jonquill, but I had not sufficiently foreseen the fact-finding ability of Frank Cody.

Turning to me, Cody said, "It is rumored that George was in the retreat master's room this very eve. We would never ask what sort of dark future plans you were discussing with Father Gloom and Doom."

So I told them all what I had done. Cody, taken aback, said, "Schwartz, sometimes you amaze me, but, dammit guy, good work."

The crowd I hung around with were all there that night, half of them smoking, all of them ignoring the smoking ban. We had been fed a diet of guilt overkill, and we were defiant against all the rules, for that moment, at least. Frank Cody sat on a sink, the class clown and the center of attention now. He had jet-black hair, blue, laughing eyes, a slim build, and general Irish good looks. Not merely a clown, he was the cynic from the east, with a Bronx accent so pronounced, I sometimes wondered if he didn't exaggerate it. Sophisticate that he was, and carefully groomed, it was a bit of a surprise that there was a little patch of hair above his upper lip, hardly enough to be called a mustache. For a fastidious man like Cody, this could not be an oversight. A real full blown mustache might have drawn anger from the faculty; this wisp of hair might have been a careful statement of rebellion.

After Gerald Fox left the washroom that night, there were the six of us, the gang, the guys who made the almost prison-like routine of the seminary livable, fun even. There were forty of us in the fourth year class; most of us from the archdiocese of St. Paul; the rest from the other dioceses of Minnesota and from the neighboring states of Iowa, Wisconsin, the Dakotas, etc. Seminary authorities encouraged class unity, to be supportive of the other members of your class. This we really did. We might joke about Gerald Fox's rigidity, and guys like Cody would kid him directly, but Fox had an honorable place in the class and if someone from another class made a negative remark about Fox to one of us, we'd defend him. While there was this kind of cohesion within the class, there were gangs inside the larger group and the six of us tended to hang together, not exclusively, but mostly.

Cody was a lot of fun, but my close friends were Thompson and Foley. The three of us went out together on three-fifteen's, those were the brief Wednesday and Saturday times when we could go off campus. We walked the pathways along the Mississippi River and usually finished with the almost obligatory malted milk at the corner drug store.

On campus we talked endlessly of our profs, our studies, our families, but mostly our futures. There sat Bill Thompson on the washroom floor, his six foot, 180 pound athletic frame too large to sit on a sink like Cody. He had his Scandinavian mother's blond good looks; almost as handsome as his sister. Pipe firmly clasped in his mouth, he was content mostly to listen that night; he pulled his pipe out of his mouth from time to time to emit deep chuckles.

Bob Foley also had a pipe with him that night; but he had it in his hand most of the time, too busy lambasting the retreat to smoke. Bob, another six-footer, black haired, dark complexioned, "black Irish," as some said, was prouder of his half-Welsh ancestry, which, he claimed was the source of his deep melodic voice. Among other things, Bob was the class intellectual; it was he who taught me about liturgy. He was a quiet and gentle critic of the way both liturgy and dogma were taught at St. Anselm's. At the moment he was not a quiet critic. "Did you hear one gospel value in the whole retreat?"

Clem Bartosh, Bohemian eyes sparkling with mischief, said, "Maybe not gospel, but solid morality; like that prime example of occult compensation; the priest and housekeeper who stripped the rectory."

Foley said, "Now what in hell is that supposed to mean?"

"Well, housekeepers are always underpaid. The same with priests. See, like the Israelites leaving Egypt. They took a few things along."

"As I said at the time," said Cody, "I value these new role models. The retreat opened whole new horizons of opportunity for me."

I said, "I can see you stripping some one-room rectory in Lost Gulch, South Dakota." Though from the east, Cody was studying for the Rapid City diocese, and his friends, all of us, wondered how this guy from the Bronx was going to fare in those tiny, windswept villages in South Dakota.

"Never you fear that ol' Frank is going to rot in some podunk. First thing I do is get something on the bishop and then make him keep me in Rapid City. "

Thompson, still sitting on the floor, took his pipe out of his mouth to say, "My favorite story was the guy who ran off with the highschool cheerleader. It gives me hope."

Tom Ryan broke in, "Do you suppose these are true stories?" I gave my theory. "I think whenever Jonquill goes back to the monastery, they feed him this stuff, 'cause they know he'll bite."

"I wouldn't be too sure. You know, when you read about celibacy in the middle ages, it was routinely ignored." That from Foley.

I said, "C'mom, Bob, then is not now. Can you imagine Monsignor Baker or old Slovene or any of these profs fooling around?"

"Who'd have 'em?" ventured Cody from his sink.

Cody was the clown; Bill the athlete; Bob, the brains; but it was Tom Ryan who was the class leader. He now got serious. "We ought not to let Slovene get by with this. Don't tell me he didn't know what Jonquill was like. The retreat sounded like old Adolph Slovene himself."

"So what are you going to do? impeach the rector?"

The door of the "can" opened, and the guys who were smoking started to snuff them out, thinking it was the dean. It was Ross Cox, a deacon from the other building. Tom continued talking as Ross waved a hello. "We can't do a damn thing, but our pastors can raise hell with the bishop, with all of our bishops. Slovene isn't very popular with any of them. It'd put real pressure on him."

Cox had just come in, but that didn't slow him down. Cox, small in stature, was big in self-assurance. He smiled at Tom and said, "You guys never get priorities straight." Before he could say another word, Cody stood up as if to leave. "Time to go, fellows, we are about to get THEE SPEECH." Cox had spent the previous years at St. John's seminary in St. Cloud, and was always comparing the two, with ours a very poor second. Cox went on, totally ignoring Cody. "A week from now Jonquill is nothing, a poor sad sack we'll never remember; if you want to raise hell, it should be about the lousy teaching you're getting."

"What did I tell you? The man from the great St. John's, the wunderkind." Cody hadn't really left.

Cox still paid no attention." We are being sent out to preach and teach with the worst scripture teaching in the country, strike that, in the world."

"Geez, Cox, I thought your gripe was theology and liturgy." From Cody, still on top of the sink.

"Those also, smart ass, but scripture is worse."

Thompson took the pipe out of his mouth long enough to say, "So he's got a sing-song voice that drives you nuts, and, yes, he's dull."

"That's not my point at all. Let me ask you, distinguished scholars, how many know what *'Divino Afflante Spiritu'* is?"

From the floor Bob Foley raised a hand."

"It's white Italian fudge," offered Cody.

"It is, dear second theologians, the papal encyclical opening up the bible to literary criticism. It's four years old and not a breath from our scripture prof."

Thompson was getting tired of Cox. "So what? The Bible is the Bible; it's not going to change. Why the fuss?"

"Because the interpretation is going to change mightily. Let me try another question on the biblical scholars. Who wrote the Pentateuch?

A chorus answered, "Moses."

He turned on Cody. "The whole thing?"

Cody with some suspicion, "This is a trick question, right? Like some scribe took it down in shorthand?"

"No tricks; the whole thing, yes or no?"

"Yes."

"How about the part about Moses death? Did he write that too?" There was a pause among us fine scholars as we faced this turn in the discussion. Clem Bartosh responded first. "No big deal. So some scribe wrote that part about his death. What us true scholars call *'obiter dictu'*, an extra line or two."

"Oh, is that so? The biblical commission in Rome has been known to call in errant biblicists and demand that they acknowledge Moses as the writer of your so-called *'obiter dictu'*. One more question before you scholars fall asleep dreaming of Jonquill's hell."

"Shouldn't you be getting back to your residence before they lock you out?" Cody smirked at Cox.

"Shut up, child, I'm on a roll. The question is 'Who were Adam and Eve?'"

Frank answered quickly, "Our first parents. I got this from Sister Matilda, in first grade via the Baltimore Catechism, number two. Although Coxie, you may have descended from some more primitive ancestors like maybe gorillas."

"I shall ignore this juvenile persiflage. The facts are that most progressive Catholic biblicists, freed from servitude by the aforesaid *'Divino Afflante Spiritu'*..."

Cody interrupted, "There's that Italian fudge again."

Cox went on, "have reached a consensus that the whole first part of Genesis is not historical, but a series of—uh—let's say parables about sin."

I said, "I don't believe that. What would happen to our whole understanding of original sin?"

Ross Cox looked at me malignly. "What indeed?" he said, as he started toward the washroom door. Tom Ryan, face reddening with anger, stopped Cox. "Don't just shoot off your mouth and run. You've made some pretty sweeping statements. My turn to ask a question. In two days you are going to be ordained, and you will take the oath against modernism. Much of what you just said goes directly contrary to it. I'd really like to know how you are going to take that oath?"

Cox looked at the angry Ryan superciliously. "I suppose

with my fingers crossed, like Galileo when the same sort of people forced him to say that the sun went around the earth." And with a chuckle he went out. Tom was still boiling. "You heard him. That's heresy if I ever heard it. I wish I were a tattletale. The rector and the archbishop ought to know. Heresy!"

Bob Foley had been sitting on the floor with a half smile during Cox's performance. "Take it easy, Tom; take it easy. That's not heresy. What he said is true, mostly anyway." Bob was the scholar in the group, but Ryan was the leader, and his anger now turned on Foley. "I've had about as much shit as I can handle this week, and now you—" Ryan was the class leader, but Foley would have been, if there were no Ryan. It was interesting to watch the struggle for primacy between them. It would grow bitter in later years. Now Foley looked calmly at Ryan and said, "Tom, it's too bad that Cox came across so arrogantly, because he's right about the Bible. Catholic biblicists are going to change a lot of things." "Not for me!" said the exiting Ryan.

The parley broke up then, and we retired to our rooms; me somewhat relieved as a non-smoker to get to the pure air of my room.

Cox had made two prophecies that night; one was dead right; the other was dead wrong. He was right when he talked about the role of scripture changing things; if we'd have pressed him, he'd have said the same about our dogmatic theology and moral theology. Even history; an entirely different Luther, for example, would arise from revisionists. Sociological change would come also, and all these factors would recast radically the stability of both our institutional and personal lives.

Cox was dead wrong when he said we'd soon forget Jonquill. Forty-five years later, I could dial any of a dozen priests who had been there and ask, "Do you remember that retreat master who began each conference with, 'I knew a priest once—'" and they'd all say, "yes." I suppose if the printed T-shirt was in vogue in those days, we'd have been wearing shirts saying, "I survived the retreat of 1947." But not everyone did. There were always a few people who announced at the end of the school year that they wouldn't be back in the fall. That June the number was doubled. Such was the effect of this sad man who, in effect, told us that a lot of us would default on our vows. Worst of all, the son of a bitch was right.

TWO

The End of the Beginning

That summer (1947) was the best summer of my life. In line with what was to happen later, it was even better than I then realized. It compares only to eight years earlier, in 1939, at the end of my first year at Dowling Hall, the minor seminary. Someone either has written or will write the history and significance of the minor seminary in the life of U.S. Catholicism. At one time, thousands of North American boys rushed off to minor seminaries across the nation; some encouraged by zealous young priests; some by zealous parents; some few almost coerced by aforesaid parents; and some influenced by nuns; and, not a few, by their own volition. The largest number were just out of grade school, pubescent and pre-pubescent, some idealistic, some already opportunistic; mostly well motivated, if generally callow and unacquainted with the ways of man and perhaps of God. Each September they came from city, and town and farm, ready to "test" their vocations, as the phrase went. Attrition was huge. Some left within the month, overwhelmed by homesickness; others gradually through the year, bored by seminary routine, finding the romantic glow dulled by reality. An exuberant freshman class of, say sixty, was literally decimated to six hardy survivors, at the end of five or six years.

The theory, the root idea, was European; to keep the youth clean and uncontaminated by worldly pleasures and ambitions, to borrow St. James' phrase, "unspotted by this world." The notion is passé now. Sometime in the '60's or '70's, it was decided by the men who decide such things that highschoolers would be better off in their parental home, the home which inspired their priestly ambitions in the first place. And so, one by one, across the United States, the minor seminaries closed like fast food franchises which had lost their customers. Some few survive, relics of the past, dinosaurs of an obsolete heritage. Many priests applauded; judging that those students, brought up in a monasterial environment, away from the "world," were singularly inept to minister to it. My own appraisal is more ambivalent. Perhaps the test of its value came when Dowling Hall was sold out of the "family," as it were, to a more robust Protestant group. We old Dowling grads were moved by a mixture of anger and sadness. Sometimes when speaking to old grads who had not revisited Dowling, I used to add fuel to the fire by claiming, with malign mendacity, that the new owners had painted out the marble chapel with a pale Protestant white.

But what was it? What was the spirit, the elixir, which arouses such warm recall after fifty years? Certainly it could not be the grounds, attractive as they were; well groomed lawns graciously sloping into Brown's Lake; or the 200 acres of woods. Nor the building itself with its wings; the magnificent marble chapel, the "crypt" underneath where the faculty celebrated (well, mumbled quietly) their individual Masses; the very plain dining room wing and kitchen which included the residence for the dedicated German nuns who served us so selflessly; the large auditorium and the library above it; the wide, bright main corridor, spacious classrooms along side and in the basement below; above were small apartments for the faculty and single rooms for the college men. Not attractive were the large dormitories where the highschool lads variously slept, snored, dreamt and often mumbled in their sleep.

That was the stage. The actors were God, the faculty, the students, and less noticed, but invaluable, the sisters and a few lay employees.

God, whom we loved and feared; the God we loved who had come down and died for us; not a word in a book, but a living God whom we prayed to and received in communion each day and who soothed us when we felt hurt by faculty or fellows; God, the center of our lives, whom we prepared to serve and for whom we studied archaic languages and obeyed our teachers in almost obsequious servitude. God whom we feared also; the judge of heaven and hell; the God who hated sin, but loved the sinner. And THE SIN was sexual. Anger and hatred and lies and grudges were wrong, of course, but the deadliest sin was SEX. And we avoided it, although fantasies stole into our adolescent minds, unbidden, but troublesome. Did we or did we not reject them? That was the question. Years later in hearing a confession of "bad thoughts," I asked the customary question, "Did you entertain these thoughts?"

"No, they entertained me."

The God of rules was invoked to keep order in the house. To disobey the seminary rules was a "venial," that is a minor sin. This use of God's majesty was variously regarded. Most of us were unconvinced. We felt sinless when talking after night prayer, (yes, the "grand silence" again) or going off campus beyond the allowed borders, or smoking or sneaking food from the kitchen.

And this introduces the next group of *dramatis personae*, the faculty. They were demi-gods, God's middle-management. We assigned them a quasi-divinity they hardly claimed for themselves. We loved and hated them. Mostly loved. Our juvenile attempts to demythologize them, to reduce their godliness to flawed humanity only embellished their power. We used nicknames to humanize them; "Doc,"

and "Baldy," and "Biff," and "Spectacles," and "Beans;" it
only enhanced their significance and their hold on us.
"Beans!" said my mother as she looked at the tall, distinguished appearing Reverend William Wells, "how inapt can
you guys be?"

"Ma, you'd have to know him."

Since only a few of them had chosen to be at Dowling and
most had simply been drafted to teach by the archbishop, it
was pure luck for us, that, almost to a man, they were both
first class teachers, as well as first class men. We learned
from them literature, history, mathematics, science, modern languages, but the greatest of all, the *sine qua non,* without which you could not graduate was Latin. The official
language of mother church, the tongue we used to talk to
God and the Vatican, mostly in that order. And so we
struggled year after year with conjugation, declensions,
subjunctive moods, passive voices, and vocabulary, with
partial success, and, incidentally learned the rules of gram-
mar for our own language.

All of this, the grounds, the building, the faculty, the
nuns, the studies were for the students. The student body
had a pecking order of its own. Merely having survived into
the college years conferred a kind of status. Inside each class,
some were more equal than others. Top scholars were, by
no means per se, leaders. Athletes had status. If one had a
strong personality, athletic ability, plus high marks, that
added up to a leadership post. Most classmates were
friendly and helpful, but there were inner and outer circles.
And this brings me to Bill Thompson and the summer of
1939.

As I have said earlier, Bill and I arrived in our third year
of highschool. Most of the class had been there for two
years and had established close relationships. As newcomers
we were welcomed and treated with respect, but we weren't
invited to expeditions off campus and usually the half dozen
class leaders gathered by themselves in the recreation room

or in the corridors. Bill and I spent a good deal of time together the first part of the year. When basketball season began, Bill, tall and fast on the floor soon led our class in beating the second, fourth and even sixth year teams. Only the fifth year men could beat us. That put Bill in the inner circle, and he took me with him. I remember the thrill of being invited to an after night prayer's party, an added zest because it defied the rules.

The party was held in the archbishop's room. The archbishop's room was never, at least in my day, inhabited by an archbishop. Once or twice a year it is possible that he used it to vest in when he came for liturgical ceremonies. To be in a party in that room established one as a member of that all important fraternity, the regular guys. Since the room was locked, there were two ways of getting in; either with a key or through a rumored of plumbing tunnel from the student room next door. An enterprising student, many years before had had a duplicate key made and if you were the right kind of guy, you could ask the current key-holder for the "key to the Vatican."

After "light's off" in the dormitory, we crept, one by one, down to the perilous priest's corridor and stole into the episcopal demesne. The party, by any realistic standard, was a farce. For us, and especially for me, it was a rite of passage, a proof of being in the "right crowd." We sat on the floor, the six of us, and sipped Cokes purchased before seven-thirty p.m., which were therefore warm and frothy. We ate cookies that had been sent in with somebody's laundry and were dry and stale. No lights were turned on for fear that a late arriving "Jigger," that is priest, would see the light and investigate. I mostly listened as the others talked about profs. Once I broke in with a comment from Father "Beans" Wells and managed his eastern accent with a fair degree of success, and I drew a laugh from the gang. In less than an hour, the party broke up, and one by one, we made our individual ways back to our dorms. I crawled carefully and fearfully back to my bed, pulled out the clothing which I had stuffed under the covers to simulate my sleeping body and got into bed. I heaved a grateful sigh of relief for not being caught and, more importantly, for having made it to the inner circle.

That was a memorable summer. I didn't try to get a job that summer and Bill and I played a lot of golf. My dad was an attorney and one of his clients had given him an old Chevy as part payment for dad's defending him. Dad lent it to me, so most mornings I drove the thirteen miles from Sioux Lake over to Deephaven where the Thompsons lived. Until I'd seen their house, I hadn't realized how wealthy the Thompsons were. They had a huge house overlooking Lake Minnetonka. More importantly, they had a membership to Oak Tree's Country Club. I got in on the family membership or so Bill told me. We played mostly in the mornings and scored mostly in the 90's. If either of us had a bad hole, the other would give the last putt, some of them in the fifty foot category. Without that little help, we might have slid into the 100's. After golf, I'd drive us back to the Thompson house. The Thompsons had a screen house, a sort of gazebo which the family seldom used. This became our headquarters as we gossiped about the profs, or shared our common interests in literature or discussed world matters we so little understood. Often his beautiful mother would come out with sandwiches and Cokes. She seldom lingered there very long, as if respectful of our need to talk in the language of youth.

Bill's father was seldom home. He was in the bond business and travelled around the country. Bill had a sister, Beth, but she was away at camp and I didn't meet her until a July Monday when she came out to the gazebo. Her mother had sent her out with sandwiches and Cokes. I can still visualize her today, a half century later as she came toward us, walking shyly, or so it seemed. She was then fifteen, long blond hair like her Swedish mother and deep blue eyes, also like her mother. As I say, she'd been at camp, and her arms and legs were tanned dark brown. She opened the screen door, set the sandwiches down with the Cokes and smiled at me. "This is Beth. Beth, George Schwartz." We exchanged greetings. She said, "Ma says there's more stuff in the kitchen." To my disappointment, she started to leave, whereupon Bill said, "Sis, stay, I haven't had a chance to hear you talk; you must have come in late last night. Tell me was 'Myrtle, the meddler' there?" Apparently this was some camp counselor who got on Beth's nerves.

Beth dropped all shyness and began. "She tried that old 'snipe hunt' stuff on the new kids, but we tipped them off and told them to meet us on the edge of camp and we all took off to the town and we had Cokes and stuff. Then we pretended the snipe hunters had got lost, and like we had been looking for them. I don't think she believed us, but she couldn't prove a thing." As she told this, her eyes sparkled, her hands moved and I couldn't keep myself from watching her well-shaped legs wiggling as she emphasized a word or phrase. "One night when we had campfire on the beach, some guys from the boy's camp across the lake canoed over and were coming—like real close to shore, so Myrtle the meddler went to talk to them, but they just got louder and louder as she followed them along the shore. Well, this was the way they'd set it up, so then another gang in a separate canoe came around on the other side of the campfire, and a few of us snuck away and met them and talked to them until the bugle sounded." Usually stories of camp pranks were on a par with a dull classroom lecture for me, but I found myself completely absorbed, watching this dazzling girl's eyes as they flashed with excitement, recalling adventures with Myrtle the meddler, whoever she was. It was with disappointment that I watched her go back to the house at her mother's bidding.

I had, in imitation of Job, made a pact with my eyes that I wouldn't look at a girl—I mean really look. It was like I had cut off half of the human race from my vision. That night, thoughts of Beth kept coming to my mind. This animated, lovely girl had broken through the frail, psychic walls of my defenses. I longed to see her again.

The following Monday, when I arrived at the Thompson home. Bill asked, "Would it be O.K. with you if Sis came along to the course?" Well, first of all, it was their course, and he didn't need my O.K., but I was so happy about this turn of events, that I thought my eagerness would give me away.

"Oh, sure, fine." I said, trying to appear matter-of-fact, although I was so pleased, I could have shouted. I wondered during that summer and many times since what it was that made her so captivating. There were all kinds of attractive girls of her age, but Beth broke through my intentional reserve. One thing that comes to me, even after all these years, was her seeming indifference to her own beauty. She did not seem to know that she was beautiful. Or if she knew it, it was unimportant to her. Was it possible that no one in the family had ever mentioned it? Did she not see the pretty girl in the mirror? I'm not sure that was it, but her natural unstudied manner affected me.

She played golf with us, not only that day, but many more times that summer. She took the game most seriously and I enjoyed watching the deep concentration with which she prepared to hit the ball. She had not yet broken 100, but was not far away from it. But I loved hearing her voice. She talked about her school and her friends, so that I came to know their idiosyncrasies as if they were my own school mates. We all walked toward our balls, but since Bill had a tendency to hook and both Beth and I were slicers, we often walked together and chatted. I could feel, as one does, that she had become interested in me as I with her, but not possibly to the same extent. It was truly a threesome, however, and Bill was in no way excluded. I was to learn much later in life that Bill was observant of our mutual attraction.

One morning, late in July, when I knocked at the Thompson door, Beth came out to say, "Bill's got a fever and Ma won't let him play." Bill's voice came from the up-stairs," I'm O.K., the sun will be good for me."

Mrs. Thompson, from inside the house, "Don't try to con your mother, William. Get back in bed. Selma Thompson had the ability to put a chuckle in her voice at the same time she was issuing a no nonsense order, "*Suaviter in modo, fortiter in re.*" as one of our profs would say. That is, smooth in manner, firm in decision. Beth was looking longingly at me, and I'm sure I reciprocated. We stood at the front door as if in a stalemate. Selma came to the door. "What's with you kids? Can't you find your way to Oak Tree without Billie?" I thought there was a twinkle in her eye, but it may have been my own eagerness.

It was a very hot July morning and even at nine-thirty, it was in the seventies. On the drive over and as we walked down the 350 yard first hole, we were both talking very swiftly. Our excitement at being alone together interfered with our golf, so unlike our usual seriousness about the game, we were indifferent to bad shots. Mrs. Thompson had packed sandwiches and Cokes. By the sixth hole the heat had gotten to us, and we needed liquids.

"Those Cokes are going to get awfully warm," she said. That she mentioned thirst at the sixth hole where, immedi-ately above, there was a leafy bower, quite hidden from the course itself may have been a happy coincidence. By way of response, I said, "Let's go up there and have Cokes and eat lunch."

Once there, our conversation had the same heightened excitement that had marked it from the start of the game. I said, "I don't know when I've played so badly!"

"Maybe it's the heat," she said.

I wanted desperately to kiss her, and I thought she wanted to be kissed, but I wasn't quite sure, and I feared a wrong move on my part might jeopardize my relationship with the whole Thompson family. I began tentatively, "Golf is not that important. I'm enjoying just being with you."

"Of all Bill's friends I like you best of all. You're so sweet." The look that accompanied those words was both warm and hungry. I didn't think that kissing her would, per se, be a sin, but I knew it didn't fit my vocation. God knows, we had heard often enough at Dowling that we were not to date on our vacations. Somehow all that did not matter. Looking backward through the years of priesthood, it is too bad that I didn't remember that moment more fully when I later dealt harshly with young lovers. At that moment of truth, as it were, I watched her lovely tanned legs which moved when she spoke animatedly and her lovely blue eyes peering out from luscious blond hair and decided to make my move. "You know, you are so pretty sitting there that I can't help wishing to kiss you."

At that moment, she dropped her habitual shyness and said simply, "Why don't you?"

I needed no further prodding. So we kissed and talked and exchanged loving words and forgot about lunch. We were there for only twenty minutes or so, and then both of us were aware that something beyond our control, something both inviting and ominous was present. We arose together and without much further conversation went on with the game, golf; that is.

And that was all. I make no claim that in another age and with another set of backgrounds, there might have been a different result, but that was then and that was it. We played as a threesome the rest of the summer, and neither of us ever spoke to each other about it, even when we walked together toward our slices, while Bill followed the left side of the fairway. But her eyes still sparkled at me. Bill and I went back to Dowling in the fall, and I saw her only rarely. Two years later, when I was at dinner at the Thompson's, Beth's blue eyes were sparkling, not at me, but at a young man across the table from me. I hated him, though I trust, in a

Christian sort of way. I told my confessor, of course, and he absolved me of any serious wrong, but gave me a stern lecture on avoiding this in the future. And so Beth and romance went out of my life. I reverted to ignoring that half of the human race, whether girls or women, who posed a threat to my chosen way of life. Beth, of course, showed up at the ordination, and I was invited to her wedding. I managed to be busy that Saturday. She was no longer to be a part of my world, or so I thought.

That summer, as I say, was full of wonder, with Beth, and Bill and golf, in that order. The summer of '47, following THE RETREAT, was very different, and really better. My father was an attorney; for a long time, Sioux Lake county attorney. Dad was a tall man, six-foot-two and when he prosecuted a felon, I saw a side of him which was not observable around the house; that is, when he looked over his glasses at the man on trial, he scared me as a child. I think he intimidated not only the man on trial, but the defense as well. Maybe even the judge. He was gentle at home. There is a line in Proverbs or one of the Wisdom books that says, "Be not the lion in your own home." It was hard for me as a child identifying my smiling father with the inquisitorial prosecutor of the courtroom. He tired, eventually, of both the low pay and the hard work of prosecution. In private practice, he got into personal injury casework; particularly against firms which were careless or indifferent toward their workers. The spring of 1947, he won a $600,000 award. In June, he said to mother and me, "I've retired as of July 1. I'll probably do some part time work, but later. Let's take a long trip around to all the places we've talked about through the years. Next year, George, you'll be in your deacon year and there'll be lots of details for you. This could be a relaxing time for all of us, and God knows, I need it."

Ma and I needed no further encouragement. We took more than six weeks; the Black Hills, Yellowstone, Glacier;

and on into Canada, Lake Louise; Vancouver; back to the U.S.; Seattle; south to San Francisco, Los Angeles, and north of Yosemite; on to Salt Lake City, and over to Denver. In Denver, Dad said, "Let's go back to the Black Hills to the lake—Sylvan was it?—and rest up from our travels." I remember especially a pleasantly cool night there at the lodge near Sylvan. Mother and I were going to walk down around the lake. Dad was occupied with a book he was reading. We strolled among the great rocks by the lake. Mother was a head shorter than dad, and, a few years younger; her dark hair was enhanced by the bits of gray then arriving. I could tell that there was something on her mind by her unusual silence. Finally she plunged in. "George, if what I'm asking is out of line, just tell me to mind my own business."

Before she had a chance to say what it was, I said, "O.K., mind your own business." She was always beautiful, but more so when she laughed as she did then. "Well, have you thought much about the loneliness of the priest's life. I suppose they talk to you about that?"

"Endlessly; why?"

"When I think of Father Walsh going into that old rectory every night, I can't help picturing you there, and wondering how you'll like it."

"You think I'd be happier married?"

"Oh, I don't say that. I guess that's what started me on this interference in your life."

"I don't think that."

"Don't you ever think of a nice wife?"

"Ma, what is this?"

She flushed red. There are children who reverse the adult-child relationship as parents get senile and feed and diaper and clean feces even as parents did for them. I was never to experience that exchange, but that evening at the mountain lake I saw my mother, for my sake, and to save me from future pain, make herself an equal, become vulnerable. She

33

said, "I think I've hurt your feelings and I would do anything not to, but I can't help worrying about your future."

"Say anything you like, Ma, it's O.K."

"Thanks for that. Uh—uh—I'm not very sure about the value of celibacy. Dad says that the—the drive is there always."

I didn't know how to answer. I couldn't or wouldn't explain how I had cut off the other part of the human race—not in the form of service—but in friendship. I said, "I've thought of all that."

She said, "What made me get into all this was at dinner in Denver. Our waitress was absolutely gorgeous. I haven't seen anyone that pretty for years, and when I mentioned it to you, you seemed utterly oblivious. You never even looked at her after that."

"You don't think I'm homosexual."

"Heavens no. I can recall you coming back from Thompson's with stars in your eyes."

"That was true. How did you know?"

"George, you always talked about Bill with enthusiasm, but when it was Beth, you were fireworks. I used to say to your dad that I thought you'd be coming home from Dowling pretty soon."

A young couple came around from a large stone formation and we were silent briefly. Mother looked so sad, so ashamed, and so beautiful. She had been so brave to challenge me, and she expected my disfavor. My beautiful mother. I kissed her warmly. It was not erotic, but it was sensual; a mother and son who loved each other deeply, soul and body.

I said, "Ma, you must know how I feel about this thing. We both admire Doc Johnson. He's a devoted doctor. He can stave off death. He saves people, but they're all going to die sometime. I hope to save people forever. Or Dad's friend, Mcguire. Since he's lost his wife, life is meaningless to him. Even when you have him over for dinner, he can't wait to get out of the house. He thinks he needs his wife. He really needs Christ. Maybe, I can get to people like that. That's all I want. That's enough reward for me."

She smiled, "I am really proud of you and happy for you!" She kissed me again. When we got back to the lodge, Dad was on the veranda, shouting "hello!" When we came into the suite, he said, "You looked like a couple of young lovers out there."

I started to blush, but he put his long arms around both of us, as if to assure me. "I'm the luckiest man in the world. I always thought that it would be nice to have a big family, but I'd never trade that for the two of you." We basked in that glow. The memory warms me now.

The Right Reverend John Baker sat on his high desk (like a frog on a log, as an uncharitable classmate had said and glared at his questioner). "Mr. Foley, St. Anselm's theory, while changed by St. Thomas, has had a wide acceptance from theologians for almost a thousand years. What is your objection?"

"Well, Monsignor, it seems to me that it makes God, the Father—uh—uh well, almost vengeful."

The classroom became very quiet. It was rare that one questioned a prof. To hint even, that, given such a theory, that it made God look bloodthirsty was unthought of. Monsignor Baker was, maybe five-foot-six, stocky, and when he walked, he swayed from side to side, and gave the impression of a farmer following a plow. He had a florid face, and wore a perpetual frown, broken only by an occasional laugh. His face, wrinkled and furrowed, seemed about to turn wrathful, which in fact, was often the case. He suffered fools badly and his world was quite filled with them. He was a man of considerable intellect and some went as far, hyperbolically speaking, as to say that if he went into heresy, they'd follow. Neither event seemed likely to occur. His face, always florid, now turned crimson.

"Mr. Foley, if you read the text—"

"Monsignor, I did read the text—"

The crimson turned a deeper red. "I'll ask you not to in-terrupt. If you read the text *intelligently*—you would have discovered Anselm's point that just as God cannot make a square circle, a self-contradiction, neither can he dismiss an infinite offense. Only an infinite being can compensate fit-tingly for an infinite offense. I use the word 'fittingly' because St. Thomas added that notion; it softens Anselm's position. I'm not gonna spend all day on this, Mr. Foley, so read the book, but intelligently."

Foley decided to leave bad enough alone. Baker, now cooler, went on in his dull, staccato monotone, like a mo-torboat set for trolling. I had mixed feelings about Baker. He was irascible. At the same time, he was basically gentle. It might have been that his anger was a defense against some sort of fear. I sensed that underneath the irascibility there was a vulnerable and very sensitive soul. There was a rug-ged honesty about him which contrasted with some of the other faculty members who struck me as playing a bit of a role, at least at times. Each of us had to choose a faculty ad-visor; mine was Baker. I think I was one of the few who chose Baker. In personal conversation, I found him honest, direct and even warm. He could have a biting sense of hu-mor. Our nickname for him was 'Duns', after the famous medieval theologian, Duns Scotus. The rector, Adolph Slo-vene, had an abhorrence of Duns Scotus, presumably be-cause Scotus and Thomas Aquinas were somewhat apart in theology. And Baker was among the faculty who disliked Slovene. While the faculty made a show of unity in front of the seminarians, they were about as successful as quarreling parents trying to hide their animosity from their children. Baker had a favorite story about the Texan at an English fox-hunt. At the end of the day, the Texan asked his host if he'd done it right. "You were fine," said the host, "but over here, when we see the fox, we say 'tally ho', not 'there goes the son of a bitch.'" Whenever 'Duns' was with one of his faculty buddies, and he would sight the rector off across campus, he'd say 'tally ho' which delighted his constituents.

We were sitting, that same night, in the rec room, the six of us and Gerald Fox and a new guy, Joe Farley. The recreation room was huge; the length of the whole building; the entire basement. There were ping pong tables, pool and billiard tables, none of which interested me. I liked to sit with the gang, sip a Coke and sum up the day. Taking a deep drag on his cigarette and exhaling, Frank Cody began, "We could have had a death right there; old 'Duns' dead of apoplexy; and it would have been your sin, Foley. Baker went from pink to red to deep purple."

"I wanted to pursue the question, but I thought it was not the right moment," said Foley.

"That would have been fatal, first for him and then for you."

I said, "Not at all. Slovene would have made you head-prefect next year in sheer gratitude."

Foley was laughing in that full throated way he had. "What it does bring up is the thing Ross Cox brought up the last day of school last year, remember? About our poor teaching?"

Tom Ryan said, "Not that asshole, Ross. Did you hear what he did in his first month—for God's sake—at St. Mary's?"

"St. Mary's? Where 'Mortar Mike' Sweeney is pastor?" ('Mortar Mike' had the sobriquet from a classifaction of pastors who were known as "brick and mortar pastors", that is builders of churches and schools etc. 'Mortar Mike' was especially active in this domain.)

"Yeah, St. Mary's. Ross was there all of two weeks when he got up at Mass, and said, 'At my Masses here, there will be no second collections.'"

Foley removed his pipe from his mouth, "Good for him. Nothing interferes more with liturgy than that damnable practice!"

Ryan came back, "Fine, if you're pastor, not if your assistant."

It was interesting for me to observe the rivalry between Ryan and Foley, good friends though they were. It wasn't simply a difference of ideas; there was a struggle for supremacy involved: like rams butting each other's brains.

"If nobody challenges guys like Sweeney, they'll ride all over every assistant."

But Ryan insisted, "The chain of command has to be preserved."

Foley merely said, "Chain—chain indeed." And dropped it.

"Anyway, 'Mortar Mike' went to the arch and Ross has been farmed out to Father Bronski at New Bohemia."

Cody smacked his lips, as if in anticipation, "That'd be a fun contest to watch."

Ryan wouldn't let go. "All this is letting you off the hook, Foley. What are you trying to do? Get 'Duns' down on the whole class?" A smile on his handsome Irish face, Ryan's tone was a bit sharp. When the rest of us argued, it was milder; when these two went at it, there was a certain shrillness; raised voices; men fighting for the same turf.

I interrupted, "To use Baker's own word, his answer was not 'apodictic'."

From Foley, "Thanks."

I continued, "You guys won't remember, but I asked 'Duns' a question when he was teaching natural theology and got the same 'go read the book' answer."

Ryan, still needing control, said, "Baker may be dull, but he's the real pro around here; the big intellect; the one you can trust to deliver the goods."

The pipe was out of Bob's mouth again, "He's bright, I agree, but within a narrow circle, Thomistic thought."

"Well," said Ryan, voice again a trifle belligerent, "isn't that what we are, Thomists? I'd like to see 'Duns' take on some atheist like Bertrand Russell. He'd have him for lunch."

Bob Foley was not done, "I'd like to see that too. But 'Duns' would find it a different ball-game; it wouldn't be with students who have to kiss ass. Anyway, I want to hear the question George asked. I think I recall it."

Ryan, giving ground, reluctantly, "Foley has decreed. You have the floor, George."

I began, "Baker was guiding us through the proof of God's existence from contingency—"

Cody interrupted, "If you're gonna talk dirty, I'm gonna go sit with the girlth." His pretended lisp was a denigration of four younger students of decidedly feminine characteristics who were seated across the room.

I ignored him as well as I could. "See if I got this right. There are two kinds of beings; necessary and contingent. Contingent beings come and go. They need not exist. The proof of that is that they do not always exist, but a necessary being has to exist; it is self-existent. Right so far?"

"O.K." from Foley.

"Since plants, animals, people, come and go, they are contingent. They cannot cause their own existence. They receive their existence from a necessary being. That being is God."

"Close enough," said Bob.

Cody's mustache seemed to have been allowed greater growth over the summer. "And there you have all heard Schwartzie's first sermon in his first assignment. They'll be on the edge of their seats."

"But what was your question?"

"In the text it says that the whole universe can't be necessary being because it is just a series of contingent beings. But I still thought that the whole system could still be the original existent being. But the author says, "Matter cannot be necessary being because it is pure potentiality; it can only receive perfections." My point was simply that you have to accept Aristotle's theory of matter and form in order to buy this argument. Baker just said 'Read the book.'"

Cody got up. "That does it. You've just destroyed my faith. I'm going over to the girl's table." And he did. There was a sort of understated cruelty to seminarians who were 'different'. We seldom used the word 'homosexual' and indeed, if the faculty believed a man to be a homosexual, he was summarily dismissed. Nor was there any recourse. We students weren't very kind, either, and it wasn't homosexuality, as such, which we abhorred. Rather, if a student was not into sports, if he were given to a little too much interest in vestments and if his movements were somewhat undulant, he was an oddball. He would not be shunned, but made to feel less than accepted. These men tended to flock together, possibly by choice or possibly by the neglect of others. All this was to change in time, but that night as Cyril Gonier, Jack Flynn, Earl Nelson and Fred Jessel sat together, I'm sure that they were glad to have Cody, an upperclassman join them.

Foley responded to me. "I'm not sure that you have that entirely right, but, you know, Aquinas never took his own arguments that seriously. He just added these arguments to cross the t's and dot the i's. I think that we really start from faith and then sort of buttress it with these. Like the pronouncement from Vatican I that declares it a matter of faith that man can find God by reason. Its a strange mixture; a sort of hybrid."

A number of the guys had drifted off by now. Only the four of us were left; Foley, Ryan, Thompson and myself. Ryan had begun to redden in the neck; it struck me, years later, that his anger was not a liability to his leadership, but an adjunct, a means of control. Now he said, "Bob, you begin to sound like Ross Cox. To deny any part of Vatican I is heresy." He smiled as he said it, but there was teeth in the remark. Foley just laughed. Thompson had not said much until then. Now he said, "Did you guys ever notice how argumentative our whole education here is? I mean thesis: *one* proof from reason, *two* proof from scripture, *three* proof from tradition. Hardly the way Jesus talked. Nor the Bible for that matter."

"You just said the best thing that's been said here all night" said Bob.

I could see Tom Ryan getting ready to argue. However the bell for study rang. Bob looked at Ryan. "Saved by the bell. Right?"

"You're damned right. Someday, I'm going to straighten you out, before you lead your people into heresy."

Study time went from seven-thirty to nine p.m., at which time we were summoned to chapel. Actually, I discovered that I could do the formal study necessary for the classroom in less than a half-hour. This left me time for the collateral reading which I found much more interesting; Belloc, Chesterton, Gill, Bernanos, Leon Bloy; these were some of the readings. We were not allowed secular newspapers or magazines. I accepted that discipline then, but in retrospect, this deprivation seemed to prepare us for an era which had passed. While we could read news when we were on vacation, the habit was gone, and so we entered our active ministry devoid of an understanding of most of the cultural, political and international events of the times.

That night, during study time, there was a gentle knock on my door, almost imperceptible. "C'min," I yelled.

A visibly upset Gerald Fox stood on my threshold.

"I—I don't even have permission," he said. The house rule, routinely ignored, was to go to the student prefect for permission. Then one was to stay at the door. I believe the idea was to prevent some sort of homosexual business, although this was never stated.

"For God's sake, Jerry, you're a fifth year man. C'min." He looked uncertain, but came in. Usually his face was a cool, collected mask; now he looked close to tears.

"What's wrong?"

"The rector called me in tonight. I might not get subdiaconate in the spring. He said—he said—" and Jerry's voice broke. "He said that I'm on trial. The faculty thinks that I'm too rigid."

I hesitated. I didn't want to make things worse. Finally, I said, "Well, Jerry, you really could, well—uh—loosen up a bit. Like all this rule keeping; I mean its O.K., but you do it so thoroughly—"

"I know, you guys think I'm strange, and you joke about me. I just wanted to do everything right."

"Wrong." I said. "We don't make fun of you."

"You heard Cody tonight making fun of me."

"Oh, c'mon, Cody makes fun of all of us."

"I suppose that's true, but I think that when I'm not around, you guys talk about me."

"Now you are being paranoid; sure, in a closed place like this, we all talk about each other, but you are liked and respected. Jerry, what is it? I know that you have a sense of humor; but you kinda keep a lid on it. Why not let it out. You have a sense of proportion. I couldn't help noticing, for example, that when that pile of gloom, the June retreat master, told us that we should obey the pastor to the point of cutting the lawn with a tweezers, that you quit taking notes."

I finally got a smile out of Gerald Fox. "Yeah, I thought that was just too absurd. But thanks for telling me that the guys don't think I'm a complete jerk. See, in my family, I'm a kind of a joke; my older brother is a state senator, and my sisters and my brothers are all good athletes, and sort of popular in school. I wanted to show that I could do things too. When I came to the seminary, I suppose I wanted to do everything right; like keeping the rules."

"You really don't think that talking in the grand silence is a sin, do you?"

He hesitated, then; "It's an imperfection; and they lead to sin."

"I don't believe it; not for a moment. I think you're trying to run before you can walk. Maybe all of us. I've been reading a book by Rudolph Allers about character. I think the idea is to develop normally and then try to take on these virtues. Not the other way around. I told Monsignor Baker that I thought we ought to read Freud and people like that. Baker's my spiritual advisor, you know. Well, anyway, he told me to read Tanquery's *Spiritual Life*."

"Did you?"

"Tried. Its the same old stuff. You got a problem with anger? O.K., so you count to ten; that kinda thing."

"What's wrong with that?"

"For one thing it's superficial; doesn't touch the real meat of the problem. What causes my anger? Maybe it's a bad self image. I can count to ten only so often. The trick is to find the cause."

"So how about my rigidity?"

"You've already answered it. You're trying to be perfect. The hell with it. Try to be human. Let go a bit."

"I'm not sure."

"Neither am I."

"Is this Allers on the list of forbidden books?"

"He's Catholic. He's in the library for God's sake."

"Maybe I'll look into him. Thanks for understanding."

And Gerald left me wondering whether the advice I gave was good or bad. I was sure that I meant it well. Maybe I helped, maybe not. Maybe the faculty warning helped, maybe not. What is for sure is that a far different Gerald Fox was ordained, and a far, far different Gerald Fox does amazing parish work today. And yet something in him remained the same. Later on, when his social justice activity raised eyebrows, that same uncompromising spirit was there; a set jaw, a kind of inability to negotiate marked his efforts and seemed to render them ineffective, at least to a degree. The very book of Allers that I had recommended to Fox expressed the point that character could change. It may be so. Gerald Fox certainly changed in those final two years in the seminary, but there was an ingrained part of him that clung to an earlier pattern.

One thing that happened as a result of the rector's warning was that Fox took a new interest in athletics. Gerald Fox was, at that stage in his life, a very slim man, so much so that he appeared almost feminine. It was known about the campus that he'd been a trackman in high school, but at the seminary, he'd shown no interest in any physical activity. Now, perhaps in response to the implied threat of the faculty, he started playing in the touch football league. Slight as he was for football, he was ideal for pass-catching. So he was picked to be on the instate team for the annual game.

The annual instate/outstate football game was one of those strange aberrations in seminary life which is hard to explain or even make sense of, because for a few days before and maybe for a few days after, this event took on a meaning and significance way beyond any commonsense explanation. Seminarians, for the most part, were strongly supportive of each other and this was particularly true of members of the same class. But for that week loyalties changed. Friends still spoke to friends, but beneath the surface there was a switch away from class loyalty to loyalty to Minnesota, if you were studying for a diocese there, and loyalty to outstate if you were studying for an outstate diocese. The game was played with much earnestness, and though it was touch football, it was an awfully physical contest, and if there were no tackles, there was plenty of blocking. Injuries serious enough to need medical attention were not unknown. Some of the faculty wanted to put a stop to these barbarities, but they were so dear to the student body that the faculty refrained. A priest friend who is a chaplain in a prison told me that the ordinary complaints in prison are often of the same variety as those of seminary days. "Why can't we have two hours of recreation, rather than one?" or "How come the guys in Joliet get to hear Johnny Cash and we don't?" In that same vein, the instate/outstate game was allowed.

I thought that I was as good a player as Tom Ryan, maybe better, but he always got picked. More of that subtle leadership stuff. That year outstate had the quarterback, Joe Casey, whose brother played for Notre Dame. And while that didn't make him a star, in fact, he was terrific. They expected to win, and Frank Cody, loyal to outstate put a heavy two dollars on them against me. The outstaters were acquainted with Fox's speed, so they put a big guy, Clarence Murphy against him. Murphy's job was to take him out of the play by laying him low.

The game went off predictably with Casey tossing two bombs to Harold Lightfoot, an Indian student, studying for the Lincoln diocese in Nebraska. Lightfoot was regarded as the fastest man on campus, but they hadn't seen Gerald Fox as yet. And the reason they hadn't seem Fox is that big Murphy was flattening him at the line on every play, so that he couldn't get down field. It got brutal. Murphy hit the scales at about 230, Fox, after a big meal, might weigh 120. It would have been bad enough with equipment, but the crunch we heard each time Murphy met Fox was bone breaking. Frank Cody, walking past me on the sidelines, quipped, "Tally ho! Do you want to pay me now?"

Well, it looked like a runaway. But the instaters managed to put a cap on Lightfoot in the second half. Meanwhile I went over to Tom Ryan who was the playing coach of the instaters, and said, "You ought to take Fox out before something happens. There could be a serious injury."

Ryan barely nodded. He wanted to win. Fox's health was a minor consideration at best. It became increasingly hard to understand how Fox could get back up, time after time, as Murphy continued to batter him. The set jaw of Gerald Fox got sharper as he arose from the ground. That same determination that had given the faculty pause frightened me. Toward the end of the third quarter, Fox came up from Murphy's block and I noticed that his eyes were glazed. I yelled at Ryan who was on the sidelines; "Take him out!" He appeared not to hear me. On the next play, as Murphy roared into Fox, Fox took a step backwards, and Murphy blocked into the air, as Fox scooted down the goal ten yards ahead of any defender. Bill Thompson, our quarterback, threw a pass that seemed well beyond Fox, but Fox somehow got to it and the game was only twelve and six. (Since there weren't any goalposts, no field goals or extra points; only touchdowns counted.) Murphy continued to abuse Fox, but Fox had discovered ruses to avoid him, and I could sense that the thing sportswriters later called "momentum" had swung to the instate team. I sought out Cody, whose half-mustache was more visible in the late afternoon sun. I smirked. "Do you want to pay me now?"

"I don't give a shit about the two bucks, but we better get an oxygen tent for Foxie. This is nuts." Fox caught two more and was carried off in triumph by the instaters.

Cody, paying me, said, "I knew he'd be carried off." Looking back over forty some years, it was all there; I mean the kind of determination that was to show later in both Ryan and Fox from exactly different points of view.

Retreats, football, theological argument, these were special moments against a background of dull routine. Those who rebelled made a practice of cynicism or partially expressed hostility; it came out in bitter comments about the faculty or the system. Most of us, however, inured our minds to the monotony, and fared quite well. I think, that only in retrospect, did we judge the system critically.

The retreat that year was delayed, for what reason I can't remember. So in early November, we gathered in chapel to size up the new retreat master. He was totally different than old Jonquill. He told jokes; he spoke admirably about fellow priests; he was a genuinely happy man. I was struggling with something that at times seemed important and, at other times, negligible. I had come to seminary life out of a sense of duty, of fear, as I have mentioned; but then, I'd loved the life, the studies, the wonderful men of the campus. I liked the focus of the vocation to serve Jesus and people; and yet, there was that nagging doubt that I had just sort of fallen into this life; that the guys around me had a more convincing calling: a better sense of priesthood. I decided that I'd go to the retreat master and see what he could make of it.

It was that same spare room set aside for the retreat master that I had ventured into so unhappily in June. The same desk. Two chairs, a cot, and a single picture of Jesus in the garden. The atmosphere was entirely different, however. A smiling Father George greeted me. "Hi, c'min." I noticed that he had loosened his cassock, revealing an open shirt with black curly hairs showing on his chest.

"What can I do for you? Confession, discussion, or do you just want to get away from the awful silence?" He was a good looking man, perhaps middle forties, heavy head of dark, curly hair and a huge warm smile.

"Maybe, all of those."

"Start anyplace," he said, reassuringly.

"Father, in a way, it's hard to explain. I'll put it this way. I'm suddenly a half year from subdiaconate, and it's like I just sort of drifted into it. I like the life, but I'm not sure that I really belong." I hesitated to fetch up the right kind of metaphor. "It's like a kid who goes to grade school, and passes from grade to grade and suddenly he's about to graduate. He just went to school because his parents sent him. I mean he never sat down at age six and planned to graduate. It just happened. Well, it's been pleasant here and I've liked it. And I'm about to commit myself for life and I'm not sure that it's right."

Father George smiled at the other George. "Whoa, lets hold on a minute. There's a whole world of excitement out there and nobody spends—how many years?—"

"Eight."

"Eight years, why would you spend eight years cooped up here if you didn't have a vocation?" He took out a pack of cigarettes and passed it to me.

"Thanks, I quit."

The good Father George took a deep and satisfying drag and exhaled a cloud of smoke. "Less than one tenth of one percent of U.S. guys would come here for the ride. And the faculty; if they thought you were taking up space, believe me, you'd have been packing years ago. The decision is partly yours, that's true, but only partly; the bishop, guided by the faculty, makes the choice. The real mistake would be for you to back out now, without some real problem."

And so it went. He was affable, reassuring, positive. Looking back, I wish I had been able to articulate that, indeed, however small the percentage, some guys might choose the routine. I left his room, relieved and partly persuaded. The winter months dragged on; up at five-forty a.m., classes from eight a.m. to noon; reading at lunch, afternoon classes till three p.m., an hour-and-a-half of recreation, study period, then spiritual conference at five-thirty; dinner at six p.m., while a seminarian preached his sermon; followed by chapel, briefly this time; an hour of recreation; and back to studies until night prayer at nine p.m.; the man had a point; who would do this by choice?

And so in June, I made the promises of celibacy and recitation of the breviary and became a subdeacon. The decision, irrevocable had been made; at least irrevocable in the sense that to break it now was sin. And Gerald Fox had been accepted. So had Frank Cody, not without some discussion back and forth between the diocese of Rapid City and Monsignor Slovene. Only Cody would have said it. Sneering at me with what was now a full grown mustache, he said, "Hey, Schwartz, we've crossed the fuckin' Rubicon."

The deacon year, the last year, was a happy, easy, and yet

restless year. Deacons, created such in early September, are on a higher level than other seminarians. They belong to mother church; so much so that, while technically they could still be refused priesthood, the church sort of owed them a living. Every day there was granted an automatic five p.m., an all afternoon absence from campus. Deacons could theoretically flunk out, but I never heard of it. We were a strange breed, half priest, half seminarian. The only substantive duty was to learn the intricate ritual of the Mass. Today's Mass is much more simple. I should think it could be learned in a couple of hours. Not so in those days. For example, there were fifty-three signs of the cross; done in quite separate ways. The signs you made over the bread and wine had to be done in a very particular way. Hands spread in prayer could only be so far from your body etc., etc. I remember being very angry over the film, "The Left Hand of God," because Bogart learned the Mass overnight. Couldn't be done. But that was about it. Studies were simple. Some guys spent an inordinate amount of time preparing for the "First Mass." If you really wanted a showcase affair, it would call for a lot of work. But the year was relatively undemanding.

Restlessness, however, was rampant. After ten or more years in preparation, we were eager to get on with it; to go into the world like Peter and the twelve, to bring the Good News. The happy comradeship and intellectual stimulation which had contented me for so many years was replaced with a gnawing impatience. This caused us to indulge in carefree attitudes toward the members of the faculty, and a less than all-out effort in studies. While deacons could scarcely be dismissed, unless for some gross misdeed, they could still be frowned upon and years of docility led us to accept frowns seriously. And so ordination to the eternal priesthood dawned. Some of us, maybe all of us, shuddered before the awful responsibility which lay before us.

THREE

✠

Launching Out

The night before ordination, we gathered in the "can" to talk it over. It was our last night as seminarians, and rules were out. I was nervous about the next day's ordination; mostly it was that kind of pleasant stimulation you might feel before a joyous occasion, but the solemnity and the irrevocable consequences were there too, and then, I didn't want to foul up by tripping or marching determinately in the wrong direction. These were tiny worries against the backdrop of the awesome power and responsibility of the eternal priesthood. I think the others felt the same. Let me put faces on them; my companions; my fellow apostles.

Jerry Fox was there; still an intense man, but the faculty had approved; his rigidity lessened or at least, under wraps enough so that it was unnoticed. He was thinner than ever; 110 pounds, slightly built, but with large intense eyes. He still listened more than he spoke. He and Cody were the only ones slim enough to sit on the sinks without endangering the plumbing.

Cody, as soon as he was made a deacon, felt safe from faculty correction, and let his diminutive mustache grow fully. It curled around his upper lip in such a way as to accentuate his cynicism. Facial hairs were important enough in those days as to cause a lively exchange of letters between

Monsignor Slovene and the bishop of Rapid City. The bishop allegedly told Slovene to keep out of Cody's hair, facial or otherwise.

Cody was the only outstater there that night. Bill Thompson, big and blond, sat on the floor. Bill, over six feet, was the athlete of the crowd. Cody, going to Rapid City on the next day couldn't resist a few parting jabs. He was occupied that night in deciding where each of us would be assigned. At the end of the ordination ceremony, a very businesslike chancery staffer would place a large envelope on each of our prie-dieux. This mysterious document would give us our first appointments. It was considered bad form to break open the seals and peek.

Cody said, "Bill, you will be sent to St. Mary's where you will develop great football teams and maybe after twenty-five years of that, you'll turn into an adult."

Bill merely smiled. Cody next turned on Clem Bartosh.

"I hear that Father Bronski kicked Cox out of the rectory at New Bohemia, and so you are the next sacrificial lamb. Bronski will turn you into a robot in six weeks. Then you will be fit only for a chancery role, or maybe a bishop."

Bartosh was used to Cody. "And you, Frank, will be sent into the deserts of Dakota, where the deer and the buffalo have fled, because life was too tedious to play. In one month the parish will hang you because they won't be able to understand a word."

Cody went on, "Now we come to Tom Ryan, who is going to study canon law and come back to the chancery, and you guys will all have to kiss his ass, because he is one ambitious guy."

This last remark got to Ryan, because he turned red, and said, "Cody, shouldn't you be packing?"

"Ah, I've struck blood. Methinks he doth protest too much. Admit it, you asked for chancery work?"

"Off of it, Frank, I'll go where I'm sent."

"And," said Frank Cody, "if the Archbishop wants you

to train for bishop, you won't refuse. Right?"

Ryan, I think, was more riled than he wanted anyone to see, but he said, "Cody, if I get to be your bishop, I'll make you perpetual pastor of 'Rattlesnake Junction'."

Bob Foley, dark-haired, tall and deep-voiced, "Cody, save your sarcasm and your wit. I've asked for a teaching job, and I'm pretty sure he bought it."

I turned serious. "Why would you do that?"

"I think the intellectual life is the cutting edge of tomorrow's church."

"What's to intellectualize about? We got an unchangeable creed, a likewise moral code, and a bible which is unalterable. Sure, you can go into small discussions on how much stolen money makes a mortal sin, but the main lines are there."

"Two years ago," said Bob, "on this very night, we heard Cox talk about change in biblical interpretation. I've read a lot since then, and our moral code, which you say is so unalterable, is in for a lot of redefinition. And that's just a beginning. There's ferment among the Europeans that will make your head spin."

Cody cut in, "Bunch of heretics, right Ryan?"

Ryan said, "I hate to agree with Cody on anything, like what day is it? But I think these biblicists are outta control. The Vatican will sweep 'em under a rug."

"The same rug they swept Galileo under?" asked Foley.

Bartosh's mischievous Bohemian eyes sparkled. "I think Cody is right. If Ryan gets to be bishop, he'll have to rein in Foley for heresy."

The conversation got cut short when the dean, a new dean, Father Joe Keeney came in. "Now," he said, "I know it's your last night, but you better get some sleep. Tomorrow is going to be a long day."

So we all went off to bed, but few slept.

June tenth, a perfect day-of-poets. No rain, fluffy clouds, a world of green from recent rains, and seventy degrees at nine o'clock. The cathedral organ roared and the seminary choir sang the majestic notes of "*Tu es sacerdos in eternum!*" (You are a priest forever according to the order of Melchisedech.) Melchisedech appears in one line in Genesis, but he offered a sacrifice of bread and wine, and also, like Christ, his origins were unknown to his contemporaries, and so he fit, somehow, the priesthood of Christ.

We walked down the long aisle in white garments looking to the right or left to catch a glimpse of a family member, because they were all there, and our aunts and our cousins and all. We were presented to the archbishop, then walked to the sanctuary and lay down on the floor to indicate our personal powerlessness, but God, in ordaining us would empower us so that we would perform the mighty works of Christ: baptizing, preaching, forgiving sins, anointing the sick and, above all, offering the sacrifice of the Mass.

The significance of individual parts of the ritual, the bestowing of chalice, of chasuble, the placing of hands in the archbishop's to indicate obedience were somewhat lost as I tried to keep up, step-by-step, with a minimum of error. I wanted to get through it all with as much grace as my awkwardness would permit. The sermon, as it was called in those days, was not delivered by the archbishop, but by the vicar-general, Monsignor O'Brien. Because I was at that point, an observer rather than a participant, phrases from that sermon come back to me. "Young men—intellects sharpened, emotions disciplined, wills finely honed by years of rigorous training—going into a world as the apostles;" that sort of thing. At that time, I really felt those kinds of virtues burgeoning within me. The years were to refine those ores, discovering a good deal of dross intermingled with the gold.

I had asked Monsignor Baker to be my "chaplain," to assist me as I concelebrated with the archbishop and my classmates my first Mass. After communion we recited a very long Latin "oath against modernism." Years later, when Beth Thompson and I had rediscovered each other, she told me, that while she read the translation of that oath, she wondered how thirty-five men could possibly have such unity of mind and thought. She had, by that time, changed from the shy fourteen year old to a very sophisticated university student, and found the oath an appealing bit of anti-intellectualism. She said she wondered how her brother Bill and I could possibly have been so brainwashed as to accept the whole thing.

It seems strange to me now, forty-some years later, to realize that Beth, the laywoman, would have difficulties with the oath against modernism whereas none of us would have given it as much as a hesitant thought, with the possible exception of Foley. For one thing, it was in Latin, granted it was church Latin, much easier than the old classical Latin, but still with pages of it, pretty hard to read intelligently. Even if it had been in English, I doubt that we would have flinched. It was against heresy, right? And so were we.

The word "modernism" is not to be confused with the word modernism in the ordinary sense. It referred to a movement of scholars, many of them Catholic, who wanted, for example, to reduce biblical studies to purely scientific and historical criteria without any dogmatic presuppositions. In this naked form, it was hardly acceptable. And yet, in many ways, it was the forerunner of much Catholic interpretation later in the century.

Mass and ordination over, we gathered on the lawns around the cathedral and began to bless people who knelt before us. First, mothers and dads, and relatives and then anyone willing to plop down on their knees on the grass.

Beth, coming upon me blessing a group of obvious strangers, said, "Hey, George, easy! You're gonna wear it out." She had changed, not less beautiful, but more so. She was with the Thompsons and also her fiancée. Exchanging greetings and congratulations, she asked, "Well, where you going?" It may seem odd, but, in all the confusion, I had stuffed the envelope with my appointment in my pocket, and I didn't know where I was to report. I suppose part of the trouble was that I didn't know one parish from another, beyond my home parish in Sioux Lake, but, nevertheless, my indifference was surprising to me as well as to the Thompsons. I quickly tore open the envelope and discovered that I was to "report to Father Michael Higgins at St. Brendan's rectory at twelve noon, on the seventeenth of June."

Bill Thompson was to go to St. Isidore's in west Minneapolis, where they were known to stress muscular Christianity; Foley, for future studies and, Tom Ryan to the Catholic U. in Washington to study canon law. (That damn Frank Cody was right.)

I ran into Ross Cox, who was going to his fourth assignment in two years. "Where to, Schwartzie?"

"Higgins, at St. Brendan's."

"Good God, I just got freed from there. He's a son-of-a-bitch."

I wasn't sure how to interpret Cox, since he had three sons-of-bitches in three assignments. Other people were more reassuring. "He's a good natured guy," said Monsignor Baker. Others were even more positive about Higgins. Mother and Dad and I were walking into the Roxie for lunch, when I ran into Cox again. "Play it cool, George, don't let Higgins fool you. He's a real jerk."

Unfortunately, the folks heard part of that. "What does he mean, George? Should you try for another appointment?"

"Ma, don't take it seriously. Cox never liked any of his pastors. Besides, I can't pick and choose. It's like the army." I felt good saying that. There was a faint echo of the heroic in that phrase; like the colonel going off to the wars. Ours not to question, but to do and to die. Dad must have caught some of the bravado in my voice, but he merely smiled.

The next day was my formal First Mass; then a week with the folks and off to Higgins and St. Brendan's. I admit to a tightening in the throat even recalling it.

It was the best of times; it was the worst of times. Mostly the best of times. I read recently an analyst of the modern day who said that a few years ago was the "Catholic Moment" in America. He meant, apparently, that by issuing the statements on war and weaponry as well as on the economy, the U.S. bishops had taken a leadership position as sort of keepers of the nation's conscience. If I remember rightly, he went on to say that we'd then blown it by an over-reaction to the abortion issue. Well, I don't know. The "Catholic Moment" to me was the year of and years after my ordination. 1949 and on through the fifties. Look at it. Catholic schools were burgeoning. People stood in line in the big cities to get their children into Catholic highschools. The same for even grade schools in the suburbs. Seminaries were rebuilt to accommodate aspirants to the priesthood. For example, Dowling Hall almost doubled its buildings to make room for new students. Schools had been added to parishes in the 1940's and after the war, at an astounding rate and they were getting paid for! No longer were we an immigrant minority attempting to "fit in." Forty million Catholics had to be reckoned with whether it was the legion of decency, guarding movie morals or the "Catholic vote." Catholic nomenclature crept in, no, swept in to the common tongue, mortal and venial sin. "Hail Mary" passes in football, and Father and Monsignor and Cardinal were cultural realities.

Catholics had not only entered the mainstream, they achieved more. Soldiers coming out of the Great War and the Korean police action went to colleges and universities closed to them in previous decades for lack of cash. The majority of us had a slice of the American dream. While Catholic historians could remind us that we had not an intellectual or political or cultural significance in accordance with our numbers, it was changing even as they wrote.

There was a notion of Catholic intellectual ferment. Mortimer Adler, not himself Catholic, pointed students to the reasoning power of Thomas Aquinas and the old scholastics. European names; Mauritain, Belloc, Chesterton, Waugh, and Graham Greene found their way onto American bookshelves. Converts like Dorothy Day, Thomas Merton and Claire Booth Luce, while espousing different points of view were united in the Church. And then the politically incredible, a Catholic president!

But there was more. Hilaire Belloc, writing in a letter to a friend, said this about England:

"Four powers govern man, avarice, lust, fear and snobbishness. One can use the latter. One cannot use the first three. Blackmail is alien to Catholic temper and would cut little ice. Pay we cannot because we are not rich enough... Threaten we cannot because we are nobody, all the temporal power is on the other side. But we can spread the mood that we are the bosses and the chic and that a man who does not accept the Faith writes himself down as suburban. Upon these amiable lines do I proceed."

This does not describe us perfectly over here, but there was the notion that we had the answer, that armed with Aristotle and Aquinas, it was only a matter of time when THEY would see that we had the TRUTH, and would turn to us for salvation, at the very least that's the way I saw it and I suggest that I was by no means alone.

Some of us had the feeling that our very strictness attracted many in society who had tired of the wishy-washiness of the mainline Protestants. Here were straight lines; mortal sin, venial sin; Mass on Sunday or mortal sin; steal a hundred and mortal sin. Doctrines were stated clearly, no room for "it seems to me that Jesus might have meant..." Our dogma, our moral code, our sacramental system were well-defined. Our very harshness was attractive. No mealymouths need apply. My idea was to gather people into the fold; the converts, the fallen aways; yes, and even the atheists; and, like the king who gave the banquet, compel them to come into the Church. Once there, the sacramental system, supported by our dogma and moral code would be like a river torrent sweeping them into heaven. Now, as I look at the lines I have written, I really can't believe that any of my contemporaries ever entertained anything quite so simplistic. Did I really think it myself? Well, at least partly.

It was the worst of times. Underneath the burgeoning, solid church were fissures which could be seen by the keen. Like a fine old building where the foundation is slipping and the beams are rotting. A comparison might be found in two books, written a half-century or so apart. William Thomas Walsh wrote a paean of medieval Catholicism, entitled *The Thirteenth, The Greatest of Centuries* in which he established that this was civilization's highest moment. A decade or so later, Barbara Tuchman wrote *A Distant Mirror: The Calamitous Fourteenth Century*. Both of these historians did their homework and set forth some convincing data. And, of course, these are different centuries. All the same, if the Fourteenth was as bad as she said, then the seeds of destruction must have been identifiable earlier.

So must it have been in the heady fifties, when we made our mark in the greater society, marching right into the White House. Our schools, so strong and so solid, were held together like plantations of the old south with slave labor of sisters, voluntary though it was. A more educated laity, aided and abetted by a more broadly educated set of theologians, began to question previously unquestioned verities. While this long-sought freedom had value, it would tend to split the Church in the U.S. into divisions, inexactly labeled "conservatives" and "liberals." These lines of divisions went from mild disagreement to ferocious hatred. Worst of all, this divisiveness stalled the effectiveness of Catholic social justice.

And there was more; alcoholism was much more rampant among the clergy than was recognized. One wonders too, how much of the obedience and loyalty of the laity was governed by fear; and, when a more enlightened and more educated laity began to repudiate fear, the love which casts out fear was not always developed. These cracks and fissures in the apparently healthy structure were to shape, at least partly, our ministry.

But all these thoughts were far from me as I drove into St. Brendan's parish on a lovely sunny June day to assume my position as assistant to Father Michael Higgins who had been variously described as "a good natured guy," a "son-of-a-bitch" and as a "real true priest". Naturally I was a bit apprehensive as to which of these designations I would discover. Yet the notion of the colonel marching to orders was there. Whoever and whatever Higgins was, I was serving Christ, and I had no deep fears. St. Brendan's was in a southern suburb of Minneapolis, in a neighborhood more rich than poor, and upper middle class homes gave way to more expensive ones as I neared the rectory.

The first view was pleasant; the rectory, a large brick colonial which I judged would have adequate space for several assistants. The suburban population south of Minneapolis was growing and, no doubt, this rectory would house more assistants. The streets, new as they were, were embroidered by elms. Beyond the rectory was a large school building. I had been told by someone in the past week that the school auditorium subbed as the temporary church. The real church had to yield to the more pressing need, the education of the children.

Then I saw him. In the front yard was a man of less than six feet. He was almost bald, florid face, Irish unmistakably.

He was near the bushes in the front yard, conferring with a man who was obviously the janitor or gardener or possibly the general factotum. As I stopped the car, he gave me a most genial smile and said, "This must be the new assistant, Father Schwartz."

We shook hands. "Welcome, welcome, and a thousand welcomes as we Irish say. Emil, meet the new priest."

Emil said, "Father, I can't shake hands. My hands are too dirty."

"Well, well, come inside. Here, let me carry that." But I hung onto my suitcase. I had just left the seminary where the lines between faculty and seminarian were strictly drawn. As we entered the house, he called out, "Jennie, Jennie, come and meet the new man." From back in the house a woman of about fifty emerged. She was a fine-looking woman and one had the impression that she must have been a real beauty in earlier days. Greetings over, she said, "Let me take you to your rooms." "Rooms" had a great sound to me, living as I had in the small double room in the seminary. I was not disappointed. There was a large sitting room, a fine bedroom with a big double bed and beautiful appointments. The sitting room had several large chairs in addition to a leather sofa. Along one side of the sitting room or study were a series of bookshelves. A large desk with typewriter completed the furniture. There was also a spacious bathroom and a large cedar closet. The windows of both sitting room and bedroom overlooked the lawn and flowers of the backyard. We had a kind of jocular saying in the seminary that "nothing is too good for Father." It certainly fit this setup.

Jennie said, "If you prefer, there's another suite across the hall, but the Reverend Cox made such a mess there, that it's going to take me a couple of weeks to straighten it out. Some of his junk is still there." From her tone of voice it was unnecessary for me to ask her opinion of Cox.

"No, no this is just fine."

I started to put the contents of my suitcase in the bureau, when I heard a gentle knock on the door. Father Higgins came in. "Father, I hate to abandon you this noon, but the commercial club has their monthly meeting and I'm the chaplain this year. But Jennie will give you lunch and we'll talk at dinner. She'll ring in about ten minutes, when lunch is ready. You like the rooms O.K.?"

"Oh, wow, just fine."

When Jennie's ring sounded, I found her seated at lunch. This was a democratic household, I could see. In most rectories, the "help" and the clergy did not eat together, so I had heard. Jennie said, "Would you say grace?" Having recited the time-honored blessing, I looked at the meal; mushroom soup, a cheese soufflé, wonderful hot rolls and a light spinach salad.

"Don't you just hate Fridays?" she asked.

"Not when I'm fed like this." She beamed. I'd gotten off to a good start with her I could see.

"Where did you grow up, George?"

Calling me by my first name rather than "Father" surprised me, but I rather liked the informality.

"Sioux Lake."

"I'm from a small town myself, in Iowa. I think small town kids have a better sense of values. Maybe, that was Coxie's problem. He's a big city type. Thought he knew everything. Tried to have me serve meat on Friday. Imagine! Said it was an antiquated law. He even bought the kids burgers on Friday. I hope you're nothing like him. We're still cleaning up the bad stuff he created around here. People wrote in to the bishop about his sermons. Heretical. I heard Mr. Schaffer—he's a trustee—have a shouting match with him right here in the dining room. Schaffer said Coxie was corrupting the youth. He was too."

"Sounds like Socrates."

"What?"

"Well, you know Socrates was accused of the same thing."

"Well, for your own good, and our's too, I hope you're a different kind of young priest than Coxie. Listen, two more years of him and there'd be no one left in the parish. He split St. Brendan's right down the middle." It struck me later that day that it could hardly be both ways. If Cox chased everyone away, who were the folks who were "split" on the other side? She went on, "He never should have been ordained. He's gonna make trouble wherever he goes."

"I should tell you, though, Jennie, he's a friend of mine." Jennie glared at me, and without another word, got up and brought in the coffee. There was no more talk of Cox that noon.

I spent the afternoon bringing books from the Ford that dad had given me, and arranging them in the ample bookcases. Later, I went for a walk in the neighborhood and marvelled at the fine houses and well-kept lawns. I wore, as was expected, my Roman collar and coat. As I passed a playground, a number of children shouted "hello Fathers" to me.

At five-thirty p.m., a buzzer sounded in my room. After fumbling with the phone, I realized that there was a separate intercom on my desk. It was the pastor. "Come on down and join us in a preprandial." I hoped that he would not be too disappointed that, under Monsignor Slovene's tutelage, I'd taken a five-year pledge not to drink. As I came into his capacious study, I saw that he and Jennie were sipping Scotches. She got up and said, "I'll leave you guys to talk about whatever you guys yack about." As she went past me, she smiled and winked. She'd had more than one drink I surmised, and her smile was almost flirtatious. I thought that if she were twenty years younger, I'd have to practice what we called "custody of the eyes."

"Would you like a drink?"

"Oh, thanks, I'm on the wagon." I answered, a bit embarrassed, although I don't know why I was.

"I suppose Adolph Slovene pushed you fellows on the pledge. Don't get me wrong; I think it's a good idea while a man is finding himself in the priesthood." Father Higgins had obviously "found himself," for he poured another good sized Scotch. He said, "I'll have to get some soft drinks. I'd like you to join me at times. It's a good time to talk things over. Jennie won't be ready for another twenty minutes, so I'd like to see how we can share some duties here. The parish has about 700 families. The arch promised me another assistant when we hit 1000. In the meantime, here's my suggestion. As you can imagine, the business part of the parish takes a good deal of my time. We'll share Masses and confessions equally. You're young, so naturally, I'd like you to take up the youth activities. Cox had a youth group, but it was out of control, so I'd like you to wait till fall, and give it a whole different title and orientation. O.K. so far?"

"Yes, sure."

"Now I take care of the women's club and the men's club. Ditto, the Knights of Columbus. So I'd like you to take the two nursing homes in the parish area. Anointing, visiting, say, every other week. As far as census, if you want to do that, fine, but I'll leave that to you. Oh, and the Boy Scouts. I go over to the school mostly to see how things are, but I'd like you to make some regular visits to classrooms. You could work it out with the principal, who, incidentally is Sister Mary George. We can talk about who does what in the fall with the convert class and marriage prep etcetera. How does that sound?"

"Great, really great!"

"Good. I'd like this to be a team. Couldn't do it with Cox. You know he's always preaching more democracy in the Church, but he resented it when Jennie took meals with the priests." He paused. "Jennie is a gem; no other word for it; a gem." There were tears in his eyes at this point. The

Scotch was making him repetitious. "A gem; she's been
with me fifteen,—no eighteen years; wonderful meals, great
housekeeper, and she keeps the books, you know. But,
most of all, always in a good mood; a treasure, that woman;
a gem."

Jennie may have heard this last part, because the aforesaid
gem now stood at the doorway. "It's time that the rever-
ends quit yacking and come to dinner."

There was a mixed-green salad, mashed potatoes, and
salmon with a delicious sauce of some kind.

"Don't you hate Fridays?" she asked for the second time
that day. And I, for the second time, "Not when it produces
a feast like this."

Father Higgins' Scotches were catching up to him, as he
said, "Now, Jennie, why couldn't we have got this fine
young man last year instead of Coxie?" He had slurred the
words somewhat so that 'this' and 'last' came out as 'thish'
and 'lasht.' For the second time that day, I said, "You know
Ross Cox is a good friend of mine." Jennie's smile, which
had responded to my compliment on the cuisine, evanesced,
replaced by a grim expression. But Father Higgins was
equal to the situation. "Jennie," he said, "you gotta unerstan seminary life. Everbuddy loves everbuddy. Father
Schwartz, you gotta unerstan, that sort o' thing changes
when you get in the min'stry. You'll see."

The late, unlamented Father Ross Cox disappeared from
the dinner conversation.

"Oh, I meant to tell you. Tomorrow, Saturday, is confession day. I wonder, George, if you would mind too
much to take it alone? Usually we do it together, but Frank
Dowd has invited me to play golf at Oak Tree Country
Club. You've probably heard of it?"

"Yes, as a matter of fact, I've often played there." I saw
my stock had gone up 100%.

"Oh, whom with?"

"The Thompsons."

Higgins eyes shown. "Of course, the new priest."

"Yes."

"Then you know why I can't turn down the chance. It's a beautiful layout. Frank is a trustee here. Wonderful guy. You'll meet him. We're having him over to dinner—when Jennie—Friday?"

"Not Friday. I hate Fridays. They're coming on Thursday, so I can give 'em prime rib."

The pastor, somewhat sobered by food, continued, "This Frank Dowd is a gem, a twenty carat gem. He's one of our better contributors. A real Catholic, and his wife too, another gem. Well, you'll meet 'em, next—what Thursday?"

"Yeah, Thursday."

"Now I know Cox is your friend, but he and Dowd couldn't stand each other."

Jennie spoke, "Who could stand Coxie?"

"Now, Jennie, that's water over the dam. We're a team again, right, the—the three musketeers—right George? You don't mind us calling you 'George' do you? A' course, when the laity are around, we ought to call each other 'Father'."

"Not me," said Jennie, "don't call me, 'Father'."

Both of them roared over this sally. I tried a mild chuckle. Unsophisticated as I was then, still I realized that people, after a few drinks, laughed rather easily.

Dinner over, Father Higgins said, "Jennie and I have some bookkeeping to do. Please make yourself at home. If you want to go out, please do."

"I have part of the breviary to say and reading to catch up on. I thought I might call a few classmates. Uh, some of them are long distance. I mean, should I keep track?"

Higgins put his arm around me. "Hey, you get the grand sum of seventy dollars a month. Least we can do is free phone service. Say, you really don't mind taking confessions alone?"

The truth was that I was scared stiff of hearing confessions. I felt the same sense of responsibility that a doctor would feel in making a diagnosis. My fear was that either too much leniency or too great a strictness could make me a bad "doctor of souls" as the textbooks described us. The fact was, however, that whether Father Higgins was in the church or not, I'd be on my own in the confessional. These fears accompanying me, I went to my room to "say" my breviary. The breviary or Divine Office was a collection of prayers and readings which we had pledged to pray each day. It consisted largely of psalms and other prayers, and readings from the Bible and church fathers, along with some colorful accounts of the lives of the saints. Even in those days, the hagiography of some saints caused smiles. For example, the story that Mary Magdalene (I think it was she) set out on the Mediterranean Sea in a boat without oars to let the wind take her where God directed and ended up in Spain? Where she preached the gospel, caused some remarks about the "boat without oars." The Office was really meant for monasteries, but was passed on to us as our prayer form. In those days, it took well over an hour and was said to be binding under pain of mortal sin, and since it was to be concluded by midnight, it was not unknown to have a priest out late at night doing a photo finish by car headlights. Each part had to be said, including a night prayer called compline which took about five minutes, and there was a joke making the clerical rounds which went like this. Three priests were sent to hell and they compared fates. One was damned because of drink. Another because of a lifetime of wild women. They turned to the third man to ask what his vice was. "I missed compline once."

So I read my Office; then I tried to read a theology book which Monsignor Baker had recommended, Scheeben's *Mysteries of Christianity*. But the turgid prose and the speculative nature of the book tired me. I started calling classmates. Ryan was already in Washington; Foley was out of town; Bill Thompson's pastor, Father Gibbons explained

"Ah, he's probably out playin' with the kids." I dialed St. Cyril's in New Bohemia, where true to Frank Cody's prophecy, Clem Bartosh had been sent. The phone rang; a harsh man's voice answered, "Yes."

"I'd like to talk to Father Bartosh."

"What about?"

"I'm his classmate, George Schwartz. I wanted to talk to him."

"Weren't you ordained?"

"Yes."

"Then your name is Father Schwartz. Didn't they teach you that?"

"Would you tell him I called?"

"He hasn't time to just gossip about pastors. We don't have money here for long distance calls. I see you replaced Father Cox. You're the same kind I can tell." And with that he hung up. It took me a while to recover from that. When I went to bed that night, I felt bad for Clem Bartosh; not bad enough to trade places. I thanked God for the good assignment I had, and I slept the sleep of the just—and the lucky.

Saturday, another lovely June day; but I was like a man sentenced to death, my first hearing of confessions. Neatly cassocked, I found my way into the confessional and turned on the light which indicated my presence. And people came, long lines of them. Sometime after Vatican II, people went less and less to private confession. Hundreds went, instead to penance services, where the onerous duty of telling sins was unnecessary; not so in 1949. My fear was replaced by the delight of absolving sinners; of rescuing sons (and daughters) of Adam from the fires of hell.

I was no longer afraid and it was to be a year before the sheer boredom of listening to whispered offenses against the good God was to make it a bit of a burden. Some things surprised me; I had not imagined the amount and degree of sexual activity which I now heard. Nor had I foreseen the depth of sincerity with which penitents spoke and accepted

the advice of a callow young priest. All and all, it was rewarding work, and I emerged, sweating, exhausted and tri-
umphant when the two-hour initiation was completed.

"How did it go?" asked Jennie as I came back through the
kitchen. "It was uh—wonderful."

"Oh, you'll get over that."

Father Higgins was to have dinner at the club, where he
had golfed, so Jennie and I had dinner together. She told me
more about Coxie, as she called him. It was to be some
months before I understood that she was, in effect, deliver-
ing messages from the pastor. It was, in a much milder
form, a little like those interrogating teams in prisons. The
pastor took the softer line; Jennie the harder. It was important, for example, that should my friend, "Coxie" say anything which might turn me against Higgins, that I be prepared in advance to reject it. So, Higgins' role was to say,
"Of course, Cox is your friend, well and good." Whereas
Jennie's role was turn me so against "Coxie" that I would
view any of Cox's negative statements as so much balder-
dash. At this point, however, I was too naive to grasp that.
Jennie said, "You know the whole parish was upset by
Coxie; letters were sent to the archbishop; people started
going to Mass at other parishes. He told lies about Father
and, well, about me also. Oh, things are going to be so
much nicer now. You do want us to be a team, don't you?
What did Mike call us 'the three musketeers'?"

"He did."

"And you do want us to be a team?"

"Uh, sure, I guess." I was beginning to wonder what part
of myself was to be given up to be a "musketeer".

The term was disturbing. When I agreed, however
guardedly, she seemed pleased, and gave me a smile that
was meant to be warm, but somehow, came across as sort
of flirtatious. She was dressed nicely that night, and when
she got up to get the dessert and coffee, I saw that she had
on a short skirt and black silk stockings. Her legs were slim

and attractive, and I decided that I had better start practicing "custody of the eyes" regardless of the differences in our ages. I said, "Jennie, you're all dressed up. Are you going out tonight?"

"No, I do this every Saturday night. I think that after a day of confessions and sometimes weddings and all, that this ought to be a festive occasion."

"Hey, that's really thoughtful."

"Thank you. We're all going to be such friends."

That night I ran through my sermon several times; I was nervous because this would be the first time I faced a real congregation; not a group of seminarians busily eating dinner, while you preached. I liked it that way. People eating dinner were distracted and less critical. It could even be fun. One of the seminary wags once preached a sermon on a saint and gesturing toward the study body, said, ". . . and while the common people starved. . . " and then gesturing toward the faculty, continued ". . . the clergy feasted."

At the first Mass, I could feel my woodenness; but I relaxed at the next Mass, and I could feel, as a speaker can, the responsiveness of the congregation. After each Mass, I shook hands at the door. There were various welcomes. One said, "We sure are glad to have you instead of that socialist, Father Cox." But it was, by no means, universal. Several asked if I knew Cox, and said things like, "We sure enjoyed him. He brought some fresh air to the place." In my own mind the vote was still out on the impact of Cox on St. Brendan's parish, despite Higgins and Jennie.

I suppose that every priest can recall, with some detail, the first week of his active ministry. I said the convent daily Mass; got to know the wonderful principal, Sister Mary George, who assured me that Higgins gave good financial support to the school. "But," she said, "the kids need a young man like you to be around, to give them a male, priestly example." That flattered me. I went to the two nursing homes Higgins had assigned me; anointed an old lady who thanked me effusively. Each night I took off my clerical garb, with Higgins' approval, and wandered down to the root beer stand, two blocks from the parish, and sipped the house specialty, root beer floats, and mixed casually with the kids. A few came up and introduced themselves.

One night, I was talking to a little group of them, when one asked, "Hey, Father, when are you gonna restart the youth group?"

"In the fall."

"Why not now?"

"Father Higgins suggested that I wait until then."

"Father Cox really had the thing going well until Higgins put the brakes on. We had a lot of fun, but he also took us down to Washington Avenue, you know, where skid row is, to let us see how the other people live. The rich guys in the parish raised hell about that. They don't want us to be what they called "bleeding hearts." You hear about that?"

"No, but we'll have to see about that." I could see that my carefulness had turned them off. Yet I didn't want to get Higgins on the wrong side of me. How could I do anything in the parish without the pastor's approval? By such hesitation are many things done in the church as well as in the state.

Mostly though, that first week rewarded me with a sense of effective ministry. I took the pastor up on census. I picked out a street not far from the rectory, and simply knocked on doors. I asked if they were Catholic; if not, I explained that I was getting acquainted with my flock. If they showed an inclination to talk, I visited for a few moments. If they were Catholic, I introduced myself. In those days, there were a lot more women at home, and they were glad to have a priest's visit. In the course of those visits I discovered a lot of people who liked Father Cox. True, there were also some who described him as "far-out" or "weird." I even found two families who were, as the nomenclature of the day defined them "fallen aways". Even with all this and Mass, breviary, and sermon preparation, I still seemed to have lots of time.

By Thursday night, I'd almost forgotten that we were to have guests, until I walked past the kitchen to find Jennie in the midst of what seemed to be a considerable culinary undertaking. She was dressed up, but more conservatively than on Saturday.

"Well," I said "this looks like a feast! I trust you are going to join us."

"I'll sit with you on a corner, like Martha, or was it Mary?"

I was still in the shower when my buzzer sounded. "Father, c'mon down and join ush."

With Higgins in the pastor's commodious study, were two couples. "Please, don't stand." I said, but everyone rose.

"This," said the pastor, pointing to a pleasant looking woman "is Grace Renner. And this," he said indicating a bespeckled, studious man in his late forties, "is Louis Renner." Then he turned to a very handsome woman; dark-hair, high cheek bones, and a beautiful smile. "Father, Norma Dowd." As I shook her hand, she gave me a dazzling smile. At last I was introduced to the man whom Higgins had called "a real gem." He was tall, well over six feet, in his fifties, a bit heavy, but fine looking in an aggressive way. His tan face suggested the outdoor type and he held me with his eyes, as if appraising my character. "I've been looking forward to meeting you. The young people here need guidance and Father Higgins tells me that you're the man that can do it. Liked your sermon Sunday; you know we've had that socialist."

I pretended not to understand, "Socialist?" I said, looking mildly bewildered.

"Cox." He spit the name out. "Do you know him?"

For the third time in a week, I said, "Yes, he's a good

friend of mine." Frank Dowd's smile faded. Mrs. Dowd's smile was replaced with a grim look. I was to notice later, that her handsome face, in repose, was sad, and while, still striking, lost some luster.

"I hope that you're not a socialist, too." said Mr. Dowd, as he gave me a questioning gaze.

Relatively unsophisticated as I was and insulated from the greater world, I recognized that the pastor's gem was being a bit of a bully. I said, "No, actually I'm a Catholic."

The Renners roared and Norma Dowd's grimness disappeared and she laughed in a deep-throated guffaw. A red flush seeped through Dowd's tan. Father Higgins kept the party on even keel. "You gotta unerstan, Frank, that everbuddy is everbuddy's friend in the seminary, so that is what it's all about."

Dowd had regained his composure. "You can all laugh at ol' Frank. That's fine, but this country is turning—hell—it's already socialistic. Worse, communism is sneaking in and guys like Cox are paving the way."

"Oh, I'm sure he's not a communist." I insisted.

"The whole government is fulla commies. We gotta get rid of Truman; he's a red."

Mr. Louis Renner, who had been quiet up till then, said, "Frank, you're not serious."

Norma Dowd, smiling again, said, "Frank's on his soap box; run for cover."

Frank threw his wife a glare, which she managed to ignore. The scene was saved by Jennie who came into the room. "Dinner is served." Jennie was obviously a favorite of the couples who complimented her appearance and in the exchange of greetings, I was mercifully forgotten.

The dinner was marvelous. Jennie always had fresh linen on the table, but tonight there were candles and special napkin rings, a floral arrangement sat in the midst of the table which had been stretched to its full length. We began with a remarkable salad, then rare prime rib with tiny potatoes and carrots. I declined the wine. The dessert and coffee followed. The other five obviously had a history and they conversed of parish matters, only occasionally involving me. Toward the end of the meal. Dowd said, "I understand that you've played our club."

"Yes, with Bill Thompson."

"I've known his dad for years. We'll have to get you and Father Higgins out some time."

"I'd like that."

And somewhat contritely, he added, "And I won't talk politics, I promise."

"That'll be the day." retorted Norma Dowd. Again, Dowd flashed her a stern look, which she again ignored. It struck me that the two Dowd "gems" had a stony relationship, or was I making too much of it? The Dowds might be gems, but I found the other trustee and his wife more likable. When the meal was over, they all went back to the study, but I pleaded some desk work and escaped.

The next morning, Higgins asked "Did you enjoy the Dowds?"

"Yes." I said, without much enthusiasm.

"He and Louis are going to head the drive for the new church. Both of them . . . a couple of gems. You'll be working with the laity, so it's good to get to know them."

"I particularly liked the Renners."

"Oh, they're fine. I know that you and Frank got in a little flap over Coxie, but the Dowds are fine people, ideal parishioners, real gems. And the Renners, too. You know I just put Renner in as trustee because of Coxie. I had a trustee, Ed Schaffer, but he and Coxie had a hot battle right here in the rectory, and Ed resigned. I think he wanted me to fire Coxie."

"I know that Cox gets people excited, but he's got something to say."

"Well, you and I will never agree on Cox. George, I think you know the system here well enough so that I can get away for a few days. Jennie too; I'm taking her down to her sister's. Then I'm going to visit a classmate in Des Moines. O.K.?"

"No problem."

"Can you fend for yourself in the kitchen?"

"Again, no problem. There were only the three of us at home. I know how to cook. Maybe, I'll invite the folks over one night. O.K.?"

"Good idea; mothers like to see if their boy has a decent place to live. Jennie needs a few days off, too. I suppose you don't know, but Jen and I are cousins."

"No, I didn't know."

"When her husband died, she was in a terrible state. That's when I suggested she try to housekeep for me. Been with me ever since. A real gem, that woman."

I was pleased that the pastor would entrust me with the whole parish. I strode around the buildings like the lord of the manse. I even gave a few orders to Emil, who regarded me in disbelief. Mother loved the place. She insisted on seeing all the rooms, even Jennie's suite, in spite of my "gee, Ma, I don't think we should go in there." I was to cook, but Ma took over; as it turned out, it gave me a chance talk to Dad alone. I told him a bit more than I wanted to share with Ma, who might make more of my ambivalence about Higgins than I really felt.

"On a scale of one to ten, how do you feel about the place and Higgins, especially?"

"I guess a solid eight."

"Maybe that's good enough. So he drinks a bit. Has it affected the way he works?"

"I don't know. I don't think so."

"So hold your judgement. However,—uh—you mentioned a man named Dowd. Would that be Frank Dowd?"

"Yes."

"May I offer a suggestion? I'm not sure that this is the man. If he is the man I think that he is, our firm was involved in some litigation against him. I wasn't personally involved and the thing was settled out of court, but as I recall the office gossip, there was something wrong, something not kosher; so I'd be a little wary. A golf game is fine, but it sets up, ever so small, a kind of obligation. Now, I've got your clubs in the car, and if you want them, fine, but it could provide you with an excuse if you can honestly say that you haven't had time to bring your clubs here. George, believe me, I'm not trying to tell you what to do."

"No, I know, and I appreciate it. I'm really too busy and too happy being busy to want to play golf." Dad seemed pleased that I bought his advice. My parents went away satisfied that I was happy and well.

The whole week was great, I worked on census whenever I had nothing else to do. So many people brought up Ross Cox, that I began to keep an informal count on a paper in my desk. I wrote a plus, everytime they said something favorable about Cox, and a minus, whenever they were negative. Cox was looking pretty good. Almost every night I went down to the root beer stand. There were two large cottonwood trees, one on either side of the stand, and in its shade gathered anywhere from ten to thirty kids, mostly highschoolers. I tried not to be obtrusive, but by and by, I came to know most of them. One night, I noticed a new girl, dark-haired, lithe and with sparkling eyes. She drew a crowd around her, mostly male. Red Hammus was giving her a bad time.

"Don't kid me; I saw you with "Gunner" in his car; don't shit me."

"Hey, that wasn't me. My dad would kill me if I got in 'Gunner's' car."

"It was you!"

"Hey, don't tell my old man."

With that, she spotted me, and, apparently not embarrassed by her remark which implied misleading her parents, came over to me and said, "Hey, you met my folks."

"Maybe," I responded, "who are they?" I already had noticed her resemblance to Norma Dowd; the same smile that was more than a mouth smile, but enlivened her eyes as well.

She put out her hand. "I'm Mary Lou Dowd. My folks liked you. They didn't like Father Cox." God knows how many times I'd said it the past few weeks, "Father Cox is a good friend of mine." A kid in T-shirt and shorts, a dozen yards away, muttered "Her ol' man was the Cox sacker." I pretended not to hear the obscene pun. "Yes, I enjoyed meeting your folks. You look like your mother."

"That's my trouble." Her smile left and, like her mother, her face in repose was sad. "I mean people always say that." Then, in a quick change of dialogue, "I hear you know Bill Thompson—oh 'scuse me—Father Thompson. His sister, Beth, was my counselor at camp. She's sorta my ideal."

"I bet you both gave 'Myrtle the meddler' a bad time."

The smile returned. "Wow! You really do know Beth, why didn't you marry her, instead of all this celibacy stuff?"

I blushed then, and blushed more deeply when I realized this sixteen year old had gotten to me. It delighted her. "Father, you're blushing!" By this time a lot of the kids were watching me. I said, "You're a little imp, aren't you?"

"Don't pay any attention to her, Father, she's always doing that." This from the lad who had made the "Cox sacker" remark. I left shortly after, feeling a bit foolish that a sixteen year old girl had made me turn red.

My office at the rectory was smaller than Higgins', but just as classy; oak desk, black leather chairs, oak bookshelves, mostly empty at that time, beige carpeting and a metal file cabinet, totally empty at that moment. I sat behind the desk with collar and coat. Sitting facing me were a future bride and groom. He was swarthy and short; Anthony Rettini. Like many short men, he was talkative, even aggressive.

"So you're takin' the weddin'. O.K. by me, but Father Higgins never told us. He's out of town?"

"Yes, he's sorry. He forgot, but he called me last night and told me to take the wedding."

"You ever done a weddin' before?"

"I'm only ordained three weeks." I threw up my arms in mock alarm. Tony laughed out loud. "Me neither, Padre, so no sweat. We'll learn together, right Lil?"

She, taller by a few inches, was quieter, but very pretty. She smiled her answer silently. I had found the marriage papers in the pastor's office earlier and everything was in order, but I was mildly provoked that he hadn't prepared me in advance. The wedding was on Saturday morning, and Higgins wouldn't be back until Saturday evening. I was not looking forward to the rehearsal and wedding for which I had only the vaguest idea as to procedures. I wondered that night whether this was a rare slipup on Higgins' part or a pattern. I was to be further informed the next morning when I ran into Father Ross Cox at the religious good's store where I went to purchase a marriage ritual of my own.

"George! my honorable replacement. How's old bastard Higgins and his bride Jennie?"

"And, how's your current son-of-a-bitch?"

"Touché, Schwartzie! I hate to disappoint you, but I like the place, so far. Let me guess. Higgins is out of town on a well-deserved vacation and the bride went along."

"You are speaking of cousins."

"George, I checked that one out. They're as much cousins as you and I. Kissing cousins they may be, but real ones, no."

"Anyway, I like the place, and them."

"I have no desire to be the snake in paradise, but do keep alert. One other thing, if you start a youth group, let those suburban kids get to know how the other fifth lives. I'm glad you're there; not only because that means that I'm not there, but because he may allow you to do what he wouldn't trust me to do. Those kids deserve more than Higgins."

I drove back a little depressed. While I didn't completely believe Cox's ideas, I wondered if, at least part of what he had said, might be true.

The wedding went off fine; at least I thought so. I took the Saturday confessions without any fears, but something there had begun to gnaw at me as I sat in the closed, hot little space exchanging whispered words with 'sinners'. What troubled me was the endless repetition of the 'solitary sin,' (masturbation). Each week, very sincere voices mentioned it with considerable shame, accompanied by what seemed to me to be resolute intention not to repeat it, only to fail again—and again. All the moral theology texts judged it a mortal sin, the devastating sin which separated the sinner from God. How could sincere kids (and some adults) go in and out of mortal sin like a revolving door? I had no answer as yet, just a disturbing question. And some of the voices were familiar ones, kids whom I'd come to know at the root beer stand; kids who were very polite, reverent even. It just didn't add up. I thought of talking to Higgins, but he didn't seem to be the right one to ask.

Higgins and Jennie came back on Saturday night; she, tanned and bright-eyed; he, a little wan. By the next morning, he was his old self again, excessively praising me for the week's work.

It was some days before I could force myself back to the root beer stand, the scene of my embarrassment. I was well rewarded. As soon as she saw me, Mary Lou Dowd came over to me.

"Gee, Father, I didn't mean to embarrass you the other night. It's just that I admire Beth so much, I just thought how neat the two of you would be." She gave me the smile, but with a touch of sadness.

"Mary Lou, it's fine. I've got some growing up to do."

"You're so honest, I really like you. I hope you restart the youth group. All the kids like you." We talked for some time, and again, I noticed that when she was listening or not leading the conversation, that she had the same sad, brooding look which I had noticed on Norma Dowd's face. Was it something in the genes I wondered? I found myself liking her very much, but with a touch of pity. I promised her that we'd have a youth group again, but later in the fall.

That summer was the stuff of dreams; that, despite moments of wondering about the life of the rectory; or puzzling over moral decisions in the confessional. The confessional came more and more to be mine, as Higgins came up with various reasons why he couldn't be there "today." I didn't mind. And I truthfully could say to Frank Dowd the couple of times he invited me to the golf club, that "I haven't had time to get my clubs here." The fact was that I was simply enjoying being a priest. Sometimes, as I say, I was puzzled, unable to respond to the moral questions. How, for example, the category "mortal sin" applied to the solitary sin. And then there was the young couple whom I had married. Anthony and Lil Rettini made an appointment a mere two weeks after their wedding. He marched into my office with Lil in tow. He never even sat down. Looking at me in that aggressive manner of his, he said, "Father, she's frigid. Talk to her!"

Then, in that same abrupt manner, he walked out of the room. This was a challenge which I was hardly prepared for. True, I'd had a course in "Thomistic Psychology," and I had, after all, ordination, which included some sort of infused knowledge. Thomistic psychology was competent as far as it went; heavily indebted to Aristotle, it demonstrated how the intellect and the will controlled the passions and emotions, not unlike a driver with a team of wild horses. I do it an injustice to leave it that baldly, but that, more or less, is what I carried away from the course. Though the fault may have rested more with me than with Aristotle, I was superbly unequipped to help a gorgeous young woman with her frigidity. Lil broke into tears, a thing I wished to do myself. But I maintained the professional manner and talked knowingly of the wholesomeness of sex, God's own plan; the very heart of the matrimonial contract, and so on. She broke again into tears, whereupon I returned her to her husband, "for better or worse." I never saw them again.

Well, not many things were failures that summer. Each morning saw me off to the elm-lined streets, doing census, and finding "fallen aways." I, like the heaven of the parable, rejoiced in the return of the prodigals, which I secretly entered in my soul account, like a miser counting gold pieces. Each evening saw me instructing, counselling or at the root beer stand. I needed neither time off nor recreation. The pastor made up for it. About every other week, Higgins would announce that the Knights of Columbus, the Sierra Club or some other entity needed him out of town. Sometimes, Jennie would go along to be taken to her sister's. When she was not to go along, I noticed her smile was missing for the first days of his absence.

His absences did not bother me in the least. I was happy to have free rein. In truth, he did not much interfere with my activities. Once, when I went to dinner with a family in the parish, he said, "George, I'm not going to tell you that you can't go there, but those people are troublemakers."

The Olsons, I discovered, were troublemakers in the sense that they admired Father Cox, and when a petition to keep him in the parish went around, they signed it. The list of signers was passed on to Higgins by the chancery, and that action put them in the troublemaker category. They were not enemies of Higgins, whom they regarded with un-enthusiastic tolerance. They felt that Cox had awoken the parish from its otherwise lethargic condition. I enjoyed them and went back several times, although I never told Higgins. My own furtiveness in this matter bothered me as did some other activities in the parish which I left undisclosed.

However, it was when I was away from the parish that I began to evaluate my uneasiness with the rectory. Higgins had said to me one night at dinner, "George, I've been selfish with you and I want to make it up to you. Why don't you take a vacation?"

"Well," I responded, "Who'd say Mass?"

"I can get the Benedictines at St. Bernard's to fill in."

And so I went to Sioux Lake and stayed for two weeks with my parents. It was there, as I say, that I found what my problem with St. Brendan's was. I had never heard, and was not to hear until many years later, the term "dysfunctional family," but the reality came to me on that vacation, because ours was a functioning family, which was, for starters, that we told each other the truth. I knew the relationship between Mother and Dad; this was not to claim perfection or that they never disagreed, but it was out in the open. If there were facets of my new life which I discussed more freely with Dad, Mom knew that she had a tendency to overreact to my welfare. Yet it was she who had dared to give me the celibacy talk. Dad would have found it awkward. But everybody knew what everybody was doing. Not so at the rectory, "musketeers" that we were. I did not know the exact relationship between Higgins and Jennie, and so was left to guess whether Cox's hint was true or vengeful, or simply wrong. Nor did I know what my relationship was to Higgins. Was I O.K. as long as I didn't rock the boat? Was his praise and friendship a carrot to keep me from looking more critically at his drinking and absences? The feel of the thing went quite beyond these analyses, however. There was a sense, a stench almost, of unreality, worse, of mendacity in that house. The snake was in Eden, with or without Coxie. I was sorry that I had fathomed this.

In my return to St. Brendan's, however, I partially forgot

all this. I was treated as the long lost son and regaled by both Higgins and Jennie with accounts of the parishioners' satisfaction and praise for me. For my part, I rejoiced at my return to the joyous work of "saving souls." It was late August, and school was in the offing. I met new nuns, enthusiastic for the new year; a joy which, for many of them, would be tempered by the hard realities of disciplining recalcitrant pupils. My own part in this was worked out with Sister Mary George. I was to visit two classrooms per week, starting with the third grade and working up. I was to ask catechism questions out of the Baltimore Catechism for forty minutes. My other work with the school was to be around at recess time and to train altar boys for the Mass. Sister Mary George, the principal, and I hit it off immediately. We agreed to call each other "George" and skip the Sister-Father bit. Sister M. George was a slim five-feet-six inches and had a lovely smile. Her face was beautiful, what you could see of it; because only her eyes, nose, mouth, and a bit of her forehead were visible, the rest hidden behind the white starch and black habit which were compulsory in those days. Her blue eyes and blond eyebrows gave promise of blond hair on her head, and I had a vague desire to see it. I decided it was time to exercise more "custody of the eyes." Her voice had a musical quality, and when she sang in chapel, she led the group. She had a good sense of humor, but kept it subdued when she spoke of the pastor. She would say things like: "Father Higgins' expertise does not lend itself to the classroom." or "Father Higgins' extracurricular duties prevent him from an active role in the school." Not even Higgins himself could possibly find fault with that kind of analysis, but it was like she was effectively criticizing his absence from any meaningful role in the school. We talked to each other in this sort of code, which we both understood. I found her attractive on several levels.

So in mid-September I stood in a warm third grade classroom. The smell of chalk and fresh new books gave way to the smell of children. Perhaps nuns like Sister Mary Stephen were inured to it; I was not. Thirty-some children had been drilled aforehand to stand as the new priest entered the room. A well-rehearsed greeting, "Good Morning Father" welcomed me. Sister M. Stephen stood off to the side, not unlike a uniformed guard at a bank, while I asked, "Who made the world?" A forest of waving hands proved that this might be a little too easy for the small scholars. I stepped up the challenge. "What is a sacrament?" A few hands went up. "You." I said as I signalled a towheaded eight-year-old boy, who answered swiftly as he rose. "A sacrament is an outward sign instituted by Christ to give grace."

"What does that mean?"

He was not quite ready for that, and sat down sadly, overcome by Father George changing the rules. But a sharp-eyed blond girl rose. "A sign is like water in uh— like—baptism, and when you pour the water, the grace goes into the baby." That was quite good, and Sister M. Stephen looked pleased that her student had answered rightly. And so it went. Who were our first parents? What kinds of sin are there? What is a mortal sin? What is grace? The third graders were well prepared. Once in a while, among the sea of hands would be an enthusiastic hand waver who thought he would not actually be called on. If called, he'd be reduced to bluffing by saying, "God." or "Grace." or "Love.," knowing that these had been right answers some time ago, and might possibly be staging a comeback. My policy in this instance was to move quickly to another waving hand, hoping this maneuver would spare the erring student embarrassment. As I questioned, I made little jokes which were uproariously greeted by the pupils who were starved for any kind of break in the routine.

The Baltimore Catechism was, like others of its genre, an attempt to summarize the main tenets of our faith in words which would obviate complexity. Nor was this specifically a Catholic venture; Luther, for one, had done the same.

Many of the words were abstract and as yet unknown to tiny scholars. The idea, I guess, was that they would retain the memorization and learn its meaning as they grew. Indeed, many retained it too well; making absolutes out of definitions of mortal sin or original sin or grace etc. in such a manner as to prevent further catechesis. This mischief would be particularly rampant in the wake of Vatican II's reforms.

On the other side of the coin, Catholic theology teachers, like Bob Foley were to lament, in later days, the dearth of even minimal knowledge on the part of students never exposed to the old Baltimore Catechism. It was a mixed blessing. In those days, I simply carried out the task without much reflection. And I did get to know the children. The towhead who answered my question about sacraments was the son of one of our most cooperative families; the Nelsons. The sharp-eyed girl who knew the meaning of the words was Cynthia Renner, the daughter of our trustee.

One late September morning, Father Mike Higgins came out of his office as I was about to "go on census". His florid face was beaming at me, usually a sign that he was about to ask a favor.

"George, I've been thinking; it's time we run the fall convert class. Would you like to do it? It might be good to have a fresh voice."

"I'd be happy to."

Then, for about the sixth time since I'd come to St. Brendan's, he announced that he'd be out of town, "for a few days."

"I'm on a committee for the canonization of Frederick Baraga, the early missionary. We're to meet in Michigan, upper peninsula. Hate to leave you with all the parochial work."

"Glad to do it." And I was. Not so, Jennie, who moped around for a couple of days. Even when she was angry and depressed, she turned out wonderful meals and kept the rectory spotless. By Wednesday her spirits were better. She served an Italian meal: spaghetti, meal balls, salad, even spumoni. She was nicely dressed; she'd had a drink or two, and was,—well—sort of flirtatious, or at least, so it seemed to me. She winked several times as she made some remarks. I was busy, despite the age differential, in practicing custody of the eyes. At one point she turned somber and asked, "Doesn't it bother you that Mike goes away so much and makes you do all the work?"

"No." I meant it. I knew of several pastors who wouldn't let their assistants get involved in what they termed "parish work." I had chancery permission to binate, that is, to say two daily Masses. I usually took the sick calls anyway; and so, it wasn't much of a burden to a young priest, who was in awe of doing the Lord's work.

Jennie, however, persisted. She sighed. "You're so young; can't you see what's happening?"

"What?"

"These expeditions of his."

"Well, this one is about Frederick Baraga. Do you know about him? He was this early missionary . . . "

"Baraga! be damned! George, open your eyes."

"What?" I said again, a bit shocked at her language.

"Haven't you seen what Mike looks like when he comes back from helping the Holy Name Society or the Knight's or Baraga or whatever?"

I suppose I really didn't want to know. I just loved doing my work and maybe I purposely closed my eyes, because, in retrospect, I had noticed a certain wanness in Mike when he returned from these "expeditions" as she called them. To her I said, "Maybe a little pale, yes."

She mimicked, "A little pale! George, he goes on two and three and five day drunks! Wake the hell up!" And then she broke into tears. For some reason unknown to me, women's tears have an erotic effect on me, and while I wanted to comfort Jennie, I was afraid of arousing myself.

But I did put my arms around her. She said, "Oh, George, I love that man, but he's destroying himself. We've got to do something. This can't go on."

Then she became more subdued. During the coffee, we talked quietly. I had spent ten years of my life learning that I must be obedient to the pastor. I was hardly equipped to guide or correct him. "Jennie, what can I do?" She ignored my question, and continued on. "I think it's guilt! That's what it's about."

"What guilt?"

She looked up from tearful eyes. "Just guilt—uh—about things."

Not much more was said that night. Actually when Higgins came back, he looked fine, and talked away about the progress his group was making with the Vatican on the promotion of Frederick Baraga to sainthood. He could hardly have made it all up. Maybe Jennie was wrong. In the rectory, things went along smoothly and, while I didn't forget what Jennie had said, I put it on the back burner.

A dinner gathering with my classmates reinforced my satisfaction at being at St. Brendan's. Bob Foley and Tom Ryan had flown back from Washington to be with us. Bill Thompson was regaling us with stories about Father Gibbons at St. Isidore's. It seemed that as long as Bill worked with kids, it was O.K. with old Gibbons, but if he started to deal with adults, the pastor would get furious, probably afraid that he would lose popularity with his parishioners. Clem Bartosh wasn't allowed to come. The pastor forbid him leaving the parish. Frank Cody had driven all the way from Rapid City to be with us. We sat in the then splendor of the old Minneapolis Hotel. Above us was the kind of chandelier which could not be found in newer restaurants. The linens sparkled, the silver, vintage stuff and the whole decor more than we could either appreciate or afford. Tom Ryan assumed his usual leadership role. "Being in Washington is where it's at; the center of government and church;

and the history; George Washington, Lincoln, Franklin . . . "
Foley interrupted, "Not Franklin, he died in 1790." Ryan
looked irritated. I noted that while the two had been thrown
together geographically at the Catholic University, their old
rivalry was alive and well.

"Well, you know what I mean. There is the Apostolic
Delegate's office." (The delegate is Rome's watchdog, and
has a great deal of sway.) Ryan continued. "And, don't forget, our own Archbishop Ireland had a big part in starting
the Catholic U. It started so small and now thousands have
studied there. Think of it, a good many bishops studied
there." Then he flushed because he saw the sly glint in
Frank Cody's eyes. Said Frank, "Hey, Tom, have they
taught you yet when to take on and off your miter, or do
you have to get your canon law degree before they make
you a bishop?"

Ryan mostly ignored him. "Canon law is a lot more interesting than I thought it would be."

"About on a par with mortuary science." offered Cody.
"It's all cut and dried; a bunch of old laws that nobody pays
attention to. It's an outmoded instrument."

"Interesting that you would bring that up." retorted
Tom, "because we just had a lecture on that. Just as American civil law is not cut in stone, neither is church law. True,
some facets of canon law are obsolete, but revisions of
canon law show the flexibility and even theological growth
in the church."

Bob Foley, his skin darker than ever from summer golf in
Washington, was smoking a pipe much to the disgust of a
lady at a nearby table. He took out his pipe to make a point.
"I'd have to agree with Tom; there's a lot more in canon law
than old rules."

"Foley in agreement with me! See what advanced education will do."

We were all in clerical garb except Cody, who was wearing a turtleneck. He was nursing, no, more like inhaling

martinis. He said, "'nuff of this intellectual crap. Here, solve this, you intellectuals. Three women apply for a secretarial job. O.K., one is very bright, but types poorly; the second is a great typist, but can't take dictation; the third takes dictation, but types only fairly. Who is hired?"

It was a dumb riddle, but we accommodated him.

"The one who takes dictation," I said, "because she'll improve her typing."

"Who cares?" from Foley, "But I'd take the best typist."

"Cody is going someplace with this, but I'd take the brightest, 'cause she can pick up the rest."

"You're all wrong." announced Cody in a loud voice, "it was the one with the big tits!"

Several things then happened; Cody mustache awash in gin, chuckled. The lady who had been frowning at Foley's pipe, surveyed us all contemptuously and turned back to her table, never to look at us for the rest of the evening. I felt my face flush red. Foley said, "Frank, how could you?" Ryan, in a voice loud enough for the offended lady to hear said, as if to differentiate the rest of us from Cody, "That was uncalled for."

Cody, unabashed, continued, "I was just letting Foley off the hook. The lady with the considerable mammalia, was glaring at Bob's pipe." Foley tapped his pipe in an ashtray and pocketed it.

"Please don't rescue me ever," offered Ryan. "Frank, what are they going to do with you out there?"

"Interesting that you brought that up," said the imperturbable Cody, imitating Ryan's earlier phrase, "but that concerns me a helluva lot. The first time I saw Rapid City, I flew in, but I've been chauffering the bishop to some of the other towns. My God, some of them don't have tar streets. We hit two places for confirmation last week and the total population was less than 100—that's for both of them."

"I once told you," said Ryan, "if I get to be your bishop, I'd put you in Rattlesnake Junction in perpetuity."

I sensed, for once, that Cody was honestly worried. I said, "Frank, how do you avoid going to one of those po-dunks?"

"Usually, the new guy gets to stay in the cathedral at Rapid for a year or two, and then off to the plains. I'd like to get a chancery appointment, but his excellency seems to have other ideas."

I thought, and perhaps, the others as well, that Bishop Finley would think twice about installing a blabbermouth like Cody in the chancery. I felt badly for him; this wise guy from the Bronx, who could handle anything and anybody, except the one thing likely to come, appointment in the ranch country west of the Missouri River.

Ryan continued to bask in the glories of Washington; he seemed to enjoy canon law which was surprising to the rest of us, who regarded it as the dullest of all of our courses. Foley thought the theology department at Catholic U. was fair to poor, but he was doing collateral reading of men like Rahner, Congar, Bouyer, mostly European as I gathered, and an American named Murray. He spoke of a Protestant by the name of Bultmann whom he had a high regard for. I had heard a few of the names, and that's about all. I hoped he knew what he was doing.

Bill Thompson, patient up to a point, cut in, "All this theory is fine, Bob, but when you're in real pastoral work, what is needed is stuff like how to carry on a good program in spite of the pastor's interference."

The lady of the anti-pipe had left and Bob was puffing again. "Maybe, that's it, Bill, theology might help to rectify a very bad relationship of authority."

"Fat chance that happening," from Cody.

"Bill," I said, "I know it must be frustrating for you, but think of Clem Bartosh who can't even get out of the house to be with us tonight."

"The worst part of that," said Foley, "is that Bartosh is tough as nails."

"Why is that bad?" asked Cody.

"Usually, guys last about six months to a year with old Bronski, but Clem'll brave it out. He'll never complain to the chancery."

I said, "Listen, we need to get out there to show our support." And that night we made some promises to get out there.

"We haven't heard from you, George," said Ryan.

"Fine," I said, "anyway, mostly fine. This is not to be quoted, but the pastor drinks a bit. The flip side is that I'm free to do what I want."

Foley took his pipe out again. "There're more rumors than drinking about Higgins." I felt defensive. "Is that from Cox?"

"Yeah, but lots of others who've been with him. How are you and Jennie hitting it off?"

"Fine, we're the—I'm not kidding—the three musketeers." I laughed. The rest smiled. Foley persisted. "Don't let him take advantage of your good nature." I smiled back.

That night, I came home at midnight. Usually, I was in bed by ten or ten-thirty. As I came toward my room, I saw Higgins in his pajamas coming out of Jennie's rooms. He looked startled, but recovered swiftly. "Jennie's not feeling well. I just gave her shum ashpirin." It flashed by me what Cody would do with "ashpirin."

"How did the reunion go?"

"Fine," I said, "but Bartosh wasn't allowed to come."

"Thas a real crucifishon he's goin thru."

"My classmate from Rapid City is fearful he'll have to go to some podunk on the plains."

"That 'ud be shomthing. He outta have shomone like Jennie to help him."

"I'll bet," I thought, as I entered my room. As I lay in bed that night, I weighed the pros and cons of my life against my classmates. I was glad that I was on the "front lines," not studying dull stuff like Ryan and Foley. I'd hate to be in

Clem Bartosh's shoes. And I certainly wouldn't want to be in Cody's diocese. And Bill Thompson's assignment was no bed of roses. All in all, I had the best deal. Evaluations like that kept me from questions about Higgins, and if that was denial, well what's so bad about that. I slept between clean and crisp sheets in a comfortable bed. And I slept the sleep of the just and the lucky.

❊

FOUR

Snakes in Eden

We kept our promise. On a chilly morning in late October, Bill Thompson and I drove down to New Bohemia to "give support" to our classmate, Clem Bartosh. In those days, the relationship between pastor and assistant was roughly that of lord and serf. The cliché-joke was that assistants had no rights except Christian burial. It was not altogether a joke. Some time in the late sixties, this began to change. The title "associate" in place of "assistant" was only part of the story. We who had grovelled before pastors in our time discovered that our assistants had acquired a great deal of independence and a lot of lip with it. The obedience which was so carefully cultivated in our seminary days must have been replaced with assertiveness courses. Of course, a lot of this obsequiousness in our day was our own fault.

I had insisted with Bill that we wear our full clerical clothes. From my phone conversation with Father Bronski, I recognized that he would be a stickler for correct priestly dress. As we drove the fifty miles from Minneapolis to New Bohemia, past lush farming land, I noticed a tightening in my throat. This was, I knew, hardly the right attitude to approach this formidable cleric. As far as I could see, Bill did not share my anxiety. The rectory in New Bohemia was a fine, big three-story house, next to an imposing church, surprising for a rather small community. My apprehension did not abate as we rang the front door-bell. The many stories I'd heard of this autocratic pastor plus my phone conversation had prepared me to see a huge man. Instead, the priest answering the bell was not more than five-foot-six, thin, white-haired and squint-eyed. I had heard a rather exaggerated description, that you could sit on his lower lip. This, along with a prominent jaw, proved true. He gave us no smile. "What do you want?" he asked in a belligerent tone of voice which intimated that whatever it was, we couldn't have it.

"We are classmates of Father Bartosh," explained Bill.

"He's not here."

We could see Clem behind the little martinet. "I'm here, Father," he said, and the pastor stomped off. Clem ushered us into a bleak parlor, explaining that he had no office of his own. The room contained a worn sofa and two other nondescript chairs. We visited in hushed tones, afraid the old man would be listening. Perhaps he was.

"How's it going?" I asked.

"Looks grim!" offered Bill.

"Nothing I can't handle."

Clem put his hand to his mouth to indicate that we'd best change the subject. So we spoke about the reunion we'd had at the old Minneapolis; about Cody, about our own assignments, about Foley and Ryan. We could not have visited for more than twenty minutes when Father Bronski entered the room without knocking.

"You've wasted enough of my assistant's time. Get out, now." We were completely taken by surprise. Clem indicated with his eyes that we best do as he said. We were both angry by now, but whether it was our fear of getting Clem in greater difficulty or whether we were baffled by this weird man, we expressed nothing and were ushered out by Clem, who said, "Thanks, guys, for coming." Years later, when I understood better the ways of man, I would have surmised—at least guessed—that Bronski was really acting out of fear. He was a small man, not only in stature, but in personality, in character, and he had found power in authority. He feared desperately a loss of that power. If he was at all sentimental, that is, kind, people might have taken advantage, and despoiled his power. At least, I suspect that that was the source of his small-time despotism.

Bill and I went to the excellent restaurant in town and tried to enjoy the fine cuisine put before us, but we felt guilty about dining well, while our friend was probably getting a dressing down for the awful crime of having us as classmates. It was hard, too, not to picture Clem as having nothing more than an absolutely grim lunch, because no other scenario in that sad household seemed possible.

I said, "What Foley said is true; one of the problems is Clem's very toughness. Other guys have asked out. Clem won't, seeing this, somehow, as the will of God."

"I'm afraid you're right. What'll it do to Clem?"

"Maybe nothing, but, in the meantime, what a life!"

The handsome, middle-aged waitress, noticing our clerical clothes, said, "Do you know Father Bartosh?"

"Yes, he's a classmate."

"We really like him here, but assistants don't stay here very long. Father Bronski might be all right for adults, but the young people need someone like Father Bartosh. I hope the bishop won't take him away."

"You think the bishop takes assistants away?"

"That's what I've always heard. Who else?"

"Sometimes," said Bill," priests ask to be moved."

"Can I speak frankly?"

"Sure."

"I know that Father Bronski might be hard to live with, but, I mean aren't that what you priest are for, to—to make sacrifices?"

We just looked at her silently. This was a judgement that I was to hear throughout the years. Possibly, part of the dual standard between the clergy and the laity was our fault for stressing the higher status of the clerical life. Actually, a Christian is a Christian; and we are called equally to sacrificial living.

On the way back to Minneapolis, Bill Thompson shared with me some of his own sacrifices. His pastor, Father Gerald Gibbons, was a hale fellow well met, and friendly, and while much easier to get along with than, say, Father Bronski, he had similar fears of his power eroding.

"As long as I'm organizing stuff for the kids, I'm O.K., but let me go visit a family in the parish, and he's on my ass."

"Did you confront him on this?"

"Oh, I guess so, in a way; well, maybe not directly enough. I don't know how to do it, or how much good it would do."

Back in my rectory that night, I thought how lucky I was. O.K., so Higgins drank a bit or more, for that matter. I was free to do almost anything I wanted in the parish, Higgins was kind; so was Jennie, even if she had moods and at times, seemed almost flirtatious. What was that compared to Clem's life or even Bill's?

That kind of happiness marked my days all through the year. The pastor and the trustees and the new church committee met frequently in the winter months. Dowd and the pastor spent hours together plotting the spring drive for pledges for the new church. I could hear them in the pastor's study as I went by to the basement where I conducted the convert class, or on my way to my office for an appointment. Sometimes, I think Higgins and Dowd enjoyed having drinks together with or without a church agenda. Over 150 men in the parish joined in the pledge drive and it was a great success. The pledges went well over the goal. The church would be under construction by the following year. While this was going on, I was mercifully spared from all this fund raising and could devote my time to the youth sodality and the convert classes, among other projects.

I hardly remembered the remark made in seminary days that Bill Thompson had made, and that Foley had seconded heartily; that a lot of our theology consisted of sets of proofs; prove God's existence from nature; prove the historicity of the gospels; prove the resurrection; prove the true church; prove, prove, prove. It was the way I had been taught. It was the way the Catholic Church had responded to the reformation and to the enlightenment. (That movement which, in effect, accepted only information from the senses and reason; small room for faith.)

There certainly was a point to all of our rational defenses, and it was a successful way to bring in converts. By the end of the first two years, I'd brought in forty-seven converts. Higgins joined in our success as the archbishop watched. Most of them were confirmed along with our eighth graders on the fifth of October, 1953. I let Higgins take the credit, as the archbishop congratulated him on the large number of converts. "Yes," he said, "Father Schwartz and I take a lot of time with them." Ryan, now the vice-chancellor, smiled knowingly at me, but I didn't need individual recognition. The fact is, I kept a running count of converts and of those I'd brought back to the faith, almost like a rich man counting his assets.

Meanwhile, Foley continued his studies for his doctorate; Thompson struggled with G.G. as he called Gibbons; Bartosh held on in New Bohemia and Cox was moved a sixth time. Worse, poor Cody got moved to a place with the incredible name of Lost Creek.

Thompson's stock with his pastor went up, because under the careful coaching of Bill, the athletes from St. Isidore's swept everything in football, basketball and baseball. By the spring of 1954, we were in the new church at St. Brendan's. With the archbishop present and Frank Dowd as toastmaster, the celebration was concluded with an inspir-

ing speech from Higgins. He praised all who had made a
success of the fund drive, and also the work of the whole
parish. I was included in the litany of commendations. Parish spirit was high and we all wallowed in it. That night, I
remember being unable to sleep, not because of any anxiety,
but for the sheer joy and excitement of the day. Pajama-
clad, I looked out the window at the garden under the light
of a full moon; the garden which was just then throwing off
winter, a few bushes starting to leaf. I was so grateful to be a
priest in this day and in this alive and wonderful parish. I
heaved a sigh for classmates and other young priests of my
time who were struggling in difficult assignments, but I
would have been too selfish to trade with them. Finally relaxed, I sank between the sparkling white sheets which Jennie replaced twice a week and I slept the sleep of the just and
the lucky. It is well that we have such moments of joy to
help sustain us when the dark and evil days come.

I had not long to wait for such days. The sacrament of
penance at St. Brendan's had become mostly mine. At
Xmas time, at Easter time, and on days when confessions
were heavier than usual, like the Thursday before first Friday, Higgins made an appearance. He no longer made excuses for his absence at confession time. For me, as Jennie
had predicted, the joy of rescuing sinners had evanesced. In
the tiny box, hearing children dealing with "distobedi-
ence," I fought sleep. Adults were not much more stimulat-
ing. Any job has such moments, and occasionally, a prodi-
gal son showed up after ten, or twenty or more years away
from the sacraments, and I shared in the joy of heaven
which Jesus spoke of in regard to repentance. But these are
not weekly.

It was a Saturday in late May, late in the confession day
also, when I heard slow dragging footsteps. There was a
pause outside the confessional as if the person, (a woman I
guessed by the footsteps) was not sure she would go

through with it. Finally, the sound of knees on the kneeler. I opened the slide, and for a moment, there was no sound.

"Yes," I said.

Instead of the usual formula, "Bless me, Father, for I have sinned," she said, "This is going to be hard."

"I'll make it as easy as I can."

The voice was the merest whisper. "O.K., I've been doing bad things for years and I haven't been confessing them." The voice trailed off.

"Well, what a good time to get this straightened out."

There was a large sigh, and then, "You don't understand."

"Uh—try me."

"Really bad things. I mean immoral . . . "

"Many things are immoral; stealing, lying, hating . . . "

"You know what I mean."

"You mean sexual."

Again a slow sigh. "Yes."

I used the customary query; "Was this alone or with others?"

"Both, but—uh—mostly with another."

"Was this only touches or was it intercourse?"

"Both."

"One person or more?"

"One."

"Have you been going together for a long time?"

Now there was such a long pause that I thought she was giving it all up. Then she said, in a choked voice. "That's the trouble. I'm not going with him."

Two thoughts, very troubling, pushed their way out of my subconscious. One, that it must be someone in her family; and a second, perhaps more frightening thought, that despite the low whisper, I knew her.

"Was this someone in your family?"

A pause. Then she choked out the words; "My dad!"

This time the long pause became mine. I had heard about this sort of thing, but I supposed it took place in faraway places, not in a Minneapolis suburb. Finally, I said, "Have you talked this over with anyone?"

"No, not until now."

"I think you have to deal with this outside the confessional. I mean it's hardly your sin, it's your dad's."

"No, its mine, too. I—I liked it."

"What age were you when this first occurred?"

"Uh—twelve, I guess."

"You could hardly be guilty at that age. I'll give you absolution now, for whatever wrong you might have done, but I think we need to talk more about this. Are you willing?"

"I guess so. Maybe that's why I came to you in the first place."

"Could you come to the parish house tonight?"

"No—no, that wouldn't be good. I could meet you some place."

"Where?"

"Do you know that little park on Logan?"

"Yes, what time? Seven?"

"O.K."

"Would you recognize me without my priest's clothes? I mean it might be better to come in civies."

"I'll know you." I gave her absolution and she left. In a reversal of form, I asked Higgins to take confessions that Saturday night, and he consented. Thank God, he didn't ask why.

That took care of only one of my problems. What on earth could I do? I had no—zero—experience with parental molesting. But it was clear to me that I couldn't just sluff it off. Something had to be done. But what? I thought of asking Higgins, but that seemed wrong. Anyway, it was still only confessional knowledge. A confessor could, without betraying the person ask questions about procedure. I thought of calling Monsignor Baker, but he had little parish experience; besides, his field was dogma not moral theology. Jennie asked where my appetite was and Higgins asked if something was wrong, but I laughed and left the table early.

I did a thing I thought I'd never do. I called Ross Cox. I'd sought him out once before on dealing with kids and the sin of masturbation. He judged it to be of minimal significance. I asked him what I should do.

"There is only one thing to do. Take her to the police station and get her to tell her story. If you go to the father, he'll simply deny it, and probably beat the daughter or God knows what. Listen, wrong as he is, he remains an authority figure in his house. You've got to put another authority figure against him."

"What about me? Aren't I an authority figure?"

"I don't think it'll work. What penalty or threat do you represent? Schwartzie, go get him."

We talked some more, but that was the essence of the matter. It was ten-to-seven when I left the house. I had awful forebodings about whom I would find there, or if anyone would show. I almost wished she would chicken out. The park is not much more than an acre in size, there were shade trees, a swing for kids as well as a teeter-totter. It was deserted that night. Suddenly she was there and my worst fears were realized. Strolling slowly, reluctantly toward me, head bowed, was Mary Lou Dowd. She said,

"Now you know it all."

"Mary Lou, I think I recognized your whisper."

"What now, Father?"

"You realize that what you previously told me was under the seal of confession. I can't repeat a word of that. If you agree to talk about this now, it'll be away from the seal. It's still a private matter, but no longer absolute. That is, for a good reason I could share that information. You don't have to say one more word to me if you don't want to. Understand?"

"God, I feel rotten."

"An adult to a child? You're guiltless."

"NO! Sometimes I liked it. When I was younger, dad used to snuggle me; you know like all fathers do. Once, when ma was out of town, he got carried away. I must have been thirteen at the time. I knew it was wrong, but still I sorta encouraged him."

"Would you be afraid to go to the police with me?"

"Good God, what are you trying to get me to do? Get the police on my dad?"

"Mary Lou, you've got a twelve-year-old sister. What about her?"

"Yeah, and I worry about that. When I'm away at school, I wonder. I heard Beth crying one night, and she wouldn't tell me why."

"I know the police sounds terrible, but . . . "

"I can't do that. Would you come and talk to dad?"

In a corner of my mind, I'd been expecting this. I hesitated. Cox's advice seemed better. The sad eyes which I had noticed when I first met Mary Lou deepened. I recalled that same sad look in her mother.

I asked, "Does your mother know about this?"

The sad eyes met mine. "I'm not sure. I think so, probably." Ma and dad hardly talk to each other, except when people are around. Dad told me I was the only person keeping him from leaving. I guess that's why, at least it might have been, why I uh—accommodated him." So that was the great Dowd, the trustee, the "Gem."

"I'm going to ask you, Mary Lou, outside the confessional, if you want to tell me what you and your father did." The same sad eyes, which could be lively at other times, looked at me.

"We did sexual things like intercourse."

"Could you say that in front of a cop?"

"No."

"Mary Lou, if you don't, I'm going to go to the Bloomingdale station and sign a complaint."

She turned white. "You can't!"

"I'm sorry, but I think it's my duty."

"Father, that'll ruin my family. I know you mean well, but this is not the way to deal with this. Why can't you come with me and confront him?"

I considered it; I really did, and if I had gone with her, I'd have saved myself a lot of grief, but I felt it wouldn't work. I had the other daughter to think of, and I suspected that Mary Lou wasn't out of the woods on this either. I said, "I'll sleep on it, and you do the same. Can you meet here tomorrow at two p.m.?"

"Promise you won't act on this."

I was told later that I had acted precipitously. It was the very opposite. I paced the floor that night. I thought of people whom I could call, my dad, Bill Thompson, Monsignor Baker. But it seemed to me that, while it was no longer under the silence of the seal of confession, it was a quasi-confessional matter, and, therefore, I should be careful about talking to too many people. I even thought of talking to Higgins, but I felt that he would be unable to believe that his friend, Dowd, could possibly do this. At last at two a.m., I fell into a troubled sleep. I surmised, even then, the kind of trouble I could get into, but I vastly underrated it.

It was a bright sunny afternoon, the temperature in the high sixties, when I arrived at the park, somewhat ahead of the two p.m. appointed time. Unlike Saturday, the park was well populated; some dozen children and adults filled the tiny park. I felt a little foolish standing about almost like some voyeur. I waited. I thought when Mary Lou came that we'd have to walk away from the crowded little park to discuss the situation. At two-thirty I wondered what was keeping her. By three p.m., I began to wonder if she were coming at all. At three-thirty, I realized that she was not coming. I went home and called their home. Frank Dowd answered. After we had exchanged a very few words, I said, "May I speak to Mary Lou?"

"About what?"

"I'd like to speak to her."

"After all, I'm her dad. What you have to say, you can say to me."

"No, I want to speak to her."

"She is not well; she can't come to the phone."

"What's wrong?"

"She's emotionally upset; maybe you know something about it."

I didn't know how to proceed. I said, "Please have her call me when she feels up to it."

I hung up. Again, I paced the room. At five p.m., I told Jennie that I'd be out for dinner. Wearing my clericals, and with a great deal of anxiety, I marched into the Bloomingdale police station.

"Yes?" asked an officer, who looked like he might be totally anti-clerical.

"I'd like to talk to an officer in private."

"What about?" He seemed to sneer at me.

"Something serious."

"A crime?"

"Yes."

"Your own or somebody else's?" he asked with a big smirk on his face. By this time, my nervousness had gone out of control. I pounded on his desk and shouted, "I want a private meeting with an officer right now, or I'll have the mayor on your back!"

He pressed a button then, and I heard him say, "There's a hysterical priest out here, and he wants to talk to you."

I was too troubled to bother about his insolence.

An officer came out of an adjoining room. He was a man in his early forties, clean cut, well-built, and fine looking. He was obviously of higher rank than the sergeant at the desk. He glared at the desk man and said, "Father doesn't look hysterical to me." There was no response. "Come with me, Father." I was ushered into a small room.

"Don't mind Shulz there; he was turned down by the diocese for a second marriage, and he's hated all of you since. What can I do for you?"

"If I report a crime to you, do you have to act on it?"

"It depends. If it's serious enough, yes. Some crimes might demand a complaint from you."

"Can I start by asking about a theoretical crime."

"Might be the way to go."

"Suppose that I knew that a girl, well, a nineteen-year-old, had been sexually assaulted by her dad?"

"I'm Catholic, Father, so I'm assuming this is non-confessional knowledge."

"Right."

"Is the woman willing to testify."

"No, I'm almost sure, no."

"Puts us in a rough spot. If I arrest him, I could be sued for false arrest. And you—you could be sued for slander. Let's say you swear out a complaint. If the father denies it, and the daughter doesn't admit it, we're nowhere."

"Doesn't the law envision a situation where the daughter is intimidated, where she blames herself as a willing accomplice, even though, in fact, as a teenager, she could hardly resist this authority figure, her father?"

"Yes and no, Father. First of all, you hardly came here to discuss a theoretical problem. So you are aware of just such a situation. I'll tell you what I'm willing to do. You swear out a complaint, and I'll go to their home. The man may weaken under accusation. What do you think?"

"I doubt it."

"Or the daughter might admit it. In either case, we'd have him. But even if both of these possibilities fail, he knows that he's under suspicion. Representatives of the community, you, and the law, me, have him on notice. It might change or at least curtail his abuse."

I sat in the tiny room and weighed the consequences. They could be pretty grave for me. On the other hand, I couldn't see how I had a choice if I were to do my duty. The officer looked at me with a mixture of sympathy and yet challenge, a sort of put up or shut up expression. Finally, I said, "O.K., I'll do it."

As I signed the complaint, I realized I had recrossed the Rubicon. I walked out of the station into the lovely May evening, and I strolled down the elm-lined boulevard where the leaves were getting close to fullness. I had a feeling of fear in my stomach, and yet it was accompanied with that peace that Jesus promised, the peace that the world cannot give. I gobbled a hamburger at the root beer stand, went home in the twilight, crawled into bed and slept the sleep of the just and the unlucky.

It broke loose the next day after lunch. Higgins had been out at lunch, and Jennie and I were sitting leisurely talking of whatever, when I heard the front door bang shut and an unsteady but heavy-footed Higgins burst into the dining room. He'd had liquid reinforcement to amplify his rage.

"You—you dumb son-of-a-bitch, you asshole, you have ruined the reputation of our finest family." I had sort of expected it, even though I had hoped for the best. Jennie looked nonplussed. He turned to Jennie. "This idiot took the confession of a troubled adolescent down to the police."

"It was out of confession. You're lying!"

"Sure, you inveigled her out of the confession, and got her to exaggerate her embraces with her dad and..."

"There was no NO exaggeration!"

"Many family members may have a passing erotic feeling while embracing..."

"Bullshit! this was far more serious. You're trying to minimize rape!"

"You shut your goddamn mouth!" and with that, Higgins made a menacing fist at me.

I said, "You make one move on me, and you'll be in the hospital, you damn drunk!"

"You get out of here now!"

"I was sent here by the archbishop and only he can move me."

"I just talked to him. You are moved. He's ordered you to report to him tomorrow at ten a.m. sharp." Then, as if realizing that I wouldn't be stampeded by his bullying, Higgins seemed to soften a bit. "George, why didn't you bring this to me? I could have told you that the girl is a very mixed-up kid whom they've had trouble with for years."

"The trouble is her dad!"

Higgins retreated into anger. "Just get out!"

Later, when I went past the kitchen, Jennie said, "Now, get all your stuff out. I don't want you coming back like Coxie." By this time, I'd recovered my composure; I said, "Why Jennie, whatever happened to the "three musketeers?"

She said, "One of 'em shit in the parade!"

"Jennie, you say that with the elegance and class I've come to expect from you."

I did take out "all my stuff." I decided to go to my parents' home in Sioux Lake. When I had finished my explanation of my moving back, Ma said, "That priest was right, who called Higgins a 'jerk', wasn't he?"

Dad said, "I did warn you on Dowd. I looked it up, but I never told you. Dowd was in investments at the time our firm got involved. He had bilked a widow out of a considerable amount. I wasn't involved with that litigation, but Dowd settled out of court, so there was no record."

"I'm not surprised."

My father looked at me, "George, how are you feeling about this?" Mother said. "How could you ask such a question? How do you think he feels after being—being—well, fired?"

Dad looked at Ma with patience; he smiled and said, "Let the witness answer the question."

I had to stop for a moment; "Mixed. I feel bad about leaving a place where I really thought I was accomplishing a lot." I sighed. "On the other side I know that I did the right thing. That means a lot to me. I guess, overall, I'm O.K."

Dad said, "I thought that's what you'd say. How does the quote go? Be true to yourself, and it follows as the day the night, thou canst not be false to any man. Hamlet, right? I mean Polonius."

"Plus, Dad, there was something not right in that household. I feel free."

And we shed no tears that night; a different set of musketeers.

I walked into the chancery just before ten, to be met by Tom Ryan, now Monsignor Thomas Ryan, Vicar General of St. Paul.

"George, I'm so sorry. I know it wasn't your fault, but the old man is furious; he thinks you misused the sacrament of penance. I tried to tell him you were as good as gold, but Higgins is an old friend. I'd advise you to let him yell, for a while. Then he'll cool off."

"I have no apologies."

"Sure, O.K., but play it cool."

With that, I was ushered into his excellency's office.

"Sit down," he ordered in a hostile voice. I sat down and looked at Archbishop Francis Dunn. He was a short man, with a round face, a face most unsmiling at that moment. He was flushed all the way up to the top of his mostly bald head.

"I have been told that you manipulated the very sacrament of penance for certain purposes of your . . . "

"Your excellency, I DID NOT manipulate the sacrament!" I surprised myself with the vehemence of my defense.

"You will wait until I have finished my statement. There is a very thin line between the seal of confession and getting someone to talk outside the confessional. Do you see that much?"

"I won't say anything about confession, but what was said to me was most certainly outside the seal."

"Young man, that is not my point. Young people can be led into strange accusations . . ."

"She was not led into anything."

"Since we are perilously close to the seal, I will say no more except to warn you away from any future imprudences. I am assigning you to Monsignor James Rogan at Our Lady of Seven Sorrows. He is known as a strong disciplinarian. You are to report next Friday at noon. He will expect you at that time, precisely. I trust you will learn prudence as well as fulfilling the promise of obedience you made to me a few years ago. That will be all."

Ryan met me outside the door. "How as it?"

"What can I say? Unjust that's it; unjust."

"I hear he's sent you to Rogan."

"Yeah."

FIVE

✥

Out of the Frying Pan

The Right Reverend Monsignor James Brian Rogan, the pastor of Our Lady of the Seven Sorrows, was known as a "breaker" of priests in the same sense that a cowboy breaks in wild horses. The analogy falls apart severely over "wild" which we were anything but. I'll pursue that later. I'd met him a couple of times; once hearing him speak in a caustic manner at the seminary; and once at confirmation at St. Brendan's. If you could, as the wag had it, sit on the lower lip of Bronski, Rogan's lip protruded like a setee. The guys who were sent there, used to say that it was the Church of Seven Sorrows in the sense that each and every day of the week there was a sorrow. Another wag had said that it was the only parish in the archdiocese where even the altar boys had ulcers. With these happy thoughts to sustain me, I drove to near downtown in Minneapolis to assume my new position, prone, I surmised.

The church was huge, as was the rectory, a formidable set of buildings. I was met at the front door by the redoubtable monsignor, or rather by his sister, who had a lower lip and strong jaw, not unlike her brother. She summoned her brother, who did shake my hand, but began, "I heard about how you manipulated the sacrament at St. Brendan's and..."

I cut him off, "I did not manipulate . . . "

But he continued, "There'll be none of that here. I was at St. Brendan's for confirmation, and I saw you preening over your converts; there'll be none of that here. No convert classes. The man who has house duty the week someone comes for instructions takes the convert through. Converts need to be taught one by one. Do you know the difference between the heresies of Lutheranism, Presbyterianism, Methodism etc.?"

"I think so."

"You think so; you should know so." With that, he gestured to his stern jawed sister who said, "Pick up your bags. I'm not going to carry them. I'm not your servant!"

I wanted to say "Nor I yours." But I kept silent. She led the way up two flights and pointed to a suite of rooms. "Meals are PROMPTLY at eight a.m., noon, and six p.m. Have your laundry here on Mondays at seven." She slammed the door as she left. The suite had a large sitting room/office, a bath and a bedroom. The quarters were large, but seemed to fit the coldness of my reception; gray walls, a kind of dull brown carpeting, and small windows. Even the bookshelves managed to preserve the austere nature of the place.

There was a knock at the door, and two priests entered, the other assistants; Greg Bowler and Tony Shulz. I knew both of them slightly. "Welcome to outer Mongolia!" said Greg.

We shook hands. "Hey!," said Tony, "you've heard these nightmare stories about Rogan and Mary, his sister. All those silly horror stories; we're here to put the lie to all that rot."

"Yes," said Greg, "the truth is that all those awful stories about this place are false, the reality is much worse." Then, they both laughed. Greg Bowler was three years behind me at the seminary and therefore could have been here no more than two years. He was a chunky, pear shaped, non-athletic looking blond. He smiled easily, and underneath his fat face, there seemed to lurk intelligent eyes. Tony had been at Seven Sorrows for a long time, which might indicate either a strong, lasting character or, conversely, a passive personality. He was at least six feet tall, handsome face, slightly graying hair, and a bland smile which was impervious to my deciphering. I asked, "How long have you been here?"

He quoted the psalm, "How long, O Lord, how long? Eight years, enough time to assure me a swift purgatory."

"C'mon, Tony, there're much worse places."

"Sure, Auschwitz, Siberia, and hell, to name three."

I was getting tired of this ghoulish Rover Boys game, and maybe it showed in my face because Tony, without any change in his inscrutable expression, said, "It's indoctrination time; what's more, old Rogan expects the old boys to explain things to the new boy. The old boy is nuts on time. He should have been a railroad conductor. So, everything starts on time. Meals start on time; confession starts on time; Masses start on time; weddings and funerals . . . "

"Is it true that you start the funeral with or without the body being there?"

"I know that's hard to believe, but wedding—or funeral—you start on time; corpse or no corpse, bride or no bride, the show must go on."

"I've heard that stuff, but it's hard to believe."

"Become a believer; you know why you're here? You're replacing Flynn. What he did was refuse to start a wedding without the bride, who was five minutes late. Rogan had him out of here before sundown."

"It doesn't make any sense. How can you have an exchange of vows without the bride present?"

"Ah," said Tony, "that's where you come in. When prepping the wedding party, you emphasize this time thing. You actually tell them that you'll start without them. It usually works." Tony began again. "Then there's Mass. It must be said exactly. Any aberration from the rubrics, get out the ritual and refresh the rubrics. Now, the next couple of weeks will be tough on you, but, also on Rogan. He'll be on edge making sure that the new boy is doing it right. So, on your toes."

Greg broke in. "As bad as all this sounds, once you get on to the system, it's not bad at all. Oh yes, meals! He does lunch in five minutes; dinner in eight. When he's done, we're all done, so we spell each other."

"Spell each other?"

"Watch us at lunch; Tony will ask questions about Archbishop Ireland or some old deal. Guy knows history, so he'll show off. In the meantime we eat like hell. Then I'll leap in with another question; then you and Tony eat like mad. Only way to survive." Again Tony broke in, "Another thing, don't even think of starting a youth program or an adult one for that matter. He doesn't believe in parish organizations."

"So what's the program? What do we do?"

"What do we do?" mimicked Tony, without a change in expression, "it's not all a waste of priestly zeal. You will offer Mass, hear confessions, anoint the sick, preach, instruct the ignorant, both here and in the school, and you'll have time to get away. It's not all bad."

"Get away?" I asked. "Like for weeks?"

"Actually, we're overstaffed. It's partly Rogan's power over the archbishop; it's partly prestige."

"I don't get it."

"Rogan wants three assistants because the cathedral has three. It has nothing to do with need; everything to do with ego. The arch wouldn't dare to cut us back to two guys. In the meantime, if you want a week off, you just ask, and usually he's O.K. with that. The same with daily life. If you're not on house duty, you can go anywhere you want."

After they left the room, I pondered this new setup as I hung clothes in the closet and put books on the ample shelves. I was still musing as the lunch bell rang. Tony and

Greg were rushing down the stairs not unlike firemen answering an alarm. Monsignor and the two of them were already standing by their chairs as I entered the large and surprisingly pleasant dining room.

"Come, come, come!" said the Monsignor, as if summoning cattle. In spite of the absurdity of it, I hurried obediently to the one remaining chair. He then said grace in the Latin form we had used in the seminary. We sat down and a bowl of soup was placed before the good Monsignor who began to attack it vigorously and not without gurgling noises. He had gotten way ahead of the rest of us, when Tony spoke up, "Monsignor, do you know the new bishop of Tulsa, uh—McMahon, I think?"

"He must be a young man, I never heard of him. I knew Farrell, of course. I once spent a week with him. He was very fond of horse racing, had to give it up when he went to Tulsa."

"Did laymen complain?"

"No, but there was no racetrack."

I ate swiftly as instructed. Then it was Greg's turn. "Monsignor, have you heard that the Pope is going to issue a new encyclical on pornography?"

"It won't do any good. Especially in this country. The secular humanists have destroyed the public conscience." Again, Tony and I ate like mad and attacked the sandwiches put before us. We were keeping ahead of the Monsignor. I decided it was my duty now. I said the first thing that came to my mind.

"Monsignor, did you know Archbishop Ireland?"

He looked at me with fury. "What kind of a stupid question is that? I've been in the diocese for fifty years. How would I not know him?"

I looked a little sheepish. "I, I didn't know his dates very well." At this point, he stood up without finishing his sandwich. Again, he said a brief Latin prayer and we all left. Tony, smiling or smirking, I wasn't quite sure which, said,

"Nice try. You'll catch the formula, don't worry."

The next morning I said the eight-o'clock Mass, with the right reverend kneeling behind me saying his rosary. He corrected several things about how I held my hands, how I mispronounced some Latin word, and the topper came when he said, "Why did you make the sign of the cross after the prayers for the conversion of Russia? Are you in charge of the rubrics? Are you inventing a new version of the Mass?"

"I thought I was supposed to."

"Learn it correctly. I will not have a sloppy performance of the Mass here."

"Yes, Monsignor."

As I look back over the space of forty some years, I try to understand my own cravenness. Or was it the climate of the times? No young priest today would put up with it. True, we were taught to obey. The whole thing was heavily military. The church was glued together with iron discipline. Pope over bishops; bishops over priests; pastors over assistants and both over laity. We spoke of the church on earth as the "church militant", and that was the model. The old testament words of God, that "I prefer obedience rather than sacrifice" could be misconstrued. It meant that rather than ritual sacrifice, God wanted loving obedience; loving treatment of others. Instead, it came out as slavish submission to superiors. Truly, it was an act of faith to find the will of God in some malicious order from a crotchety monsignor or from a whimsical mother superior. If it defied common sense, so much the greater virtue. Besides, if one chipped away at the system, would not the whole deck of cards collapse? The question is still being addressed. If this chain of command helped us in humility, what happened to the superior? Or does the old dictum not hold; "power corrupts, and absolute power corrupts absolutely."?

I found that not only was Rogan my boss, but his sister of the same granite jaw, was as well. She would march out of the office with a printed address and say, "Go to this home and give the Last Sacraments to so and so." And we did. After a while (maybe a month), Rogan quit attending my Masses. Apparently, I'd passed inspection, at least for now. I was even given a certain reluctant response when I asked questions at meals. I could slow down the pace at meals, whether to prevent starvation or indigestion, I'm not sure which.

And the guys were right. If ministry at Seven Sorrows was restricted, it was good sacramental duty. Nor was freetime to be despised. I took time to arrange lunches with Bartosh; with Thompson who was suffering Gibbons; and with Foley when he came back to town. After I'd been there for six months, I asked and got permission to visit Cody out in Lost Creek, South Dakota.

The monsignor let me take the six a.m. Mass on Sunday, so I could get an early start for Lost Creek. I had not looked forward to the long trip across the flat, dreary plains, one I had taken twice before. In seminary days I had listened to endless debates between the Dakotans and Minnesotans about the flat, treeless, barren lands of Dakota. I chuckled when recalling that both of them used the same words, "You can't see anything." To the locals it meant that there was nothing to see but bare, empty land stretching to the horizon. The Dakotans said, "You can't see anything," meaning the trees and hills restricted your views. When I had travelled with my parents, we had sometimes played a betting game. When we sighted a grain elevator in the distance, we'd wager how many miles away it was. I think twelve miles was the winner.

Despite the fact that I had no companions and the radio held nothing of interest to me, I was surprised at how pleasant the trip was. The solace was retreat-like in my being able to examine and sort out my disturbed thoughts. I really was concerned about Frank Cody; the tough little Bronx kid whom nothing fazed, except being sort of imprisoned in

the loneliness of the village of Lost Creek. What would become of this lippy little Irishman? However, to be honest, I
was more concerned about myself. I have known people
who seem to suffer more by what happens to others than to
themselves. Whatever is missing in my psyche, I confess to
a greater care for myself. There was much to sort out. The
day before I left on the trip, I got a letter from Mary Lou
Dowd, in which she explained what had happened. Up to
that point, all I knew was in bits and pieces.

Dear Father Schwartz,

I feel so sorry about your leaving St. Brendan's. I know you
did what you felt was best. When the police officer came to our
home, he asked my mother to leave the room; then he told dad
that someone had signed a complaint about sexual molestation.
Dad demanded to see the complaint, and there was your name.
Dad got VERY angry, and denied it. Then the officer turned to
me. I couldn't bring myself to betray my dad. My dad was
shouting at the officer who explained that he had to act on a
complaint. Then dad called Father Higgins who talked to the
cop. I guess Father told him that you were obsessed with sexual
sin and easily would mistake paternal embrace as immoral, and
that you hated dad. All the kids miss you here, and most of
them don't know what happened.

I know I'm partly to blame for what happened to you, but I
did tell you I couldn't go to the cops about dad. Please forgive
me. Don't write to me because the folks are opening my mail.

Love,
Mary Lou Dowd

It was hardly a fulsome apology. As I drove past the brown
November fields, I wondered if I would do what I did, under the same circumstances. I decided that I would. There
was a sense of the early martyrs in my thought. I had fought
the good fight; I had kept the faith. I could live with the

consequences. I felt the small and barely rewarding comfort of having done the right thing; and yet that cold comfort was enough; like the sun momentarily breaking through the bleak November clouds and giving a dash of color to the grayness.

Thoughts came too, about my new place. A hundred some miles away from Seven Sorrows, the whole sick setup seemed hilariously funny; black humor, if you will, but so absurd that I laughed out loud, zooming across the open highway at seventy plus per hour. An old martinet of a monsignor and his sister, ruling over three adult males as if we were medieval serfs. I thought, too, of my companions in grief, my co-assistants, Greg Bowler and Tony Shulz; we had a bond of mutuality formed from having a common enemy. I wondered if we would have been friends in some other setting. Tony possessed a pleasant cynicism which fitted the place, and while he talked and joked a lot, I could never quite know what was important to him. He worked hard and seemed to be a devoted priest; but what was his motivation? He was an articulate preacher, but lacked passion. He trained the altar boys so well that they were like a drill team; he responded to sick calls immediately. His performance of weddings and funerals was flawless, but again, without much personal warmth. He was always willing to take my place on a golf day; all in all, a pleasant man.

Greg was a warmer person; outgoing and friendly to parishioners. He shared our common cynical humor, but he was so laid back that his considerable intelligence seldom got expressed. Like Tony, Greg had no interest in golf or any sport. He sometimes walked over to the nearby park, book in hand, to read by the small lake. Once, when Foley came to visit, the two of them got into a theological discussion and I realized that Greg was conversant with many of the European theologians which Foley was pursuing. But that was a rare occurrence; mostly our talk was on shared duties or persiflage about Rogan or his sister.

I thought, too, of my parents. When I was at St. Brendan's, mother had gently hinted that my home visits were rare. I now had less to do and so almost every week I would go back to Sioux Lake for lunch or dinner. I kept up also with Bill Thompson and Clem Bartosh. Gerald Fox, too. Gerald who was going down to El Salvador on a five-year program with some missionary order. I hoped that he knew what he was doing. These various thoughts were like a constant conversation as I drove the treeless plains. The gentle flat plain changed to more rugged hills and valleys as I neared the Missouri River. The dark November day turned darker after I had crossed the Missouri and headed off the main highway onto a decidedly secondary road which led south to Lost Creek. Soon, it was pitch black without the occasional warmth of farm lights. All I could see was the blacktop and its yellow midline. I had the eerie sense of being the only person in this dark world. I shivered involuntarily. What if I blew a tire? The last two hours of the trip were the most difficult, and the tiny roadsign, "Lost Creek" was most welcome.

I had no trouble finding the church, even though the streetlights were dim (all three of them). There was a cluster of houses; a "downtown district" consisting of a general store, a bar, and a gas station. Only the bar and connecting restaurant was open. I turned off downtown to see if I could find the church; my headlights picked up a building with a cross; a surprisingly fine building, small, red brick. The house next to it was a small white frame building, which had to be the rectory. I had told Cody that I'd be in at mid-afternoon, but it was now evening. Cody answered the door, bright-eyed and a bit wobbly.

"Midafternoon, huh? It is now past six. If I'm a trifle sloshed, the fault is yours, old friend. I have wiled away the hours with a sip or two of Scotch; speaking of that, would you have a drink?"

"Is that the most welcoming words you can give to the weary traveller?"

Then, gesturing in a circle at the tiny living room, Frank said, "Behold, the manse! Fit for a king. A sort of down-and-out king. But come into the commodious kitchen, where I have prepared cuisine unknown, yea, undreamt of in these parts."

The kitchen, although a mess of pots, pans, and utensils, gave the smell and appearance of a gourmet's product. I held up my hand to halt the overly generous Scotch poured into my glass, while Frank poured twice the amount into his own. His moustache was now in full bloom, almost concealing his mouth and nose. I said, "You look like a Mexican general.

"And, you, poor boy, look like a refugee from Cannery Row. How is life with the good monsignor? As I recall from seminary conversation, Seven Sorrows, so aptly named, was where all of you St. Paulites wished to be elsewhere of. So why? Of course, Bill told me of your breaking of the seal of confession..."

I glared at him, and Cody put up his hand defensively. "Hey, hey, you know I'm not serious. I meant to soften your blows with a bit of humor. When ol' Frankie imbibes, he's been known to droop a bit in the sensitivity department."

"I should have remembered. But to answer your question, strange as it sounds, Seven Sorrows is not as bad as guys claim." I went on to describe the place as I had thought about it as I drove that day. I ended by saying, "I burst out laughing today just thinking about the absurdity of it all."

"Laughing about it is what ol' Frankie does here." Then, turning serious, Frank said, "In winter, when the wind blows day after day, I worry that the mind is leaving. Then comes a few days, so quiet that I can hear my heart beating. Then I know I'm nuts."

Thus did we spend the evening commiserating with each other and recalling old school days and companions. I had finished my five-year pledge of not drinking, but I was still very careful, keeping in mind Higgins. Cody was under no such discipline, and as the evening worked toward morning, his words became more slurred. Maybe the good part was that he no longer put on the show of being the cool, unflappable guy of seminary days, and his vulnerability and his pain surfaced. His loneliness was evident and he made no attempt to hide it as the liquor loosened both his tongue and his emotions. It came out that his total congregation consisted of twenty-seven families in Lost Creek and another fifteen in Elk Head; most of his people lived on ranches, some as far away as twenty-five miles. Priests were good at visiting, and that helped, but "ol' Frankie" as he called himself had turned a few off by his caustic wit. The congregations could not support themselves, but the Extension Society, a charitable organization, kept things going.

The next morning I heard voices as I got up and Frank, looking surprisingly alert, introduced me to his housekeeper who came in from time to time to clean house and to cook. Her name was Rosie and she was quite attractive; red hair, cute pug nose, green eyes, beautiful teeth and a nice figure. She said, "Well, you're Frankie's classmate, he says. Tell me, how bad was he in school?"

Frank gave her a studied look and she said, "Oops, I mean Father Frank."

I answered, "Very bad, but I managed to keep him out of major problems. How bad is he here?"

She laughed. "Nobody could figure him out at first, but now we love him."

Again there was some wordless communication and she started working in the other rooms while Frank fed me bacon and eggs.

"Rosie is cooking for us tonight. Good western fare; steak and taters."

"She help you every day?"

"No, she comes in two or three times a week. You know, laundry, housecleaning, sometimes a meal. She's good company, too. Rosie can talk about something other than the cattle, loves a joke. I'm lucky to have her."

"Listen, Frank, don't let me keep you from your work. I can walk around town or read; don't think you have to entertain me." Cody laughed, "My work! Once a month I bring Communion to an old-timer back on a ranch; lives with his son and family. My work, last year I had a funeral; this summer, a wedding. I'm burning out. I counted the collection yesterday, this aft we'll go to the big town and deposit the whole bundle, seventy-six bucks."

"Don't you visit the people?"

"Sure, but they get tired of my big fat face."

"I can understand that!"

"Well, they do. Not all of them. Like old Finnegan whom I bring Communion to. After the prayers, he brings out a jug, prime stuff; Jack Daniels. Sometimes I stay for dinner."

"How about hobbies? Grow a garden; raise bees."

"Not ol' Frankie's style. Not the rural type." He was not as open as he'd been the night before, however. He was the Frankie of old; the cool kid whom nothing bothers. He said, "Actually, I like it here. It took a little getting used to; the guy before me, Miller, was very formal. When I started clowning around, they didn't know who's on first, but ol' Frankie brought 'em around. Hell, I could be mayor."

Rosie came back into the kitchen, saying. "Frankie—uh—I mean Father, I counted thirty-one cigarette butts in the two ashtrays. Now, what was the promise? No more than a pack a day."

"Rosie, haven't you got something better to do than count butts?"

She raised her eyebrows and grinned mischievously. "This will be reported to one of the trustees, tonight."

"Her husband, Jim Hogan, is one of my trustees." It answered a question which had been pushing its way into my head. She was married. She said, "Jim, wants me to monitor his health. Jim thinks we've never had anybody quite like Father Frankie."

I said, "I hope not."

"She smiled. "You know, Father Miller was a dear, but he was so formal. And now . . . this . . . "

"This what? asked Frank.

She deepened her voice, "This s-t-r-a-n-g-e person!" I noticed her retreating sway as she left the room. Very attractive. He shouted after her. "Omelettes for lunch. You got that?"

"Yassa, master."

Perhaps, having been around Higgins and Jennie brought me to notice that people with close relationships throw out a lot more signs than they are aware of. Or was I reading more into this than there was? For his part, Cody was always informal and it was certainly not out of character for him to have a perfectly innocent, but unconventional friendship with a young married woman. He seemed neither embarrassed nor guarded about Rosie. We continued to reminisce about the sem days and to share our mutual dilemmas. But Cody was talking differently than he did the night before. It was the old cocky Frank Cody whom nothing dismayed, the man who could handle it all. There was no mention of the solitude he had pictured as he sipped Scotch a few hours earlier. We only broke up our discussion as Rosie called us to lunch. As I led the way into the dining room, we passed Rosie and I thought I saw Frank pat her arm. At lunch he called her, "the bishop's wine." She raised her eyes toward the ceiling. "Wow, the bishop's wine."

"What's this 'bishop's wine'?" I asked.

"Oh, it's a little joke. When I have the priests in, we serve ordinary wine, but when the bishop comes for confirmation, we serve the best stuff. The old guy is a connoisseur, so we give him top dollar."

"Father, see Frankie has put you on the same level with the bishop."

That afternoon, as we drove up to Missouri City to bank the collection, I decided that it was almost a duty to ask, "Frank, what's with you and Rosie?"

Frank looked angry, but quickly caught himself, and smiled beneath his mustache. "Hey! hey, big guy, you got us in bed already."

"It's not an accusation; just a question."

"For starters, Schwartzie, if ol' Frankie runs off the reservation, it won't be with the country milkmaid."

"She seems to me to be quite the sophisticate."

"Maybe, Twin Cities' sophistication; not New York. Anyway, you can ease your conscience. You've done the fraternal correction bit. Rosie Hogan's husband is six-four, 230 pounds and can pick up a tractor end with one arm. Trust ol' Frankie."

It did ease my mind, and that night at dinner, a more restrained Rosie served salad, steak and fries. Had he talked to her? Rosie went home after serving dinner and Frank and I again talked far into the night. I left on Wednesday, a little earlier than I planned, partly to spend a couple of days with my folks, but partly, too, because Frank's endless chatter was getting to me. In the sem, you'd hear him for an hour or so, but here there was no interim. Also, though Frank denied anything between Rosie and himself, and, I had never known Frank, despite all of his talk, to lie, I was uneasy about their relationship. Frank really hated to see me go, and I almost reconsidered. When I said my goodbye, Frank, the little Bronx cynic was near tears and thanked me effusively.

Driving back across the barren plains of November, I replayed my earlier concerns; my being ousted from St.

Brendan's; my current status; how long would it be? I'd
hate to spend eight years there like Tony. The only youth
work there was the altar boys, which Tony clung to. Nor
could I put so much effort into turning altar boys into mina-
ture drill teams. Then there was Maria. Maria Nelson had
come to Seven Sorrows a month ago. She had a black eye
and other facial bruises, a present from her husband. In
those days there were no homes for battered women; at least
I knew of none. I called the police who said that they could
act only if she signed a complaint. She was unwilling. She
called me a few days after her initial appearance to tell me
that he had promised to change. Then she returned to the
rectory one night a few weeks later, badly beaten and her
face bleeding. I had a talk with him then, he agreed to go to
a counsellor at Charities, and she seemed to think that all
was well. Even then, I wondered how lasting his repentance
would be.

Then there was a very small personal matter hanging over
me, small and yet bothersome. Beth Thompson had invited
me to her wedding, and I didn't want to go. I tried to understand my own emotions, but I couldn't. The couple had
dated for years. He was a budding attorney, and they
seemed ideal as a pair. I seldom thought of Beth those days.
And yet was I, in some weird way, jealous of her husband-
to-be? It couldn't be. But when Monsignor Rogan assigned
me a wedding on that very date, I was relieved. And I pondered over Frank Cody. In loneliness and booze what might
happen? Or was I overreacting? These ideas accompanied
me as I drove into the eastern sun, past small towns, small
but mostly larger than Lost Creek.

When, after a few days stopover with my folks, I returned to Seven Sorrows, I learned the good news that
Monsignor was to be out of town for two weeks. The climate of the place changed dramatically. We sat at lunch and
dinner for an hour, if that was our mood. We drank wine at

dinner. We told jokes and lingered over coffee. We talked of things which were forbidden when he was present. We were like kids freed suddenly from parental supervision. I'm not sure that we recognized the stupidity of it, grown men letting this old man reduce us to buck privates under a sergeant, and happy when we had a brief surcease.

When I returned, I had a number of phone messages, one from Maria. I returned the call to be told by her husband that she was out; a second time he said that she was busy. I called a third time and got the same response. This time I said, "I want to talk to her!"

"Father, we don't need your help anymore. Everything is fine. We're in counselling with an expert, so don't call anymore." He hung up. I doubted him, of course. I wondered if I should go to their house and insist on seeing her. I was indecisive.

The second week I was back, Tony said, "George, your turn with house duty." This duty required me to be around the house during the day to take house calls and to connect the night phone in my room and, therefore to take sick calls which might occur at night. On Sunday, I had two emergency calls at Wright Hospital which was Seven Sorrows' responsibility; one at midnight, another at three, a pretty sleepless night. But the rest of the week proved uneventful, until Friday night. The man on duty also had the front doorbell connected, so that it rang in his room. Usually, we turned it off at nine p.m., because otherwise we might have to run down three flights only to find some drunk demanding to "see Father" at two in the morning. For some reason, that fateful Friday, I forgot to turn it off when I went to bed. At two a.m., the doorbell rang. Mistakenly I grabbed the phone and my sleep paralyzed hand dropped it. I was then awake enough to recognize that it was the doorbell. The doorbell sound must have been designed by the monsignor, because it had a shattering effect. I stumbled over to the closet, donned a bathrobe, and decided, that since I had to go downstairs to turn off the bell, which had resounded again, I might as well have a peep at the drunk who had blasted me out of sleep. I peered through the peephole to see, not a drunk, but Maria. Maria was a rather plain looking woman, but, at that moment, she looked horrible; her nose was bleeding, there were cuts on her lips, and a large bruise across the left side of her face from her eye down to her cheek. She was shaking and crying and babbling almost incoherently. I ushered her into one of the offices and tried to calm her down. I wiped some of the blood from her face with the tissues in the desk there. She stammered, "When—when, he—he went to get another drink, I ran from the house, that's why I'm only partly dressed. I ran all the way down here." At this point she sobbed and shook uncontrollably. Instinctively, I held her in my arms as I'd seem mothers hold a sobbing child. As I held her, her shaking subsided a little. We were face to face, and with no plan on my part, and I think, none on her part, our lips fell together for a moment. Her breath, whether from fear or cold or grief, or all of these, came in gasps.

At this juncture, the Right Reverend Monsignor James Rogan, suitcase in hand, opened the door. He had come home a day early.

"Get this trollop out of here!" he said.

Poor Maria, dazed and confused, said the first thing that came to her mind. "What's a trollop?" she said, somewhat irrelevantly. I said, "Maria is not a trollop. She has been badly beaten by her husband. Can't you see that?"

"Get this woman out of here, and come to my office! Immediately!"

"No," I said, "I am taking her to a motel. She dare not go back to her violent husband."

"You leave here and the door will be chained." I knew this was no bluff on his part, because he used to chain the place when he had a couple of partying padres as assistants. I said, "Stay here, Maria, I'll be right back." I went to my room, put on clothes and took all the money I had out of a drawer, thirty-seven dollars, and went back to the office where Rogan was still shouting at the terrorized woman. I finally blew my stack. "You dumb horse's ass, can't you, once in a lifetime, have some human compassion?"

He said, "Your possessions will be in the back yard when you come back." I was later to learn that he told the archbishop that there was "lingual contact" going on between Maria and myself. I drove Maria to an all-night motel, paid twenty dollars, for her room, and gave her the rest of my cash. I sat with her for an hour until she had regained her composure. She said, "What is going to happen to you? It's all my fault!" I thought she had enough to worry about, without worrying about me, so I fibbed, telling her that I'd be fine. I gave her my parents' address and got in the car and drove until seven a.m., when I returned to the rectory to find all of my worldly goods piled neatly by the back door, just as Rogan had threatened. A light rain was falling, and the little miserable heap of books and cassocks and suits and the box of lesser garments, getting slowly soggy, seemed to fulfill the biblical admonition to travel lightly. Only my golf clubs were incongruent with Jesus' command to take only the necessities. Mary Rogan must have supervised the removal, because everything was in order, including the radio I had brought into the rectory replacing the ancient one that had been there. To their credit, Tony and Greg, risking the old boy's disapproval came out to assist the renegade pack his car. I tried to explain what had happened, but I could not erase the image the Monsignor had painted of a half-dressed priest amorously hugging a half-dressed woman at two in the morning. They both shook my hand and Tony said, "Keep in touch." I had no money and barely enough gas to get to Sioux Lake. Worst of all, my parents had trouble understanding what I had done.

"But," asked mother, "why were you dressed in a bathrobe?"

"Ma, it was two in the morning. I just went down to answer the doorbell."

"I thought you turned the bell off at night."

"I forgot to."

"Then this was not prearranged?" said dad.

"Please," I almost shouted, "she had run from her husband who was beating her. She was all bloody, so I let her in."

"But why did you kiss her? pursued mother.

"She was shaking and sobbing like a child. I was trying to calm her."

"But," said Dad, "you have to think of appearances." I started to cry, and mother put her arms around me. "We love you. We're just trying to understand."

"For God's sake," I shouted, "try a little harder!"

"Don't shout at your mother!" said Dad.

"Maybe, I should leave!" It was a bluff on my part. I had no place to go and no money.

"Let's all calm down," a tearful mother said. "Let's have breakfast." I drank orange juice, played with the bacon and eggs; all the time preserving a laconic monosyllabic anger, replying with "yes" to the question "Would I call the bishop?" and "no" to the question "Did I know what the bishop would do?" I finally said, "I need to rest." In spite of my worry over the future, the night had worn me out and I slept the sleep of the weary and the unlucky. At ten, I awoke, went downstairs and called the chancery. "The archbishop is busy and Monsignor Ryan is away from his desk." announced the receptionist.

"Well, this is Father Schwartz. . . ." I began, but she interrupted, "Oh, just a moment." Her voice had taken on a new note of urgency. I didn't know if this augered good or bad. In seconds, Ryan was on the phone. "George, what happened?" I explained carefully, only to receive the bleak message, "Well, that's a far ways from Rogan's account. George, I hate to tell you, but you've been suspended, until further notice."

"Suspended! What the hell for?" I screamed into the phone as two parental heads in the next room bolted up in dismay.

"George! George! a little patience. You've got to understand, you're in a jam. Rogan claims that the girl was panting amorously and that there was, in his words, "lingual contact.""

"For God's sake, listen! She wasn't panting; she was shaking and breathless in fear and pain. Nothing erotic about it."

"George, I argued for you on the Higgins' affair. You've got to start thinking about appearances. You can explain 'til the cows come home about comforting the sorrowful, but it's not going to sell with either Rogan or the archbishop. Face it, you were in a very compromising situation. Verbal support, fine, but embracing a scantily clad woman, is—is imprudent."

It was Tom Ryan at his monsignorial worst; the guardian of that middle morality, appearances rather than what Jesus called the "weightier measures of the law, justice and mercy and charity." These can get in the way of ecclesiastical preferment. I sputtered in anger. "And you, do you believe my account?"

He paused, "What I believe doesn't cut it. I can't bail you out of this one. The boss won't even talk to you. There's nothing I can do. You've got to start taking care of yourself. By the way, have you got a place to stay?"

"I'm with my folks. And I do not, NOT, need any help from you, old friend!" I hung up.

Mother asked, "What's happening? What's suspension?"

"Please," I said, "grab a cup of coffee and sit down. I

want to talk to you, both of you. I need you now. I need you to understand what I did, and maybe more, what I didn't do."

We sat at the diningroom table, and I said, "Suspension means that I'm not to officiate as a priest, for a while."

"How long?" asked mother.

"I didn't even ask. That's bad enough, but I need to have your understanding that I didn't do anything wrong. It was not erotic. I let in a crying hysterical woman and when she shook so wildly, I held her as you would a child. "I looked into their tense faces, wanting desperately to believe me, and not quite making it.

Dad said, "We talked this over while you were sleeping, and we know that we should have reacted differently, but we just uh" "Weren't prepared," mother finished for him. "We do trust you, you never lie to us."

Dad cut in, "It's just,—well—just that you have to think of appearances. You should comfort women with words, in a case like that."

"Dad, given the same setup, I'd do it again."

I saw the sadness in their faces, straining so hard to believe me. Dad looked at me carefully. "We back you totally, and maybe it's a bad time to bring up the law, but the law tends to judge not intent so much as what happened. I don't want to be insincere when I say that prudence is as important as sympathy."

I guess it was the most I could hope for, so I dropped it. We didn't talk about it for the rest of the day, except indirectly like; "George, you know it's nice to have you with us." It was like one of those lunches after a funeral, where everyone is cheering everyone else with easy banter, and nobody mentions the name of the deceased, which is why they came together in the first place. Still exhausted from the long night, I tried to nap, but I couldn't. I took a long walk. It was one of those unusual Novembers, when well into the third week of the month, there was no snow on the ground, and it was warm, about the high forties. I didn't want to meet anyone I knew, so I walked down past the old brick works, and into a country road that was all but deserted. Some people take pills, some get massages, when they are depressed. My therapy is to walk.

There was much to think about. I really wanted to know how long I'd be suspended, but a curious pride prevented me from calling the chancery. Here I was, ready to carry the word to the nations, the twentieth-century answer to St. Paul, and I was benched. "Benched," I repeated the word aloud. Benched, the great ballplayer, the rescuer of battered wives and abused children, made to sit on the bench. What was happening to Mary Lou and Maria in my absence? And how could I stay here? In any other context, I would have been delighted to be with the folks, but with us tiptoeing around my suspension, it was just too uncomfortable. I began to form a plan.

That night Ma went all out with my favorite dinner, roast chicken, mashed potatoes, gravy and dressing, topped off by chocolate pie. My sadness had not conquered my appetite. We were sort of quiet; no mention of my situation. We talked of the unseasonable warmth, the death of one of my dad's law partners, Aunt Helen's waning health and the Eisenhower administration. My father liked Ike and I did not, but I wasn't prepared to argue about it. The quiet evening gave me a chance to notice the folks close-up. I noticed that they were aging. A few years ago, there were a few strands of gray hair on my mother's head, now the gray predominated. Dad's craggy good looks were still there, but there were new lines about his eyes and mouth. I noticed, too, that his hearing was less sharp.

As we sat sipping coffee, I laid out my plan. The folks owned a small cabin on Pinecone Lake, north of Brainerd. I said, "Can I use the cabin?"

"Now?" asked Dad.

"Yes."

"But next week is Thanksgiving."

"I've thought of that, and I'm sorry, but I need to get away."

"What would you do?" said my practical mother.

"Hike, fish, maybe hunt, read." I shrugged. The word "hunt" must have sent warning signals to my mother; guns.

"Wouldn't you get depressed up there alone?"

"Ma, I'm not suicidal, if that's what you're thinking. I want to hang around to get even with the bastards."

"George!"

Dad, however, loved my response; and for the first time that day, laughed heartily. The various wrinkles in his face grew together in a big grin. He always loved a fight and he was glad to see my determination.

"Go ahead and use the cabin."

"There's another problem. I've got less than fifty dollars in my bank account."

"Will five-hundred dollars be enough?"

"More than enough."

The rest of the evening was spent in the details of advice on the woodstove, getting the cabin phone turned on, how to get the water turned on; how to keep warm etc. The next morning I was ready with clothes packed, some food from Ma, and my breviary and a few books which Foley had recommended, but I hadn't yet read. I said "goodbye" to a tearful mother and a misty-eyed father.

It was colder north of Brainerd and there was snow on the ground. It took a while to settle in; to get the woodstove going and the fireplace warm; and to get the water turned on. It was five p.m. and dark before I had time to walk on the crunchy snow and look at the snow covered lake and the tall pines. There was a crescent moon, and the stars, clear of city smoke, were as bright as I remembered.

If I were asked to say what happened in those weeks, I suppose I'd say, "very little." I hiked. I chopped wood. I chopped holes in the ice and fished. I read authors Foley had talked me into buying. Rahner, Congar, some articles by an American Jesuit with the highbrow sounding name of John Courtney Murray. They opened my mind somewhat, but I was frustrated with their complexity. In retrospect, I wonder what my percentage of comprehension was; forty, fifty, sixty, percent? Certainly under eighty percent. Each day I called the folks or they called me. I had moments of loneliness and sadness. These events, except for an occasional phone call were the pattern of my days, the outer, superficial pattern. Deep in the psyche where ideals and emotions and ideas like justice dwell, I guess much more was occurring. Sometimes, in later years, when counselling people in the process of divorce, I would hear one partner say, "She's bringing up stuff that happened twenty years ago. I thought she'd forgiven and forgotten long ago. God, it was my one infidelity!" Somewhat like that, the foundations of my marriage to the Church had been shaken. I was still the loyal soldier. Suspended? O.K., I could handle that. The will of God came through superiors, and I never doubted my obedience. This was on a conscious level; below, beneath, things represented by words like "loyalty," "honesty," "fairness," were carrying on another dialogue, which would surface years later.

I had told mother to be selective about giving out my phone and address. Thompson called, asked if I wanted company. I told him to wait. The same from Foley, Foley who now taught at St. Anselm's. Fox suggested that I go with him to El Salvador. Cody, typically, had found out about me, and called. His usual banter was absent, and I could see he was careful not to offend me, even though, he called at night, and his tongue was well oiled. He, like the others, offered to visit. Unlike the others, he argued about my insularity. I suppose that all of them, including my parents felt that my seeking isolation was on the sick side, but it was healing for me. Possibly, there were angers and rages festering within, but that was not what I felt. It was more that I'd entered a world away from my sorrows. Oh, memories pushed their way into consciousness at times and brought sadness with them. But mostly I was occupied with the stuff of immediate living. Chopping wood, catching fish in the still waters of the lake beneath the ice, keeping the cabin warm, going to the town for groceries. Then there was the peace of long walks in the cold air and sometimes under the brilliant canopy of the stars. At the end of ten days, it was enough. Mother had cried on the phone on Thanksgiving day, and Dad had hinted that my absence was causing both of them some pain. So, a few days after Thanksgiving, I decided to go back to Sioux Lake, and also to check into my clerical status. I tried to call the folks on Sunday and when I couldn't get a response, I thought they must have driven down to Aunt Helen's, and may have stayed overnight to help her in her illness. That there was no answer on Monday began to worry me.

Monday night the phone finally rang. It was Father Krause who had taken Father Walsh's place at Sioux Lake. As soon as I heard his voice, the adrenaline rushed through me. There had to be something wrong. He began, "George, I didn't know how to reach you until a few minutes ago. I have, I have some bad news, very bad news. "He hesitated, and I said, "About my folks?"

In retrospect, I can see that he was preparing me for a shock; that he was reluctant, afraid almost to tell me the extent of the bad news, but at the time it was frustrating.

"Yes." he said.

"What?" I screamed into the phone.

"George, you know that rail crossing on Spinner. They either didn't hear the train or couldn't stop."

"Bad accident?"

"Yes." Again the maddening hesitation.

"How are they?"

"George, they're dead." Quickly, he tried to ease my pain. "They didn't suffer; they died instantly." He paused.

"NO!" I screamed. In ministry, when I had to inform a spouse about death, that "no" had seemed affected. It is not.

"After I could breathe again, we talked about arrangements, funeral home etc. I said, "I'll leave right now."

I explained things to my neighbor, Ned, who lived down the road, and had a key to the place, and asked him to keep the cabin warm.

"I'll do better. Do you want me to get Dupre to put electric heat in the place?" I said "yes," and drove through the snowing night, oblivious of that or anything other than the black, empty hole in my life. It would have been safer and wiser to go in the daylight, but I didn't care about safety.

I can only recall bits and pieces of the funeral days. Even when I managed to sleep, the awful ache in my heart was there. Awake or asleep, that huge weight stayed in body and soul as if I had somehow swallowed moistened cement which then hardened in my stomach. I have heard that people under great stress can have hours or even days wiped out of memory. Not quite for me. Parts of the funeral are retained. The relatives came. Priests came. All of the local classmates, except Fox who was already in El Salvador. Cody had flown in from Rapid City. Ryan was there; I remember thinking that he looked sheepish when he said, "The boss is at the bishop's meeting, but I'll get this suspension thing taken care of." And he smiled as he said, "Gotta get you back to work!" It meant nothing. Technically, a suspended priest cannot say Mass, but no-one seemed to notice as I offered the funeral Mass. In those days, we didn't often preach at funerals, but Bill Thompson did, and I'm sure he did a good job, but I can't remember. Beth and her mother were there too. Mrs. Thompson said, "Why don't you come and stay with us for a few days?"

I made some excuse as I did to relatives and others who invited me. Cody had to catch a plane and so couldn't stay for the funeral lunch. As he shook hands, he said, "Rosie is divorcing her husband. I don't know what's going to happen." At the time, I just couldn't respond. I wanted to be alone with my grief. Frank Griffin from my dad's old firm said, "I'll need you to sign papers."

"Later." I said, "Can you get me a couple of thousand? I'm going back to the lake." He mumbled an affirmative. Beth Thompson, now Mrs. Tom Kelley, was the only one to break through my reserve. She said, "I am coming up to see you whether you want me to or not." It seemed O.K. I stayed a day after the funeral at Griffin's request to sign papers, to get my money, and to hear him say, "Father, you realize that you are a wealthy young man." It meant nothing. When I got to Pinecone Lake, it was night. The electric heat had already been installed. I stretched out in the big bed, and, for the first time in days, slept soundly. Looking back to that time, I still do not know why, like the elephants of legend, I wanted to be alone with my grief and my anger. My sadness and almost despair, were abetted by the fact that my parents, try as they had, had not really accepted my explanation of comforting Maria. They believed me, but not totally. My suspension rankled, too, but at that moment, it was relegated to some far-off part of my brain.

At Pinecone, I dealt with my grief by the daily toil of living. I cleaned the cabin. I chopped holes in the ice and fished. I chopped wood, (even though I now had electric heat). I went to town (also Pinecone Lake), to get groceries. I helped neighbor Ned with his farm work on occasion. I took long walks in the cold, crisp night air. I developed a new habit, too. Each morning, if the weather was good, or even half good, I drove to the little eatshop in town, bought a Twin City paper, and read it while breakfasting. Newspapers had been denied us as students. Now I rediscovered an interest in national and international affairs. So I poured over the Trib, or the Dispatch while eating bacon and eggs. Sometimes I joined in the conversations around me if they were general topics like cold weather or fishing or mild political arguments. Rural America has scant trust of Congress. Mostly, I read my paper, beginning to form opinions of the Cold War, Korea, China, labor and capital, and Hubert Humphrey. My fastening on these events seemed to take me out of my grief, at least for short periods. Some of the people there knew who I was; the waitresses and the manager too. They assumed that I was up there on some sort of a rest. One big overalled farmer, who ate with his cap on always asked, "Are you feeling better?" This judgement seemed better than to explain that I was suspended, so, without lying, I let the impression stand.

Then, one early January morning, it happened. There was the glaring headline; PROMINENT BLOOMINGDALE BUSINESSMAN ACCUSED OF FRAUD; SEXUAL ABUSE. I know that I must not wish revenge. God says: "Revenge is mine." The idea being that God will avenge or justify us. However wrongfully, I let out a whoop, which turned all of the cap-wearing clientele toward me, and brought my favorite waitress, Judy, over to ask what was wrong. "Somebody I know," I said by way of answer. I read on to discover that "Divorce trial turns ugly as Norma Dowd accuses her husband of sexually abusing their daughters." The article went on to say that Frank Dowd is alleged to have defrauded the Church of St. Brendan's of an amount exceeding $100,000. The pastor, Father Higgins, was thought to have been an innocent dupe in all this, but he had been sent to an alcoholic rehabilitation facility, and there was some diocesan question about the large travel expenses he had taken from parish coffers. As I said, revenge is wrong, but, my God, how I enjoyed it! I sat there in that tiny restaurant, sipping cup after cup of coffee, as I read and reread that news item. May God forgive my enjoying the suffering of my enemies, but it was sweet. I drove back to the cabin, and with an ugly and growing hubris, called Monsignor Thomas Ryan at the chancery.

"I've been trying to get you for weeks." he began, "The arch lifted your suspension two weeks ago. Where the hell have you been?"

"Busy reading the papers."

"O.K., O.K., George, Dowd and Higgins are on the shit list, but I've got a good offer. Monsignor Baker is going to retire from the sem in June, but he's already pastor of St. Christopher's in downtown St. Paul. He'll both teach and run the parish until June. Now he specifically asked for you as assistant. What do you think?"

I somehow wished for more of an apology, and I wanted the arch and Ryan to eat a little humble pie, but I decided to skip it. Besides, it was a good offer, and I thought I'd like to work with Baker. In addition, it was as close as a chancery gets to acknowledging guilt, by giving me an "offer" rather than ordering me to St. Christopher's. I accepted.

A few days later, I sat in Monsignor John Baker's office, and listened to his plan. Going from being a seminarian to being a priest sets up an amazing change in relationships to former profs.

"George, this is going to be a partnership. I want you to call me 'John,' well—except when the laity are around. And we'll split the work evenly." I always liked Monsignor Baker, and I trusted him, but there was a touch of déjà vu in this, inasmuch as Higgins had talked this way when I came aboard. Even though Baker was a more honest man, I sat there silently, not responding. Baker must have read my mind, at least partially, because he said, "I know you've been through the ringer with pastors; I remember telling you, on ordination day, that Higgins was a good-natured guy or something like that, but what good would it have done to tell you that I thought he was a lush? As for your trouble with Rogan, well, I've heard both versions, and, George, I can see him honestly misinterpreting your actions. But to get on with it, I'll still be teaching at the seminary until June, so you'll get the lion's share of parochial duty till then. I guess that means funerals, weddings and hospital visitation. Afterward, we'll have a week each of house duty. And George, you've had more parochial experience than I, so you and I will discuss projects and changes; naturally, as pastor, I'll have the final say."

"Naturally," I assented, with a very slight grin.

"Did I catch a little cynicism in that 'naturally'?"

"You are dealing with a man who has been pushed to a little cynicism." But I smiled warmly, I hoped.

"I'll get you over that. Now for the next four months, I'd like you to cover the front door. Marge, you've met her, the secretary tells me that eight to ten people come to the front door to ask for a priest. Some want to go to confession; some for spiritual counsel, and many for money. As I understand it, the policy here has been to give out tickets for the mission. The first one gives them meals and another ticket gets them a night's lodging. Then, at the end of the month, we pay for the tickets. I guess its $200 or $300 per month. We don't give any other money."

Just then, the buzzer sounded in Baker's study. I heard him say "yes." He turned to me. "I guess you start right now."

"O.K., Monsignor."

"Name is John."

"O.K., John." But it felt awkward.

The man in the front office stood up when I came in. He was a street person, but looked fairly clean. A middle-aged man, but with bad teeth, unruly hair, and a heavily lined face.

"Father, I'm not here for money."

"Good." I said, "'cause I don't have any to give." We both smiled. I saw him carefully eye me before he continued.

"I gotta uncle down in Virginia; he made 'monsignor.' Maybe, you heard of him, Monsignor O'Neil?"

"No."

"Well, I got this problem. I'm a diabetic, and I'm outta insulin."

"Gee, too bad. Won't they give it to you at the hospital?"

"You kiddin'? They want $20, or no insulin."

"I thought you didn't want money."

"I don't. I just need insulin." He took out a moldy bill-fold and extracted a picture of a priest. "This is my uncle, Monsignor O'Neil. I know he'd give a man insulin. It's a matter of survival."

I hesitated, remembering Baker's orders. "See we just give tickets to the mission." I hid in parish policy.

"If I can't get help from my own church, I don't know where to go."

He was wearing me down. Besides, I'd just learned that my inheritance was close to a million. "Well," I said, "this once I'll give you $20, but we can't make it a habit."

"Father, thanks, you've restored my faith." After he left, Marge said, "That was quick. You must have given him money." She looked at me accusingly.

"Well, it was for medicine. Vital medicine."

"The insulin scam. Father, he hits all the parishes in downtown once a month. Catholic, Baptist, Methodist, you name it."

"Why didn't you tell me?"

"Sorry, I was on the phone. How much? We'll repay."

"Nah, maybe I'll learn this way." But she insisted.

"The problem is that now we'll have a flock of them coming in to take advantage of the new man. I'll tell 'em you're out." That was my introduction to downtown St. Paul. The scene would be repeated hundreds of times, but I was to become a more skillful dodger. Back in my room, as I unpacked and stacked the bookcase, I thought that Marge would prevent any further house calls. About eleven a.m., she buzzed.

"Somebody looking for money?" I asked.

"Ooh, I don't think so. It'd be worth you're time, just to come and look." Marge was a tease.

In my front office, there she was, looking more gorgeous than ever, Beth, now Mrs. Kelley. She smiled as I kissed her lightly, and then she frowned at me. "I drove all the way to Pine—whatever—and you were gone; all this in twenty below weather. Took me all day, so you're on my list. You know what kind of list."

"Things happened so swiftly."

"Anyway, congratulations. But do you like it?"

"C'mon, first day. Looks good. So do you."

We chatted on, some things about losing the folks, my chancery problems, and so on. Then she said, "Don't wanna dump this on you. Can you handle some grief?" She was still smiling.

"It's second nature for me."

At that moment the gay, smiling facade dropped and her blue eyes turned bleary. "Maybe, you've got enough to deal with."

"Beth, what is it? Your marriage?"

She nodded as tears now coursed down freely. After a moment, she regained her composure and her voice. "Marriage," she spit out the word, "it's no marriage, just a legal contract."

"Beth, what is it?"

"You know that Tom and I dated for almost ten years, I really loved him. He was *so* honorable!" She said it mockingly. "When we hugged and kissed, He'd say, 'we'd better stop now.' I was proud of his restraint. Such a noble man! To be honest, there were times when, virtue be damned, I wished he were less moral. I wanted him, all of him! Do I shock you?"

I shrugged my O.K. She went on. "The honeymoon was a disaster. Turns out, he doesn't like sex, at least not the normal kind."

"He's homosexual?"

"I don't know. Hell, I know I'm reasonably attractive." I was weighing this understatement as she continued. "I've never seen any sign of homosexuality, but..."

"Why did he marry you? Do you have a clue?"

"Uh, yeah, I guess. Maybe successful attorneys need to be identified as regular; well, something like that. It wasn't money; he makes plenty. I help him entertain."

"How is he otherwise?"

"Other than that, Mrs. Lincoln, how was the play? Well, we talk together; he treats me with great respect. I'm the ornery one. Ornery and horney; oops, 'scuse me."

"What will you do?"

"You mean—leave him? I don't know; I'm Catholic, you know, till death do us part. I suppose that's why I'm talking to you. My brother, Bill, well, it's hard to talk to family."

"If you do leave, there're decrees of nullity built around this sort of thing."

"Like Catholic divorce? I'm not ready for that. I keep praying to St. Jude for a miracle. Do you know if people like Tom can change?"

"I've not run into much of this, but I gather that it's rare."

We talked some more about it, and then she said, "You know you're not the only guy with problems with pastors. Brother Bill is fed up with Gibbons. Seems like he's restricted to working with kids. He likes that, but he wants to be a part of the bigger scene. No dice." The time, as the adage has it, flew by. At eleven-thirty, Marge banged on the door. "You gonna say the noon?"

I'd forgotten that we had confessions at eleven-thirty, Mass at noon. I wanted to take Beth to lunch after Mass, but, in those days, if you wore the collar, accompanied by a raving beauty, it caused comment. If you went in secular clothes, it might look sneaky. Besides with my reputation... So I bid her a reluctant farewell.

"Wow, who is that?" teased Marge.

"Father Bill Thompson's sister."

"Now that is a typical priest's explanation. The woman has no identity of her own, just 'Father Thompson's sister.'"

"O.K., then, my old flame whom I gave up to serve mother church."

"That's reasonably heroic."

Mass at noon, another at five, so was my first day at St. Christopher's in downtown St. Paul.

❖

SIX

Growth or Decline?

I spent five years at St. Christopher's in downtown St. Paul and I loved it; well, mostly. Baker was a man of his word. We really worked together, and he trusted my pastoral instincts. He made final decisions, but never without consulting me. The first night, at dinner, he said, "You know we'll be busy during the day, but there's little night work. I'd like this to be a priest's haven. If any of your classmates or friends want to have dinner here, just call a day or two in advance. Mildred, (the cook) says that that's fine with her. And I'll have some of the sem guys in. You know you guys always thought we were dining like kings. Institutional food is institutional food, no matter where." And so I'd call Bob, who, as a matter of fact, did teach at the seminary, and he'd come down. So did Bill Thompson. It was an unwritten law in those days that you didn't gripe about pastors in the presence of other pastors, so Bill would do all of his griping about Gibbons in my room, and not at dinner. It was fun to watch Bob Foley and Baker together. When Baker and I were together, I deferred on all matters of theology to Baker's expertise. Not so, Bob, who, after all, had the same doctorate. The first night that Bob was there, I thought they were going to start shouting at each other.

"Sure, Bob, theology can grow, 'develop' to use Newman's word, but the parameters can't change; the Council of Nicea or Vatican I for example."

"You picked a poor example. Infallibility was pushed onto the bishops. There was no real consultation. It was forced down their throats. Nor is it necessary. It's only been used twice, in the full sense, for the declaration of infallibility itself, and for the Assumption a few years ago."

"You said, 'in the full sense,' and that's a good point. The full use of infallibility is rare, but the doctrine of infallibility gives greater authority to any papal statement."

"John, that's my very fear; that quasi-infallibility, or creeping infallibility. In effect, it narrows the teaching power of the Church to a very small theological set, the men of the Vatican, the Pope, and his school. Any other theological insight is not taken seriously, unless the papacy endorses it."

"Bob, that's the way it ought to be. What good is non-infallible truth?"

"The same value that statements from authorities in other fields have; legal experts; scientific or historical authorities; experts in many disciplines."

"Bob, I recommended you for further study." Baker smiled. "But now you scare me. If you put the Vatican on the same level with theologians all over the world, you'd have heresies springing up like weeds."

"And if you hold on to the present structure, theology can't grow. It's like the iron shoe for Chinese women. You will admit that as science develops, moral theology has to respond; like we have increasing ways of keeping people alive."

"And the Vatican has responded."

"O.K., but how about birth control? Our present stance is, at least partly, based on primitive biology, mistaken biology. Why not give it at least some discussion? As you must know from parish work, it's a gigantic problem for much of the laity." Monsignor John Baker was accustomed to students who did not argue. A red flush of anger rose from the back of his neck and took over his face as he said, "That's natural law, and, there, immutable!"

Bob Foley, tall, dark, "black Irish," and with the deep Welsh voice, was not intimidated. "John, whose natural law? That there is a natural law, I don't deny. But are Protestant leaders denied an understanding of the natural law? They come up no problem with birth control."

"That's precisely what I'm trying to straighten you out on. They have no infallible leadership, no real authority, so they just cave-in to whatever their people want."

Now it was Bob's turn to get angry, and despite his dark, Irish-Welsh complexion, a dark flush joined a deep frown.

"Straighten me out! Listen, Protestants have the same ability, simply by being human, to discern the natural law. How come they come up with another answer?"

"Because their consciences have been darkened by heresy!"

"Oh, for Pete's sake, you're too smart to believe that!" They were glaring at each other by then. The birth control problem was of more than academic concern for me, since I was dealing with it in the confessional almost daily. However I had to break up this fight, because that's what it had become. I intervened. "You two have given me enough to think about for a month. If I were a debate judge, I'm not sure how I'd vote. I think you both made some telling points. By the way, Mildred told me that she had to get home early, so I'll get coffee if you want some. John? Bob?" They both assented, and by the time I came back from the kitchen, they were laughing like old friends.

Not everything in St. Christopher's was dinner and discussion. There were lots of confessions, three Masses a day, hospital visitation, convert classes, and the endless procession of the hungry and the unemployed, like the man who came in after I'd been there a couple of months. He was waiting for me when I arrived at about eleven p.m. "Are you the priest? Nobody answered the door."

"Well, it's pretty late. We're closed."

"I don't want money. I got word that my father died down in Nebraska, and I just want to talk with a priest."

I'd been downtown long enough to recognize that there was something not quite kosher, but I invited him in. How could I turn down a man who'd just lost his father? So I listened to his story and prayed with him. May God forgive me a dishonest prayer! After about twenty minutes, he said, "The funeral is in Lincoln, Nebraska, and I've got twenty dollars, but I need forty more to take the bus. Can you help me?"

"I thought you said that you didn't want money."

"I don't, in the usual way, but I want to go to dad's funeral."

"Sorry, we've got a policy here. We give meal and bed tickets to the Mission, but we can't give out money. We get too many requests daily."

The man was dressed poorly, but not sloppily. He was in his mid-thirties, I judged, and while unshaven, he had a good face. It was even possible to believe his story. He looked more disappointed than angry when he said, "The nun in grade school always told us that if we were in trouble, to go to the priest. Now I wonder."

"Look, I've listened to you, prayed with you, but I can't give money. First of all, I have no way of telling whether all the stories we hear are true or not." That was a mistake on my part, because he drew out a faded telegram which said, "Dad died today. We'll wait funeral services until you arrive." I did notice that the date had been ripped off. I fell back on my role as assistant.

"Only the pastor can give out funds."

"Is he here?"

"I'm sure he's in bed by now."

"This is very important. Can you get him up?"

"No. Tell me this. Why don't you take some of your

twenty dollars and call your mother and have her send you money."

"She's very poor; couldn't afford to."

"Well, I'm sorry, but I can't give you money."

He got up angrily and said, "I'm quitting your goddamn church, you son-of-a-bitch." He banged the rectory door shut as he left. It was not an unfamiliar pattern; the Catholic claiming his rights. I wondered if he'd told the same story in Protestant rectories. Yet these guys never failed to leave me feeling guilty with the faint possibility that their stories just might be true.

Along with this self-doubt, was the fact that I had inherited a considerable amount of money. Dad's old partner, Frank Griffin, whom I trusted implicitly, was in charge of the funds. I liked having the money as a kind of old age protection, but I didn't want to deal with it. At his urging, I parceled out gifts to various religious orders, and some anonymously to St. Christopher's to be used "for the poor." If Baker suspected that it came from me, he never said so, but it enabled us to cover the expenses of the Mission and some other worthy causes. Downtown ministry was not confined to the poor. Businessmen, old lady shoppers and people of all ages came to the three Masses, and many liked to go to confession and seek counsel away from their home parishes. The parish was a real cross section of Catholic society.

June, 1959, was our tenth anniversary as priests, but it wasn't until September that the six of us gathered in the Roman House in Minneapolis to celebrate. Our conversations as seminarians focused on common ground; studies, profs, sports and future plans. Now, each one of us had separate agendas. Bob Foley, a touch of gray in his hair, was excited over the new Pope and his plans for a council.

"It's the biggest church event in centuries. Its going to revolutionize the way we lead our lives. A new look at other

Christian faiths, a new look at seminaries, priesthood, liturgy, you name it."

We were all dressed in civies except Bartosh, but Cody, still mustached, was sporting a necktie. He said, "Bob, Bob, you can get excited about the damndest things. All this council is is a bunch of old guys sitting around and saying the same stuff they've said for a thousand years. Dullsville Rome."

I had pretty much the same picture. So, I think, did most of us that night.

Bob took the pipe out of his mouth, smiled and said, "What if they dropped celibacy, Frank?"

It was a better shot than Bob realized. Cody had just been moved from Lost Creek to Buffalo Hill. I wondered if it had some connection to Rosie's divorce. Cody said nothing about that to the group, but I was to learn more later.

"Well now," said Cody, "that's sounds a little more interesting, but it has the chance of the proverbial snowball."

"True, but not absolute. Pope John is bent on opening some doors. How about Mass in English? Liturgical reform? Larger use of scripture? A Vatican foreign policy based on the American experience?"

Bill Thompson, big, blond, and still athletic, said, "How about trimming the power of the old pastors?"

Bill was still with Gibbons, was strictly being used as the "youth priest," and still smarting under the role.

"Anything could happen, although I think the pastor-assistant thing is something we have to do on our own." The long-suffering Bill looked angry, "How, just disobey orders?"

"Well, even the moral theology of our day in the sem left room for commonsense. If the pastor gives an unreasonable order, don't do it."

Bartosh, who was the epitome of the obedient assistant and who had outlived old Bronski and now had a good appointment, said, "That kind of talk is what we don't need. Obedience is the key to everything. If priests don't obey the pastor, and take it further, if bishops don't obey the Pope, then the laity will start going their own way, and the whole unity breaks up; bingo, we got protestantism."

Bob, cool and smiling, said, "What's so bad about that?"

Tom Ryan, Monsignor Tom Ryan, Vicar-General, and everybody's guess to be the next auxiliary bishop, turned red, "Bob, you really get to me. You're always on the edge of heresy. Clem is right; the great mark of the Church is unity, a consistent pattern going back to the apostles."

Bob broke in, "O.K., O.K., I was indulging in hyperbole, but if you are looking at church history as Christ's will through the centuries, you're guilty of a bit of hyperbole of your own. There's a lot of human sin wound into that history. Take that 'unity' you speak of; we've paid a high price for some of it. Trent was necessary, yes, but the subsequent four centuries have made us a medieval church, inept to deal with the twentieth century, much less the twenty-first."

I had been silent up to then. "That, it seems to me, is a major role for the Church; I mean to keep alive the eternal verities in a random world."

"Eternal verities are fine, George, but much of what the Church has is baggage from medieval values; a monarchical papacy, a liturgy weighted down by Byzantine court ceremonial, a one school theology. Let me give you an example. How are bishops in say, St. Paul chosen?"

"We all vote for Ryan," offered Cody, "or he'll never speak to us again."

Ryan was defensive. "I know where you're going with this, Bob, but after all, letters are sent out to both priests and laity, asking for candidates."

Cody again, "I'm reminded of when I was a kid, my dad used to have my sisters and me write out letters to Santa. Then dad would take us down to the furnace and say, 'we'll put these in the furnace and Santa will read the smoke. I suspect that the letters about bishops get a similar action. The archbishop puts the tierna, the three names down, and the Vatican picks Ryan. So much for democracy."

Bob said, "Be that as it may, bishop selection used to be from the local church."

"Yeah," said Clem, "like Ambrose. The crowd in Milan shouted his name and that was it."

Bob again. "I don't think I'd like to go back to those days, too much room for demagoguery, but there has to be a greater democracy in bishop selection."

The waiter arrived with the salads, and Cody ordered another martini.

"My God, Frank where do you put it all?"

"Right, your eminence, I'll make room, right now," said Cody as he went toward the men's room. Conversation became more general, then, and broke into smaller pairings. Bill Thompson turned to me quietly. "I've been counselling an old friend of yours."

"Who?"

"Mary Lou Dowd. She feels bad about the way you were the fall guy for her. At the time, she just couldn't go against papa. She needs a lot of recovery from those days. It was Beth who steered her over to see me."

"I often wondered how that all came out."

"Well, as you know, papa Dowd did a year in Stillwater. The marriage broke up. Incidentally, old Higgins apparently feels bad about his treatment of you."

"I'll have to go see him, I bear him no ill will, now, anyhow. I hear he's doing great work in alcoholic counselling."

There was more to come. Cody was staying at St. Christopher's with me, and as I drove him back, he said, "Georgie, I don't know if ol' Frankie could tell you this, if I hadn't had a few, but you see I got driven out of town by Rosie's husband who accused me, in court, of breaking up the marriage. Bishop moved me just in the very nick. Rosie's hubby was about to put a two-by-four through ol'

Frankie's head. I'm in deep shit. Word's around the diocese. Truth is I mighta been part of it. I think they'd have split sooner or later anyway. Classic mismatch. If you think ol' Frankie has bedded her, you're wrong, but I guess I'm in love with her, and vice versa. She's getting a big settlement, and she offered to put me through law school."

"Frank, you can't be serious that you're considering it."

"George, ol' friend, I'm not sure. Donwanna lie to you."

I kept on talking, why he shouldn't, why he couldn't; even brought up his ma back in New York. I did my best, but I knew Frank would make his own choice.

After Frank left the next morning, Monsignor Baker said, "I don't know what to make of Cody, never did. I'm not supposed to talk about old faculty meetings, but I trust you not to talk. Fact is, Frank Cody almost got canned. Slovene wanted to dismiss him. I guess that anytime Slovene was for something, I was against it, and any time, he was against something or someone, I was for it. I don't mean that's the whole story, but I fought to keep Cody. Sometimes I wonder. Is he doing O.K.?"

It was a question I avoided. "I guess he'll always be Frankie."

"I worry even more about Bob. Was he there last night?"

"Yes."

"I always liked him. I recommended him for the seminary. He scares me. I know he's a good man and bright, but this new theology is like new whiskey. It's not based on Aquinas or what you guys used to call me, Duns Scotus, or any other solid tradition. We could have heresy or even schism. I hope this council puts on the brakes."

I didn't say anything to that, but if Foley was right, the council would do anything but.

I chose the fall that year for priest's retreat. It was down at the new retreat center on the Mississippi. The leaves were beginning to turn, and the grounds were beautiful. Bill Thompson and I walked along and kicked leaves. It was like old seminary days, only without the restrictions. The retreat master was good, the best in years. He touched on something that was poised on the edge of my mind, but that I hadn't fully acknowledged. He gave titles to his talks (conferences), and this one was called, "But Do You Love Them?" The idea was that there were many "successful" clerics, who built churches and "saved souls," but who really didn't love their flocks. It struck home. In the four years I'd been at St. Christopher's I'd made over eighty converts. I'd helped nearly that number back into the faith. It had become a kind of spiritual materialism, if you will; adding up souls the way a miser added gold. But did I love them? Or was it like making points in a ballgame. Even though an old cloud hung over me from the Rogan days, time had diminished it, and my standing was good. Baker expressed his satisfaction with me in glowing terms. People were warm in praise for my sermons, and I heard more confessions than most priests, and had a large number of counselees. In a word, I was a "success." A success and yet there was this little gnawing notion in my heart which kept asking, "What are your real values?" When I tried explaining it to Bill Thompson, it was clear that it meant nothing to him. He had concerns which seemed more important. He said, "So I went to Tom Ryan and told him that I had to get out of St. Isidore's. He got me to see the bishop and Dunn talked me into staying."

"Does he still keep you out of parish activity?"

"Not so much, but the problem is that he's nuts. The other day he told me to paint the church. When I explained to him that it took professionals, he blew up. Of course, by the next day, he'd forgotten all about it. Then, a few weeks ago, I had to keep him from going down to city hall to run for mayor. And when I tell this stuff to Ryan or the arch, they just dismiss it as Gibbons' sense of humor. His mind is gone."

After I got back to St. Christopher's, I remembered my

retreat thoughts, but did nothing about them.

Late in the fall, the announcement was made: Monsignor Thomas Ryan was to be auxiliary bishop of St. Paul, and titular bishop of Gronus, Egypt, an inactive see. All five of us were invited to take part. Even Cody was invited into the ceremony. To my surprise, Bob Foley was the speaker. He told me that, to avoid bad feelings, he had submitted the whole sermon to Ryan so that he could change it if some of it was unacceptable. Ryan red penciled a few things. It was a magnificent ceremony and we all basked in reflected glory. Archbishop Dunn was in failing health, so, for all practical purposes, Ryan was running the archdiocese. He was regarded as a shoo-in as next archbishop. Priest gatherings happen for a number of reasons; funerals of brother priests, clerical meetings (some mandated, some optional), and ordinations, especially episcopal ordinations. Some priests go to all of the above, some to the mandated stuff only, and some of us are selective. Prior to the luncheon, we strolled about greeting old friends, and as one wag put it, "renewing old hatreds." I ran into Ross Cox, all five-foot-two, alive with the pleasure of a new parish. He beamed at me.

"I'm so glad for you. I hear you and Baker are hitting it off well."

"And you? Tell me if all the stories about St. Dismas are true."

"As you know, the chancery didn't know what to do with me. No pastor was willing to take me. So they sent me to develop a new place in West Bloomingdale. There's a lesson in there for you, Schwartzie. Assistant priests get the idea that if they are suitably obedient, they'll get rewarded with their own parish. Wrong! The real idea is to be such a bastard that they don't know how to place you, and then, you get a place of your own."

Little guy that he was, he wore the mocking grin that was his signature. "Tell me the story of the naming of the parish."

"I wanted a title which would symbolize Jesus with the outcasts, the tax-collectors, the Samaritans, the prostitutes; well you know the Scripture. And I want to identify with the outcasts of our own day, you know, the same old prostitutes, the homeless, the people in prison, but it goes deeper than that. How welcome in parishes are the openly homosexual, the mentally unstable, or for that matter, those whose 'crime' it is to be of another race? And the visibly poor? Or the peacemakers, those who demonstrate against nuclear weapons?"

"I think you forgot my question."

"I'm getting to it. So when I proposed St. Dismas, the arch and our newly-born bishop went berserk. In effect, what would such a dismal name—forgive the pun—be doing in a wealthy suburb such as West Bloomingdale? I kept on arguing, so finally they agreed to St. Dismas, but wanted me to drop the surname, 'the Good Thief.' Anyway, I won."

"Great, I guess. So what's all this untraditional stuff you're doing?"

"Untraditional? Nonsense. The problem is that these people don't know their own traditions. For instance, those paper-like wafers which most parishes use for communion. Some scholar wrote a paper which averred that they weren't real bread, so that all those millions of Masses were invalid. I don't go that far, but Jesus said, 'Take and eat' not 'inhale.' So I use good old cracked wheat, that you have to chew. O.K., then on occasion at daily Mass, I share the wine with the folks."

"That's against canon law."

"But Jesus said, 'Drink my Blood.' So who is disobeying whom?"

"Ross, you'll never change; rebel to the end."

"What really scares the chancery is that I'm sharing power. Like maybe that'll start a trend, so that the episcopal power will be less absolute. The parish trustees are elected by the people. Then we have the parish committee. Nothing substantial can be done without their consent."

"How did they ever approve of your nontraditional church building? I hear it's circular, with the altar in the middle."

"It took all of my powers of persuasion. Maybe I cheated a little. I told 'em that's what the arch wanted."

"So much for democracy."

And with a last wink he was gone. At that moment, I had no idea that my future would be tied in with that conversation. We classmates of Bishop Ryan sat together at the banquet. Bill Thompson began it. "It's funny how we know a guy all through the seminary, but who *really* knows Tom Ryan? Cody, you'll say that he's ambitious, and maybe so, but none of us would be a good bishop, even our eloquent speaker of the day, right Bob?"

Bob Foley, who had had a morning of praise for his sermon, laughed agreeably. "I think it depends on how you see the Church. If the present Vatican Council shakes off the dust of the ages, we'll need another kind of bishop. Incidentally I don't see any of them in the wings."

"I meant, 'natural leadership.' Ryan always had it," Bill responded.

I said, "Your original point, Bob. Tom is ambitious, maybe so, but there's a warmth in him too. I was angry at him when I got thrown out of Seven Sorrows. He's more than apologized since. He's very human, but the job itself forces him to be analytical rather than humane."

"That's not a great defense, Schwartzie," said Cody, "but I'd have to admit, I'd rather work under him than under my bishop."

I wondered what Cody had done now. Clem Bartosh, dark eyes flashing under dark brows, didn't like the direction of the conversation. Clem had smarted under years of exact obedience to Bronski and he thought everyone needed that sort of thing, something like boot camp. He said, "To me the Will of God is spelled out in just that, obedience. Without that, the Church becomes one more wishy-washy organization, well-meaning and ineffective." It had become Clem's speech, and nobody responded. We had come to expect the 'obedience' declaration from Clem. It never occurred to me, in those days, to analyze how we six priests, all who had taken the oath against modernism, and who were once more-or-less of one mind, had begun to go our separate ways, at least, intellectually. Tom, whose very position in the Church had fed into his institutionalism, into a stronger conservatism; Clem whose life experience had brought about a similar stance; Cody, always a rebel, but now, from perhaps loneliness, turning even more away from institution. Bill and I were in the middle some place; mentally still babes in the womb of Mother Church, but changed more than we were aware of. Bob was different from the rest of us. Tall, dark, "black Irish," proud of his half-Welsh ancestry, which he felt gave him his deep resonant voice, he had freed himself, even in seminary days, from our vision of church. We mostly identified the kingdom of God, the will of God, with the institutional church, the Vatican, in effect, the will of the Pope and his "kitchen cabinet." Not so, Bob. He had made the distinction early on between the administrative church and the Spirit-guided people of God. Perhaps because of that, he was to be less affected as changes: sociological, theological, and, yes, those from Vatican II, broke into our lives in the sixties and seventies.

Other things were said by us classmates as we sat at the banquet in honor of the new bishop. We responded to Bill's remark about "not really knowing Tom Ryan," but I think all of us missed the mark. It's much clearer to me now, with thirty-some years of hindsight. Ryan was married to the Church in a way that we were not. His identity was commanded by the Church, not the people of God as much as the church of chanceries, the church of committees, and

Vatican offices. That very identity limited his compassion, for example for me, when Rogan had assumed that I was having "lingual contact" at two-thirty in-the-morning with some street woman. He was compassionate enough to be concerned that I have a place to stay, but not concerned with my emotional destruction at the hands of Rogan. The appearance of the Church, to use the biblical phrase, "without wrinkle or spot" was more important. It was a limitation widely shared by bishops.

I spent the rest of the day with Bill Thompson and Frank Cody. I wanted to ask about Cody and Rosie, but I couldn't with Bill there. I did ask Bill if he were still counselling Mary Lou Dowd. "No, but I still see her. We've become very good friends." I wondered what that meant. Our conversation wandered to world events. We shared a fear of communism, support for the "containment policy" of the U.S., concern over Cuba, and the feeling that secularism was destroying U.S. values. Even though I had become an avid reader of the newspapers and *Time,* I realize now that my skills at political analysis were severely limited. The same naive trust that I had in church authorities I carried over to the U.S. government. I trusted that their decisions were well thought-out. We were all excited over the Catholic candidate, Kennedy.

Cody's comment to that was, "Nice try, but no cigar. No Catholic can be elected in this country."

"Right!" was Bill's response.

"One-hundred dollars says he'll make it." I challenged.

"Moral theology forbids me," replied Cody. "Can't bet on a sure thing. Immoral."

"If you're serious, I'll take you up," said Bill.

That night on the way to the airport, Cody finally talked.

"When I get off the plane at Rapid, I'm staying overnight. In the morning I'm going to see the bishop. Matter of fact, he'll be on this flight. Georgie, I'm saying goodbye to priesthood. Rosie and I are going to be married in Chicago.

I'm already accepted into the law school at the University of Chicago. I hope we can still be friends." I was hardly shocked. I'd been expecting this. I simply said, "We'll always be friends."

I knew that it would be futile to attempt persuasion. I did say, "Don't answer if I'm too nosey, but is this anything like loss of faith?"

"No, ol' Frankie has faith like the rock. I'll go to Mass even though I can't go to Communion. Maybe you wanna blame this on loneliness or my bishop or Rosie. None of the above. In a way, I was happy at Lost Creek. They loved me. I'd go down to the bar for my weekly jug—oh, O.K., bi-weekly—and I'd kid the guys.

Like this time I walked in and there was the biggest brawler in town, Ned Eggers, six-foot-two, 230 pounds, iron-jawed, and meaner 'n hell. He wasn't a member of my church. We'd never met, but he knew who I was. I went up to him and pulled out a cigar, and I said, 'Here, Ned, take this cigar. It'll make a man outta you.' The gang roared, and so did Ned. The story went all over the country."

"Frank, you'll never change."

"Trouble was, and this is not meant as an excuse, after a little kidding like that, conversation was cattle prices, weather, machinery parts—not much for Frankie."

"You once said that Rosie . . . "

"I know, I know, I said that I wouldn't run off with the village milk-maid. You were right, Georgie, when you said she is a sophisticate; not educated, but highly educatable. She's going to college down there, too. Anyway, as I started to say, don't blame the Church or the Bishop or Rosie for that matter. I love her and that's it—like Edward and Wally."

I left him off at the airport and felt like crying. I couldn't sleep that night, and so, I got up and knelt by the bed for an hour and prayed for Frankie, and Rosie.

It's strange how things that were so important for a day

or so recede into the background, as my thoughts of Frank's troubles did. I got caught up in the needs of downtown ministry; the poor at the door, the pious confessions of old ladies who had missed their morning prayers, or the not-so-pious confessions of businessmen who had cheated on their wives and did not want to share that with their pastors in the home parish. Then it was trying to improve the convert classes or trying to create an interesting sermon or attending to the sick. Thus did I "measure out my life" as the poet says "with coffee spoons."

It was like that in larger, global matters too. I had shaken off my seminary habits and had become an avid news reader, but the Cold War, nuclear weapons, China, the economy, etc. were worried about and thought about in a vague background way, almost like pictures in a motel room. As one poetess wrote, "Strange that an earthquake far distant, though shocking / Disturbs me less than a run in my stocking." I was like a fish swimming in the sea where there was a terrible storm on the surface. I was totally unaffected. There were other things too. As much as I liked Baker, and as kind as he was, I had to fight the petty annoyance that he, unwittingly aroused in me.

I had a standing invitation to watch the news with him every night, and every time the broadcaster would say, "This is C.B.S." Baker would say, on cue, "A lotta b.s., if you ask me."

Why this repetitive remark would bother me, I haven't the slightest, but it did. Then, though he prized Mildred and her cooking, he would say, always! "We'd better have a couple, so we can stomach dinner."

I suppose married people get tired of each other's repetitive words. But I know I overreacted to Baker's, even though I really liked him. Maybe part of it was that I'd been an assistant for almost a dozen years, and I wanted my own parish. I can imagine a navy guy wanting his own ship, and most of us felt the same way.

I was struggling with some other stuff. That retreat master who had challenged us with the question, "But do you love them?" was on my mind, yet I didn't know what to do with it. I served people every week in a hundred ways, but "did I love them?" It was a good question. There were the partisans of the "cold love" theory who would hold that serving was the test, not some emotional feeling about it. I couldn't buy that.

I meant to bring this up to the retreat master that fall, but he turned out to be the wrong man. The retreat that fall, (1960) was in election week, and we were released on election day in order to vote. That afternoon the retreat master said, "Now you have done your civic duty, you have rendered to Caesar, but I have directed the housemaster to close the T.V. room this evening. I know that you're interested in how Kennedy did, but we're here for a retreat, "to render to God the things that are God's" He wasn't dealing with pasty-faced seminarians, but with pastors of parishes, long-time assistants and even a seminary professor (Bob Foley). We overrode him and that night all twenty of us sat and cheered every time Kennedy got a majority and booed when Nixon did. I had a hundred dollars on Kennedy with Thompson and we took turns jabbing each other as our fortunes went up and down. At midnight it wasn't clear at all who was going to win and I was worn out, and in addition, had been sipping bourbon and so I went to bed. It was far into the next day before I knew that J.F.K. (and I) had won.

Bill Thompson handed me a check and smiled, "You don't know how glad I am to give you this. I never thought this country would allow such a thing to happen."

Foley said, "It is a milestone of sorts; a once despised and feared minority have come into acceptance. It's still naive to think that this will have great consequence. We'll have to see what Kennedy can do." In retrospect, the whole scene seems strange to me. We acted as if some basic change had taken place, almost as if it were a spiritual triumph.

The retreat itself was a loser for me. I was so turned-off by the retreat master that I didn't talk to him about the matter that was affecting me, how I was loving or failing to love the people whom I served. For the next year or so, I wasn't able to step back and look at my ministry. I simply responded to the needs of the moment. Hours passed into days, days into weeks, weeks into months, and the sequence got lost like the waves in the wake of a ship. I wish that I'd kept a diary, so I could sort out the numbers of elderly whose hands I held in sickness, and whom I buried, the young ardent lovers I united in marriage, the troubled I consoled, and the divorces of some of those same ardent lovers, all the while wondering if I truly loved them. World events passed similarly. The two K's, Khrushchev and Kennedy crossed swords in Vienna and the Cold War got icier. The Cuban invasion fell apart and Castro was stronger than ever. People predicted a communistic world, and we all feared it. Mayors in St. Paul came and went. Governors the same. Rachel Carson told us that we were poisoning the earth and some listened. Archbishop Ryan prepared to go to the Vatican Council and Archbishop Dunn decided that he was too sickly, but took on the harder task of running the archdiocese.

A few personal things stand out. In early December I got a call from Frank Cody.

"I'm staying at the St. Paul. Can I take you to dinner?"

"Sure, when?"

"Uh—six—uh, Rosie is with me. Uh, O.K.?"

"Sure."

When I got there Frank was working on at least his second martini. He excused himself to go to the men's room. Rosie looked frightened. "I suppose you hate me."

"Rosie, Rosie, nobody hates you. We all know Frankie. He does what Frankie wants to do."

"I do feel guilty. He was a good, warm priest, and everybody loved him. I turned down his proposal half-a-dozen times, but, but . . . I love him too much not to be with him. Do you think God will understand?"

Thank God, Frank came back at that point, because I didn't know how to answer. The next day they went to Chicago and I wondered if I would ever see Cody again.

Other things happened. I went out and got reconciled with Higgins. He was terribly pleased. He told me that Jennie had died. He was a great success at working with alcoholics. While asking my pardon for events at St. Brendan's, he seemed to write it all off as alcoholic behavior. Although I didn't contradict him, I never really believed it. Monsignor Rogan made no attempt at reconciliation and died, apparently still convinced that I had had "lingual contact" with Maria.

Reports came on preparations for Vatican II. Foley was excited over it and got me to read Hans Küng on the coming council. About my only interests were that I hoped they would put the Mass, the Divine Office, and other sacraments in the vernacular, and that some new reading on birth control be done. Life went on at the rectory and each evening Baker continued to follow the announcement, "This is C.B.S." with "A lotta b.s., if you ask me," while I silently ground my teeth.

The Vatican Council had hardly begun when I got a call from Foley. "Got some bad news, George, very bad. Ross Cox was killed in a car accident in Rome."

"Oh, oh, oh," I said in shock. I'd really come to love the little guy. He was a gadfly in the seminary, and an episcopal thorn, not to mention the pastor's bane, but his genuine care for the poor, his élan, his sense of humor—yes, his wisdom and goodness had won me completely. After I had partially come out of shock, I asked how it had happened.

"Well, you know Coxie. He waded into one of those streets in Rome. You haven't been there, have you?"

"No."

"The traffic is unreal; all speed and horns blowing. Well,

this was on the 'Corso', by the Victor Emmanuel monument, the so-called 'wedding cake'. Ross, all five-foot-two, walked into the heart of the autos in that cocky way of his and got blind sided. It was instant death, at least he didn't suffer long."

That wasn't much consolation.

Archbishop Thomas Ryan, himself, came back from the Council to preside. It's strange how death changes things. There was almost an ongoing battle between the chancery and Cox, all through the years, and Ryan seldom spoke of Cox without anger. At the funeral he praised him, calling attention to his espousal of the poor, his liturgical progressiveness, his calls to justice and so on, hardly words that he ever said to the living Cox. He praised the architecture of Cox's church. I had never seen St. Dismas before and I found it so different that I couldn't appraise it. It was circular in form, but while the altar was in a central position, no one was behind the celebrant. The walls were Mankato Stone, the ceiling, again circular, had a series of windows below the cupola which gave a great deal of natural light.

After the Mass, I didn't go to the cemetery, but with Bill Thompson and Bob Foley walked about the parish grounds. The rectory was small, in keeping with Cox's idea of priestly poverty, and was strictly a living quarters. The parish offices were in the building connected to the church which also housed a large dining hall; not the usual spare dining hall, but a warm room with gaily colored carpeting and nature scenes painted on the walls. Cox had told his flock, "There is no need to celebrate our post-Eucharist gatherings in a dingy place." As I looked over all of this, I had no idea that these surroundings would play a part in my future.

When the funeral entourage returned from the cemetery, we all had lunch in the splendid hall. I sat next to Bob and Bill. About halfway through the meal, Ryan came to our table and tapped me on the shoulder. "George, finish your meal, but I'd like a word with you after you are done."

"Yes, Archbishop."

"Name is still Tom." I knew he had to catch a plane right after lunch, so I hurried through the cold cuts and excused myself. Since Ryan had spoken a word to each of the others, they hadn't noticed his request to me. I found him at the front table. He said, "George, let's walk out in the corridor." Once there, he said, "You realize that Ross's death puts us in a bit of a bind. Of course, I heaped praise on Cox at Mass. '*De mortuis, nihil nisi bonum*'." (He was employing an old Latinism; Say nothing about the dead unless good things.) "I meant what I said, but not everything that he did was prudent. Archbishop Dunn and I want to preserve the good stuff without keeping some of his wilder ideas." I wondered where Ryan was going with all this, but I guessed that he wasn't telling me this for no reason.

"To make a long story short, we'd like you to go there." I looked at his freckled Irish face with the strong jaw, and I said, "Is this a reward or punishment?"

He laughed, "Maybe both, although I prefer the word 'challenge.' Frankly, we need someone who is flexible enough to suffer a few fools, but firm enough to rein in the crazies. I think Cox himself was beginning to wonder where it was all going." He paused for a moment, then, "George, I'm not proud of the way we treated you when you got bounced you from Lady of Sorrows. I hope you can forgive and forget. I think that at the time I was pretty much into bishop-pleasing." The candor and the warmth of that statement took me by surprise. It was Ryan at his best.

He continued, "I wish I could say, 'Take a few days to think about it,' but I have a flight to Rome in a couple of hours and you know that Archbishop Dunn would stew over this. His health is fragile. It would take a load off of his back."

It was too fast, but I wanted a place of my own. I said, "Count me in."

"George, I'll never forget this." And so it came to be that I became pastor of the parish of St. Dismas, the Good Thief, in West Bloomingdale. This was the first time in my career that I had a pleasant farewell, a party moreover, and a purse which I did not want nor need. There were things left undone at St. Christopher's. I never got used to Baker's "Well, I suppose we'd better have a few bumps if we're going to tackle Mildred's dinner." or "That's a lotta b.s., if you ask me." whenever C.B.S. identified itself. But those were minor matters. We'd never solved how to take care of the poor without being taken for fools. The even heavier question was the persistent one for me, do I really love the people whom I serve. Baker honestly hated to see me go. We had a fond farewell and I went to MY OWN PARISH!

✖

SEVEN

St. Dismas, the
Good Thief

A priest with his own pastoral! Is there a happier man or moment? I imagine the joy of a young lawyer, accepted into the bar, but, better yet, accepted into the firm. Or a young couple who rented for years, now owning their own house. All fine I say, but can it compare to the young pastor taking over a parish? I heard that a bishop once said to a priest about to found a new parish in the suburbs, "It's like having a baby. You can train it the way you want." My baby had already been formed; it was more like an adoption, but I was singing "You are my sunshine" as I drove past my old assistantship in East Bloomingdale on my way to West Bloomingdale. There are suburbs and there are suburbs. Some fit the song about "ticky-tacky" houses, but not West Bloomingdale. The Minnesota river flows nearby, and there are hills and dales and splendid houses overlooking the river. Builders preserved the old trees which had grown in the farming country before man, the builder (or man the destroyer) came.

I drove up to the now familiar church-office building and rectory. I did remember then the same happy, excited feeling I'd had when I came to St. Brendan's, but no thought of déjà vu could frighten me or minimize my joy. "Mine!" I said to myself, "All mine!" It was exactly three weeks after Ryan had appointed me that I opened the front door of the rectory, carried my "stuff" into the house and went out and got groceries. There had been no housekeeper for Cox and I meant to keep it that way. Then I walked about my new manse, gloating over the splendor of it all. I made a modest supper, really too excited to eat. I took a few books out of boxes and placed them in the ample bookshelves. I gave the house one more tour. It was small, but well-furnished. There was a living-dining area, a small but adequate kitchen, and a small den-library. Upstairs, there were two bedrooms and a large bathroom. I was wallowing in this splendor when the front doorbell rang. Ah! the welcoming folk. Two men and a woman stood at the front door. A young, professional-looking man faced me and quite without smiling, said, "We are a delegation from the St. Dismas committee. I am Charles Dawson. This," he said, gesturing at a woman of imprecise age, "is Bonnie Farrell, and, pointing at a finally smiling bald-headed man is Henry Taft. We are here to see you if that is convenient."

"Certainly, come in."

Once seated, the serious young man, still unsmiling, said, "George, we may as well come to the point." I was surprised at the "George," but maybe that's the way Cox had taught them. I said, "I like people who come to the point." As I said this, I realized, unhappily, that Bonnie's nose, indeed, came to a point, and since I had said this as I was staring at her considerable probiscus, I had made a poor beginning. Lamely, I added, "And what is the point?"

"Frankly," replied the unsmiling man, "we'd like you to resign." I have no memory of what sort of facial expression I bore at that moment, but it could not have been pleasant. Mr. Taft, who seemed a bit more friendly, hastened to add, "Please, Father, this is not personal. You might say this is more directed at the bishop. You see . . ."

The nonsmiling Charles Dawson said, "Oh, don't be so apologetic, Henry. The fact is, George, that neither you nor the archbishop consulted us. You come to our community without our consent, or without knowing a thing about our clergy needs."

Henry entered in, "So that's my point. It's not personal. You might be just fine, but we don't approve of the process, where appointments are made without consultation. It's not your fault."

"Oh, isn't it?" said nonsmiley, "he accepted it, didn't he? and that just perpetuates the system. Taxation without representation."

I was boiling by then. "You people are damn rude to come into my house and demand my resignation before you even know me."

"Your house? your house?," Dawson was finally smiling, really more sneering. "Our money, not yours built this house. As a matter of fact, it was more than money. I helped Ross Cox and some of the local builders to put this house up. Your house, indeed. But to come back to the point, if you don't resign, we'll go over your head."

"The bishop sent me here, and he alone is going to move me."

Now, Bonnie, the pointed nose, spoke. "Do you have the sense to see how you are part of a suppressive system? The bishop, by himself, should not have the right to send anyone here. We are going to the people, over the bishop's head."

"So," I said, "when Paul was sent to preach to the Gentiles, he should have first gotten permission from the Gentiles." This stopped them, for a moment. Then, Dawson, "Don't try to play logic with me, George, I can out debate you with half-a-brain. Your flaw is that we are not a pagan community, but a sophisticated Christian community, and we have Christ present already. What we are looking for is a proper celebrant. You were not our choice, and you have confirmed our worst suspicions."

I said, "We are not a congregational church, but hierarchical. And..."

Big Nose cut in, "Right this moment the Vatican Council is poised to give back power to the local assembly as it should, and as Ross Cox taught us, we have to..."

This time I cut in, "If the Council does that, fine, but at this moment in Church practice, I am the duly appointed pastor and now I'll ask you to leave."

"I'm not leaving!" said Dawson.

"I ask you to leave, and if you don't, I'll throw you out on your asses."

"Come," said Bonnie, "this uncouth person is also violent."

I noticed with some satisfaction, that my violent look had taken the smirk off the face of Mr. Charles Dawson, and my threat had cowered him. As they left, Charles shouted back, "You haven't seen the last of us!"

I sat in dumb amazement after they had left. I looked at a picture of Cox, still smiling on the office wall, and I said, "Damn you, Coxie, God rest your soul, but what a mess you set up for me!" He grinned back from the photo in that impish way of his. I was not amused. But these people! They had taken away all of my joy. With one swift kick. In later years I was to realize how my "erroneous zones" worked in parish life. That is to say that if two people praised you on a given day, it seemed like the whole parish was behind you, but if three people attacked you, it seemed like the whole parish was out to get you. At that time I had not arrived at such a philosophical stage, and it just plain hurt. Worse than that, they had pierced my fragile armor. I had sworn at them, lost my temper, and they had further shamed me because in a sense it *was* their parish more than mine. Did I love these people I was to serve? I hated them! I paced up and down in my? (their?) small house. I couldn't sleep. It must have been well past two a.m. that, worn out from the arduous work of moving and the emotional highs and lows of the day, I fell asleep in a chair in the small study. I was awakened at seven by a loud pounding on the front door. "Don't tell me they're back," I said to myself, but it was a tiny old lady, who spoke in a timid voice. "I hope I haven't disturbed the father. I heard that you were here, and I wondered if we would be having daily Mass now?"

My ready-to-go grumpiness evanesced. "What time was Mass?"

"Uh, well, at seven."

"If you wait, I'll be right over."

"Thanks, Father, uh—I hope I didn't—"

I smiled. "Thanks for alerting me."

There were three other elderly ladies at Mass. I said a few introductory words and promised to start Mass on time in the future, that sort of thing. Then I smiled, and they smiled back. I had four on my side as opposed to the three against me, but it didn't seem that way to me at the time. I spent the rest of the morning settling in. A small lunch, a walk, and I was feeling better. At three, the phone rang. It was Father John Muldoon at the chancery. "Hey, George, things must be pretty quiet over there."

"What?"

"We got all your parishioners over here. They're walking up and down with signs. Like, 'Schwartz is not our choice.' What did you do, take away their wine?"

I groaned. "I just got here, and had a delegation last night asking me to resign. What are you guys gonna do?"

"Nothing. These things get to the old man. Dunn got himself put in the hospital. Interesting you should ask. Len Smith wanted to call the cops." (Len was the new man on the chancery staff.)

Muldoon continued, "I went out and said, 'You people can walk up and down, even on our lawn. But I just called the chief of police, and he said that he can have a car here in

two minutes. If you block the door or come in here and interfere with our work, I'll have you arrested, and I'll personally prefer charges. So if any of you want to be martyrs,
I can get you ten days in the pokey.'"

"Did you really call the chief?"

"Nah, it's just a bluff. This is the fourth one of these I've
had in the three years I've been here. Half of them were in
protest against Coxie."

"How many of my loving flock are out there?"

"Oh, 'bout twenty, mostly women. I can see 'em from
my window. One of 'em, fact I know the guy, is carrying
a sign saying 'Taxation without Representation'. That's a
joke. I looked up the amount Good Thief gave to the annual
appeal; one dollar. That was so Coxie couldn't be accused of
not taking up the collection."

"How about the assessment?"

"Glad you asked. You're two years in arrears."

"What have you guys done to me?"

"Not me, it was your classmate who sent you there."

"I'm wondering whether I want to stay here. What'll
come out of the protests?"

"Nothing. These assholes don't read the papers. The Arctic Clipper is on the way. In two days, it'll be twenty below
and windy. The whole deal will die of attrition. People get
sick of trudging through the cold. Except maybe Dawson."

"That's the guy who headed the delegation last night.
You know him?"

"In the sem with me. Slovene threw him out for being
too rigid. Cox converted him from a rigid conservative to a
rigid liberal. They're worse, as you know."

"All this doesn't make me any easier."

"I always heard you were a worrier." I felt insulted. I
said, "You gotta lotta lip for a guy out three years."

"Hey, George, don't take me seriously. And don't take
the petty persecution seriously. Hell, we got more angry
mail against Coxie than they ever had in the history of the

chancery. Hunker down; this'll blow over." I was looking
for a little sympathy, I guess, and I said, "Geez, I couldn't
even sleep last night."

"Got a remedy if you're interested. Old folk remedy
from grandma."

"What?"

"Three double Scotches, neat. Slept like the old log."

"I heard you were a smart-ass. They got that right."

"Only way to be on this job. Can't wait for Ryan to get
back and send some other poor slob to take my place."

"Then what? A parish?"

"Nah, see, the nice part of this job is that, once out, you
get to go to school."

"Why school?"

"So I can teach or do charities work, whatever, just so I
don't have to go to some parish and have some dumb shit
like Dawson pushing me around. Incidentally, he hasn't got
any backing. I wouldn't worry about him. If anybody follows him, they have to be as dumb as he is. Anyway Ryan
knew you could handle this crap, so have a good day. I
gotta annul a few matrimonies. G'bye."

I did feel better after talking to this wise-guy. I didn't
quite make the three double Scotches, but close, and I slept
the sleep of the just and, maybe, just maybe, the sleep of the
lucky.

I prepared well for Sunday. I plotted the course with care.
I wanted to be ready for anything. I admit to some anxiety.
I sweated armpit-wise, whenever I as much as thought of
Sunday. On Friday, Father Muldoon called. "Smart-ass,
here, the 'clipper,' as you know arrived on time. Well, in
the midst of the storm, three people arrived, all women,
started parading up and down, freezing their large butts off.
I got ahead of 'em; got an ex-cop, friend of mine to show up
in his old uniform. When the women tried to come in to un-
freeze aforesaid butts, he said, 'no'. They went back outside, talked angrily for about ten minutes, got in their cars.

Protest is over, at least here. Good luck on Sunday."

"Was Dawson there?"

"No show. He's got a marginal job somewhere. Forget what, but he hadda go back to work, I guess. We had a few phone calls, but I just told 'em that I'm low man here, and Ryan is in Rome, and Dunn in the hospital. Actually, he's back here, but you don't hafta tell 'em everything. Have a happy weekend."

And so Sunday loomed. There were a few picket signs as I walked through the snow to church. At sermon time, I said, "I am Father George Schwartz. I am not Father Cox. He was my good friend and I admired him a great deal, but I am not the same. A delegation came to me before I was even unpacked and asked for my resignation. I'm not going to do that. I'm sure that Father Cox taught a great deal about charity. I'm not even asking for that; merely justice. Perhaps, some day, congregations will have more to say on the choice of pastor..." I heard the unmistakable voice of Dawson, "Let's start now!" There was a smattering of applause. I continued, "But that's not how it is done as yet. I took a vow to obey my bishop, and he sent me here. I intend to stay here." Again there were a few boos. "I will suggest that I stay for a year..." A small chorus of 'NO's' made me aware that I was loosing control, not only of the congregation, but of myself. So I said, "Could we have a little courtesy, please. At the end of a year, if the majority here don't want me, I'll ask the bishop to move me." I went on in that vein for ten minutes. At the end, there was a smattering of applause. So, I thought, not everyone is opposed to me. The next Mass was about the same. After the last Mass, at eleven, I went back to the rectory, ate a small lunch, and realized that I was exhausted. I lay down on the couch in the study, put a blanket over me, but I was not to sleep, because the phone rang.

"Is this George?" It was a man's voice.

"Yes, who are you?"

"A parishioner. I heard your feeble defense today and I can tell you that a year from now, we won't like your anemic bullshit any more than we do now. Resign, now!"

"Who are you please?"

"A follower of Ross Cox . . . "

"I don't talk to people who don't give their names. Bastards are ashamed of their names." I hung up. I was having trouble loving my parishioners. There were four more calls before I took the phone off the hook. Two were negative, two positive. One, especially buoyed me up.

"Father, this is Stella Brown. You were magnificent today. I don't know how you kept your cool, with all those discourteous people."

"Well, thank you, Stella."

"A lot of us are glad to have you here. It was O.K. with Father Cox, but I didn't buy everything that he did. You know a lot of people who objected to Father Cox will be coming back. Don't loose heart."

That was the pattern of the first few months at St. Dismas. It was a roller-coaster ride; up one day, down the next. It was at St. Dismas where I learned that the pastor, generally, is in a winning spot. You pick up chits, credits, if you will. You baptize their kids, you marry their kids, you visit their sick. Unless you are a complete dolt, you are making a positive impression on the flock, family by family. Take Henry Taft, for example. He was one of the delegation which confronted me the first day. He called one day, his voice in tears. "Father, my wife had a heart attack. She's very ill." I had just sat down for my evening meal. I said, "Where is she?"

"Father, she's at General. I—I don't want to disturb your dinner. Maybe tomorrow . . . "

"I'll go right now."

And I did. I visited her several times in the hospital and after she went home. I brought her Communion every week for several weeks. On one of my last visits, Henry saw me to the front door and broke into tears. "You have been so good to us, and we treated you so badly when you'd just arrived. I feel so ashamed of myself..."

"Henry, don't. We're friends now, right? And that's good enough. O.K.?" That is how it went. Of course, some quit the parish. Dawson wrote me a mean letter, announcing his new allegiance to St. Brendan's, where he said, "I understand you also screwed up..." I never saw pointy-nose again. And there were others. Gradually I felt acceptance, and that young smart-ass, John Muldoon turned out to be right. It really had become "my parish" and I was enjoying it. I knew that I couldn't excite an audience like Coxie could, but I gave honest sermons. I taught converts and made a large effort to recall fallen-aways. I wrestled, with the aid of the trustees whom I appointed, to get the debt under control. At the end of one year, I thought of sending out a ballot asking if they wanted me out or in, but I decided it wasn't necessary. It was increasingly fun to be pastor of St. Dismas.

In the meantime, Vatican II continued to make strides, and I began to see that there were good things coming out from there. Soon, we were saying part of the Mass in the vernacular, and also the Office. Protestant-Catholic marriages took on a new cast, less one-sided than the old promises. We began to have laymen readers (lectors), at Mass. Mother Church was not ready for women near the altar yet. I had stalled having a meeting of the famous committee for more than a year, despite phone calls and people asking about it when I ran into them casually. I suppose I was afraid that most of them were like Dawson. I called that smartass, Father John Muldoon at the chancery to see how the letters, pro and con, were going.

"We had so much anti-Schwartz mail that we had to open a special room to stash it."

"Be serious."

"Nah, maybe a dozen letters."

"Negative?"

"George, for God's sake, people who are satisfied don't write. Not often anyway. Interesting, you should call; Ryan called from Rome yesterday. Among other things, he asked about how you were doing; I told him, great. You owe me a lunch for that."

"Thanks, I think."

"One question, G., and that is what the hell is this 'committee' which your parish writes about?"

"Oh, that was Cox's creation. I've been putting off meeting with them."

And I decided that it was time to face the music, but I needed to do this with some care. The opportunity to get advice on making a move happened on the golf course. I had joined Oak Tree Country Club along with Thompson, and we played most Mondays. This particular time we had Foley with us. The first hole is an easy starter, 350 yards, with traps out about 250 yards, and therefore no problem for me; and traps near the green, but not too close. I hit first, about 210. I was pleased. Bill Thompson was next, 250 yards, dead center. I had expected that. Years ago, we played even, but now he was much better. Bob Foley surprised me by going past me a good twenty yards. Being a prof had given him a good part of the summer to get his game in shape. It was like that all day. Bill coming in with 78, Foley with 86, and I was lucky to stay under 90, with an 89. Along the way, I tried to get both of them to react to my dilemma on having the committee meet. Foley was mostly theoretical. He said, "It's the right of your people to have the major role in decision-making."

Bill was absorbed in his own problems and less communicative those days. The game itself defied any sustained conversation. About the time I was ready to explain the committee, I'd have to march off to the right to field my slice from behind a bush. It was not until we were in the club grill with drinks and steaks that they gave serious consideration to my plight. Bill was now administrator of St. Isidore's, since Gibbons had finally been put in a rest-home. It was uncertain whether he would be made pastor when Ryan came back from Rome, and as I said, he was preoccupied with his own life. But that night, he came out of it enough to give me a better idea.

"George, why don't you invite the old committee to a meeting, but include anyone in the parish who wants to come. Put out a parish letter which calls for more democracy. That ought to disarm Coxie's army. How can they gainsay a fuller voice of the parish? And this gives people who left in Cox's day, and others who merely tolerated Cox, a chance to speak up. It gives you a lot of allies."

"It has the feel of stuffing the ballot box," said Foley.

"You've been a prof too long." retorted Bill, "you don't understand pastoral survival." I bought it.

I sent the letter out in the middle of August, and set the meeting on the third Tuesday in September. I had no idea what would happen, and perhaps, that was just as well. I had asked some of the committee members to act as hosts and so we had coffee and donuts set out in the beautiful meeting room designed by Cox. The members of the committee who hadn't quit the parish were there, almost to a man (and woman.) I was concerned that I might face a mostly hostile crowd if only the old and neglected committee members showed up. They were there first, but as the hour of seven-thirty p.m. approached more and more people came. I saw Charles Dawson come in and sit with some of his old cronies. I thought for a moment of saying that only the members of the parish were welcome, and since he had quit, he had no right to participate, but I decided to let democracy reign.

The meeting opened with Mary Lamb with her guitar leading a song. Then I arose and spoke.

"I'd like to welcome all of you to a gathering which I

hope will be repeated many times. Our purpose tonight is not to make decisions so much as it is to collect ideas. We need suggestions; things and services which you think are needed in the parish. Not every idea will be implemented immediately. Not every idea will be implemented ever, but this is an opportunity to express these needs and ideas. "I intended to say a few more things, but Charles Dawson broke in.

"George is right where he's been since he came here. This is a pretense of community choice. Sure, he'll listen, but he'll do what he wants regardless of what we want or need . . ."

A young man, a pipe-fitter by trade, John Gerson, then broke in.

"Shut up, Dawson, I heard you're not even a member here anymore. What gives you the right to speak . . ."

He, in turn, was interrupted by another man, who said, "I'm a member, and Dawson speaks for a number of us here. We're tired of this beating around the bush. I didn't always agree with Father Cox, but we always knew where we were at. This sneaking around the bushes . . ."

This time, I cut in, "What sneaking around the bushes? Be specific."

"We have a properly elected committee at Dismas. You've been putting off meeting with us, and now you're going right around the committee with this phoney 'gathering' as you call it."

There was a smattering of applause. I said, "Glad you brought that up. (I wasn't really.) Because that is a problem for me. The first time I met some of the committee, they asked me to resign. As I've said in the pulpit, we are not a congregational church. Just as we priests don't choose our bishop, you don't get to pick your pastor. Some members of the parish committee seem to think that they, and they alone, are to decide parish policy. Well, as a famous man said (and here I pointed at myself), "The buck stops here."

I'd like to see a newly elected parish group who would understand that they are advisory, and I'd listen, but retain decision making..." I was interrupted by loud boos. Another florid gentleman spoke up angrily. "I am a businessman, and we put in money, thousands, Father, and we haven't seen one report since you came."

Again, I said, "I'm glad you asked that. Business-wise, there was some confusion when I came—frankly, our checks were bouncing—and I took over the books. I admit I'm not very good at it, but we couldn't afford to hire a bookkeeper, but we have one now..." The businessman broke in again. "Why do you need a bookkeeper? A lot of us do our own bookkeeping. What do you do with all the time you have? I understand you are seen a lot out at Oak Tree Country Club."

I turned beet red. "I've never kept track of the exact hours that I put in each week, but I assure you its a damn sight more than forty hours!"

"Well, when will we see this report? I know there was a lotta funny business over at St. Brendan's next door..."

"Are you making accusations about me?"

"I'm not accusing anybody, but as a contributor, I'm entitled to see..."

I broke in again, "You'll get you're report in a month," then I looked over at my main trustee, "right Earl?"

Earl Michels stood up. "Right, Father, maybe earlier." Then to the businessman, he said, "You'll get your godamn report, Joe, and you can shove it up your ass!" I saw that the meeting was almost totally out of control. So was I, but I stuffed it and said, "Now we have to act as Jesus would. St. Paul told the Corinthians to love one another, and we must do the same. Let's all cool down." I said it as much to myself as to them.

A lady stood up. I didn't know her name, but I recognized her black hat from Sunday Mass. She said, "I'm Miss Henrietta Reade." (Somehow the "Miss" was unnecessary.

You knew it.) She went on. "I've heard too much business tonight. A parish is for the spirit. I want to ask, Father, if we could have, as we used to, the Rosary and Benediction each Sunday night?"

"We'll have to consider that. I'll think about it."

"Well, you didn't have to consider whether you'd have a financial report; why does this take consideration?" I said, "We'll let you know." I was having trouble loving my parishioners.

Henry Taft stood up. "Father, these people should know what you do. I was one of those who asked you to resign. I'm really sorry now that I did that, but listening to these people tonight, maybe you'd like to resign. Listen folks, when my wife had her heart attack, Father Schwartz was right there, and for weeks after. He deserves our support." And he started to clap. About half the crowd joined in. The meeting went on for another two hours. Several people spoke. Henrietta spoke twice more. She said, "When Father Cox came here, I didn't like what he did, but, unlike some of you who are here tonight, I couldn't go to some other parish. I don't drive. But I listened to Father Cox, and I began to see the sense of a lot that he had to say about justice and charity, like Jesus, really. But I saw something else. I have an M.A. in history, and what I saw was that he was moving us from the nineteenth century Church to the twenty-first, without enough time to adjust. A lot of prayer forms which we grew up with were taken from us. That's why I'm asking for Rosary and Benediction."

There was a small mixture of boos and claps. I was beginning to like her. I decided that I'd accede to her requests, but I wouldn't say so that night. I realized the reason I'd held off is that after the last Mass on Sunday noon, often Thompson and I would go off to Oak Tree for golf and dinner. I'd compromise, rosary at one p.m.

Mr. Joe Bonini got to his feet again." I got put down by Earl Michels, but as a businessman, I have responsibilities, so has Father. For example, how much does the parish take in in a year, like $100,000?"

"More like $250,000."

He looked surprised, but went on. "Then you're a business, a big one and you are responsible for that money, and we deserve a report. I keep my own books, so I know what is going on."

Earl, sitting next to me, said, "He runs a little spaghetti place. With a shoehorn, you could squeeze in twenty people. He's got his wife and a couple of part-timers. He's got plenty of time to keep books."

"I do know what is going on; is it Joe?" He nodded, and I went on. "Yes, we're a business, but primarily, as Henrietta says, we are spiritual. My sermons may not seem that great, but I put lot of time in on them. I need to read, to study, to meditate. Right now the council in Rome is going to force us priests to relearn a lot of things."

But Joe wouldn't let go. "Father, we businessmen have to keep up too. We gotta keep up with state and federal laws in taxes, employment; in my restaurant, the prices of food, the hygiene rules, so don't give us this study bit. We all have to do that."

Earl Michels cut in. "Oh, nuts, Joe, spaghetti prices don't change that much." Joe was on his feet again, but I'd already recognized Lillian Roth. She was a slim, dark-haired woman in her thirties. She was nice looking, but had a mean look which compromised her good looks. She smoked furiously on dark cigarettes. "Father, what this parish needs is a school." There were boos and claps. Divide and conquer, I thought. And I remembered what St. Paul did when confronted by a hostile Jewish crowd. He saw that they were a mixture of Sadducees and Pharisees. So he got an argument going between them, and got off the hook. Now this unpleasant woman was going to do it for me.

"How many of you attended a Catholic School?"

Most of the hands went up. "There," she said, "and why shouldn't our kids have the same opportunity?"

There was some applause and some audible disagreement. She continued. "And it's Church law, isn't it, Father, that a parish MUST have a school?"

"Well, the Council of Baltimore put out a kind of law, but obviously this depends on the ability of the parish to pay for it. Right now, we have a debt of $400,000, and we are barely able to keep up the payments, so unless our income increases, I don't see how we could maintain a school, much less build one."

Joe Bonini was on his feet again. "If we didn't have to pay for bookkeepers and staff people, maybe we could afford a school. We need a hard-working pastor. Less time on golf; more time at work!" I tried to keep my rising anger under control. I answered, "Joe, I have no family. My parents are dead. I have no brothers or sisters. I need family and my family are other priests. That is largely what my golf is about. I'm not going to drop it for you or anyone else!" There was loud applause, but Lillian of the mean eyes was up again. "Oh, spare the violin, Father. This doesn't get you off the hook. We could find the money if you were willing to look into the school matter."

I said, "As I said earlier, we are not going to make decisions tonight. We'll put that on the future agenda."

Henrietta raised her hand, "I'm a librarian in the public school which embraces a good part of this parish. It's a good school. Your children are well-cared for. You can run a parochial school, fine, but it's financially possible only if you underpay your teachers and deprive other parish programs of money. I'm a single person; an old maid if you wish, and most parishes have no special programs for us. I'm all for children, but there are other needs and other values."

Well, it went on—and on. After two hours, I said, "As I said earlier, our purpose tonight is not to finalize anything, but to hear needs. I am going to set up an election for a new parish group. Anyone in the parish can file, but you must be a member. It will be an advisory group or committee or whatever." Dawson had left, but some of his cronies were there. One shouted, "Can't you people see what he's done. Father Cox gave the parish members some rights. He's taking them away..."

"Meeting adjourned!" I said. "There's coffee and cookies for those who remain." Then, *then,* people came to me and said things like, "Gee, Father, I'm so happy you're here!, or "They were so rude, and you were so patient." And I wondered why they had been so silent during the meeting. After they'd gone, I locked up the room, went back to the rectory, took Muldoon's grandmother's remedy of Scotches and slept the uneven sleep of the partially just and the partially lucky.

The next morning, Earl Michels called. "Father, it might not seem like it, but you won. It's all over. You faced up to them and they know who is in charge." I wasn't so sure, but it turned out that he was right. My parish had become mine.

Oh, there were letters sometimes, but the very rudeness of some had turned others toward me.

And so it was that I could truthfully tell my classmates that all was going well in my parish as we gathered to celebrate our fifteenth year as priests. Actually we celebrated in June of 1965 which was our sixteenth, but our schedules the year before had clashed. Thompson and I hosted the gang at Oak Tree Country Club, and we drove over together. I looked at him as he drove. He still had the fine features and Scandinavian good looks which both he and Beth had inherited from their mother. He was still the good athlete, but he had fleshed out a bit. There were strands of gray in his once totally blond hair. The emotional changes were more noticeable. He smiled less, and, while not taciturn, he spoke less and when he did, it was often quietly negative. He said, "I hear Ryan isn't coming because Frank Cody will be there. That gives me a pain in the butt."

"He told me that he had nothing against Cody, but being archbishop, his presence might suggest approval of Cody's leaving, and therefore cause scandal."

"Shit."

"Shit. Is that all you're gonna say?"

"Shit meaning hypocritical. Ryan and the chancery ought to get their own act together before they get scandalized," Thompson replied.

"Like?"

"Like the way both you and I were treated."

"Time to forget and forgive. Besides Ryan sort of apologized to me."

"Well, he's never apologized to me. When I think of the times I called or wrote Ryan and Dunn to tell them that Gibbons was out of his head, and they paid no attention until his cousin told them that Gibbons had asked her to drive to Ireland with him. Then they put him away."

"And now you're in charge, so why not enjoy?"

"I'm still only the administrator of St. Isidore's and you're a full pastor."

"Why not ask them?"

"Beg a favor from Ryan? Forget it."

At the dinner, there were other changes among us. Cody came, dressed to a tee. Pinstripe suit, conservative tie, no mustache, and the manner of a businessman. Instead of gulping martinis, he nursed two of them slowly. Bill Thompson went the other way. He gulped down a Scotch before the others came, and then hit at least three more at dinner. Clem Bartosh was the only one in clericals, but his booming good nature hadn't changed. Bob Foley was more enthusiastic about Vatican II than ever. "Do you realize," he began "what John and the council have accomplished? Mass and sacraments in the vernacular; a much broader use of Scripture; new roles for the laity in worship, but also in church life. An openness to the world; a warm relationship to Protestants; a foreign policy (if you can call it that), built on the American experience. Those are only a part of it."

"Mother Church is just beginning to catch up with the rest of the world. They might begin by changing seminary stuff. Think of what little robots they made us into," said Cody.

Foley, a bit of gray in his jet black hair laughed. "You of all people! They would have had to lobotomize you to make you into a conformist. But wait a minute. Look at you now. Pinstripes, no mustache. The law has robotized you, at last."

"If you think I'll give you a 'touché' for that, you're wrong. Ol' Frankie hasn't changed on the inside. I dress this way 'cause the law firm of Stein, O'Brien and Schmidt pays better than being a public defender, and so I suit up for the suit, as it were."

Foley wasn't finished. "How about the endless conformity of the law court? The judge dressed like Mother Superior? The oyez, oyez, stand up his Honor is coming? And to top it off, they brainwash you guys into thinking the best justice is served by the adversary system?"

"You were going well 'til you hit that one. The adversary idea is proven stuff, the only way."

Bartosh cut in, "So the rich can hire the best attorney and always win. So much for justice."

I thought the unflappable Frankie was getting flapped. "Clem, there are public defenders and inexpensive lawyers winning suits against the big guys every day of the week."

Bob said, "My main point is that even the pre-Vatican Church was not any more couched in conformities than most institutions."

Still sipping Scotch, though our salads had arrived, Bill said, "All this Vatican II hoopla is fine, Bob, but I've got reservations. As I get it, we are going to have parish councils, fine, but what'll happen is that the flakes are gonna run and get elected. George could tell you. Right?"

I said, "At least some flakes. The thing is that Cox was such a dominant personality that he could control it."

"Don't be modest. You took charge."

"Right now, I wouldn't trade St. Dismas for any other parish. I love it."

Bill still hadn't got to his salad. "To come back to my point, we are gonna have to take orders from the laity. In the meantime, we are little slaves of the bishops."

Bob gave Bill his black-Irish stare. "Don't exaggerate, Bill, you've got a lot of freedom in parish life."

"How the hell would you know, from your ivory tower?"

I intervened, "As your mother would say, eat your salad." Bill started to give me a dirty look, but laughed instead, and began eating his salad.

"What I can't understand," I said, "is why the council didn't deal with the birth control issue."

Foley answered, "Pope Paul just took it away from 'em."

"And celibacy!" said Bill. "Who is going to take an honest look at that. I don't see any point in it."

Bartosh looked shocked. "Are you trying to say that the Holy Spirit doesn't know what He's doing?"

"You still believe in Santa Claus?" from Bill.

"No, but I believe in celibacy and that the Holy Spirit inspired it."

"Let's ask the theologian." I said, hoping to keep peace.

Foley was willing. "Let's answer that by analogy. Do you guys remember a short-lived theory in Scripture that the Spirit dictated word-for-word the Bible?"

There was a chorus of yeses. "While we in the Church have freed ourselves from a biblical literalness and fundamentalism, mostly we cling to an ecclesial fundamentalism. As if every papal decision is from God."

Clem said, "That's close to what I think."

"There's a lot of human opinion woven in. And," continued Bob, "I'm not always sure where the boundaries are."

Cody was working on his steak. "Tell me, Schwartzie, are there any lawyers in your club? All this church stuff is giving me a stomach reaction."

So I asked, "How is Rosie?"

"Interesting that you ask. She got her teaching certificate last year and is still at it as we speak. One more week in June. Sends her love. Sorry she couldn't be with us." I looked over at Clem and thought that maybe it was just as well that she couldn't come. Conversation slowed as we ate our entrees, and it got more general. I noticed Cody pass on the after-dinner drinks, but not Bill. I worried a bit as he drove me home, but he managed. I asked him if he didn't think he'd become a bit cynical. He got defensive, "I haven't changed my spots, no, but I've got ideas about authority, and—uh, other things which—yeah, I suppose have changed me."

"Like what?"

"Like maybe I'll tell you sometime, not tonight." He smiled.

"When will you share these so-called ideas?" He hesitated. "Next time you beat me in golf."

"Like never." We both laughed. As he dropped me at St. Dismas, he said, "Oh, I have a favor to ask, or Beth has. She has her divorce, but she wants to go for a decree of nullity. Being I'm her brother, I suggested that it would be better if some other priest applied for it. She wondered if you . . ."

I must have looked unwilling, because he said, "Look, if you don't want to, she'll understand."

"No, no, I'd be glad to. Should I call her, or will she call me?"

"She'll call you. You sure now . . . ?"

"Sure." But I wasn't so sure. It wasn't that I didn't want to help Beth, but I wondered where it might lead. I even talked it over with old Father Johnson, my confessor. He looked at me in that gentle way that he had, and said, "You don't have any, uh, designs on her?"

"No."

"You deal with many attractive women, no? Just keep your usual professionalism. You'll be all right. The very fact that you asked me shows your good will."

There was even a more compelling thought. For years, I'd been wrestling with the feeling that I was serving people, but was I loving them? I thought that if I couldn't help Beth, whom I was sure that I loved, well, what was the point of it all? All the same, there was an electricity in the air as I thought about seeing her again. The other side of my brain kept saying, that I was now forty years old, and I'd been tested. What is to worry about? Maybe those people who kidded me about being a worrier were right. With these thoughts did I prepare to meet Beth again.

It was a nice time in my life. The parish was responding to me. People seemed excited about the parish election. The few who opposed me were not very intrusive. Some had voted with their feet, the rest were subdued. Most of the parish was with me. Perhaps, after years of struggle and anxiety, relaxation was so unaccustomed, that it seemed akin to boredom. The days were busy. I found myself working from early morning Mass to late night meetings. Sunday afternoons (after Rosary) and Monday were a kind of weekend for priests. Bill and I would check on each other toward the weekend to see if either had a Sunday wake, followed by a Monday funeral. Once, when I had run Monday funerals three times in a row, Bill asked facetiously, "What's with these people of yours? Do they think they can die any old time that they want?"

On this particular Sunday night, Beth Thompson (Kelly) was to see me at eight p.m.

❖

EIGHT

Beth and Others

It wasn't that I hadn't seen Beth in recent years. I had had dinner with the Thompsons, Beth, Bill and their mother. (Mr. Thompson had died.) It was usually on Bill's birthday or Christmas or sometime. But I really hadn't been alone with her. It's strange, too, how insufficient images from memory are. I still had an image of fifteen-year-old Beth, blond and tanned, walking toward the gazebo and later, so-phisticated Beth at Bill's and my ordination kidding me about blessing everybody. "You'll wear it out, George." Then later, when, in tears, telling me about her unhappy marriage. I realized how pale and incomplete those pictures were, when Beth came up the walk to my rectory on that July evening. The sun was still up as she stopped on the path to reach out her hand to the rose bush as you might to a friendly dog or cat. She drew a section of the bush to her nose, inhaled, smiled and patted it, indifferent to thorns. All of this in seconds; then she smiled at the house as if she knew that I had been watching. I had a mental picture of blue eyes, blond hair, fine features, but what was missing in memory was the peculiar grace, the élan, the person behind the beautiful face. She knocked lightly at the door, as if she knew that I knew that she was there. I shook her hand.

"I used to get kissed," she said plaintively. So I hugged

her and kissed her lightly on the cheek. (I was being professional.) We made small talk for a while. I asked about her new job, something in the then new field of computers. Then I took out my pen and began the matrimonial questioning. "I can't recall," I said, "all of our conversations of some years back, but I'm wondering if we can raise the nullity claim on *non-consummatum.*"

"If that means what I suppose it to mean, close, but no cigar. We did have intercourse twice; once on the honeymoon, once later. I don't want to be vulgar, but there is more, uh, *amore,* in say, a horse breeding. He went through the motions like a man sentenced to marriage. And that was the end of it, nor would he talk about it."

"Is he homosexual?"

"I don't know; I really don't know. I visited him a couple of years ago, and he was living in a shared apartment with another guy, and he took some pains to show me that they really had separate apartments, even to individual living rooms. They had only a kitchen-dining area in common." She sighed, "He might just be an asexual being; I dunno."

"There's a kind of new nullity approach called psychic incapacity. I think, from your description, it fits your case to a tee."

For an hour we talked about the case and I wrote. Then I said, "I'll type your testimony up and have you sign it. Then I'll send it to the diocesan tribunal and they'll assign a priest as a sort of lawyer for you."

"You mean you're not going to follow this through?"

"See, I'm not on the tribunal." She seemed terribly disappointed. Her blue eyes, so joyous and alive, turned sad. I said, "I could ask to get on the court. they're always looking for people. Trouble is, they don't want you for just one case. I've got all I can handle here, although I'm promised an assistant soon."

"George, I don't mean to increase your work load." She stopped for a moment as if trying to find the right formula to explain, and then said, "What I'd really like is for us to be friends. I mean just friends. I respect your celibacy, even though I think it's nuts, but I mean lots of men and women are friends, not sexually, just friends. Like maybe Bill and Mary Lou Dowd.

"Like who?"

"You mean Bill doesn't talk to you about Mary Lou? Well, I don't want to be the family tattletale, but they see each other two, three times a week. Funny, Bill doesn't tell his best friend."

Funny, I thought also, funny indeed. She continued.

"Hey, celibate, anything wrong with dinner once in a while with an almost virgin?"

She was wearing pants, not the skintight kind you see a lot of today, but the lovely contours of her legs were well outlined. She was not quite the slim fifteen year old I once knew, but close enough. Age had ripened her favorably as it does some women. Her eyes had a glamour which only age can confer, and they looked out at me teasingly now, but a moment after, somber, begging for the simple response of friendship. The old tape that had run through my head in recent years came to me, "Do you love them?" Meaning, of course, the people I serve. She spoke quietly then. "The last thing I would want is to damage you or for you to feel compromised."

I was clinging to my professionalism less and less. I *knew* I loved her. Why couldn't I offer her a pure and celibate love?

"I don't see why we can't have lunch sometimes." When she smiled as she did now, she smiled not only with her mouth and teeth, but with her eyes, her whole face suffused with evident pleasure. When, two hours later, I kissed her goodbye, I'm not sure that old Father Johnson would have termed it "professional."

Other people came back into my life at that time. One August morning, the doorbell rang. I opened the door to a tan, smiling, and even thinner, Gerald Fox. "Well, what the hell?" I said.

"What the hell yourself, George, meet the new assistant."

"What?"

"Just joking. Back from the wars. Ryan won't let me go back to El Salvador. I've become too radical. Seriously, if you want me as your assistant, just call. Today, though, I just want to visit. If you want me as assistant, you'll have to ask. I don't want to put you on the spot—like help the old friend."

"Coffee?"

"Sure. Uh, wait, what brand?"

"I dunno—you allergic or something?"

"Only politically," he said, as he accompanied me to the kitchen to check the source of my coffee. "Yeah, this O.K." he said, then added, "Actually none of it's O.K., all coffee growers have exploited the Latin Americans, but some are worse than others."

"Jerry, for God's sake, what are you talking about?"

"Exploitation. I forget. Our seminary education didn't include the evil effects of U.S. colonialism in Latin America."

"You just got here, and you're on some soapbox." I poured him a cup of coffee. "Do you use cream and sugar, or do those exploit some farmer?"

"Probably, but I drink it black."

"I don't want to spent my whole visit with you, after five years, on politics, but I'm curious as to how buying coffee from El Salvador or wherever hurts people. It gives 'em a market, employment, no?"

He smiled as he sipped the brew, but the same intensity of the rule-keeper and the touch footballer was in his eyes.

"George, you're a neat guy, and I'm sure if you experienced what I did, you'd have the same response. Use coffee as the example. U.S. firms go to Central America, and buy up land. Sometimes, families have lived on that land for years. They grew maize, beans, fruit, for local consumption, but they often did not have formal deeds to their property. Along comes good uncle Sam, and they are tossed out. Now coffee is grown there. The coffee goes north, the money goes north and the natives go—go hungry. Do you see?"

"You make it sound so simple. Aren't you leaving out something? Like the Central American governments could protect their own people. Why blame us?"

"Sometimes we control those governments. Take Nicaragua. We put the Somozas in power and they own everything and the peasants have poverty which you can only imagine."

"Why don't they revolt?"

"They try, but we've beefed up their military so much, that it's futile. They even train their beasts up here on our bases." The anger in his voice was rising.

"Same old Jerry Fox," I said.

"I know, I know, I'm supposed to be the zealot, but I defy you or even Ryan to live there, not among the rich, but in the *barrios del pobres,* for six months, and you'd be as outraged as I am."

"What's the *barrios* etcetera?"

"Sorry, that's my Spanish, it means the slum areas."

"Not to change the subject, but how's your health?"

"Fine. I went through all the Montezuma ailments down there, but I must have developed immunity."

"You're as thin as a rail."

"Comes with living with the poor. I eat what they eat. Not much."

"What's this bit about looking for a job?"

"Hey, I don't wanna put you on the spot. Ryan won't let me go back. I think he thinks I'm some kind of Communist."

"Well?"

Jerry laughed. "In El Salvador, or in Latin America generally, anyone who helps the poor, oh—like teaching them
to read, is called Communistic. There's even some kernel of
truth in the charge. If you are starving and your children
sick, and all this is the result of the capitalist system, you
look for an alternative system. Communism is the only one
in place."

"Are you then saying that you're attracted to Communism?"

"You sound like Ryan. No, I think the Commies don't
have it either, but some form of socialism, yes."

"Enough politics, for the moment, anyway. Would you
really like to come here?"

"Don't decide today. Don't even feel the least bit of pressure for old time's sake. Think of the parish and yourself, is
it a good deal?"

"I'll do just that."

And we chatted on, about the old days, but I noted that
he could hardly stay away from the burning question of El
Salvador. After he left, I weighed having him. I loved being
alone in my little house. "My house!" It had become mine.
I'd earned it, by pulling the parish together, keeping the
good stuff that Cox had done, quietly eliminating the ex-
cesses. I wondered what it would be like to share a house
with Fox. Zealot or not, he was a man of very strong convictions. Fine for a morning visit, but day after day. Also I
hated to give up my privacy. On the other side, I did need
an assistant. The parish had grown to 1500 families. Try as I
might, I was short-changing them. But another thought
kept protruding; how would a fairly well-off suburban parish deal with Jerry's sermons which would inevitably touch
on the U.S. induced poverty of Latin America? The flip side
was that, while I occasionally preached "prophetic" social
justice sermons on racism or poverty, maybe the parish
should have a stronger diet of social values, and Fox could

and would provide it. I had a rare evening without appointments, so I had invited Bill and Bob for dinner. It was an opportunity to get their advice on taking on Jerry Fox.

"Jerry was always a little goofy," said Bill. He was heavily into the Scotch, and when drinking, I noticed his judgements were careless and often unfair.

"Oh, that's not so," said Bob, "he did have a tendency to go overboard, but he's right on Central America."

"How about our late, martyred President? Didn't he start some 'Alliance for Progress' or something?" I said.

"Oh, I don't think it matters much which party, Democrat or Republican, we've pretty well ripped-off the Latins. Coolidge stated it concisely when he said, "North Americans and their property are a part of the general domain of the nation, even when abroad."

"Which," said Bill, "brings us back to Vietnam. I've got a simple litmus test for right or wrong in international disputes; namely who is on those lands. That goes back to the Europeans coming to the Americas and it applies to us in Vietnam."

"How about stopping the spread of Communism?" I asked.

"In the name of anti-Communism, we have intruded into a nation seeking independence from the French, from us, from whomever," Bob said.

"How about the people there who are against Communism?"

"I wonder how numerous they are, George? They have all of our mighty backing, yet, they're losing."

"And the Chinese and Russian powers are behind the other side. So it's like the global battle between Democracy and Communism is being fought over there."

Bill snorted, "The crucial thing is nationalism, not communism. Mary Lou and her bunch are forming an anti-Johnson campaign and I think I'm going to be part of it." It was the first time since Beth had told me about his closeness to Mary Lou that I heard him mention her name, and I looked at him quizzically. He ignored my stare.

I asked, "What will Ryan think about that?"

"I could care less. It's time we priests got involved in the political process."

I said, "Maybe that's why I ought to hire Jerry Fox."

"The problem is," said Bob, " is how he goes about it."

"I'd hate to have him at St. Isidore's. If you get Jerry as your assistant, you're in for trouble."

I thought about it for a couple of days, and made up my mind. I called the chancery and got Muldoon.

"You wanna do what? You bring him in and those women will be walking up and down in front of the chancery. And this time of the year, there's no arctic clipper to get you off the hook. However, George, Foxie has gotta be someplace, so you may as well be the sacrificial lamb. I'm sure your honorable classmate will approve."

When I told Fox, he sounded pleased. "I hope you're not just being a good guy about this." I assured him I'd made a deliberate choice. Then I sat in my den saying my Office and getting distracted from my prayers by thinking of how I was giving up my privacy. There was going to be more than that.

After Jerry Fox's first Sunday sermon, the phone rang frequently.

"Who is that Communist?"

"Did he say he was going to be here permanently?"

"I was mortified by his anti-patriotism." And so on.

Well, I'd been warned. I suggested to Fox that it might be better if he waited until people got to know him better. He took the advice, but not totally. We had a few people leave the parish, but, after the initial shock, he soon found a following. He was a hard worker and it made it easier for me to get away more often. And one of the things I did was to have lunch with Beth. I guess that I'd never had anyone with whom I could relate better. As much as I enjoyed her brother and Bob Foley, Beth was a real soul mate. The lunches flew by so we took to walking together to prolong our time with each other. By now, I felt unworried about any physical involvement. After all. I'd been tested, and that for many years. It was just a marvelous new friendship; one which colored my whole life. I explained to my retreat master that the relationship with Beth had helped me in loving my parishioners; something I had been struggling with for years. Did I really love them? I found that it was easier since I had formed this friendship. He balked at that.

"The proof of love has always been doing God's work, not feelings, not emotions. Jesus said, 'If you love me, keep my commandments.' As you said earlier, you always tried to serve your parishioners well. This new emotion isn't necessary. Might even be dangerous. Is she attractive—I mean in the physical sense?"

I answered with an understatement that was close to a lie.

"Some people would say so."

"I'm not going to tell an obviously mature person what he can and can't do, but I ask you to give prayerful consideration to what you told me."

I told him about how living with Fox had changed my lifestyle. I'd lost my privacy.

"Is he hard to get along with?"

"No, he's the soul of kindness." I sighed. "He's a good conversationalist, but, well, he's tough to celebrate with. If I invite him to play golf, he'll say, 'that's a bourgeoise sport.' If we have steak for dinner, he'll turn it down, too expensive. When he cooks, ugh, it's rice and beans, stuff like that. He shares the poverty of the Latin poor, even though he's up here."

"Do you argue with him about these matters?"

"Not very often. He always wins. I guess he's got truth on his side."

Usually, Bill and Bob and I arranged our schedules so that we could be on retreat together, but this year Bill skipped the retreat for some reason. It gave Bob and I the chance to talk a lot. As we kicked the fall leaves on the retreat house lawn overlooking the Mississippi, I told him how strongly I used to preach against birth control, but when I saw the problems in homes, both economically and psychologically, I kept wishing the council would do something about it. Bob took the pipe out of his mouth.

"George, Pope Paul took it out of their hands, but, two things; one, in saying that intercourse has a legitimate purpose in marriage quite apart from conception, they broke new ground. The old Augustinian notion that only the desire for children justifies lovemaking has gone the way of the flat earth theory. So, it seems to me that a different attitude toward birth control is inevitable."

"You said, 'two things'. What's the other?"

"The Pope has, as you may know, set up a commission to reevaluate the issue. Since there are laymen, and even more significantly, laywomen on the panel, I think we'll see a less rigid stance."

"And in the meantime, what do I say in the confessional?"

"Some of the moral theologians seem to be approving of the pill. You can't preach it, but in the confessional, uh, it might be the just thing to give absolution, uh, readily, and ask them to come in and talk, outside the confessional. There, you can help them put the whole thing in perspective. If they have six kids already, for example, they don't seem to have a contraceptive mentality. I think we've tended to see morality in single actions. We need to see it in a broader context, like a series of actions."

"O.K., let's say they have a bunch of kids; then what? The rules no longer apply?"

"I'm not a moral theologian, as you know, but if I'm reading Haring and some of the Europeans correctly, they might suggest something like the pill."

He stopped to reload his pipe. "I understand this smoking is connected to both heart and cancer."

"I'm glad I quit back in sem days."

"I'm trying to cut down. But maybe the pipe is my way of coping with celibacy." He laughed.

I said, "Tobacco and celibacy! A new article for the priest magazines. Let's get back to the subject. Say some more about the council and birth control. They really didn't deal with it."

He relit his pipe. "Yes and no. You remember that Augustine, after his conversion, saw sexual activity as a pretty crummy business, so that you could justify this nastiness only if you wanted to beget a baby. That attitude has hung over the Church as a pall for all these centuries. Even in recent times, Von Hildebrand had to back off a position which claimed that the normal sequence is for couples first to express their love, then conceive the child, rather than the other way around. The council has said almost the same thing. Now, once you establish the making of love in marriage as a value in itself, not dependent on the intention of having a child, it seems to me that we are on the road to approval of some sort of contraception."

"Well, it would sure solve a lot of pain for a lot of parishioners."

"George, I wonder if you have noticed a change in your approach to pastoral questions? You seemed to me, in the past, to be a little like Moses coming down from the mountain to impose the law. I'm exaggerating somewhat. Now I see you working from the needs of your people. I think you're growing, you old legalist."

I told him about my efforts to love my people, not just to serve them. I told him about my love for Beth, a chaste love, I assured him.

He took a deep drag on his pipe. "I don't know about that. George, it looks chancey to me. I know a number of priests who are in these 'chaste loves'. How come you guys never have these 'chaste affairs' with some old ugly granma?"

I didn't have much of an answer.

After the retreat I went up to Pinecone for a few days. Jerry was taking all the Masses that weekend. It was a nice rest.

I came back on Tuesday to find our usually calm secretary, Madelin Hart, in a state of high dudgeon. She glared at me as she handed me a sheaf of memos with names and phone numbers. "These are the ones who gave their names. I would give you some of the anonymous messages, but I don't want to swear at a priest."

"Hey, easy, Madelin, what's this about?

"*Your* dear assistant preached against the Vietnam war on Sunday. Not only that, he attacked the whole foreign policy of the U.S. for a hundred years. Listen, he makes Coxie seem like a conservative."

"I'll go talk to him," I said, as I started to the basement which humble Jerry had set aside as his office.

"You can't see him now. He's got a line-up of young men. He's counselling draft dodgers. That's the other thing; in his sermon, he invited draftees to see him first."

"I knew he felt strongly about the war."

"A lot of other people are feeling strongly. Gimmee that stack a minute." She fished through the memos. You better start with this one from the chancery. Monsignor Muldoon. The chancery is being bombarded."

I poured a cup of coffee and retreated to my office. I could see that it was going to be a long day. As Madelin had suggested, I started with the chancery. I got Muldoon.

"When the cat's away, the mice will play," he began. "Come to think of it, the mouse has roared. Foxie has outdone Coxie."

"So I understand."

"You mean that's the best you can say? We've had a

couple dozen calls. Your very reverend classmate is not amused. Does the names Charles Polson mean anything to you?"

"Of course, he's our main contributor."

"Wrong tense, G., he *was* your main contributor. Worse. He had accepted chairmanship of the Annual Appeal. He now will resign unless as he says, 'the mess at St. Dismas' is cleared up."

"Oh shit, one sermon."

"Not according to Polson. He says that his ulcer kicks up every time he runs into Fox's Mass. But let me turn you over to Ryan. He's growling back in his office. Hasn't had his meat for the day. Have a pleasant visit."

Ryan was on the line. "George, what the hell is going on?" Before I had time to answer, he went on. "I thought you'd have been able to control Fox; I misplaced my trust . . ." It was my turn to get angry. "As a matter of fact, I agree with Fox. I probably would preach a little more carefully than Jerry, but this war is nuts."

"Let me ask you this. Would you now be ready to build your school without Mr. Polson?"

"So, this is not about whether the war is just; it is about money." There was a period of silence on the other end of the line; then, "You can be moved, you know."

"Yes, all powerful one, but where are you on this war?"

"I'm for the containment of Communism, but that's neither here nor there. I'm not a politician, I'm trying to keep a diocese from falling apart. If you can't run your parish, there's a few rural places open."

I said, "You do what you have to do." And I hung up. It was the first time I'd ever hung up on a bishop. And then I worried. An hour later, he called back. "George, I guess we were both a little hot under the collar." I wanted to say, "Especially you," but I held back. He continued, "What has he said to you?"

"I haven't talked to him yet. He's busy counselling draftees."

"Shit," said the archbishop.

"I don't want to back into another argument with you, but Jerry has strong convictions about the war, the U.S. policy in general."

"So have a lot of people; like we fear the spread of Communism. I'm thinking of letting him go back to El Salvador."

"He might not want to go anymore."

"Well, talk to him."

It was four p.m. before Fox was free. I said, "Jerry why didn't you talk to me before your Sunday blasts?"

"And find out what my convictions are? George, I'm sorry if I got you into trouble, but isn't that what we're about, telling people what Jesus would say if He were here?"

"What makes you so sure that you are representing Jesus' ideas? You think Russia and China are what Christ had in mind?"

"This isn't about Russia or China. This is about an independent Vietnam."

"I half agree, but still I think we need to correlate our ideas to some extent. How much force will either of our ideas have on our people if we are opposing each other?"

"It's the old story, isn't it? I'm the zealot. Sorry if your parish is mad."

"Not to mention Ryan."

"Really?"

"Really. He wants to send you back to El Salvador."

"I'm not sure I want to go now."

"That's what I told him."

"Gee, I'll think about it, though."

And he did, and he went. We had a warm parting. And Polson's quarterly $7,500 check arrived. The world might

be going down the tubes, but St. Dismas and the archdiocese were safe. However, I was without an assistant. I called
Muldoon and he said, "Um, um, we got somebody but
maybe Ryan should talk to you." I didn't like the sound of
that. A day later, Ryan called.

"George, you once worked with Tony Shulz at Sorrows.
Did you hit it off O.K.?"

"Yeah, O.K. was about it. Nothing great, but it passed."

"Right now, that's all we got."

"Thought he was pastor in Walton."

"Well. I want to level with you. He got in some trouble.
Homosexuality. We sent him out to that facility in New
Mexico. The psychs there are satisfied that he's O.K. now.
His homosexuality was connected with alcohol, and he's in
A.A. now. You willing to take a chance?"

"Let me think about it. Would he live here?"

"No problem; he lives in a halfway house for alcoholics.
So your precious privacy would be intact."

So it came to be that Tony Shulz came to St. Dismas, and
I had time to be with Beth and continue our "chaste friendship."

We sat at lunch at the Lex, and this made me a bit nervous, because the Lex had become a hangout for priests, and
while some of them would recognize Beth as Bill's sister,
others might raise an eyebrow or two. I told her about Jerry
and his sermon and Ryan's reaction, and how I ended up
with Shulz.

"Men!" she said.

"Men, what?"

"Just men. If the archbishop were a woman, he would
have been pleased with anti-war sermons."

"How do you get there?"

"Women are always against war."

"Is that so? How about Molly Pitcher?"

"Oh, for God's sake! That's a myth."

"Heck it is. Betcha five dollars."

"It's beside the point."

"How about Joan of Arc?"

"I'm talking about most women."

"There were even women calling about Jerry's sermon."

After I said that I remembered that only Henrietta had called, and she was in favor of Jerry's sermon."

"How many?"

"Who counts? Some, anyway."

"This Shulz a new guy?"

"No, as a matter of fact, he's older than I. I was with him at Seven Sorrows."

"Then how come an older guy gets to be under you?"

"He got in some trouble."

"What kind of trouble?"

"I suppose I can tell you, but keep it *subsigillo*."

"That means 'keep it quiet'? What'd he do?"

"Something about homosexuality."

"Something? Don't you know what?"

"Anyway he's better now. He was drinking at the time. Now he's on the wagon."

"Shouldn't you know more about it; for your parish, as well as you?"

"You're in a funny mood. Kinda negative."

"I resent that." She looked genuinely angry. "I'm only concerned. If I had somebody working for me, especially in a nuturing job like yours, I'd wanna know what he or she did. Like did he get caught by the cops? Did he make the advances? What age was the other person?"

"Look, the archbishop is satisfied that he's O.K. now. Maybe, he needs my trust."

"Maybe, he'll do something in your parish, and you'll get stuck with it. Did you think of that?" I hadn't, but I was getting tired of her nagging.

"I repeat, 'what's with you today?' I know what I'm doing. I haven't had a mother for some years telling me what to do." Now the usually smiling face turned sullen.

"What's with ME? What's with YOU? Can't a friend even make a suggestion?"

"It seemed more like an order."

"Hey, are we having a quarrel? A lover's quarrel?" Then she laughed. She had said the last part loud enough, so that someone at the next table looked over with a smile. I felt my face flush. This made her smile more than ever.

"This is wonderful; it's a real growth in our friendship. We're close enough to fight." I began to relax. I loved her too much to really quarrel. Then she changed the subject.

"I've got some good-news, bad-news. I have a chance to supervise a revision of the computer setup of a big medical complex. More money, more prestige."

"Gee, that's great! How can there be a bad side?"

She sighed, "It means I'd have to move to Rochester, for at least a year or so."

I was still feeling a little ornery. "What's so bad about that?" Now her face showed anger again. "You mean you wouldn't care? You wouldn't miss me?"

It was my turn to smile. "Of course I would, but I wouldn't want you to miss an opportunity like that."

"I haven't decided yet. I don't need the money, but wow, the career!"

And so, Beth did decide to take the offer, and she moved to Rochester, but not out of my life. We met in halfway places like Red Wing or Faribault or Wabasha and had lunch; usually followed by a walk. Once, when we were going to have lunch at the old hotel in Red Wing, she showed up, looking particularly stunning. She was in a tight red skirt, her golden hair at its longest, and a blouse which somehow emphasized her endowments. That's the day that a parishioner came over to our table to greet "Father." Later I said, "You know that you look smashing today, and meeting for lunch around town is one thing, but meeting so far from the homebase makes it look like, well, like a tryst or rendezvous. I'm not trying to tell you what to do, but I guess I'd feel a little less guarded if you were uh, uh—dressed more conservatively." I thought she might resent me telling her that, but she said, "Oh. I really understand. You don't suppose that guy was scandalized?"

"No, but I appreciate your understanding my position."

Two weeks later, we met in Owatonna. As I walked in past the bar, an elderly woman with her hair in a bun and dressed in black was faced away from me. Something about her caught my attention, and then this dowdily dressed woman turned toward me. It was Beth! Beth, without a dab of makeup or lipstick, and not a smile on her old maid's face. She really broke me up. Then she roared.

I said, "That proves it. All your good looks comes out of cosmetics and dress."

"For that remark, you don't even get kissed." I never told her how to dress again.

She was full of enthusiasm that day about her job.

"They want me to stay on. And they'll almost double my salary. That's not important, but it's what I always wanted to do. I hate being away from Ma and Bill and you, but I'm thinking of buying this beautiful house right on the Zumbro River; it's a classic, very private; maybe you could come and stay sometimes." I raised an eyebrow. "Oh, don't be so—so celibate. I'm not gonna rape you. There's a whole separate wing; you could be like a monk in a hermitage. Oh, its got a swimming pool too."

"We'll see." I said.

"How is your Reverend Shulz working out?"

"Interesting that you should ask. Chancery took him away. They said he needed further evaluation. Now, all I got is a weekend guy, at least till June."

"There's something more than they're telling you."

"Could be. I never saw or heard anything strange, while he was with me. What might have happened in his halfway house I can't even guess."

1968. I heard a theologian describe it as a year of extraordinary events, a watershed year, like 1492. He had convincing statistics, but I can't remember most of them. He was right, though, 'cause in June, 1968, I beat Bill Thompson in golf! A solid seventy-nine versus his lousy eighty-six.

After drinks and dinner at the clubhouse, he said, "Remember my pledge?"

"You gonna quit drinking?"

"You sound like Ma or Beth. Maybe you got that from hanging around Beth. You did know that I knew that, didn't you?"

"I suppose so."

"Anyway, a while ago, I told you that, if you ever beat me in golf, I'd tell you of certain changes in my life. I was going to tell you anyway, but this makes it a good opportunity. I think Beth has hinted that I was seeing a lot of Mary Lou Dowd, whom you tried to rescue a decade ago. Uh— to make a long story short, I'm going to marry Mary Lou. I'm leaving priesthood." I had had premonitions of this, but the reality hit me like a winter wind. The first thing which came to me was not about Bill and Mary Lou, but the thought that if this could happen to them, it could happen to Beth and me. For want of a better thing to say, I said,

"What will you do?"

"As you know, Dad left me enough so I don't need to do anything, but I'm already into the 'Bellows Real Estate' firm. I'm in training and should start in the fall."

"Have you told Beth or your mother?"

"I'm not sure Beth needs to be told. She and Mary Lou are pretty close. Telling Ma is not gonna be easy. You were hard enough, old buddy. But you don't look too shocked."

But I was, although I didn't demonstrate it. We chatted on about this new development, about Mary Lou, and some of her problems, going back to her father's abuse and her mother's slow response. I finally asked him what I'd asked Cody.

"If I'm asking stuff that you don't want to talk about, just tell me to butt out, but is there any problem with faith in this decision?"

A little loose from three Scotches, he answered, "Maybe, just maybe, yes. I don't say I don't believe. You know some of this new stuff that Foley and you and the others talk about has played some part. Like I never read this Bultmann, except derivatively. I'm talking about demythologizing Scripture. Basically, how far do you do that? I see some of these fundamentalist outfits like, what is it? The Missouri Synod people? They want Jonah in the whale's belly. Right? I read in the paper one of 'em saying 'If you start getting away from literal interpretation, where do you stop?'" He paused, sipped some more after dinner Scotch. "Then, then, there're those proofs we had or have. Like the historicity of the Bible, the Resurrection, etcetera."

"Hold it," I said, "these are for nonbelievers. We've got our faith."

He paused, rattling the ice in his glass, as if musing whether to get another drink. "My faith. True. But maybe it had to be buttressed with those arguments from history, or the stuff about God in natural theology. I liked those arguments. Now, now—they don't seem to be what Monsignor Baker called 'apodictic'. I still have faith, I suppose. Maybe, it's on hold. Like that summer grass that turns brown in the heat. The lawn people say that it's sleeping, not dead. Perhaps my faith is sleeping."

I didn't know what to say. I wished I hadn't asked him about his faith. I looked at my friend from Dowling Hall days; tall, fine-looking like his mother and Beth, still athletic, if a trifle heavier; blond hair a bit paler, with a few strands of gray. My longtime friend and I feared he was making a terrible mistake that I was powerless to prevent. So I continued asking questions, although I didn't want to.

"Stop me if I'm getting too personal. But the doubts came first or Mary Lou?"

"Boy loves girl. Can't have her with the faith. So he dumps the faith. 'Take the cash, and let the credit go.' *Benedicamus Domino.* Well, Father Confessor, that's a little simplistic, don't you think? I'm not saying there's no connection at all. I was there for Mary Lou when she needed me, but she was also there when I needed someone. Don't think I'm blaming you or Bob or anyone. You all had your own problems, but Mary Lou listened when life with Gibbons was almost intolerable."

"Are you angry at the chancery? At the Church?"

"Put a name on it, yes, at Ryan. When I think of how often I wrote or called Ryan about Gibbons. Today they term it 'Alzheimers.' I'd never heard the word in those days. Gibbons had all the symptoms. On top of that, he was an ornery guy to start with. It was godawful."

"How long were you with him?"

"About a dozen years; seemed longer. But you're asking if these things are the cause of my questioning my faith. Maybe, but I think they're on separate tracks. Perhaps my faith was always weak. Needed bolstering which I got from rational proofs. Then, as I said, the proofs didn't seem all that absolute anymore. You know seminary life was a big support for belief. We were like a little island in a secular sea. All of us with the same ideas, the same creed; no newspapers, no magazines. A kind of medieval castle."

"Aren't you getting poetical!"

"George, I don't know how it all fits together. Mary Lou is my reality. That's the bottom line. The one certainty I have is my love for her and her love for me. I don't want to say any more."

"Nor I."

I went back home to the rectory. I hadn't cried for years, but I did that night. The next day my new assistant arrived.

I was vesting for the seven a.m. Mass, when this smiling, freckled, handsome young man opened the sacristy door.

"Hi George, I'm Joe Bass."

I shook his confident hand, as I said, "The new assistant."

"Please, the new associate. Gotta get you up to date. Mind if I concelebrate?"

"You know I haven't gotten around to that."

"Just do it your usual way and I'll guide you. Time you joined the post-Vatican church. Are you homilizing?"

"No."

"Mind if I do?"

"Uh—I guess it's O.K."

The Gospel that day was about Jesus feeding the crowd with the loaves and the fishes. The new Father Joseph Bass began by introducing himself. Then he said:

"Many of you grew up, I suspect, with the notion that the Evangelists, John, Mark, Luke and Matthew sat down shortly after the resurrection and wrote these gospels as memoirs. Actually, they came out of years of some early community's reflection about Jesus. Maybe after decades. Some scriptural experts claim that not one actual word in them is really a direct saying of Jesus. And the Gospel writers were not above rearranging events to make a point. Take this Gospel today. Did a real miracle take place? I doubt it. Maybe Jesus just got these people to share. Or maybe this is just a Gospel to make us aware of Eucharist. And the point there is that we are to share." He went on in this vein for more than ten minutes.

After Mass, I asked, "I'd like to discuss that sermon, or homily as you say, with you over breakfast."

"Do you have a cook?"

"No, I mean a lady comes in three times a week for dinner. In the morning, I just have juice and cereal."

"Do you have granola?"

"I don't think so."

"I see there's a pancake house a few blocks away. O.K.?"

I studied him as he was eating his granola. He was certainly more sure of himself than I was at a similar age. Or than most of my classmates. I began telling him that it was an intriguing homily.

"Intriguing. Intriguing? Does that mean that you didn't like it?"

"Uh, put it this way. I don't know enough Scripture to affirm or deny what you said. The Scripture of my day was, let us say, deficient. Yet I do know that most of the people there today were hardly ready for what you said. In a class on Scripture you could gradually lay a foundation, and then they might put it together."

"Jesus didn't do that. He just laid out the truth, take it or leave it."

"Well, if what you said at Mass is true, we don't know what Jesus said, much less the manner or way in which He said it." His laden spoon stopped in front of his mouth. "That's not what I meant. We do have a pretty good notion of what he said by—by the whole Christian movement."

"Well, that's what you seemed to say, and I'll bet that is what the congregation picked up. Don't you think we should talk these things over first? If you say one thing and I say another, that will just lead to confusion."

"What's so bad about that? Confusion often leads to growth."

"You may have a more up-to-date biblical know-how, but give me credit for almost twenty years of parish ministry. Most confusion of that type leads, not to growth, but to indifference or they may leave the parish or the whole Church."

His smile was a bit belligerent. "Would you like me to submit my homilies to you in advance?"

"I don't think that's very fair of you to put it that way. There's a difference between my trying to dictate your homilies and my asking that we talk it over. You preached this morning without asking me anything about your hearers. Take the time factor. A lot of them are on the way to work. I usually get them out in twenty minutes or less. That's an expectation on their part. A two minute homily is long enough."

"That's the problem. Catholics are a Eucharistic folk; they need to become biblical, people of the Word of God."

"I think that we ought to meet at least once a week just to discuss these matters."

"O.K. by me. While we're having this frank conversation, let me say that I was surprised that in this parish, founded by the legendary Cox, there is still an altar rail, kneelers, and a grandiose altar. I guessed that you must have changed a lot of things when you replaced Cox."

"Cox was a very good friend of mine. That doesn't say I bought everything that he did. The altar, etcetera is what was here, for that matter. I dropped some things and preserved others. Our justice committee is one of the best in the diocese."

"What's the justice committee's budget?"

That stopped me. "No budget; they're all volunteers."

"To me, the budget reveals your priorities. No money, not much dedication. What's your school budget? There's your priority. Kids over adults. Jesus blessed the children, but preached to the adults."

"Or so some later generation guessed," I countered.

"You're taking my words in too absolute a fashion. My point now is that we've spent enormous amounts on kids, but ignored adults."

"School versus adult education, eh? There are some other factors. Children are a captive audience. I've seen some very well prepared—and expensive adult programs die from lack of response."

Bass continued to volley. "We've always got the Mass as the means of education."

"This is where I came in. You're back to your morning

homily. I'd like to go back to your crack about money, because that was the very argument that I threw at the archbishop when he was disturbed at a sermon that Father Fox gave. A very large diocesan contributor was..."

"You mean you weren't the one who got Fox out of here? That wasn't the scuttlebutt at the sem. We heard that you were the one who got him moved."

I got up from the table and grabbed the check. "Not everything you hear in the sem is true."

"Touché, George. When do we meet?"

"How about Monday mornings at, say nine o'clock."

"I was thinking that might be my day off."

"We haven't even talked about work, and you already want time off?"

"First things first. Speaking of which—would you mind if I lived away from the rectory?"

"Fine, if you can clear it with the boss, I love my privacy."

"I could get something decent for a couple of hundred."

"Whoa, who's gonna pay for this?"

"The parish. I don't have any money."

"No deal. we're back to priorities. Our people come before our comforts. Here's a key to the house. See you later."

After meeting Joe, I thought of calling the chancery and asking for another assistant (associate). Instead I called Foley.

"I just met my new assistant—oops—associate."

Foley laughed. "Well?"

"What ever happened to the nice docile guys like we were?"

"Don't blame me. I just teach here. How is he?"

"I'm seriously thinking of calling the chancery to swap with someone. Or are they all like that?"

"No, there're some really docile types. Joe is as good as we got. A bit brash, but bright and up front."

"Up front. Call it effrontery. Lippy kid. D'you guys teach 'em that?"

"I don't think you'd like the more docile ones. Joe is O.K."

So Joe Bass came to St. Dismas, and I had time to golf and to see Beth. Except I didn't. I found excuses not to see her.

She called after I had not met her for a month.

"I know why," she began.

"You know why what?"

"You know why what?"

"I know why what?"

"You are finding excuses for not seeing me, because you fear the same thing could happen to us as it did to my brother and Mary Lou. It's true, isn't it?" It was true, but I didn't want to admit it. "I've just been inundated with work."

"And you with a new assistant."

"He makes it worse. Besides, you gotta call 'em associates now, or they won't do anything."

"Enough evasion. When will we have lunch? I'll wear my 'Mother Machree' outfit, if that'll help. George, we're not Bill and Mary Lou. We've agreed on the limits."

And so I made a date and we were back seeing and listening to each other's woes. We met in Red Wing and she talked about Bill's impending wedding. "Are you going?"

"I guess. I wish Bill could have gotten laicized first."

"To be honest, I'm less worried about that than about Mary Lou. I think she's still mixed up from her dad. But the older brother is not gonna listen to this little sister." I told her about Joe Bass. "He kinda grows on you. I didn't like him at first, but we get along fine now."

"Once you let him run the place?"

"It's not that at all. I'm in charge."

"It didn't sound that way."

"You're not gonna tell me how to run my parish again?"

"Po' li'l me tell Father how to do things? I would never presume to. Priests know everything."

"Flattery will get you nowhere, and sarcastic flattery less."

"Anyway, you know the wedding is going to be at my house above the Zumbro."

"Is your mother coming?"

"Most reluctantly, but yes, after I pleaded with tears. This brings up another point. Mother is staying over with me after the wedding, so would you like to also? I've got oodles of room."

I hesitated. She looked at me teasingly. "Ma would be an absolute chaperon."

I decided it would be O.K.

1968. I wish I could recall all of the reasons why Foley's Latin American friend, the theologian, said that 1968 was a watershed year. It was for a lot of U.S. Catholics, clergy and laity, alike. I know one reason for sure. For, after a period of time where we all felt there would be an authoritative softening of the birth control issue, the encyclical on the subject, "Humanae Vitae" came out. It was a hot July morning and I was putting together a few words for a funeral at ten, when Madelin buzzed me.

"I know you said no calls, but the Reverend professor would not take 'no'."

"O.K. put 'im on."

Foley's usually placid voice was anything but. "You got time to talk?"

"Not really. I'm preparing a funeral homily, which I will deliver about forty-five minutes from now."

"Didja hear about the Pope's encyclical on birth control? Just on the wire services."

"How bad is it?"

"Bad, but I can't give you a short summary. Have lunch?"

"No. It's one of those times I have to go to the funeral lunch."

"Later? 'Cause I want to see you about this, and what we're going to do about it."

"Busy day. Tell you what. I can change an evening appointment. Come here for dinner—no, Bass will be in. I'd rather see you at Oak Tree. Six p.m. O.K.?"

Bob Foley was so into his subject that his Scotch sat idly while I sipped a gin and tonic.

"I have only the bare bones of the encyclical from the news, but I heard the quote that states that every conjugal act must be 'open to conception.' That's the bottom line."

"I'm just wondering how we handle this in parish life?"

"Or in academia. That's partly why I had to see you. We are putting out a letter from some priests to be given to the media. Mike Murphy from the College is preparing it. His field is moral theology, you know."

"I don't see what good it'll do. *Roma locuta est, causa finita est.* (Rome has spoken, the case is closed.)"

Foley looked at me fiercely. "They're not using the infallibility bit. Nor could they. Anyway, the letter will say something like we find this difficult to implement pastorally from a conscience point of view. We've got fifty-seven signatures already. You'll sign, of course?" He finally paused long enough to sip his drink. I looked out through the huge window of the clubhouse at the eighteenth hole shimmering in the July heat, while we sat in air-conditioned comfort in the splendid dining room; the place where Gerald Fox would never go with me, because the whole wealthy scene was offensive to him. The well-manicured lawn, the shiny bar, the elegant clubhouse, all of it was a kind of symbol of this country as well as the birth control dispute. I would sign, of course, but with mixed feelings. I was concerned about my parishioners and their consciences. They had, in effect, already voted. Twenty years earlier, a parish of 1500 families would have many, many baptisms per week. Either most of my parishioners had decided that it was not a sin, or they were sinning, or they were exercising great self-control, because there weren't that many baptisms. How much of this was conviction on their parts and how much was it the need to preserve a luxurious life style, one that I shared in? I guess Fox, in the brief time he'd been with me, had gotten into my own conscience, my moral sense. This series of thoughts took only a few seconds, but it must have come to Foley as a hesitancy on my part, for he quickly said, "Hey, I'm not urging you. If you are worried about how this will set with the chancery or your parish, that's up to you. Maybe it's against your convictions."

The waitress took our orders. We both went with the walleye.

"Look at us," said Foley, after she left, "getting health conscious. A sign of age."

I returned to the matter at hand. "I'm going to sign, and that with conviction. Let me put it this way. I could sign with a lot more enthusiasm if I were in a poor parish."

Foley drained his Scotch. "I know what you mean. You know my brother, Ned. He's got a big salary. So does Jane. They got two kids, and a summer home in the north, the big boat, the whole schmear. Is that a contraceptive mentality? I dunno. Maybe two is all they can handle. Still."

"You started to talk about Rome."

"Pope Paul, 'Hamlet' as Pope John once called him. A sincere man. I wonder what agony this cost him? And yet, he and a handful of one-sided theologians are legislating for the whole world, and that includes Jerry's El Salvador and starving folk all over." We sipped our second drinks quietly for a moment as we watched a weary foursome coming up the hill on eighteen.

"The worst part, George, is that this decision is based,

not on moral theology, but on the fear that any change would seem to jeopardize the magisterium."

"You mean like those documents which begin by saying, 'As we have always held...'"

"Like that. The fear is that if new biology or newer insights of any kind cause us to change a teaching, the whole teaching authority of the Church is compromised. The majority on the commission wanted change, but the Pope accepted the minority view."

After the waitress brought the salad, I said, "What will our classmate archbishop do with this letter of ours?"

"He'll be pissed."

"I think you should stay out of this. Let us parish guys voice our problem with applying this to our laity. I don't know if he'll do anything to us, but a seminary prof?"

"I've thought of that; I have indeed, but I can't back off of this."

Two days later the letter with over a hundred names appeared in all of the Twin City papers. I got some indignant phone calls and letters, as I think all of the signers received. A week later, a broken-voiced Foley called me. "Can you come over, tonight?"

"I've got a seven p.m. appointment. I'll come right after." I suspected I knew what it was about, but I also knew the phone was not the right place to discuss it.

Foley was not his usual self. He had been sipping (or more likely gulping) Scotch. In a very subdued voice, he said, "I should have listened to you, George; I've been fired!"

"NO! Ryan?"

"Ryan, yes, our most reverend classmate. He's mad at all the signers, and I think he would have called us in, one by one, but there were too many; would've wrecked the archdiocese. It was wise to have over 100 signers."

"But how about you?"

"About what you said last week. A seminary prof, says

Tom, forms the minds of future priests. In this case, heretical." Bob was near tears. It was no time to say "I told you so."

"He told me that he'd had a number of calls from Monsignor Brown (the rector who replaced Slovene) and that Brown had complained about my theology as near heresy. This was the final blow. He asked me why I couldn't at least stay out of moral theology which isn't my field. I told him that you can't seal these things off hermetically. The faith vision has to be integrated."

"What did he say to that?"

"I don't think he understood."

"What happens to you now?"

He sighed; big, strong, black Irishman, vulnerable now with the vulnerability of a child. "He offered me a couple of parishes, not too flattering. I said how come parish people are less corruptible than seminarians. No answer. I'll have to make a choice."

"Will you stay in the Church?"

He stared at me under black eyebrows. It was the stare that had often stopped outspoken seminarians in their tracks. "I thought you knew me better than that. Ryan can send me to Rattlesnake Junction, as he used to say to Cody, and I'll go. I'm in to stay. It's not Ryan's church; it's our church, and nobody's going to drive me out of it. I might make them uncomfortable, in fact, I hope I do, but it's my church as much as Ryan's." He looked at me fiercely. "I'm in for the duration!"

It was conviction, I have no doubt. Possibly aided and abetted by Scotch, but the reality of his strong conviction was unquestionable. That was partly why I got an appointment to see Ryan. Bill was to come along. Archbishop Thomas Ryan was surprisingly amiable—at first.

"Bill, George, classmates; like old times! Well, I can guess why you're here. It's about Foley, right?"

Bill spoke first, perhaps a mistake, "It's not about crazy

old Gibbons, this time. You never listened to me in those days, and I wonder if you can hear anything now." The atmosphere of the room got instantly hotter or colder, depending on your metaphor.

Ryan, his face turning hot, red, said, "I've never claimed to be above mistakes. The past is the past. I haven't a choice in the matter of Foley. You don't know how many times I've refused Monsignor Brown's DEMANDS to sack Foley from the seminary staff, but this is too much. I'm angry at all of you who signed that damn fool letter, but the seminary is no place for revolt against the Holy See!"

"Tom," I said, "two things. There is enough question among moralists to put this matter in dubious territory. Secondly, if there is doubt, one is not always bound to follow the stricter side. If you bishops heard more confessions, you might see how very earnest Catholics are forming their consciences honestly toward birth control, and that, seemingly with the help of the Holy Spirit."

"We're a hierarchical church, not a democracy. Too many of you guys seem to think we just obey the Vatican because we are ass-kissers; we want advancement. Nonsense! Somebody has got to hold this community called the Church together. You guys don't think that I read too, and question things? I do, but what I fear is a Church slipping into anarchy. You got to have rules and laws."

"Like maybe the days of the Inquisition?" offered Bill.

"O.K., there have been abuses of authority, but moral chaos is worse. I worry about the future of the Church in this country for that reason; a Church unable to command a moral consensus."

"Consensus?" I said, "that's the point. There hasn't been an honest search to read the consciences of most Catholics. The very fact that the majority opinion of the birth control commission was rejected, prevents consensus."

And so it went with a bitter exchange on both sides. We were powerless to do anything for Bob Foley, and in due time, he was sent to my old home parish in Sioux Lake. Two weeks after that meeting, Bill returned to drop his bombshell on Ryan. The wedding was set for the middle of November.

It was a small gathering down at Beth's home on the Zumbro: Beth and Bill's mother were there, but the latter looked very unhappy and even angry; Mary Lou's dad, who was out of prison after a short stay, had not been invited, nor even informed. Norma Dowd seemed happy by contrast to Mrs. Thompson. Her eyes, which had looked sad in repose when I had met the Dowds, years before, were now consistently joyous. There were two of Mary Lou's friends from work. Foley and I were the only priests there. Bartosh had been invited, but declined. Cody was tied up in a demanding personal injury case, and sent regrets and a very expensive gift. Bill did not want to put me on the spot by asking me to perform the ceremony, so he had a justice of the peace do the bare bones ritual.

Beth's house was huge and after a nicely catered lunch, we wandered through the capacious rooms and chatted. Norma Dowd sought me out as I sat in the rec room before a blazing fire in the huge fireplace. "Father, all these years I've wanted to come to you, and apologize for my not backing you when you set the law on Frank. I knew what was going on, but I—I guess I just plain lacked the courage to act."

"It's tough to go against your own husband. Even the law recognizes that."

"But, Father, you started things in motion. Mary Lou and I began to talk, to face it. I should have said this to you long ago, but apologies seem so feeble in the face of what you went through."

"Thanks. It wasn't that bad. In fact, I was an enabler, too. I liked working at St. Brendan's so much that I blinded myself to Higgin's boozing. It was important for me to get out of there. Anyway, you look so much happier now than when I first met you."

"I was brought up to think of divorce as the greatest evil. Now I know that in my case it was the only answer."

The wedding and the aftermath were low-key. There was a kind of sadness that hung over the day, despite Mary Lou looking gorgeous and Beth straining herself to make it a happy occasion. Selma Thompson found me in the kitchen sipping coffee.

"George, I wish I felt more like celebrating. I know I'm the proverbial wet-blanket, but it can't be helped."

I wasn't feeling that happy, myself, and I couldn't think of anything good to say, and so, I merely said, "Let's hope they'll be happy."

She fixed her still dazzling eyes on mine and said, "I hope this is the last of these I'll have to be part of." How much, I wondered does she know about Beth and me? Does she think that we're heading in the same direction? I answered blandly, "I see what you mean." Although I really didn't see. At five o'clock, the honeymooners left and shortly after everyone else, including Selma. I'd understood that she was staying over, the "chaperon". She had changed her mind. So Beth and I sat before the magnificent fire and talked far into the night. We kissed a very brother sister kiss at one a.m. and I slept in a bedroom in a wing of the house which was half a football field away from Beth. When I got up at eight the next morning, there was a note by my bedroom door, telling me where the orange juice, coffee, etc. were. At the bottom of the note she had written. "Last night was special. Thanks." And so it came to be that I spent occasional two-day escapes at Beth's. Escape was the right word because, while I'd grown to appreciate my associate, he'd sort of taken away my privacy, even the parish to some extent. Father Joe Bass was as good as Foley had promised. For example, he gave homilies against the war, but he had a flexibility which Fox lacked. The parishioners warmed to him, but I recognized my envy and refused to let it get in the way. He was personable and good company. Some would call him cocky, but that was unfair; he was simply superbly self-confident. The house, the rectory, was another matter. A lot of his young priest friends gathered and they'd talk and even sing, sometimes until quite late. All this was fine, but our house was too tiny to prevent me from being an un-willing listener to their high-spirited soirees. The flip side was that he was a real worker and took over when I was gone. One refuge was Pine Cone Lake, but that was at least a three hour drive, whereas I could get to Beth's in half that time. Beth worked long hours, so I could read, prepare homilies, even plan parish business in her absence. Some-times, I had dinner ready when she came home, and then I'd light a fire in the rec room, and we'd talk into the night. I might have known that it could not last.

In the meantime, world and Church events swirled a-round my barely aware consciousness. The war ground to a halt. Nixon was caught with his hand in the cookie jar and resigned. His vice-president was caught previously. It was a large cookie jar. The Supreme Court permitted abortion and peoples consciences toward slaughter was forever dulled. The OPEC countries discovered their power, and gas went higher and higher. The idealistic sixties (or so some considered them) gave way to youths who wanted it all. Ford replaced Nixon. Some regarded him as a states-man; some of us felt he was a political hack. Many other things happened, and as the Evangelist, John, wrote. "Not all of them could be written in this book." On the local Church scene, there were deaths. Slovene died and I went to his funeral, but I did not weep. Higgins died and I went to his funeral and did not weep, but I rejoiced that he had, in his later days, "found himself." Baker died and I went to his funeral and I did weep. I tried to get the old gang together for a dinner, but now that Ryan was willing to come even though Cody was to be there, Foley wouldn't come, because Ryan was going to be there. Bill Thompson had lost interest, and Bartosh was busy, so we skipped it. The wag who called reunions, "renewing old hatreds" was right, I guessed. These things took place around me, but I missed most of it, caught up in my corner of the Gospel. Mary Lou Dowd (Thompson now), came to see me about Bill's drinking. "He isn't doing his job. He thinks he has no problem; that I'm just a nag."

"Does he hit you?"

"No, no never, but the verbal violence..."

I promised to talk to him. Once, after golf, I broached the subject as he was inhaling, or so it seemed, his third Scotch.

"Bill, it's none of my business, but you seem to be drinking a lot more than you used to."

"You're right on the first part; it's none of your business. And I know where this is coming from. Mary Lou has talked to you, and I know that because she asked me a short time ago why I never play golf with you anymore. So she told you to talk to me. Right?"

"Don't get mad at an old friend. She did talk to me, yes. But doesn't it bother you that she thought it necessary? We've both dealt with alcoholics. Classically, the alcoholic is the last to know, so the role falls to observers."

His voice became sharper. "George, lay off; you don't know what Mary Lou is like. She's still identifying me with her alcoholic dad."

"I'll shut up after I say one more thing. I think you are drinking too much."

He got up from the table. "I don't know about golf next week. It's a pretty busy week." I knew it was resentment talking, not schedule. I returned to the rectory, feeling bad. Was my gang breaking up? Who was next? Ryan? Or, despite his strong conviction, Foley? Joe Bass picked up my sadness at the dinner table. "Bad game of golf?" he asked.

"Can you keep it under your hat?"

"Sure."

"I'm concerned about Thompson's drinking."

"It probably has to do with his guilt."

"Guilt?"

"Because he got married. And that's too bad, because in a few years it'll all be over. Celibacy is a dead issue. Have you picked out anybody yet?" And then he laughed. I found him irritating. "How do you come by this?"

"George, everyone knows it."

"When will all this happen?"

"Ten years at the longest."

"Joe, there are some things which you know that I don't, but there is no way in hell that you know that the Church is going to dump mandatory celibacy for priests."

He merely smiled in his supercilious way. I was more irritated. I said, "You know you really make angry when you do that." To his credit, he wiped the smirk off his face and said, "You've always treated me fine and I don't mean to make you angry."

"Let's call it a draw." I said, as I got up from the table.

A draw was better than I usually got arguing with Joe Bass. But he'd put a notion in my head. What if the Vatican dropped celibacy? Would it include guys already sworn? Would I really make a play for Beth? I dismissed these thoughts as juvenile and unworthy. I continued to visit Beth once or twice a month. I drove down there on a snowy December day. Beth was off work a few days, and so we were going to spend Sunday, Monday and Tuesday together, with me returning home on Wednesday. We hiked in the snowy woods, swam in the pool, tackled each other in the yard. We talked, we laughed, we dined in splendor. I can't think of three days in my life which were happier. The last night we sat before a roaring fire and sipped Irish Mist. We sat together on the leather sofa, and, after a bit, we snuggled. I embraced her and kissed her as I had many years before on a hill on Oak Tree Golf Course. About midnight,

I realized this was getting out of hand. "Well, well," I said, emerging from a deep, warm kiss, "It's midnight, and tomorrow we both go back to work, so we better get some sleep."

She was disappointed, "Oh, what's the hurry?"

"I don't want to fall asleep on the road tomorrow. Goodnight."

"Goodnight," she said reluctantly.

Now safely in my wing of the house, a good fifty yards from Beth, I was just dropping off to sleep, when there was a light knock on the bedroom door. "Yeah?" I said, sleepily. She opened the door. "Is there anything more I can do for you?"

Then she turned on the light. She was absolutely naked. I had never seen a naked woman in my life. My first reaction was not anger, but lust; but the anger followed in split seconds. "If you don't get out of here in one second, I'm going to leave."

She retreated into her imitation Southern drawl. "Oh my, I do declah, I plum' forgot my robe!" With that she left. I didn't sleep well and the next morning at six, I sat at the breakfast table, responding in monosyllables. She finally said, "Aren't we the ol' bear this morning! For God's sake. It was just a joke."

"Oh, is that so? Suppose I'd said, 'yes'?"

Again she was the Southern belle. "What could po' lil' me do if such a hansum' genl'man wanted me?"

We parted more or less amiably. I gave her a brotherly kiss, and as I drove back home I made a decision. I had to break it up. For a month I refused to respond to her apologetic letters. Ditto phone calls. Finally, one night, Joe called me on the intercom. "There's a lady in tears on the phone. She sounds desperate. You better take the call." It was Beth, of course.

"George," she sobbed, "I'm so sorry and so ashamed. Can't we be friends again? You wouldn't have to come here. We could meet for lunch like we used to. I won't, I swear, I won't try to tempt you."

"Beth, I do love you, but there's too much at stake here; for you as well as me. You've got your decree of nullity, but I'll bet you're not even dating."

"No, I have, a couple of times, but no vibrations yet."

And so we began meeting at river towns like Red Wing or Wabasha. Something had changed though. There was a restraint between us which prevented the ease and natural exuberance we had formerly enjoyed. She said, "I curse the night I came to your room. It really destroyed something. You know I really did tell myself that night that it was just a gag, but I don't know if I was kidding myself. If you had responded, God knows what?" This kind of honesty started restoring our mutual trust.

Here, I must go back and try to understand what happened. There were, first of all, preconditions. I really loved Beth. I still do. There was the sight of a naked Beth in my bedroom. It was an image which grew, whenever I tried to erase it. Priests were dropping like flies, most of them to get married. Did it give a kind of permission to the hitherto forbidden? There were the whispered voices in the confession, hinting of a joy that I could only imagine, a joy denied me. I recall one of S.V. Benet's lesser poems, "The Breaking Point" where, having conquered the strong temptations of hell, he then found:

> The grass began to whisper things—
> And every tree became an elf,
> That grinned and chuckled counsellings...
> One snaky word, 'What if you'd done it?'
> And I began to think...

I hate it when people make excuses, my own as well. Did the treatment that Bill got from the chancery play a part? The way Foley was treated? The way I was misunderstood? Did the intransigence of the Vatican, a bunch of old men unyielding play a part? As I say I hate excuses. Be that as it may.

Is a decision or a course of action the result of a single act of the will? Or is it a compilation of a hundred experiences; a jumble, or perhaps a jungle of values and disvalues vying with each other below the level of consciousness? What are the building blocks of sin? On a conscious level, I'd long ago forgiven the mistreatment I felt I'd received both at St. Brendan's and at Seven Sorrows, but was there a residue of outraged injustice? There were other things. There was the stark memory of the committee robbing me of joy on my first night at St. Dismas. The boos and the catcalls at my first parish meeting. I'd finally won that one. St. Dismas had become mine, not that any pastor "owns" the parish, but I was now accepted enough so that the work of the parish could carry on well; Sacraments, catechesis, works too of charity and justice. The leadership of the parish had gone now more to Joe Bass than to me. I tried not to be jealous; to understand that youth will be served. That, just as Higgins, despite his alcoholism, had given me free rein to do the works of Christ, so I must yield to the dynamism and zeal of Joe Bass. When parishioners praised the work of Bass, I tried to rejoice in it. He was bringing a dimension of freshness and new insights which I lacked. Just as I had attracted the youth of St. Brendan's, twenty-five years earlier, so Joe Bass was doing now. As parents saw this, they too were attracted and pleased. And I did understand. What was important was that the work of Christ go on.

Who got the accolades, who got the credit was not important. And yet. And yet. There was a sense of loss. There were issues, too, in the larger Church; the intransigence of the Vatican in the birth control matter. It seemed to me, and others, that the power of the Vatican was more the issue than the morality of birth control. The oddity was that that very authority would have been better maintained by an open and honest investigation of the morality of birth control. They were losing the thing they wanted to hold onto. And would not any organization which was losing hundreds of its leaders not take a look, at least, at celibacy?

It was with these things churning in my mind that I walked and talked with Bob Foley on the snowy pathways at the retreat house on the Mississippi in January of 1978. Foley had adjusted well to parish life, as I thought he would. But he said, "And I used to think all stupidity was confined to seminarians. Plenty of it in parish life. A lot of 'em seem to think that the exodus of priests and nuns is the result of Vatican II. If we'd go back to Latin and birettas and meatless Fridays, all would be well."

"Maybe they're right. Would Bill Thompson still be here walking with us if there hadn't been a Vatican II?"

"C'mon George, you know better than that. Vatican II may have provided a forum, a site, if you will, for an exchange of ideas, but the sociological, economic, and cultural changes were happening anyway. Take the psychological; how much of the old Church was governed by fear? The Protestant early American, Jonathan Edwards had a sermon, 'Sinners in the Hand of God' and his was an angry God. Actually Edwards was a deep man despite that unfortunate title, but that's beside the point. We heard plenty of those kinds of sermons in our own pulpits. How often did you find one of our lightweights taking that biblical phrase about 'Many are called, but few are chosen' into a proof that most people are going to hell?"

"Maybe that scared 'em into doing the right thing. A lot of my old-timers ask why we don't preach that way anymore."

"Exactly, and mine too. And then, how do you build a love of God out of that kind of craven fear? If perfect love casts out fear, does perfect fear cast out love?"

"Or, if we've relied on fear, once you pump out the fear, won't a lot of folk just steal away? I see fewer and fewer kids

at Sunday Mass. I'm not making that the litmus test for being a Christian, but, as St. Paul says. 'How shall they learn
without a preacher?'"

Bob continued, "As for Bill, I think there's a lot more in
his leaving than fear, or for that matter, Mary Lou. I think
he's got questions which were never answered."

I didn't want to share Bill's conversation about faith with
Bob. I felt I had no right to do so. I simply said, "I think a
lot of Bill's decision could have been changed if he'd have
been treated differently in his days with old Gibbons."

I didn't say anything about Beth and me to Bob, and that
says something about the direction of my own life. I talked
to the retreat master, also, but never mentioned Beth.

So I kept my relationship with Beth to myself as I walked
and talked to Bob or Clem Bartosh. Talking with Bartosh
was almost the exact opposite from talking with Bob. Still
slim and as handsome as ever, and as quick with the quip,
Clem was not happy with the new Church or at least elements of it.

"Take this new assistant of mine," he paused, "—Yeah,
please do take him, as that comic says; well, anyway, he
says daily Mass, but he doesn't believe we should do it. And
confession? We oughtta drop it says he. Early Church didn't
have it, he says, except for excommunicated sins. His idea
of religion is to gather the teenagers and play the guitar and
tell stories of God. Jeez!"

"Maybe, it works. Ditto my guy. Only I call him 'associate'".

"That's another piece of shit. Why can't these guy work
their way up the way we had to?"

"C'mon Clem, you don't want to do a Bronski on him,
do you?"

"Nothing like that, but things are getting too loose. More
people are going to Communion than ever; fine, but are
they in the state of grace? No fear of hell; so we overdid the
fear motivation. Now, kids go out on Saturday night,

screw up a storm, and go to Communion on Sunday, that is, if they come to Mass in the first place."

"Aren't you painting an overly dark picture? I see a lot of generosity in youth, and a sense of responsibility toward, well, toward the war, poverty, the environment, stuff like that. You gotta admit we never thought of stuff like that."

"Fine; they want to tell the government what to do; the Church what to do; but take no personal responsibility for what they do," said Clem, obviously unpersuaded.

On retreat, I made a list which I kept until recently. Relationships:

- To the universal Church; mixed, uneven, questioning, worried that the gains of Vatican II may be reversed.
- To the local church; mixed again. Still smarting from its treatment of me earlier. Very disturbed about Bob's firing.
- To Bob, Bill, Clem, Ryan; mixed; half lost Bill; can't communicate as well with Clem or Tom Ryan. Bob, fine, except he's not much available. No substitute for parents.
- To Beth; *very mixed;* love her. Too close? What would I do without her? Where is this going?
- To associate; mostly good. Am I jealous? Work on it.
- To parish; mostly good; question; if I died or left there, would it really make any real difference to them? I don't know.
- To God; wish it was closer. How do mystics get there? Lots of work and prayer needed.

Like most plans and schedules that I made in my life, this remained mostly an unused blueprint.

✖

NINE

Fiery Furnace

Three or four times a week, Helen O'Brien, a parishioner, cooked dinner for Joe and myself. On those nights, rather than rushing about the kitchen, we sat in my small den and watched the news. I, somewhat akin to the Paul Revere story, drank one martini, if I had night appointments, and two, if I had a free evening. Joe drank Coors beer which he informed me was made from the purest water. It was a good time to clear up ideas; almost a staff meeting. Our differing reactions toward the news of the day was a gauge of how far apart (or close) our ideas were. What seemed to me a growing violence upset me a great deal more than it did Joe.

"George," he would say, "you've read a lot of history. It was always this way. People are always looking back at some 'good old days' that never were."

"Could be, but I think it's getting worse. You're gonna say that's a sign of my age."

"Funny you should say that. I think that's right."

And then we would both laugh. The local news was particularly violent that night. There had been two rapes the night before; one ending with a brutal beating. A convenience store clerk had been shot and was hovering between life and death. And even in a rural area, there was violence.

A thirteen-year-old had been murdered in the small town of Braddock. I made my case again about the increasing brutalization of society and Joe merely said, "George, all this was going on in your seminary days, but you guys were denied information about the greater world; like prisoners in a Soviet prison camp." He laughed. "No wonder you're so out of it."

"But think of the discipline you missed. No wonder you're such assholes." We both laughed and cleaned up our language before we went into the dining room to eat Mrs. O'Brien's dinner.

Two days later, I'd turned on the T.V. just in time to hear the homilist at the church in Braddock making a few final comments at the funeral of the thirteen-year-old boy. It went something like this:

"And so we all feel bitter toward the assailant, maybe even toward God. Revenge, hard as it is for all of us, must not be our response. . . . God gave Allen to us and especially to his family for a short time, too short for us, but we did have this magnificent person with us for a while. We are thankful for that much . . ." and here the preacher broke down. The T.V. broke to a commercial and I said to Joe, "Do you know who that was?"

"We cut in too late. They must have given his name earlier."

"That's Tony Shulz."

"I heard of him. He was here for a while, wasn't he?"

"For a short time. I was also with him at Seven Sorrows. He's really grown a lot. He was always bright and competent, but kind of—uh—cold, but today he seemed to have become more human, warmer."

Then later again, it was early May and I was on Beth's patio overlooking the Zumbro. The Zumbro River is a sleepy, peaceful little stream most of the year, but in the spring runoff, or in heavy rains, it can turn into a roaring monster, sweeping all before it. Beth's home was well above flood level. On this balmy, May late afternoon, it gurgled quietly, thirty-some steps beneath the patio. Beth brought her portable T.V. out so that we could, as we said to each other, share the masochism of the news.

The T.V. turned from a dull game show to the five p.m. news. I was studying mostly the river, only half attending to the news, when I was startled out of my lethargy by the unmistakable form of Tony Shulz, handcuffed, being escorted by two lawmen. Beth, seeing my agitation, turned up the volume, only to hear; "The Reverend Anthony Shulz was arrested today for the murder of Allen Schmidt of rural Braddock." The T.V. commentator went on to say that the Sheriff's office in Twin Falls had been investigating the April murder for three weeks. Charges would likely be filed tomorrow. "He is being held in the Twin Falls jail." As the T.V. turned to a commercial, I almost shouted at Beth, "Do you know who that was?"

"Was that the man who was your assistant at St. Dismas?" I sighed, "Yeah, the one you told me to find out more about; that's him."

It was no time for Beth to give me the "I told you so routine," and she refrained. I sat there, alternatively feeling sorry for the victim, for Tony, and, yes, wondering if anything had happened at St. Dismas in the few months that he was my assistant.

"Shall I turn it off?"

"Please."

We sat in silence for a few moments. Finally, Beth asked, "What will happen now?"

"Beth, I haven't the faintest... I could wish for police mistakes, but, there's a sense of... "

"... of finality, of the cops being sure." Beth finished for me. "Did you ever witness any violence or even a hint that he could...?"

"No, nor did I dream that he was close to being a pederast."

Eventually, we dropped the subject as I broiled steaks on the grill. But my mind wouldn't let go. When Beth told me that her brother Bill had gone into alcoholic treatment, even that only partially dented my consciousness. Happy as I was to hear it, I was struck with the horror of the evening news. Beth sensed that I could hardly deal with anything else, and she asked, "What kind of man was he at Seven Sorrows?"

"Competent; uh, droll sense of humor, friendly in a cool, detached sort of way. Worked well; easy to be around. This doesn't figure at all. I should have listened to you. But the big thing is what happens to him."

"What will you do?"

"Been thinking of that. It's why I'm bad company tonight. One part of me says 'go see him.' The other part of me wants to stay out of it. Do you have any idea how far Twin Falls is from here? I know it's on the southern side of our diocese."

"That's where he's being held, huh? Oh, maybe forty miles. They won't let you in tonight, will they?"

"I suppose not. O.K., if I stay over? I'll see him tomorrow."

"Fine."

I had some trouble getting in to see him, partly because I didn't have my clericals. "You don't look like no priest." This from the suspicious deputy. I showed him my card. Although I hadn't talked to Ryan, I said, "The archbishop wanted me to see him."

"What makes you guys think you have special privileges? You think you're like an attorney?" I must be in an anti-Catholic town, I thought, or was it the horror of the murder. I continued to look at him with what I gauged was sufficient superiority. Grudgingly, he rose, got out his keys, and said, "Gotta frisk you." This he did with roughness, but I stood, stoically, like an early Christian martyr. He led the way into the cell block. There were four cells in the block, all empty except Tony's.

"You wanna go in?"

"Yes." He reluctantly opened the cell. "Lawyer's comin' in fifteen minutes, so make it brief." Actually I was glad to hear of this time limit, because I hadn't the least idea of what I was going to say.

"Hello, Tony," I said, reaching out my hand. We shook hands, and he said, "George, thanks for coming." He sat on his cot and I on a chair. We were silent, and then he asked, "Can I go to confession?" I was surprised, but I nodded.

He started out lamely, hardly able to talk, and then, it came tumbling out, a torrent, going back to Seven Sorrows, to Walton, and, yes, to my further dismay, to St. Dismas. Well, it's under the seal. After absolution, I asked, "Do you want to say anything outside the seal?"

"Yes, I know you won't misuse it. I can't justify any of it; none of it! But, this poor kid!" He broke down.

"Hey, it's O.K. if you don't want to say any more."

"No, I want to. This kid, Allen, he was a charmer: not just physically beautiful, but he had a nice kid personality. He'd obviously been abused sexually most of his life. The marks were there. Not physically, I mean the characteristics; you get so you can read 'em. He liked it, the sex I mean. It might be hard to believe, but he initiated it; he flirted; I suppose it takes one to know one. He read my eyes as I read his. My little return to his flirting really turned him on. You could see it. I did it with him only twice, only TWICE! Then, he hit me for a $100. Oh, he said, 'That's a starter. Got you by the you-know-whats. Doesn't matter who says what. The adult is guilty.' I paid him like four times. His smart-ass act got to me. I hit him. God, I never even knew I could make a fist. Must have caught his temple or whatever. He went down like a load of cement. I jumped to the floor and tried his pulse. Nothing. I tried artificial respiration. Nothing. I panicked. I put him in the car and ran him over to Rainy Creek. That's where they found him. He must have bragged to other kids. The kids talked. They found blood in my car. I confessed; they didn't want to hear my explanation." He cried then. "Oh, George, my folks are still alive; in their eighties. What will happen to them? I wish I were dead!"

At this point, the jailer came with the lawyer. I said, "I'll be back." As the jailer led me out, I said, "He's terribly depressed. Are you—well, he might be suicidal. Are you taking precautions?"

His gruff voice turned to loud anger. "Who do you guys think you are? How about the kid he killed? How about the kid's parents? For my money, priest, it would save the state money if he hung himself. And the town would get rid of a murderer."

I said, "I never realized the red-neck zone went this far north until now."

He glared, "Oh, you are smart, aren't you?"

"And you are dumb!" I retorted as I walked out. I stopped at the chancery on the way to St. Dismas and demanded to see Ryan. The receptionist balked. "He's busy now." I put all of the furor I felt toward the cop, toward the whole sick world in my voice. "I've just seen Father Shulz and I must see the Archbishop now!" She walked away angrily, but returned and said, in an irritated voice. "The Archbishop will see you now." I filled him in and went home.

Three days later, I got the call from Ryan that Shulz had hung himself. I wondered to myself if one could sue the sheriff's office for failure to listen to me.

The funeral was held at St. Dismas, my place. It would not have been wise to hold it at Braddock. It was a small group who came. Father Bass, Father (now Monsignor) Muldoon, and I kept the press out. A few priests came; his classmates, Greg Bowler (from Seven Sorrows days) and not many others. Tony's poor, aged parents huddled like lost souls in the front pew. Ryan, who always faced the tough ones head on, gave the homily. It was Ryan at his best, not minimizing, and yet reminding us that Tony had done a lot of good service. "As for the events of the past month, a prison chaplain once told me that it's too bad when all people can remember is five minutes of an otherwise good life." With words like that did he try the impossible, the comforting of the frail, elderly Shulzes. We went to the cemetery; we had lunch at the parish hall; I told the Shulzes that I'd be in touch, but I could grasp that they really didn't want to see me. And so, it was over; at least I thought it was over.

A lot of things happened that year. Cocky John Muldoon, who told me, years before, that he couldn't wait to get out of the chancery to go into charities or whatever, never did escape the chancery. Instead, he got made an auxiliary bishop. He was a popular choice among the priests and we all went to the ordination. It was said by many that he told the dirtiest stories among the world wide episcopacy, except for some cardinal in the Orient.

Lay participation got heavier in the parishes. A storm raged over that oxymoron, girl altar boys. Since Cox had started it way back when no one else did, I simply let it be. The chancery wrote letters to you if you had girl altar boys, but only if parishioners complained. I suppose it was to cover their ass if word got to Rome. Since Cox had scared off all those kind of people years before, and girl altar boys were a fixture at St. Dismas, nobody protested. Women lectors were accepted variously at St. Dismas. What complicated it more was that some women lectors refused to read passages like St. Paul's admonition for women to obey their husbands. Another problem in the new Church was that while I had set up an advisory council rather than a decision-making one, this was tested intermittently when a strong liberal or a strong conservative got elected to the council. Once in a while, one of them would resign rather noisily and would write to the chancery and make a big splash in the parish. The thing that saved us was that, despite Father

Bass being more new Church than old, and me being more old Church than new, we usually worked out a united stance about such things. After a bit of a hassle and maybe the exit of a few parishioners, the storm would blow over. In those days of right-left agitation in local Churches, ours was a relatively united congregation. It was one of the calmer periods of my ministry.

On a late September morning Madelin buzzed me from the parish office. "Your friend, Father Thompson, or do I say, Mr. Thompson? is on the way over to the house." I was delighted. I hadn't seen him all summer. He swept into the house and picked me off the floor and gave me an *embrazzo* which almost was a rib breaker. "George! it's been too long!" He had lost that flab which I had noticed in recent years. Strong blue eyes like his mother's and Beth's, were bright and unclouded.

"God, you look good."

He pointed to a pin on his lapel. "Know what that is?" I knew, but decided to let him tell me. "My six month pin."

"Beth did tell me you went into treatment."

"Treatment? treatment; it seems like such a weak word. I spent a month at Hazeltine, and then I asked for two more weeks. I tell you, George, that's the kind of thing we shouldda done in the sem. Which reminds me, will you hear my confession?" It surprised me, since it wasn't too long ago, he'd sounded like an agnostic. I knew, too, that he and Mary Lou were not married in the Church, but I decided that was up to his conscience. It's under the seal. After absolution, he said, "I learned so much about myself. My dad was a wonderful man, do you remember?"

I said, "I'm sure he was, but I never saw much of him."

"Precisely, good man that he was, he wasn't around much. He was all over the U.S. and Europe, for that matter, making a fortune. In effect, I was raised by Ma; not all bad, but not much male bonding. Ma was a convert to Catholicism, did you know that?"

"I guessed it. With that Swedish background, I figured that she was originally Lutheran."

"Right! and a devout one. She was one of those converts like we've known in priesthood. All of the strong Lutheranism she had she carried into Catholicism, like totally. My mother, as you know, is a very balanced human being, mostly anyway. When I say that her conversion to Catholicism was total, I mean that her devotion, her spirituality, her love of Christ became centered in the Church, in the hierarchy and the Pope."

"Whoa! Whoa, hold on. Last few times that I listened to you, you were a kind of an agnostic. What...?"

"Oh, I'll get to that. But what I'm coming to is that Ma very much wanted me to be a priest. It was a kind of culmination of her life. She never urged me, or anything like that, but it was there. And I wanted to please her. I don't believe all that Freudian crap about how every son wants to get rid of his dad and marry his mother, but, I really loved and do love her, enough to have picked up the signals and responded by going to the seminary."

"Oh, but I heard you enough to know that you really wanted to be a priest."

"Sure, and I'm not denying that, but what the psychologists got me to see was that, at least a large hunk of it, was pleasing Ma; to fulfill her dream. That's why it was so hard for her when I quit priesthood. She's come a long way to accepting my leaving, especially now that I've applied for laicization." I was glad to hear that, but Bill was too wound up to stop.

"Do you know what a fifth step in A.A. is?"

"Yeah, I've heard a few, but you're way ahead. What's the earlier one, what? the second? where you see the need of God?"

"I am flowing at the mouth, aren't I? When I realized I couldn't cope with booze, and went to Hazeltine, yeah, I was a sort of agnostic."

"You said your faith might be like the summer grass under a high temperature, not dead, but asleep."

"Did I? well that's close enough, but when they started talking about turning my life over to a higher power, I was sort of blank for a while and then I started to pray, to really pray." He smiled. "It might sound funny, George, but I think I've had mystical experiences. I've never had such strong faith. But the fifth step is what our confession really ought to be. I was into blaming old Gibbons, or Ryan, or Mary Lou for that matter, but I found, at least I think I found, that I was unhappy because I didn't want to be a priest, and these people were—well—just scapegoats for my anger."

I felt awfully good about him, but I didn't know what to say. I did say, "This is all fine, but the golf season is almost over. Where were you when I needed you?"

"All in good time. I need at least a month to put the business back in working order. As soon as I get things in order, I'll be back beating you as usual. And Mary Lou and I want you over to dinner, and oh, will you marry us when I get the laicization?"

"Sure." And then, with a wave, he left.

My brief, but happy conversation with Bill had so buoyed me up that I was humming a song which I gradually recognized as "Amazing Grace"; *I once was lost, but now am found*. I was happy about Bill on two levels; first, he'd been my golfing companion since highschool days. But it was more than that. While Beth was special, and I confided almost everything to her, I wanted male companionship also. Foley was still close to me, and we'd played golf a few times that summer, but I'd always had a closer relationship with Bill. Through the years, we could almost read each other's minds, that is, until Bill had started drinking heavily. And now he was back. I hoped his present ebullience wasn't a passing enthusiasm.

On the second level, Bill's seeming loss of faith had disturbed me deeply. Mary Lou might be great, but she was no substitute for God. I felt his return to faith was on solid footing.

That fall and early winter turned out to be one of the happiest times of my life. Joe Bass and I had become a team. I was careful not to let his evident success in the parish make me jealous. This, incidentally, is a very undiagnosed reality in parish life. I recall that I once raised the issue at one of those open retreats, only to find that no one else saw it as a problem. I think that they were heavily into denial. Its ugly head emerges in funny ways. At any rate that ugly head was not present between Joe and I at St. Dismas. Joe had grown, too. He understood people like Henrietta and her need for Rosary and Benediction. Though these were not his prayer forms, he took his turn at those kinds of devotions. His Christmas children's Mass was a work of art. The parish debt, mostly from establishing the school, was being paid off. There was a feeling of euphoria in the parish, and I glowed in it. I doubt that I'm unique in the matter, but those kinds of highs always seem to lead to lows, as if there is some sort of cosmic rule that happy times must be repaid by dismal events. So it was that I came back from a week of golf with Foley to be met by a couple of downers.

The day after my return, Joe Bass came into my study, and with uncharacteristic hesitancy, asked, "Could I take you to dinner tonight? There is something I want to talk to you about."

"Sure. Six?"

"O.K., thanks."

A nice dinner invitation; so I wondered why it upset me all day. Was Joe going to apply for another parish? Why was he so serious about this?

I ordered my usual martini and was surprised that Joe, instead of his usual beer, ordered a martini. When the drinks came, he said, "I guess I needed something stronger for what I have to say."

"What is it? What's this mystery?"

"George, you have been the ideal pastor. I talk to class-mates and guys around my age, and most of 'em bitch about their pastors."

"Well, I'm not trying just to return a compliment when I say, I run into the same bitching about associates from the guys of my times. I'm very fortunate to have you."

"I guess there's no easy, gradual way to tell you this. George, I'm leaving priesthood."

I sat there, twiddling my martini glass, and feeling stupe-fied. Lamely, I said, "I don't know what to say."

"Do you remember our conversation about celibacy? I was sure it would all be over in ten years?"

I nodded. Joe continued, "I realize it's not going to change. No matter how decimated the ranks of priests. To get to the point, I'm leaving to get married."

"Have you talked it over with your confessor? or spiritual director or anybody?"

"Wouldn't make any difference. My mind's made up."

"The woman anybody I know?"

"Yeah, Melanie White."

"Not Frank White's daughter?"

"The same."

"What has Frank said?"

"Doesn't know yet. It'll be World War III, when we tell 'im."

"Frank will kick your ass!"

"He's the easier one. Frances is the one we're concerned about."

"What will you do?"

"George, no problem. Would you say I'm a reasonably talented guy?"

"Reasonably talented? No, I'd say 'unreasonably,' ful-some, terrific, and that's why we can't afford to let you out of the priesthood."

"Unh—unh, George, no debate; it's over."

"Can't blame me for trying."

"O.K., but you can see I'm not worried about a job."

"Guess not; and I'll give recommendations."

"Thanks. I know that I promised celibacy; and yet it ought to be separate from priesthood. It shouldn't be a package deal. It's none of my business, but I see that gorgeous blond who comes to see you. A fella can't help wondering." He smiled warmly, but sardonically.

"Oh, no, there's no physical relationship between Beth and I."

"What a pity. The reasons they give for celibacy are a crock. Take that sign of the kingdom bit."

"What's wrong with that? The kingdom is here when people are willing to give up marriage to serve Christ."

"That's the intention, but what happens? You get guys like your friend, Tony Shulz. Other guys leaving in droves; and a heck of a lot of guys just plain cheating. What sort of garbled sign is that?"

I sighed, "Maybe it's like any other rare thing; the less of it, the more valuable it becomes."

"That's as good an argument as I've heard. Not good enough, though."

It was a steak house that Joe had brought me to, and after our steaks came, our conversation changed to parish topics almost as if he were staying. I finally asked him when he was leaving.

"About three months; I'll see you through Holy Week."

I was always sort of surprised that when men left, they continued on. Maybe I was too judgemental, but it didn't make sense to me. That night as I sat in my den, nursing a Scotch, I dealt with the bad news. I couldn't imagine that there was anyone who could replace Joe. Worse, from some of the horror tales I'd heard about associates, I wondered what kind of an idiot I might end up with. It was not the last piece of bad news.

The winter thaw came early that year, and I was out in

the yard in mid-March, trying, with the aid of a shovel, to unblock some ice, so that the run-off would go away from the downstairs windows, when a tight lipped gentleman approached me.

"Are you Reverend George Schwartz?"

"Yes."

Without a further word, he handed me an envelope. I had never before met a process server. I tore open the envelope and read:

STATE OF MINNESOTA
COUNTY OF HENNEPIN SUMMONS

JOSEPH PLINTER
PLAINTIFF

VS.

REVEREND GEORGE SCHWARTZ
DEFENDANT
STATE OF MINNESOTA
TO ABOVE NAMED DEFENDANT

You are hereby summoned and required to serve upon plaintiffs attorney an answer to the complaint, which is herewith served upon you, within twenty days after service of this summons upon you exclusive of the day of service.

The rest of the paper dealt with what would happen to me if I did not respond and also the charge, which was my failure to prevent Father Shulz from sexually molesting the Plinter lad.

I stood there utterly baffled. How could I be blamed for something I never knew happened?

I called the chancery to talk to Ryan. He was attending some episcopal committee meeting, so the receptionist put me on with Bishop John Muldoon.

"John, George Schwartz. How are you?"

He ignored the question. "So you have heard about our suit?"

"What d'ya mean 'our suit'? How about my suit?"

"You mean you're being sued on this Shulz affair?"

"For one million smackers."

"Piker, the archdiocese is being hit for three million. For yourself, why worry? They can't get blood outta a turnip?"

"Fact is, I might be worth that, up to now, anyway. But what is Ryan going to do?"

"Our diocesan lawyer says he's seen these before. Not to worry, at least to that amount. Says they'll settle out of court, and for far less."

I heaved a sigh of relief. "I'm glad to hear that much."

"You haven't heard the worst of it. Are you sitting down?"

"Yeah, what?"

"Lawyer for the plaintiff is a guy by the name of Frank Cody."

"Our Frank Cody?"

"Yeah, Ryan is boiling. I hope he cools off for the bishop's committee meeting, or he'll blow his standing in the bishop's conference."

"You sure you got that right? Frank Cody?"

"Sure I'm sure. You shudda heard our chief. I can't handle language like that; I'm entirely too delicate."

"I'm sure you are. Can you swallow a little of your well-known delicacy to tell me what he said, and what he intends to do?"

"I'll leave out the worst words, O.K.? He said, 'Cody always was a Goddamned son-of-a-bitch; now he's a bigger asshole than ever!' What'll Tom do? Use the diocesan lawyer, I guess. You want our lawyer?"

"I dunno; I'll think about it."

I called Cody's law office in Chicago. He was occupied. I left a message. Then I thought what if "our lawyer" is wrong? Have I got a million? I had left all of my finances in the hands of dad's old law partner, Frank Griffin. I vaguely remembered that Frank had told me some time ago that he was turning things over to his son and I had signed a paper which gave that power to the son, Frank, Jr. Then I wondered how the lawyer for the Plinter kid would have guessed that I had some money of my own. I called Frank Griffin, Jr. "I haven't had a report from you lately on my investments." There was a pause on the other end of the line.

"It's been a tough market. I'd have to check. I think your portfolio is down a bit, well—maybe quite a bit."

It was my turn to pause. "I'd like an early report."

I called a lawyer friend in the parish and told my story. "Father, I don't like the sound of that. The market's been up, mostly up. If you give me power of attorney, I'll go down to Sioux Lake tomorrow and get, not only the listings, but the stock certificates, well, whatever instruments there are."

"Instruments? Is that how you people talk?"

"That's how we talk, yes. How well do you know the younger Griffin?"

"I don't. My dad had implicit trust in Griffin, Sr."

"So, lets hope like father, like son. Frankly, Father, I don't like the sound of it. Most portfolios have had a major boost in recent years. But I'll go down tomorrow and demand the records."

Troubled by this information, I waited around the rectory for a call from Cody. It came at four p.m. He was using his playful voice.

"Georgie, it's been too long! How are collections among the thieves of the parish of the Good Thief?"

"You know why I called. I can't believe you're doing this."

"Doing what, old pal?"

"No games," I said in a hostile voice, "making money suing the Church. Have you no shame?"

"My turn to be angry. Your boss, our esteemed class-mate, knowingly sent a pederast to your parish, thus endangering the lambs of your flock. Your anger, proper as it is, is misdirected, old friend. If I may use a simile, it is like dumping nuclear material in your backyard."

"You trying to tell me that you are altruistic in this? How much of the three million will rub off in Frankie's hands?" Again the mocking voice, "The laborer is worth his pay." Then he turned serious. "Do you have some idea of how widespread this abominable practice is? I refer to moving these miscreants from parish to parish, destroying young souls by the dozen? It is sad, but true, that the souls, and bodies for that matter, of youngsters have not been sufficient motivation to change this deplorable activity. It has been necessary to bring in the ugly subject of dollars to cause repentance."

It was a sobering thought. It did not erase my angry feelings toward Cody. I said, "And are you the lawyer against me also?"

"Certainly not, George, although that offer was extended. Because of the legal implications, I won't speak of this further. I do hope that these legal matters will not jeopardize our friendship. I don't know about you, but your friendship means much to me. I was hoping, that amidst these unfortunate proceedings, we might share a meal in some quiet eatery."

"Cody, I'm too much in shock at this moment to reply."

"As you say. The ball, now, is in your court." With that, he hung up, and I sat there wondering what the world had come to. There was some force in what he said, yet, suing his old classmate; how could he justify that?

The other bad news came from Michael Lang, my new attorney. "Father, bad news, your portfolio has gone from well over a million to about $600,000. Now, you told me that you are being sued for a million. Not the parish?"

"Me personally."

"And so the question is, how did someone know that you had this kind of money? As a parishioner, I never dreamt it. Did Griffin, Jr. give out this information? Maybe, we'll never know. One thing for sure, we'll have to have a better explanation as to what caused the value of your portfolio to shrink."

"Will you represent me in the trial?"

"No. I'm not into that area. I'll make some recommendations. I imagine this will be settled out of court, and for far less; don't you think?"

"I don't know; that seems to be the attitude of the chancery people. I guess the only thing I fear is the loss of the cabin on Pinecone Lake."

"Good news on that. Do you remember Griffin, Sr. getting that place homesteaded for you?"

"Uh, I guess—"

"Even if you lose the case, I don't see how they can take that property."

I heaved a sigh of relief. I could do without the money, but Pinecone was to be my retirement home.

The March thaw turned into a warm April, and after Easter, Joe Bass, whom I once thought to be brash, and whom I'd come to love, left St. Dismas, and me, and priesthood. We all mourned. The attitude of the laity had gradually changed in regard to a priest's departure. The first reaction was horror; a kind of Judas judgement. By the time that Joe left, there was disappointment, but the negative judgement was more bitter toward the institution which allowed such talent to be lost. (Not all felt this way, of course.) Spring turned into summer as I worried about who would replace Joe Bass. If even half of the horror stories about the newer associates were true, a new associate could be more trouble than not having one. Those were days when parish staffs were proliferating like rabbits, since the average parish of two priests was being cut back to one, and long-standing three priest places were lucky to keep two. To replace that loss, laymen and laywomen were hired. In earlier days, a big place like Seven Sorrows had four priests, but only a secretary, a janitor, and a choir leader who doubled as organist. The newer staffs included such people as parish managers, liturgists, adult educationists, catechetical directors and lay ministers. Having watched some parish budgets go out of control from over-hiring, I had refrained. Finally, I decided, rather than ask for a full-time associate, I'd settle for a weekender to say part of the Masses, and so I hired a business manager. So I was free, at times, to play golf with Bill and Bob.

That summer was spoiled by the constant thought of the trial hanging over me. The fact that I was guiltless gave some cold comfort. The easy words of the diocesan lawyer that the case against the diocese would be settled out of court proved to be wrong and the trial date was set for late July. Nor was my case to be settled amicably. To add to my troubles, it turned out, that Frank Griffin, Jr. had indeed used some of my money to buy stocks which had faltered. In respect for Frank, Sr., I would not prefer charges and my lawyer managed to get about $200,000 back, which was roughly half. Beth tried to understand my low spirits, but she was frank enough to let me know that I wasn't great company. I did appreciate her abstaining from reminding me that she had told me that I ought to find out more about Shulz before accepting him into the parish. In late July, Cody came to my door, not the least apologetic, and simply asked, Well, am I taking you to dinner or not?"

Old friendship won out over my anger at him for suing the diocese, and I consented. At dinner, I discovered that he'd been involved in pedophilia litigation all over the country. I noticed that he drank sparingly and that he really saw his work in terms of a sort of crusade to move people in authority, including bishops, to make a stronger policy in the face of pedophilia. He was also making a heap of money. The trial was to start in two days. I decided to watch part of the diocesan trial to get a feel for what I would be in for in the fall. I waited until such preliminaries as jury selection were over and arrived on a very hot day at the end of July to discover they had already started questioning a witness. Cody's change in demeanor from the wiseguy to the serious lawyer was almost shocking.

"Mr. Zarth, what is your work in Walton?"

"I teach civics and I coach in several sports."

"And how did you first learn of Father Shulz's abberant sexuality?"

The diocesan lawyer was on his feet. "Objection! objection! counsel is leading the witness and, further, is calling for hearsay."

Judge Donovan hesitated, and Cody quickly said, "Your honor, I can restate the question to satisfy the first objection, but I think there is a difference between hearsay and the report by the victim of a serious sexual invitation." It struck me that Cody had managed to describe Shulz's activity in dark colors before eliciting an answer. The judge was not amused. He turned to the jury and said, "You are to disregard Mr. Cody's last statement." And then to Cody, "Mr. Cody, you are not to give testimony. I will allow you to question the witness, but not by leading him and also to refrain from assuming victimization for the student involved."

"Thank you, your honor. Now, Mr. Zarth, what first brought your attention to Father Shulz?"

"A former member of the football team came to me and told me that Father Shulz had acted amorously with him."

"Amorously? In what way?"

"He said that Shulz had hugged him and had kissed him."

"What did you do with this information?"

"I went to Father Shulz and faced him with this allegation."

"How did he respond?"

"He told me that his own family was very warm and frequently hugged and kissed one another and that he'd never thought of it as sexual. He had been drinking that night, and so I gave up talking to him."

"Were there further reports?"

The diocesan lawyer rose, "I object again on the leading nature of this line of questioning."

"Sustained."

"What happened next?"

"Objection. What kind of question is that? Is this a fishing expedition?"

"Your honor, the witness has much more evidence. I'm not sure that I can ask any question which defense will not object to."

"You may proceed, Mr. Cody. And, Mr. Schroeder, your objections have less and less substance. I suggest you exercise a greater abstinence."

"What happened next?" repeated Cody.

"My former football player must have talked, because, within a few days, there was a parade of people in my office with similar complaints."

"A parade?"

"Sorry, that's an overstatement. Two young men who had been altar boys for Father Shulz came in to tell me they had been accosted, when they were younger. Shortly after that, a couple came to me and said that their son claimed he'd been fondled by Father Shulz."

"Did you then go to the authorities?"

Zarth squirmed at that moment and said, "I know that I should have, but—but the two football players had made me promise that I wouldn't tell the authorities. As for the parents, I thought that they felt the same, and maybe his action would not seem definite enough to hold up in court." He sighed, "I guess I should have done more. Maybe being a Protestant coach in a Catholic town made me hesitate."

"What did you do?"

"I decided that I should go to his superior. So, I tried to

get an appointment with the archbishop, but the best I could do was to talk to one of his chancery people, Father Walsh."

My God, I thought, Walsh is dead, killed in a car accident two years ago.

"And did you tell Father Walsh everything you had heard?"

"I did. He assured me that he would tell the archbishop the whole story. And I got a letter a week later, signed by the archbishop, thanking me for the information. I have it here."

The letter was accepted as evidence. Allan Schroeder cross-examined Zarth without much result.

Apparently, the lawyers agreed that they would not call all of the victims of Father Shulz, only the first one who had contacted Zarth. I was not present for his testimony, but I heard that he supported Zarth's story. A few days later, defense had decided to put Archbishop Ryan on the stand. I went to the courtroom that day with some anxiety, both for Ryan and for myself. The questioning had already begun when I arrived. Cody looked perfectly calm as he faced his old classmate. Ryan's color, usually on the florid side, was deep purple and he looked at Cody with undisguised contempt.

"Archbishop Ryan, do you recall being briefed by Father Walsh in regard to the sexual accusations of Mr. Zarth?"

"I recall some parts of that conversation, yes, but that was some years ago."

"I regret that Father Walsh was killed; but that means that we have to try to get at this matter as best we can. Did Walsh tell you that Mr. Zarth had told him that Father Shulz had accosted some youths of the parish?"

"Youths? uh—well I know he said that there were homosexual allegations."

"Did he tell you that the youths involved were under-age?"

"Uh—this was quite a long time ago. I deal with dozens of problems daily, so I can't be expected to recall everything exactly. I do recall there were allegations of homosexuality, yes—but the age of the young men . . . " And he threw up his hands.

"And, of course, a matter of such trifling significance as one of your shepherds engaging in pedophilia with some of the flock would scarcely stay in your memory, busy as you are . . . "

Mr. Schroeder was on his feet. "OBJECTION! he is badgering the witness and pedophilia has not yet been established!"

If the phrase "not yet established" came through to my non-legal mind, I was sure that all the officers of the court had picked it up. The judge was visibly angry. "The jury will disregard Mr. Foley's last comment. And Mr. Foley this is my last warning. If you persist in giving testimony, I will cite you for contempt."

"I apologize," said a meek Cody. He had nevertheless put the thought into the minds of the jury people that the archbishop had been largely indifferent to the endangered youth of Walton and of my parish. Cody, hardly fazed by the judge's words, continued.

"I have a copy of a letter, already admitted in evidence as exhibit one. It was written by you to Mr. Zarth in which you thank him for his timely warning and you stated and I quote: 'Since I realize the grave danger to the young people of Walton, I have removed Father Shulz from active duty and have placed him in a treatment center in which he will receive help for both his sexual problems and alcoholism.' Did you write this letter yourself or was this from one on your staff?"

Since Ryan had already been half accused by Cody as "indifferent" to the problem, Cody had him in a tough place. He responded, almost eagerly. "I think I wrote it, myself."

"When you used the phrase 'young people,' did you have in mind any particular age?"

"By young, I meant no particular age. It might have been young adults."

"You don't remember precisely what age these people accosted by Father Shulz were?"

"I don't. As I said before, this was a long time ago."

"Mr. Ryan, aren't we being disingenuous? This was ten years ago."

Mr. Schroeder started to get up, but refrained. No use, I surmised, making the archbishop look as if he were enjoying special favors. The title, Mr. instead of Archbishop had gotten to Ryan, as well as Cody's crack about being "disingenuous". His purple color got even deeper and he glared at Cody. Cody continued as if he were asking the time of day.

"As the letter indicates, you sent Father Shulz to a treatment center?"

"Yes!" said between clenched jaws.

"And how long did he remain there?"

"About two months. I think."

"And you felt that he was rehabilitated in two months?" Ryan stopped momentarily. "I suppose in retrospect, it could have been longer. At the time, they, the people at the facility, said he'd joined A.A., and seemed to have changed."

"And so you sent him on to St. Dismas? Did you then inform the priest there, Father Schwartz of Shulz's problems?"

"Of course." I wished at that moment that I had the power to object. But Cody took up another direction.

"Are you familiar with the phrase '*Sacerdos in aeternum*'?"

"Objection. No proper foundation."

"Mr. Cody?" asked the judge.

"In a moment, the relevance of that question will be evident, if I may continue."

"Proceed."

"It means that a priest is ordained forever. So, for example, if one left the priestly office like Judas, he is still a priest."

"Or if he were to become aware of a different calling."

"In either case, he would have reneged on his vows."

Judge Donovan banged his gavel severely and said, "Gentlemen, there will be no more of that! I think I know what is going on here. You will not use my courtroom for yourr personal vendettas. Now, you may proceed, Mr. Cody, but you both will refrain from these *obiter dictus*."

Neither Cody nor Ryan looked very penitent. Unflappable Cody continued, "And so, *Sacerdos in aeternum,* means that a Catholic priest is a priest forever. Does this mean that your archdiocese has financial responsibilities to him even if he would be guilty of a crime?"

"Yes, although if the crime were grave enough, he could be defrocked, that is, stripped of his office." As soon as Ryan had said this, I could see that he wished he had stopped at a simple "yes." Cody pounced on it, just as he might have in seminary days.

"And, of course, the destruction of the moral and psychic life of youth would not be considered grave?"

"Of course it would be, but we sent him twice to rehabilitation centers." But Cody had made a damning point with the jury. Judge Donovan mercifully declared a recess at this time, and I left the courtroom, unwilling as I was to talk to either Ryan or Cody.

In subsequent days, Joseph Plinter, the youth in question was put on the stand. I wasn't there, but from the news account, he corroborated the claims that he had been molested. I understood that the diocesan lawyer attempted, by cross-examination, to paint the youth as very willing and even as leading Shulz on. He was terribly ineffective. I was surprised that I was not called by one side or the other, but also relieved. The jury debated for three days, a length of time which created hopes for the archdiocese, but, alas, they awarded the whole three million to the plaintiff. A few days later, I read that the archdiocese appealed. The result of the trial hardly dispelled my anxiety, and Beth and others found me a bit of a drag. The parish, too, suffered, because I found the increased job load difficult enough without the trial hanging over my head. On retreat, that fall, Bob Foley tried to get me out of the doldrums, and only partially succeeded. The attorney whom Michael Lang had obtained for me, John Manson, sat with me in my house and prepared me for the forthcoming trial.

"Did someone on your diocesan personnel board talk to you before you accepted Shulz as assistant?"

"No, they were not involved. Ryan was the only one who spoke to me."

"Now what precisely did he tell you about Shulz's past?"

"He said that Shulz had had some homosexual problems and that it was associated with a drinking problem, but that was changed because Shulz had gone into A.A."

"That's it? Nothing more?"

"That's it."

"I've examined the transcripts of the other trial and the only word from your archbishop in regard to you is a terse 'of course' in response to Cody's question, 'Did you inform Father Schwartz of Shulz's activity?' Did no one else in the chancery inform you further?"

"No, the only word I had was from Ryan. I don't know if this will help, but a friend of mine, Beth Kelly, told me, at the time, that I ought to find out more details about Shulz's homosexual exploits."

"How good a friend is she?"

I started to blush. "If you're asking is she sexual partner, no, but she is a very good friend."

"I don't mean to embarrass you, but the plaintiff's lawyer might try to suggest that she is lying for love. Then, of course, the opposition might use this as an indication that you were careless about hiring Shulz. I mean ignoring her warning." He hesitated. "Still—it could help establish your ignorance that Shulz had engaged minors. Now, Ryan is a problem. He pleaded that he either never knew the age of Shulz's victims or he forgot. The archdiocese lost the case largely because the jury, in effect, didn't believe him. All in all, I think we'll put him on the stand. What do you think?"

"He's a truthful man, no question of that, but he handles hundreds of details a week. He can't remember everything."

"I think we'll use him and your friend, Beth. And you can testify exactly what you knew and didn't know."

And so the trial began on All Saint's Day, November 1st, an appropriately dark, cold and cloudy day. I had Mass at both seven and ten, so I skipped the preliminaries, such as the jury selection. The plaintiff, Joseph Plinter, repeated the same statements that he'd made at the earlier trial. It struck me that the young man (now) might have been very willing as an underage kid to accept Shulz's caresses. I guessed that that was not the point as far as the jury was concerned. Nevertheless, my defense lawyer, made futile attempts to draw this out. I looked over at the Plinters, once my friends in the parish, now out to strip me of everything. Their looks were hostile as if I had done something wrong. I wondered if there had been sexual abuse in their family, a preconditioning for Shulz. It was several days before I was put on the stand. Manson asked me; "What had the archbishop told you about Father Shulz's problems?"

"Only that he'd had some homosexual problems and that the treatment center people had concluded that this activity had been connected to alcoholism, and since he'd gone into A.A. they felt he'd be O.K."

"Did he maintain sobriety when he was with you at St. Dismas?"

"As far as I could observe. He didn't live at the rectory,

but in a halfway house, but I never observed him drinking."

"You also worked and lived with him years earlier at Seven Sorrows Church, is that right?"

"Yes."

"And at that time, did you observe any sexual conduct with young boys on the part of Father Shulz? Uh, let me rephrase that. Did you observe any tendency toward boys, like a sort of fondness?"

"Quite the contrary; he trained the altar boys and was very strict with them."

"And how long did you serve with him at Seven Sorrows?"

"About six months."

"So you had no reason to fear that Shulz was any kind of threat to the young people of your parish?"

"Yes."

"In addition, Archbishop Ryan had assured you that there was no reason to worry about Shulz's conduct?"

"Yes."

The Plinter attorney, Orville Swanson, attempted to demonstrate my indifference, even carelessness with the young of my flock. At one point, he asked, "Did you ask the archbishop what age Shulz's sexual partners were?"

"No, because he had indicated that these were problems of the past."

"So, you took this dangerous man into your parish without any further words than your bishop's claim that he was now O.K. Do you think this was responsible shepherding for your flock?"

I was angry. I said, "Both by the fact that I had never observed anything strange in Father Shulz's conduct when I worked and lived with him and because of Archbishop Ryan's assurance, I never dreamt that he would be a problem to young people. Nor did I observe any conduct while he was at St. Dismas that would disturb that trust."

"And yet you had brought a murderer into your parish. Father Schwartz..."

My attorney, Manson, was on his feet, but I motioned him down.

"I'm glad you raised that point, because I can demonstrate that Shulz was not an intentional murderer. He..."

"No more questions."

My attorney came forward, "Redirect?" He looked at the judge.

"Proceed."

"What were you saying when interrupted by Mr. Swanson?"

"Objection. This is not the Braddock case."

Manson said, "Your honor, learned counsel has introduced that pejorative word."

The judge said, "Mr. Swanson, you did just that. You'll abide the consequences of raising that issue."

"Continue," said Manson.

"When I visited Father Shulz, he told me that Allen Schmidt was blackmailing him, and ridiculing him and that he only meant to hit him, but, by chance, hit him in the temple. The blow was only accidentally fatal."

Swanson was screaming, "This must be stricken. It is irrelevant to this case!"

The judge said, "It was irrelevant, Mr. Swanson, until you introduced this prejudicial, and indeed, highly volatile word 'murderer,' you must accept, as I said earlier, the consequence of your introducing this line."

Having made the point, Manson dropped the matter. Swanson certainly didn't want to pursue it. Manson had decided to use Beth. Beth was dressed in business attire and it was obvious to me that she had made a studied effort to project a demure image. It was not to be. Her conservative dress and staid manner, as she approached the witness stand only served to heighten her glorious femininity. The eyes of every man in the courtroom were upon her as she recited the oath. Manson questioned her.

"You had a conversation with Father Schwartz at the time that the archbishop asked him to take Father Shulz into St. Dismas?"

"Yes."

"This was the day after Father Schwartz had agreed to take in Shulz?"

"Yes."

"What did Father Schwartz say about this appointment?"

"Objection; hearsay."

"Mr. Manson?" asked the judge.

"I don't think it is hearsay; I'm trying to establish the mindset of Father Schwartz as he responded to the archbishop's request."

"Proceed."

"He said he'd been told by the archbishop that Shulz had gotten in trouble with homosexuality, but that it was associated with alcoholism, but that he'd now joined A.A."

"Did Father Schwartz know that these homosexual activities were with minors?"

"Objection. Calls for a conclusion."

"Sustained."

"What did you say, at this time, to Father Schwartz?"

"I told him that he ought to ask the archbishop more about these incidents."

"And what was his response?"

"I don't remember the exact words, but he said that the bishop would have told him if there were any dangers. He seemed to trust the archbishop completely."

Swanson cross-examined Beth. "What is your relationship with Father Schwartz?"

"Objection. Irrelevant."

"I'll allow the question."

"He's a good friend—of me and my whole family."

"Well, Mrs. Kelly, he must be a very special friend to

share these confidences with you . . . "

"Objection. Counsel is trying to suggest something conspiratorial. Witness answered the question."

"Sustained."

Beth stayed in the courtroom when the archbishop came to the stand. I had had some reservations about Ryan being called, but Manson had assured me that he would be useful in demonstrating that I had no knowledge that Shulz's exploits were with minors.

"Archbishop Ryan, did you ask Father Schwartz to accept Father Shulz as his associate?"

"Yes."

"And you would not have sent him there if you thought that he was any danger to the young people of St. Dismas?"

"Yes."

"You felt he had been rehabilitated at the treatment center?"

"Yes."

I noticed that Ryan had become more disciplined in answering. He added nothing more to the questions Manson now asked.

"You told Schwartz that Shulz had had some problems with homosexuality, but that now that he'd joined A.A.; that these problems were in the past."

"Yes."

"Cross-examine."

"Archbishop Ryan, you have spoken of Father Shulz's 'homosexual' conduct. Did this take place when Shulz was pastor at Walton, Minnesota?"

"Yes."

"How did you learn about these actions?"

"A coach-teacher from Walton spoke to one of my chancery staff about these matters and he told me."

"Did your staff person tell you the ages of those whom Shulz had made advances to?"

"He might have."

"He might have. Hmnn! Well I know that you have many affairs to deal with, but perhaps I can refresh your memory. I have a copy of a letter that you wrote to Mr. Zarth, the coach-teacher whom you spoke about, and in this you spoke of dangers to young people. Does that refer to underage people?"

"In the Catholic Church, we hold that homosexuality is wrong, regardless of age, so I don't think I had in mind any particular age."

"Well, the fact that the informant was a coach-teacher and your use of the words 'young people', while not conclusive, would seem to indicate *very* young people, would it not?"

"Maybe, it was a long time ago."

"Did you inform Father Schwartz all you knew about Shulz's actions in Walton?"

"Of course, he knew whatever I knew."

I sat dumbfounded. The jury had to be persuaded that Ryan, despite his waffling, had known that these were young people. And now he had testified that I'd been told the same. There were further questions, but I was too disconcerted to follow. Manson tried to patch things up, but Ryan stuck to the story that I had been informed. I noticed that he did not look at me as he left. Beth was furious. "He sold you out! He never told you a damn thing! I wanted to spit in his face.

"Beth, I don't know what to say. Is it possible, he really thought he told me everything he knew?"

"He was evasive with the Plinter attorney. He must have known about those kids. And he failed to inform you. I can see why Bill hates him!"

"Beth, he's not a liar. I think he just forgot."

The Plinter attorney had a field day painting me in dark colors as a pastor indifferent to the souls in his parish. My attorney, by contrast, described me as naive (I hate the word boob) so innocent of common sense that I never really caught the difference between homosexuality and pederasty. I realized it was a necessary defense, but it left my self-image in a deep hole.

The jury debated for four hours and the entire million was awarded. Manson asked, "You'll want to appeal?"

"I don't know. They can't get that money, anyway. I don't have it, not all of it anyway."

"That's my point. We might or might not get a complete reversal, but I'm almost sure the punitive damages won't stand." So we appealed.

Three days after the verdict I was summoned to the chancery. Bishop Muldoon greeted me. "Boss is in Washington at a meeting. He asked me to relay the message. Maybe we should start here," he said, pointing to a large pile of letters. "These are from your flock." I picked up a few at random. One of the remarks remains burned in my head.

"As long as this wolf in shepherd's clothing remains as pastor, I cannot, in conscience, attend St. Dismas." It was signed by a parishioner in whose house I had been a frequent guest. There were a few letters of support, but the majority called for my resignation. Muldoon looked at me with the kind of pity that one has for a dying dog, and then he exploded, "Ryan knows that I say what I think, and I'm doing it now. This meeting in Washington is as necessary as a snowblower in Panama. He hadn't the guts to face you, after leaving you to the wolves. And you can tell him that I said that. We're barely talking as it is."

"But what do I do?"

"You can refuse to do what Ryan asked me to ask you, that is resign, and if you appealed to the apostolic delegate, Ryan would be up to his ass in shit. Candidly, if you stay, I'm afraid St. Dismas is gonna be St. Dismal for you. I counted the letters, fifty against you, five for. Phone calls were worse."

"Oh, I'll resign, but then what? And when?"

"Have you followed our sabbatical policy? You can have three months off with pay—in this case, I'm sure six months would be fine. At the end, I'll make sure you get a plum of a place. When? Today. But I'll do anything for you that I can. Ryan ought to be doing the resigning. Don't forget I was here when you called for an associate, and I knew what Ryan was setting up for you. Remember?"

"Yes." I thought for a few moments and said, "I'm reminded of the movies where they put the guy in a room with a loaded revolver and wait for the noise." He sighed. Finally, I said, "Can you get someone there for Mass tomorrow?"

"Yeah, me."

"I'm going up to Pinecone Lake."

❖

TEN

Pinecone Lake

I have trouble deciding when anger is no longer mere anger, but hatred. As I drove north on 169, I knew that I was angry at Ryan, but it felt deeper. He had asked me to take in Shulz, he had not told me what he knew about him, had deserted me in court, and then, admitting no guilt on his part, had let me bear the brunt of the malaise caused at St. Dismas, and finally, asked for my resignation. Usually, as I left the Twin Cities behind, I felt a lessening of the tensions of parish life; not this time. Even the sight of Pinecone Lake, set below the pines, white with early December snow, eased neither my throbbing headache nor the less aspirin-treatable hurt in my soul.

Through the years, I'd added much to the cabin. I could now provide private rooms for a half dozen in the cabin, plus a sauna, an extra bathroom and a small cabin near the main one. I turned up the electric heat, carried my belongings into the cabin, and built a fire in the fireplace. If I had any peace at all, it was in knowing that I had done nothing wrong. Well, possibly I erred in not taking Beth's questions seriously. And then there was that nagging doubt which assails people of fragile ego like myself that, maybe, just maybe, the whole Shulz episode was somehow my fault. Two Scotches of Muldoon's grandmother's size and a small dinner did not dissipate the inner ache. I took a walk then, in the cold December air. I seemed always to be coming here in the winter. Just as well, though, because in summer, the lake is fairly inhabited, and people might invite me to dinner. Why I seek aloneness in pain is not very clear to me. I even ran it by a counselor later, and while we went round and round about it, we never arrived at an answer. In succeeding days, I chopped wood and forced myself to chop holes in the ice and to try to fish. The bitterness remained in me like undigestible food. I've never known, at least I don't think I've known, clinical depression. This was close enough. After five days, I gave up the fishing, the wood chopping, hiking and reading. I sat there in my self-imposed prison and was beyond tears or anger. Neighbor Ned's well-intentioned invitations were evaded, and I mostly sat and watched the daily dregs of television: dreary soap operas, dull games and endless weather reports. I had not arranged for telephone reconnection. I took a perverse joy in observing these sick symptoms, feeling myself slipping from human to animal and then to a kind of vegetable existence, a revenge on an unjust world. I drank, I ate, I slept; all badly. I slept fitfully, whether because of booze or low spirits or whatever. That pattern must have continued for ten days or so.

Those ten days, as I say, passed in a sort of haze. I sat, on a Friday night, as a snow storm roared outside, and sipped Scotches and fried a hamburger, while watching the news. The storm had a calming affect on me. Perhaps it was the contrast of the warm, wood fire and the forbidding outside. There was a soft knock on the door, so soft that I wasn't sure whether it was storm induced or human. In doubt I opened the door to see a person of indeterminate sex, wrapped in layers of clothing. A scarf covered the face so thoroughly that I could see only the eyes, blue Scandinavian eyes, blue as the deep lakes in the Swedish highlands, peering under blond eyebrows, eyebrows now frosted with

snow. It was Beth, of course, and I knew it before she low-
ered her scarf, to reveal a timid Beth, almost like the fifteen-
year-old bringing sandwiches to the gazebo. She was shiv-
ering as she asked, "Can I come in?"

"Of course." I said, as I hugged the bundle of Beth and
heavy clothing. Despite my welcome, her timidity continued.

"George, I know you like to lick your wounds in private,
but I can't help it. I won't let you. Look, I can stay in the
little cabin by the lake, and I'll only see you when you want
me." This all tumbled out as she shivered and breathed
spasmodically.

"I'm so cold; my heater went bad and I tried to get here in
daylight, and then I got lost and I've been driving around
with the windows open so I could see past the frosted
glass." Then, again in her little girl voice, she asked, "Can I
stay?" I said exactly what I felt. "You are the one person in
the whole world that I want to see."

Her timidity vanished like a summer squall. She whipped
off her coat and jumped into my arms and hugged me,
pushing her body against me. I said, "I'll turn off this miserable meal and I'll go down to the other cabin and turn up the
electric heat. Why don't you go and turn on the hot water?
A warm bath will thaw you out."

When I came back from preparing the smaller cabin, she
was emerging from the bath wrapped in a floor length robe,
and had on her feet, fluffy pink slippers. I asked, "Would
you like a hot buttered rum?" She would. She sat in front of
the blazing logs and slipped her delicate feet in and out of
her slippers. When I brought the steaming glasses of rum
and sat by her, I noticed, as I said, her timid face had been
replaced by a pleasant insolence, and the little creases on the
corners of her mouth were curled sensually. While the
heavy robe concealed the marvelous contours of her body,
it gave promise, as a neatly wrapped present affords promise to a child. I couldn't take my eyes off her. I said, as we

sipped rum, "I've got to get you something better than hamburger for dinner."

"Nonsense, hamburger sounds fine. Just add a little because I'm as hungry as a teener." So we sat, not at the table, but by the fireplace, and we ate hamburgers and fried potatoes and sipped rums and talked and laughed and I could feel my despondency oozing away. At ten, she said, "I better go down to the other cabin and let you alone."

"This is silly. I'm going down and turn down the heat. You stay here." And I led her to a room next to mine. After we'd cleaned the dishes, we sat and I poured two stiff Irish mists, and we watched the flames leaping and sending to us the smell of pinecones. "Does this remind you of anything?" I asked.

"The night I almost lost you. I promise to keep my robe on." I found this vaguely disappointing, even though it was right, of course. I let my fingers play in her long golden hair. In normal times, I would have been more guarded, but I was coming off a severe bout of the lows, a sadness which was compounded by memories of the past; bad treatment at St. Brendan's and at Seven Sorrows, memories of my parent's deaths, which were forever mixed in with those events, and now, what seemed to me, the ultimate injustice at St. Dismas. I hate excuses for wrongdoing: this is no excuse, only a partial explanation. Frankly, as Clark said, I didn't give a damn. We snuggled and kissed as we did as teenagers on a hill above the sixth hole at Oak Tree Country Club; and again at Beth's place above the Zumbro. I made the seconds of Irish mist smaller, but this didn't diminish our ardor. It was Beth who blew the whistle this time.

"George, I'm not about to risk losing you a second time. It's time we went to bed, separate, but equal."

But I couldn't sleep. Whether it was the booze or the past ten days or the advent of Beth or our cuddling, I was wide awake at two p.m. I rapped lightly on her door. A sleepy voice said, "Yes."

"Are you asleep?"

"No, I can't sleep."

"Neither can I."

"I guessed that."

"Can I come in?"

"It's your house."

I came. I saw. I hesitated. I said, "Why not sit by the fire as long as we can't sleep."

This time she skipped the long robe and her shorty nightgown bared her shapely legs, still tan from a California trip. I lied to myself that we were just going to talk. Our communication was nonverbal. We snuggled and kissed, but much more ardently. In the midst of a long kiss, she suddenly pulled back. "George, I'm not going to cause you conflict with your conscience. The oldie about hating me in the morning is part of it, but, more, I know you and this could wound you permanently."

"I am the master of my soul. Who said that? Henley?" I held her to me, bookends sans books, a perfect fit. She demurred again, but faintly. I carried her into my room, set her gently on the bed, and removed her nightie. I have no basis for comparison, but her breasts were round and perfect, and larger than I had expected, her pubic hair as golden as her head and brows. Heedless of God or promises or pregnancy, we were as careless as teenagers. We made love two more times that fatal night and then slept far into the morning. When I awoke, she was looking at me quizzically. "Well?" she said.

"Well what?"

"Was it worth it?"

"What a question."

"What an evasion."

"O.K., it was the most wonderful experience in my long life."

"Well, you didn't ask me. I'd rather have breakfast." I hit her with my pillow. At breakfast, she said, "I meant to tell

271

you, I told the man at the farmhouse back there that I was looking for my cousin's cabin, Father Schwartz's. Was that right?"

"By all means. No need to get funny ideas in Ned's head."

And so I, who never found it necessary to lie, began a trail of deceptions. I remember later reading F. Scott Peck's book, "People of the Lie," which had as one thesis that wrongdoing is inevitably accompanied by lies. Nor does it work. A few days later, running into Ned, he said, "I see your cousin is staying a long time." And he winked. I went into town the first day after Beth came to get the phone reconnected, which Beth needed for her business, and to get food. I bought steaks and fish and chicken and pasta and soups and vegetables and, not to be neglected, Irish Mist. She said she could stay for ten days. Glorious days. We feasted, we hiked across the snow-covered lake in the moonlight; we wrestled in the snow; we fished, we made love shamelessly. Well, almost. When we drove into Mass far away from the little church at Pinecone, so I could be anonymous, I didn't go to Communion. So Beth didn't either. On the way back, she said, "You think this is wrong, don't you?" I didn't answer. She went on. "I could have gone to Communion today. What we're doing is loving. I can't believe God is against it." I didn't know what to say. So the joy and the love and the glory were bittersweet. But we didn't talk about it. Well, Beth tried, but I was silent when she raised the subject. A heavy snow was falling on the morning which marked the seventh day that Beth had been there, she came into my room and I reached for her nightie to slip her out of it, but she said, "Unh-unh, we got to settle something. I'm O.K. with our lovemaking, but you are not. I want to marry you. I don't think I could marry anyone else, but you can't leave the priesthood, can you? And something is hurting you deeply. Last night I heard you cry out in your sleep. You shouted 'No!' so loudly that it woke me." I had forgotten the dream, but that recalled it. I dreamt that I was standing outside my rectory at St. Dismas. My parents were inside, looking out the window. A man with a bulldozer was moving toward the rectory to tear it down. I stood in his path and blocked him. I shouted "No!" and it woke me too. Years later, a counsellor would ask me what the man looked like and I said that he was faceless. "That man was you." He helped me to see that I was overturning both home and church values. But that day I evaded Beth's question. I said, "Beth, maybe it takes me a little longer to face up to things." We made love that morning anyway. Beth had intended to stay for ten days, but she stayed two extra days even though her work was being neglected. That cold December morning, when we bid tearful goodbyes, Beth forced me to level.

"George, I wanted to be something good in your life, but it's not happening."

"Beth, you rescued me from a deep depression."

"And started you on a guilt trip. I love you too much to cause more pain." And she broke down. I had to admit the basic truth of what she was saying. I would not leave priesthood and I couldn't maintain a lie. I finally said, "Maybe we can go back to the chaste friendship we used to have."

"Maybe," she said. After she drove out, I went back to the cabin and sat before the fire and faced the facts. Beth was right, of course, and I had been into heavy denial. I did feel enormous guilt. Perceptions of morality in society and even in the Church were changing. The emphasis was less on isolated actions and more was put on the morality based on relationships. One could put it, for example, that neither Beth nor I was hurting ourselves or anyone else. That thought did not assuage my guilt. I had emerged from a moral matrix which put personal sexual morality almost as a center. I had kept it scrupulously. I had never masturbated or deviated in the least, and now I'd tossed it all overboard. My attempts to blame my infidelity on the various injustices I'd received was futile. I knew I was wrong. I had a trusted priest friend in the Benedictine order at St. John's in Collegeville, and I drove there that day and confessed my considerable sins. Father Adolpho was the essence of kindness and care, but he warned me that I must not see Beth again.

"But for years we maintained a chaste friendship."

"I'm afraid that has all changed now. I must tell you it is too dangerous to try to return to that." I agreed, but in my heart, I thought that I knew better. A week later, feeling strong, I called Beth and we met for lunch in Minneapolis. We kissed in a brother-sister sort of way, and I felt virtuous. Still another week later, I drove to Rochester and stayed overnight at Beth's without incidence. I felt we'd won. About a month later, I drove to Beth's and this time it was she who was down, something about a difficult assistant at work. I was comforting her in my arms, and suddenly, we were pawing each other with abandon. The next morning it was Beth who said,

"George, we can't see each other anymore. I love you too much to let this go on. This is the hardest thing I've ever done, but it has to be." I made some feeble protest, along the lines of trying again, but she was adamant. We both cried our farewells, and I drove back to Pinecone, and was more desolate than ever. I was there a week before I realized my despondency was becoming dangerous, and so I tried to set up a regimen for change. The only thing which seemed to help was a long series of walks. I purchased snowshoes so I could navigate the deep snow of the lake. This made me so tired that I slept. Gradually, and not without backsliding, I created a series of meditations and prayer. Toward the end of a month, I felt a lessening of tension and even a desire to go back to work, but I was still too proud and angry to call the chancery. The call came in late February. It was Bishop Muldoon. "How's the sabbatical? Usually, you know we insist on a planned schedule of learning."

"Knock it off, John, you also know this is no sabbatical. I'm in exile."

"Ah, we can relieve you. St. Elizabeth is open."

"In Farmville?"

"Yeah."

"Hmn, how many families, what's the debt, and do I have to build a church?"

"Whoa, whoa, George. I don't know all these matters. Let's see; maybe close to 1800 families; uh—debt?—large, I think; the church is built. D'ya know the area? Farmville ought to change its name. There aren't any farms left. It's all suburbia."

"Does an assistant go with it?"

"Not at the moment; let me be honest; unless we luck into a student, like from Asia or Africa, I doubt that an under 2000 families parish rates two guys. There's a big staff, though."

"Is this another punishment from my dear classmate, Ryan?"

"C'mon, G., time to forgive. I think he feels pretty bad about old Dismas. He and I are talking, so maybe I'm feeling positive about him. Anyway, he had no part in this. Come's from the personnel committee, of which I am the peerless leader. In simple words, you were my idea. Why not go give the place a look?"

"Who was there? Wasn't it Bartosh?"

"Afraid you'd ask that. Clem, good man that he is, is still fighting Vatican II. Got on the wrong side of his own staff. Nobody pushed him. He just asked out."

"Maybe I'll get on the wrong side of the staff, too."

"Maybe, maybe not. What's to lose by taking a look?"

"I'll drive down today."

"You want a place to stay? I'm sure Ryan has room."

"You're still a son-of-a-bitch aren't you?"

Muldoon laughed. "I'm just a peacemaker."

As I drove toward the Twin Cities, I noticed that it was warmer. The piles of snow in the fields were decreasing. I drove south and east of Bloomingdale and I had knots in my stomach as I wondered if this would be one more debacle. Muldoon was right about Farmville; there was an occasional farm, like an oasis fighting a desert of apartments and developments of single homes. I went past lanes with horticultural names, Lilac Place, Rosemary Lane, Pine Street, Hollyhock Drive, and then I found it, Sunnybrook Road. Do I turn left or right? I chose left and was right, for within a half mile I saw the sign, St. Elizabeth Church. It was a very large brick structure, one of those new churches, of which old timers invariably say, "It don't look like no church!" The doors were open and I wandered into the main part of the church which was massive, the small altar area dwarfed by the large aisles containing chairs and no kneelers. It must seat well over a thousand, I decided. The organ and choir seats were to the left of the altar. The altar area was lower than the rows of chairs which rose upward to give everyone a perfect view. O.K., I thought. There was a large gathering area, a sort of hospitality enclosure which went all around the church area. I walked through that space and into a series of offices. I had not worn my clericals and as I walked amongst the people going back and forth, no one spoke to me. As I came toward what I guessed was the back door or one of the back doors, there was a smiling lady at a desk which I guessed was a sort of reception area. Sure enough, she said, "Can I help you?"

"I'm Father Schwartz; uh—well, the chancery has asked me to look into the place."

"Wonderful. I'm Cynthia Ryan. Among other things, I'm the receptionist. Would you like me to introduce you around? Or should we get the whole staff out here?"

Cynthia was blond and pretty with lovely blue eyes. I thought momentarily about her offer, and said, "No, I'll just go and acquaint myself. I hear you have an administrator. I'll start there. Where would I find him?"

She pointed down the hall. "First door on your left."

He was a big man with a fine face accented by large, bushy eyebrows like Pierre Salinger. "I'm Father Schwartz. The chancery asked me to give a look-see."

"Sam Bertrand. And what would you like to 'look-see'?"

"Let's start with the debt. How big?"

"Umm, right off hand—I just don't know."

"Well, if you'll give me a copy of last year's report to the diocese, it'll be there."

He hesitated. "If you were pastor. I don't know that I should just show that to anyone. Father Bartosh left that sort of thing in my hands . . ."

"I may accept the chancery offer. I may be pastor here. It behooves both of us that I see it right now."

He frowned, but went to a file and with distinct displeasure handed me last year's report. He did so with a menacing twist of his wrists, almost as if he were feeding an unfriendly dog. I read quickly. The debt was over $800,000. That past year, they'd paid off $40,000. Their total receipts were $420,000. Expenses ran over $350,000. Staff salaries were over $200,000."

"Wow!" I said. "Do you need all these people?"

"Perhaps you'd like to go around and see what they do. Most of the staff is here now." I had a notion that he would like me elsewhere.

"Shall I take you around?"

For the second time that day I said, "No, I'll introduce myself." He was glad to see me go. I continued to work the left side of the office row. "Hello," I said to the bright looking lady in the next office; "I'm Father Schwartz. I'm sort of looking over the parish at the request of the chancery. What is your job?"

"Job? I guess you could call it that. I'm the liturgist. I

work with the liturgical committee, and with the clergy on liturgy; things like that. I also work with the catechetical department and the hospitality committee."

"Choir too?"

"Sure. Now, if you'll excuse me, Father, I have to prepare a liturgy for this afternoon."

"I guess." I said as I exited. These people, I thought must think they have terrific job security to toss me off so glibly. I crossed over to the right side of the office row. Maybe, I'd run into a more cooperative bunch. In the course of an hour and a half, I met the coordinator of religious education for grade schoolers, the coordinator for junior high and the adult education coordinator. This last, a woman who looked like she was in her twenties, a Ms. Golden, explained that she set up programs for senior high students and for adults.

I asked, "What are your current programs for adults, I mean, out-of-school adults?"

"We are finishing a program on parenting. Another on biblical studies and a third on what we call, 'modern Catholicism'."

"How many attend the parenting thing?"

"I don't know exactly."

"Well, about?"

"Oh, maybe ten."

"Again approximately, how many in the Bible study class?"

"Fifteen."

"And modern Catholicism?"

"About twelve."

"And do you teach all of these?"

There was amazement on her face. "Me? I'm too busy coordinating these programs. We hire people."

"Roughly, what's your budget for the year for these programs?"

"I really don't know."

I looked it up later in the administrator's file. It was $19,400. I hadn't met all the staff, but I stopped at one more office. It belonged to the parish counsellor.

"I've done a certain amount of counselling myself." I said.

"Oh, really," he said, "Where did you study?"

"St. Anselm."

"I mean psych?"

"I think experience has been my main teacher."

He smiled superciliously. "I see."

I decided I couldn't handle any more interviews that afternoon, so I went to Sioux Lake and rang the rectory bell. Foley opened the door and hugged me. "Old lonesome George. Can you stay?"

"I need a bed."

"George, I called up at Pinecone, but your phone was out. I wanted to go up, but I couldn't get away. Busy pastor that I am. I heard Bill's sister was going to see you. Did she find you?"

"Yes." I answered. I did not elaborate.

"Are you coming out of hibernation? Oh, excuse me, I meant sabbatical."

"You may be looking at the future pastor of Farmville. I just gave it a look."

"And—?"

"And I never saw such a staff in my life."

"That's what you can do, when you're not saddled with a school. I envy them." He sighed.

"Would you really have all those people? My God, they even have a hospitality coordinator. And a full-time counsellor who looked down his nose at me. A pretty snippy bunch! If I go there, I think I'll fire half of them."

"Go easy. You fire one of them without due cause and they'll take you to the diocesan reconciliation court. And if that fails, they can haul you off to civil court."

"Maybe I won't go there at all."

"C'mon, old timer, you are in need of a challenge."

"No wonder they're such a snippy bunch. They got tenure."

"George, it's the other end of a system that was unfair the other way. Just think how often a pastor came in and fired the whole staff. How fair was that?"

"You got a point, but I'm gonna watch 'em closely. If any of them are goofing off, they're dead in the water. But I haven't made any decision."

But I did, and shortly after. By Easter week, I was the new pastor of St. Elizabeth of Hungary in Farmville. Things were rocky from the start. Mr. Samuel Bertrand, the administrator, saw himself as the man in charge. I was hired to lead the liturgy. At the first staff meeting, he presided. After dealing with some routine matters, he said, "Now you've all met Father Schwartz, our new pastor. Maybe, you'd like to address the group."

"I would indeed. Well, everybody, I'm delighted to be here. I hope to interview each of you at some length, but first I'd like each of you to prepare for me a detailed paper spelling out your responsibilities; a job description if you will . . ." Bertrand cut in. "That seems to me to be my department, Father. I've already done that. It would be duplication. God knows, we've all got enough to do around here without doing something over and over . . ."

"You interrupted me. And with the job description, a personal evaluation as to how this was fulfilled in the past year and how your work fits into the overall well-being of the parish."

It got very silent. I added, "Did you say, Mr. Bertrand, that you have such job descriptions?"

"Yes."

"Would it be convenient to put them on my desk by—say two p.m.?"

"Not really. I have many things to do today."

"Well, consider this top priority. Also, are there contracts for each member of the staff?"

"There are, and they are two-year contracts."

"I'd like those on my desk also at two."

Sam's bushy eyebrows were knit closely together. "Father, I have a meeting this afternoon at one with the janitorial staff. I mean everything can't stop so you can look at these papers..."

"I fail to understand how moving some papers from a file will throw off your whole schedule."

It got quiet again. Then, one of the religious ed coordinators, June Olson, started to giggle. She tried to turn it into a cough, and coughing fiercely, she left the room as if to bring the cough under control. She came back in a few moments, red-faced, whether from embarrassment or the result of fake coughing, I couldn't tell. By this time, Sam Bertrand had recovered his composure, and continued the agenda. The other items, something about the parking lot and a staff party went by swiftly. I think my words had put a bit of a damper on the party idea. I left the room abruptly as Sam declared adjournment. I was back in my office for only a few moments when June Olson tapped on the open door.

"Got a moment?"

"Sure."

June was about thirty, dark-haired and yet her features seemed to me to be Scandinavian, perfectly formed nose, sensual mouth, and a smile out of Hollywood. "Sorry, I interrupted the meeting."

"No, it broke the tension."

"May I close the door?"

"Sure. Sit down." As she sat down, I envied her husband. Maybe, I decided, she wasn't Scandinavian at all; that's probably her husband's name.

"You know I really wasn't coughing?"

"You were laughing; a healthy thing to do at most meetings."

"See, I don't mean to be talking behind anybody's back, but Sam is sort of—uh—bossy, and when you pointed out that all you wanted was a few papers out of a file, it just broke me up."

"I enjoyed you enjoying me."

"Thanks. And good luck." She left and I was sitting there smiling when a louder knock came on the door. It was Sam Bertrand. He was red-faced, but not in embarrassment. The bushy eyebrows sat above angry eyes.

"I need to talk."

"If you've got the time, I have." It was my way of reminding him that he had earlier stated that he didn't have time to get a few papers out of his file. He caught the sarcasm.

"Oh, I'm busy all right, but we've got to get a few things straight."

"I couldn't agree more."

"For a staff to function well, there has to be clarity of roles. Who does what? And who does the other. Now in the past it was my understanding that managing the staff was my function. Your actions this morning were very disturbing to me."

"And your response to me was disturbing."

"Well, is running the staff, your job or mine? Let's start there."

"I don't know yet. Put it this way. I've been my own administrator most of the time. When I hired one at St. Dismas, his work was mostly financial. I ran the staff. I don't say that's the only way to go, but I'm ultimately responsible for the parish and that includes finances. It's a huge staff and it is sucking up most of the revenue. I feel it's my duty to find out whether we need all those people."

"And I've got most of two years left in my contract, and I mean to stay at least that long. Bottom line, I won't go quietly into the night. I'll take you to the grievance committee, if I'm unjustly fired."

"I assure you, if you're fired, it won't be unjustly. Now I would like those job descriptions, today."

I got the papers before two p.m. The job descriptions and the contracts did not mesh perfectly. I wondered how far I needed to go into this. The staff was cooly courteous, that is except Sam Bertrand. He did not try to hide his feelings. A few days after the staff meeting, he came into my office.

"I wonder if we could set next week's agenda for the staff meeting?"

"Sure, but I was thinking; why don't you take one week and I'll take the next. That way we could both get across items from our different points of view. Like this week I'd like to have an open agenda on how our various ministries come together. Next week, you could set business which you see as important."

"Well, I don't know—I suppose so, O.K. After all, you're the one with wide experiences." He thought for a moment, then, "Gee! you've been at St. Dismas, St. Brendan's, Seven Sorrows, St. Christopher's..." I think it was his way of letting me know that he'd done a bit of research on me, and without mentioning it, wanted me to know that he knew I'd been less than successful in many parishes. I nodded. "Experience teaches a fella a lot about people." Let him think about that! My meeting on the consolidation of our ministries was a bomb. Hardly anyone talked. I went back to my rectory at noon and realized that the staff, at least most of them, were in quiet revolt. The rectory was a large colonial house, a good three blocks from the church. From the beginning, I had decided that it would be a home, not an office, and if I had evening appointments, they would be in my office at the church. I decided to take the day off, a kind of one day retreat, in order to discover where I should go with the staff and the parish. I had few calls for appointments so far. In addition, the house phone was unlisted. If there was an emergency, the secretary would call or give my home number. Ditto, the answering service at night. Otherwise, the calls stayed in my mailbox at the church office. I had noticed that ordinarily a new priest gets few calls for appointments until the folk have looked him over a bit. There were exceptions. At St. Brendan's, I had a lot of calls because people recognized that Higgins was interested in the administration of the parish, not much in the problems of individuals, except for special parishioners, his pets, as it were. Weddings at St. Elizabeth were my ultimate responsibility, but the hospitality lady, Ruth Merrick, did much of the prep work, including the tests for marriage readiness which then were given to Dr. Merwin, the counsellor, who went over them with the couple. Because it took a good part of weddings off my hands, I knew whomever I fired, it wouldn't be her. So I paced up and down the big, well-appointed house thinking about my future at Farmville.

The people I'd met at the Sunday Masses were friendly and accepting, but I couldn't ignore the fact that a bad relationship with the staff would wreck everything. Strange, I thought, I'd come here, humbled by my sin with Beth, penitent even, and now I was throwing my weight around with the staff. Was I being unfair with Bertrand, for example? And then I was off to a very bad start with the liturgist, Jennifer Brand. She had stopped into my office about the second day I'd been there and announced that the liturgy meeting was scheduled for Tuesday night. I said, "You don't expect me to be there?"

"Of course. How can we plan liturgies without the celebrant?"

"What do you do at the meetings?"

"We take two weeks at a time. We go over the music and the homilies."

"The homilies? I'm accustomed to doing my own."

"We can't very well coordinate the music and readings

and the whole Sunday experience without critiquing your homily."

"I've never worked like that in my life."

She shook her finger at me in a schoolmarm fashion, "Oh my, it's high time we moved you into the twentieth century, isn't it?"

"Let me begin by saying that I'm not use to being talked to that way . . . "

"Oh, excuse ME! But I am in charge of liturgy here!"

"Me too. For example what do you have in mind for next Sunday?"

Her smile had lapsed into a frown, but she did answer.

"As you probably know" (I caught the sarcasm) "it's the feast of the Good Shepherd. We've gotten hold of a shepherd's staff, well really it's like the bishop's crosier. My plan is to have you come down the aisle carrying the crosier with four children dressed in white cassocks in front of you, like lambs."

"Maybe we could get a German Shepherd and dress him like a wolf and I could beat him over the head with the crosier. It would add some more realism."

"I don't think that's funny. You know, Father, you may think you can alienate us staffers, but we've got friends in the parish and you'll find that you're not going far without us."

She turned around and slammed the door behind her. Needless to say, we didn't do the shepherd thing, and, sure enough, I got calls from a couple of the mothers of the kids who were to act in the procession. There was also Evy Golden, the adult ed coordinator. We hadn't had any bitter exchange as yet, but I couldn't see much happening for the $25,000 a year we were paying her. I had done some checking and hardly any senior high kids were involved in her programs and the adult fare did not seem to draw many people.

Then there was Patrick Sweeney, organist and choir director, again a $30,000 job on which he seemed to spend about ten hours a week. Like some musicians I'd known, he saw himself as the main actor in liturgy with the priest as an unfortunate, but necessary adjunct to liturgical action, something like the king of England, a ceremonial position at best.

I added up the people on the staff who seemed to like me or at least, ones I could work comfortably with. There were at least three; June Olson, the giggler who was the junior high coordinator; Mrs. Lucy Farrell, grade school coordinator and Cythia Ryan, who was receptionist and who did much more. Ruth Merrick, in charge of hospitality seemed to earn her keep, and I had no vibrations from her, pro or con, as to how she related to me.

The next thing I considered was how much of the malaise was my fault. I had felt that my dalliance with Beth, whatever the negative elements, had taught me to be more loving. That old tape from an earlier retreat was still playing in my head, "but do you love them?" If I was loving the staff, it was certainly in a cold, cold way. I invited Foley over for dinner, and he was able to come.

"Well, well, well, what a nice rectory! Hidden from the folk, so that 'Father' can get away."

"Father might want to get further away."

I had a crock pot dinner stewing in the kitchen, as I poured us both generous portions of Johnny Walker. (Red that is.) I told him about the good shepherd and the lambs. He didn't blink an eye. I went on.

"I had the secretary give me the file on last year's liturgical fun and games. Know what they did at Pentecost, last year?"

"Let me guess. They got people to read the passage from Acts in four or five languages, French, Spanish, etcetera, simultaneously."

"How did you know that? Somebody report it to you?"

"No, but that's what we did last year."

"You mean you believe in this stuff?"

"I believe: Help my nonbelief."

"Meaning?"

"Meaning, don't be uptight. I don't know. I guess some of it's good. Like the Pentecost thing. I have some sympathy for what they're doing. I think that they are trying to prevent boredom. The problem is they may be creating new boredom—like, what little liturgical games will we have this Sunday? I mean that's what the congregation may be saying. You know sameness is not necessarily boring. The same folk, at least, some of the same folk who want a crackerjack surprise for the congregation each week can sit around and repeat a mantra like 'ohm, ohm, ohm,' over and over to meditate with. How many times have people heard the 'Our Father'? and yet people enjoy saying it. Why? Do they think of the meaning of each phrase? Not most of the time, but what it does is to recall a whole lifetime of events when it was used; back in the Catholic schools, in their homes, in church. I don't mean that they have full memory, possibly it's more of a subliminal memory."

"Good Lord, professor, I didn't want to turn on a lecture, but you touched what I vaguely thought, but wasn't able to put into words."

"That's what professors are for, to articulate half-assed ideas, 'to open the eyes of the blind.'"

"Thanks, asshole."

"Really, George, how's it going?"

"Not so hot. I'd like to can half of my rebellious staff."

"So soon?"

"So soon. Yeah, I guess that's why I called you. I don't know what to do. I'm O.K. with part of the staff and not O.K. with most of 'em. I was toying with the idea of calling Bartosh, but I'm afraid that he's still smarting from St. Elizabeth's, so why reopen the festering wound?"

"What is it, bad vibes, bad chemistry, or different pastoral values?"

"A little of both. The liturgist and I are oil and water. The administrator and I are locked in a power battle."

"You want to ventilate or you want a second opinion before you cut open the body?"

"Advice."

"Two ideas, not necessarily opposing. One, if you wait too long to act, it gets stickier. Two, if you shoot from the hip, you look trigger-happy. So it depends. If it comes to a suit, how good a chance do you have? And where will the parishioners stand? That's what I meant by acting too quickly. The members of the staff probably have constituents on their side. You might be perceived as difficult to get along with. On the other side, the longer you wait, the more it will look like a sudden quarrel."

"These are my thoughts too. Come and eat."

We settled nothing that night.

A few days later, I thought everyone had gone for the night and was about to lock up when there was a knock on my office door. It was Cynthia Ryan. "Got a minute?"

"For you, anytime. Come sit."

"Actually, I need more than a minute. O.K.?"

"Sure." As she sat down and crossed her legs, I noticed their shapeliness. I had made a new pact with my eyes not to look at women, I mean really look. It was obviously not completely operative.

"In fact," she added, "I told Joe I might be late for dinner." It was good for me to learn that she was married.

"Can we speak very frankly?"

"Please do."

"I know that you are experiencing some difficulty with some of the people here, True?"

"The phrase 'staff infection' comes to mind."

She laughed prettily. "And yet they're not all bad. I know I'm talking behind their backs, but it's important. I've thought this over carefully, even talked it over with Joe. Like Jennie Brand. I know you find her difficult; so did I at first. She's a 'new woman', a feminist and very sure of herself, but she's aggressive because she feels herself in a man's world, a hostile world. That's why she comes off so blatantly. Actually she and Sam do not get along. They sorta came together when Father Bartosh was here, because they were both fighting him."

"And now, they've got a new enemy to share, me."

"I wouldn't deny that. But let's go back into ancient history. As you know, perhaps, St. Elizabeth was a little country church over a hundred years ago. In the late forties the city spread out and began to devour the farms. But the parish really hit its stride later, oh say the late sixties. By 1975, it was apparent that the old pastor could no longer handle it, so the bishop sent out Father Scott; did you know him?"

"Only slightly. He was a late vocation."

"Right. He'd been in business. He built the church and gradually assembled the staff. Then, unfortunately, he died. When Father Bartosh came, the big staff was in place. Well, let me describe the situation from my point of view. When Bartosh arrived, there was plenty of strife on the staff. I know he's your classmate, and you know he's a strong man. I think he would have solved the staff situation, but for an added problem. He was mostly a pre-Vatican II man. So the staff malaise, and I'll deal with that in a minute, looked more like old Church versus new Church. He's a wonderful man and he brought precious gifts to this parish, but the battles raged around stuff like girl servers and women preaching and this obscured the real problems of staff incompatibility. I guess he finally decided that either the staff should go or he should. Being the gentleman that he is, he left. I cried and so did most of the people. And that brings me to you. This place needs you."

"You think I'm ready to throw in the towel?"

"No, no, I hope not, but my point is that people in this parish are hurting. Not much financially, but there's divorce and drugs and a hunger for the spiritual. I think you can help a lot. Don't let the staff discourage you. Father Bartosh gave solid homilies, about commitment, Christian values, that sort of thing. But people like Jennie and Pat Sweeney judged them to be obsolete. The liturgy meetings turned into brawls. Bartosh refused to alter his homilies."

"Not to interrupt, but how do you relate to Jennie and Sam and Sweeney?"

She smiled. "O.K., I asked for it. I like Jennifer. I understand where she's coming from. The Church is a man's world. She's bright and she's honest. That doesn't mean I buy all this theatrical liturgy, but what do I know? I'm an English major. Sweeney is pompous, but I seldom have to deal with him. Gosh, I hate myself gossiping, but you asked, and you shall receive. Evy, I don't know, she's in a dream world. I'm fine with Lucy, and June has become a best friend."

"You skipped a big one."

"I wanted to duck that one, but O.K., you asked. Sam and I get along NOW. Once I let him know the boundaries."

"The boundaries?"

"Sam has little habits of being affectionate. He is not above a little pat on the derriere. He did that to me once. I said, 'my husband is an ex-Golden Glover. You do that again and you're history'. That was the end of that. What else? If you read his job description, he is to keep the books. He has me do most of it."

"Go back to his habits. Has he done that with other women here?"

"I'll leave that to them. You might ask June or Jennie. Jennie offered to take him to court." The devious part of my mind was working shamelessly. While I should have been thinking of the women on the staff, I was really thinking about what that information would do if I fired Sam, and he refused to go "quietly into the night."

"Well, well, well," I said.

Cynthia smiled her gorgeous smile. "I knew you in a previous life."

"I know. You were the Queen of Sheba and I was Solomon."

"Not quite that long ago. My maiden name was Renner."

"Of course, there was some sort of memory when I saw you. You were the smart little girl in grade school, and your dad the trustee."

"We cried when you left St. Brendan's. You sure get the deals, don't you? You know my dad is the one who blew the whistle on Dowd. And you blew a whistle of your own on Dowd."

"Déjà vu. How are your parents?"

"Fine. Listen, I'm going to ask you to come to dinner with Joe and me. O.K.?"

"Sure. And I appreciate your courage in coming here and telling me this."

"I feel like an old gossip, but I didn't want to see you go again." She kissed me on the cheek and left. My spirits were considerably higher.

The weeks that followed were made easier by what Cynthia had told me. I did go to liturgy meetings and I listened, but I continued to make my own homilies. My dealings with Sam were cool, but correct, both of us straining to keep a fragile peace. Jennifer Brand and I made no pretense of understanding one another. Evy Golden, the coordinator for older youth and adults, seemed oblivious that I was observing her mediocre output. Both Sweeney, the music man, and Dr. Merwin, the counsellor, continued their patterns of smug superiority. I had constantly to remind myself that I must not let my personal dislikes get in the way of an objective evaluation of their performance. It did not always work. I was guilty of not loving a good part of the staff. Worse, I was concealing it from them; planning their demise in the secret parts of my mind and heart. I've often wondered if the famous quarrel between Sts. Peter and Paul was entirely theological and ideological or if two strong egos were involved. I know that I was having difficulty separating my concern that the parish get a fair return from its salaries, from my personal animosity.

The parish council did not meet in the summer. At the first meeting in early September the council head, Myles Printon, listened to my motion with mild surprise. Myles was a fine-looking man in his early fifties. He carried a few more pounds than he needed on his five-foot-seven frame. Partially bald, he had a face which smiled easily and an air of easy command. I understood that he was a banker, by trade, and scrupulously avoided having the parish do business with his bank, an attitude which bolstered my trust that he was a very fair man. He waited until I had finished. "As I understand you, Father Schwartz, you wish to form a committee to study whether we can, in your words, streamline the staff to reduce expenses. Is that correct?"

"I'd like to see more bang for the buck."

"But we are making expenses and even paying off our debt."

"Very slowly. As the parish grows, we may have to add a wing to the church. I'm convinced that we could combine some functions in the staff, and drop some positions which, I think, are marginally productive."

Lillian Roth said, "And maybe we could start thinking about a grade school." A groan went up from the members of the council. Apparently this was Lillian's constant speech. Indeed, I remembered her as making the same push when she was a parishioner at St. Dismas, and a pain in the ass, then also.

Someone said, "Are you having trouble getting along with the staff?"

"No more," I answered, "than my predecessor, I think." That shut her up. There were still mixed feelings about Bartosh's exit.

"Do you want some volunteers from the council?" asked Myles.

"No, I think the trustees and I can look into the matter and come back in a month to you with recommendations."

"That soon?" Myles asked, with the air of a man who judged that I'd made up my mind. And so we passed on to the rest of the agenda. I knew it would be useless to tell the council to keep this *sub siggillo,* and so within a week the staff was discussing this amongst themselves. At first none of them talked to me about it. Sam never brought it up. But Jennifer came storming in about a week after the meeting with the council.

"I'm sure, from your homilies, that you consider yourself a Vatican II man, and yet you are thinking of terminating some of us without even dealing witth it at staff meetings. And you've been against me from the start. I'll beg you to remember that we've got plenty of supporters in the parish. You do your Lone Ranger act and you'll be with Bartosh."

"As you know, Ms. Brand, Bartosh is a gentleman and quit on his own. I'm sure you'll agree that I'm no gentleman and I'm not resigning. And it'll be a curious question in the chancery and to our priest personnel board to have two victims from this staff in less than a year." She slammed the door again. Forgive me, Lord. I think I was enjoying this. Hubris? Maybe. Dr. Merwin told me that, if fired, he would definitely take me to the grievance board. I reminded him that if we dropped the position, that would be a tough one to win. The music man said nothing to me, but I noticed that he was around a great deal more.

The two trustees were ideal for my purposes. Owen Fallon had been a trustee from Father Scott's time and had protested mildly about the ever-increasing staff. Jack Hilger was a young businessman who made sure that his own employees proved their salaries. He was amazed at the staff's meagre productiveness. By mid-October, we came before the council and made our recommendations. They were to eliminate the administrator's position, letting me run the staff. Cynthia, who was doing it anyway, would keep the books. Jennifer and Patrick would be let go and that job would be combined. Evy Golden's job, adult ed, would be scrapped. The counsellor's job would be discontinued. All the rest would be preserved. When Jack Hilger finished his presentation, the council members sat there stunned. A few staff supporters, not on the council, began to shout at me and the trustees. I said, "The three of us will leave the room to let you discuss this motion by yourselves." The session went on past eleven p.m. Then we were asked back into the room to hear the vote. We lost nine to seven. I said, Well, you've heard our recommendations and I've heard yours. I'll consider what you've said, and I'll make my decision."

Two weeks later I passed out the pink slips. Sam said, "I told you once that I'll take you to the grievance board, and failing that, I'll see you in court."

"Well, well, court might be the best place, because we might be there on another matter at the same time."

"What's that suppose to mean?"

"Oh, there's some rumors about sexual harassment that I've been meaning to look into."

His face turned ashen. He never carried out his threat. Jennifer did, of course, and so did Dr. Merwin. In the meantime, parishioners, friendly to the fired staff members called and raised hell. Nobody picketed the chancery, but Muldoon called.

"George, you are a genius! There six months and you've managed to alienate half the parish."

"Are you speaking for yourself or are you Ryan's messenger?"

"Good question. To answer, both. That is, as personnel head, all this stuff comes to me. Ryan also, however, is pissed at you. You know that half your council has resigned, including Myles Printon, who is a buddy of Ryan's. Ryan is mad at you, but he is hesitant to be on your case again. How come you ignored the parish council?"

"'Cuz I'm like a bishop. I'm in charge and these babies don't seem to know that."

"Why so many?"

"It was like a dysfunctional family, but, in addition, the staff was sucking up a disproportionate amount of the budget."

"We're getting a lot of letters and phone calls." He sighed.

"So am I. But I've got a lot of support. When the staff and Bartosh parted company, most of the parish were with Clem. I can ride this baby out." There wasn't much more to say.

A few days later, the phone call came.

"George, this is Tom Ryan. Can you come to the chancery at two this afternoon?"

"I'm sure I'll need my resigning pen as usual."

"George, this isn't about parish. I need your help and Foley has already agreed to come. Please come."

"I will."

※

ELEVEN

Gerald Fox

A leaden November sky gave promise of an early darkness as I parked in the chancery lot. As I walked in through the heavy chancery door, I saw that Bob Foley was already there. When the receptionist saw me, she said, "I see you're both here. Just go right in. The Archbishop is expecting you.

Ryan rose to shake hands. It was a stiff, formal exchange. Ryan said, "I know that both of you have some unfinished business with me. My apologies are overdue, but I'm leaving for the airport in an hour-and-a-half, and we have limited time. This isn't about you; it's about Jerry Fox. Our bishop's conference has close ties to the Jesuit University in San Salvador. The other day the secretary got a routine notice about a meeting from there, and, in fact, it was so pointless that he considered not filing it, but later that day, after another routine call about the meeting, the Jesuit in San Salvador said, 'Oh yeah, and be sure and check the acrostics.'

'What?' he said.

'The acrostics, be sure and check.' So the secretary pulled the letter out of the file and the acrostics spelled out; 'Gerald Fox—imprisoned, tortured.' Now I'd go there myself, but for this reason. I'm chair on a section of the new economics pastoral coming out soon. That meeting is tomorrow. If I don't show, the vice-chairman, Bishop Grey will chair it and, believe me, he could gut the thing. It'll be the same old innocuous bilge, asking the rich to share, and all the teeth will be pulled out of it. So I have to be there. Now can you both leave tomorrow? Whoops, I'm getting ahead of myself. Are you willing to go?"

"For Jerry, you bet." I said.

"Count me in," was Bob's retort.

"I presumed as much." He reached in his desk and pulled out several envelopes. This one contains your tickets to El Salvador. This one is your introduction to the Jesuits. You are to stay there. The next is for the embassy. It includes a letter from Vice-President Mondale. There's a separate one for the El Salvadoran government. The Jesuits will fill you in. Now, the U.S. ambassador, Robert Alban is a fine guy. Unfortunately, he is on vacation in the Bahamas and we can't locate him, so you'll have to deal with a Colonel Pierce, the number two man. The Latin American guy in the bishop's conference gives him low marks, so you'll have to use all the influence we can muster. That's why I've made you both Monsignors." He smiled. "You can toss that out after you come back. Our man in the bishop's conference thinks it could be helpful in dealing with both the U.S. embassy as well as the El Salvadoran government. Oh, and you are momentarily my staff; Bob, Vicar General and George, Chancellor. It's all official, but like Cinderella, you gotta give it back when you come home. Questions?"

Bob asked, "How bad off is Jerry?"

"We don't know, but the way the Jesuits handled this, it sounds bad."

"How much cooperation can we expect from the U.S. embassy?"

"God knows. If Alban gets back, it should go well, but, in the meantime . . ."

"Jerry hasn't done—uh, well—anything unlawful, has he?"

Ryan shook his head. I hope not, but you know Jerry. He is one determined guy. If I should finish off the economics meeting, I'll fly right down. Well, if there's nothing more, I'm on a short leash." We said our goodbyes.

The flight was to Miami and then a change of planes and on to San Salvador. On the way, Bob filled me in on Salvadoran history.

"You know what's happening in El Salvador lately?"

"A little. We're backing the wrong horse down here. All in the name of anti-communism."

"There are certainly Marxists in the F.M.L.N. No question, but the Salvadoran government is terrible. The so-called death squads are certainly connected to the government and the army. This is a place where the army runs the government rather than the other way around. They kill their own people by the hundreds, maybe the thousands. Anyone who teaches the peasants to read or to have self-respect is called a communist. The U.S. has consistently supported the Salvadoran government and army. I think, without our having aided and abetted the army, the rebels might be in place by now."

"What do you suppose got Jer in prison?"

"Doing the right thing. What else?"

"The trouble is, he does things so—so uncompromisingly."

Like Jesus?" asked Bob.

Bob's question, half-serious, half-facetious, like so many of Bob's questions, pushed into deeper ground. After a few moment's thought, I said, "Like Jesus, yes and yet, no. Uncompromising like Jesus, but Jerry has an obdurate side, sort of impractical."

"While I'm asking questions, why us? You and I?"

"Both classmates and friends."

"There's more to it than that. I speak passable Spanish. But why you? I'll tell you why; Jerry trusts you; in the sem, Jer came to you when he was troubled. He came to you when he was looking for a place in the diocese."

"I guess that's true, but what good is that down here?"

"We'll see," said Bob, and left it there, inscrutably. He changed back to El Salvador. "The name means 'Saviour', and the people surely need Him. They call the ruling oligarchy, 'The Fourteen Families', certainly, an underestimate. But the wealthy few control all the sources of revenue. Historically the Church has been no help, but our hosts, the Jesuits, are just part of a growing Church-led push for justice. The new Archbishop, Romero, was thought to be an old-time conservative, but he's been a pleasant surprise, speaking out against the government. There is a great deal of fear that his life might be in danger. I'm sure Jerry is part of a new Church, one fighting for the peasants. Things are complicated in that the rebels, pro-peasant though they are, are also heavily Marxist, which puts both the U.S. government and the Vatican in the opposite camp. In fact, I've heard that the Vatican is questioning Romero's leadership which makes him all the more vulnerable." Our meals came then, and we talked of other things. It was twenty-four hours after Ryan had spoken to us that the plane set down in the El Salvador International Airport. The airport was sunny and hot and so infested with uniformed men, heavily-armed, that it seemed like a military post. Our papers briefly looked at, we were met by Father Alfonso López, who greeted us warmly, packed our luggage in his van, and spoke to us in quite good English during the surprisingly long drive into San Salvador.

"You understand that our fear is that your friend is being tortured. This will be denied, of course, but we further fear that he might be killed, on account of the torture. It might make headlines back in the U.S., where there is, at least, the beginning of cynicism of your country's support of the murderous army. He could give witness to his brutal treatment."

I asked, "How can they get away with it?"

Father López's unhappy smile showed in the rearview mirror.

"There are so many ways. A body shows up in a dump or on the street for example, or the vultures buzzing about on the shores of Lake Ilopango brings discovery. The police, the army, some arm of government investigates. They simply write it down as a murder by unknown forces. They, themselves, have probably done it, so, obviously, they are not going to solve the murder. Or they may try to put the blame on the F.M.L.N. In any case our friend is in grave danger." With such sobering conversation, we were brought into the Jesuit house.

I remember that night at the Jesuit residence well. Their faces are blurred in my memory now as are their long Spanish names. Four of them were to be murdered along with two other of their fraternity a few years later. Those two were not there that night, but Father Jon Sobrino, the world reknowned liberation theologian, was present. He happened to be on a speaking engagement in the U.S., I think, when the six Jesuit brothers were killed. It was a pleasant meal and a pleasant evening, but amidst the wine and the laughter, there hung over the group of us a sense of mortality. Perhaps it was like the British and American fliers during the worst of the air wars over England, where each week there would be vacancies. Vacancies to be filled by fresh blood, in every sense of "fresh blood." There was talk of Jerry Fox, of course, and of the continuous slaughter of their friends, their students, and parishioners. In spite of all the grisliness, there was an aura of hope and even lightness. It was more than mere bravado, whistling past the cemetery. It was a joy springing from deep within the human psyche where faith and the courage of Jesus dwells. In retrospect, it may have been very like the emotions of the Last Supper.

It was not all talk of death. Bob Foley had just read Jon

Sobrino's book on Christology, and they entered into a deep discussion of it which I only partially grasped. I had read a short article of Sobrino's entitled something like "To Be Poor in El Salvador Is to Be Close to Death." Our discussion of this hardly lightened our spirits. We retired to our simple cots anxious and apprehensive for the morrow, but we were so tired that we slept well. The next morning, after a Spartan breakfast, we were driven to the U.S. Embassy.

The officer at the desk looked bright and had an engaging smile. "But you cannot see Colonel Pierce for the simple reason that he is not here."

"But the appointment was made by Archbishop Ryan two days ago," said Bob Foley.

He shrugged pleasantly. "Monsignors, I'm sorry, but that's El Salvador! It's like a bad dream, constantly changing. Colonel Pierce is at the airport to meet some U.S. Congressmen. He had no choice."

I said, "Our concern is not some ceremonial meeting. We have reliable information that, a priest of our diocese is in grave danger. We want him out now!"

"Even if the Colonel were here, I'm not at all sure that he could do anything about that. We're not in charge of the country."

"Oh, it's my distinct impression that you are." Bob said, and drew the letter from the Vice-President from his coat. "This is from Vice-President Mondale. It instructs you people to give us absolute priority. You do recognize the Vice-President as your superior, don't you?"

The pleasant smile had vanished, replaced by a smirk.

"Well, he's Vice-President at the moment anyway."

"When will Colonel Pierce be back?" I asked.

He shrugged, not pleasantly this time.

"I don't know. Probably this afternoon."

"We'll wait." I said.

"No you won't." He said, "We'll call you when he gets back." He called to a young marine in the lobby. "These men will be leaving now." The marine came toward us uncertainly.

Bob said, "We are not leaving until someone arranges for us to visit the prison where Father Fox is being held."

"I'll see who is here," said the officer, as he went through a doorway leading inside. In a moment, he was back, accompanied by an older man, a trim, gray-haired man, a very military looking gentleman, with a back as stiff as if it were made from steel. "The Colonel came back through the back entrance, so I didn't realize he was here." We exchanged introductions. The Colonel eyed us cooly and suspiciously.

"Yes?" he said sharply.

We explained our mission. He appraised us sternly. Bob handed him Mondale's letter. He was visibly unimpressed by it, and handed it back with the comment. "I'm not able to get you in to see your priest."

"Look," said Bob, "we can get President Carter to call you if necessary."

"Your priest friend is a known gunrunner for the Commies. He's probably in solitary."

"Nonsense!" I said, "We're his classmates. He's absolutely incapable of anything which would contribute to violence."

Bob said, "We are not here to argue politics. We are here to get our priest out of danger."

"You clerics think you are giving orders. A priest gets involved with Communists, gets arrested for illegal activity and then you expect us to get him out of trouble."

"Let me start with your claim that Fox is a Commie." I said, "I had a conversation with him a few years ago, and he assured me that he thought that it was a mistaken theory."

"People change."

Bob said, "You can get us in to see him, can't you?"

"I really don't know. I do know that he is in trouble with the law."

"Do you know Father Fox?" asked Bob.

"I know of his activities and the kind of dissidents he hangs around with. I'll find out if the Colonel will talk to you."

When he came back, he said, "Colonel Mendez will see you at the prison. But, listen to me, contrary to what some of you think, we do not have the power of getting you in to see your priest, much less get him released." He made no offer of a ride, and since the Jesuit brother who drove us to the embassy had not stayed, we ordered a taxi. An orderly met us at the front desk of the dingy prison. He had introduced himself as Jesus Maria Jose Morazin.

"Good God," said Bob, "the entire Holy Family!"

The orderly must have heard it and understood, because he glared back at Bob. We were ushered into the office of Colonel Hernandez Mendez. He rose, unsmiling from behind his desk. He did not put out his hand, but nodded toward a couple of chairs. We sat down and he said simply, "Yes?"

After that the conversation turned into Spanish, so I was pretty much out of it. Bob later described the conversation which went something like this.

"I am Monsignor Robert Foley, the Vicar General of the Archdiocese of St. Paul and this man is Monsignor Schwartz, the Chancellor. You have a priest of our archdiocese in custody. We wish to see him."

The Colonel was utterly unimpressed. He said, "You cannot see him. He is a most dangerous man. (I recognized the word, "peligroso.") He is in security lockup. As I say, he is too dangerous for us to let you see him. Besides, we could not get him ready." That sentence confirmed Bob's worst fears.

"What do you mean, 'you can't get him ready'? Is he being tortured?"

"The Colonel ignored the question. "Monsignori, I regret that you cannot see him. Now I have other matters..."

Bob said, "We have a letter from Vice-President Mondale here demanding that you cooperate with us..."

"He is not MY vice-president." He finally smiled, but scornfully. "I do not take orders from your vice-president. We have our own."

"People back in the States know about our mission. There will be headlines!"

Again, the mocking smile. "Headlines! what do we care about headlines in North American newspapers? We've had them for a dozen years. Even your own people don't read them. Why should we care?"

Bob didn't give up. "Congress is getting very tired of your killings and tortures. Once we get the Congress to halt aid, your government and army will collapse like a punctured balloon." Bob made a gesture of a balloon bursting apart.

The Colonel got angry. "These are threats to scare women and children. Good day, Monsignori." And he had the orderly escort us out of the prison. As we left, dejectedly, I noticed a worker, an obvious peon, also exiting the prison. He paid no attention to us and went down the street in an opposite direction. As we were about to look for a cab, the same worker had come back and without as much as looking at us, muttered some Spanish words. I thought I heard the words like, "Venga con me." Bob told me later that he had prefaced this with, "Don't speak or look at me. Just follow." Bob poked me in the ribs, "Don't follow too closely."

The man led us to a large building, which we entered. Why we trusted this man so implicitly is hard to explain, but we did. He spoke no English, but led us up the stairs of what was an apartment building. We followed him into a room and he explained to Bob that we would see our friend from a distance. He handed Bob binoculars and pointed at one side of the prison.

"Right through that window," he gestured. Bob looked and gasped, and turned the glasses over to me. I looked through the grimy window at a group of dirty men for some time before I recognized Jerry. His face, as well as his clothes, were dirty. He was even thinner than when I'd last seen him. Although it was difficult to see much detail, the Jerry Fox signature was there, a jaw implacably set. The worker explained that he was a flunky in the prison, cleaning cells and bringing food to the prisoners, and that he had tried to help where he could. Even though I knew no Spanish, I saw him gesture toward his penis as he explained to Bob that they had applied electrodes to Jerry's penis. He explained to Bob that it was necessary to get him out soon, because they would cover up their tortures by killing him and then, perhaps blame the death on unknown assailants.

He had us leave by another door. As we stood waiting for a cab back to the Jesuit house, we were near despair. Back at the Jesuit house, we cursed ourselves for not getting a phone number in Washington for Ryan. Finally, we decided to call Bishop Muldoon in the hope that he might have his number.

"So how's the rescue going?" asked Muldoon.

"Terrible!" I said, "how do we get in touch with Ryan?"

"Better than that. He's on his way. I was about to call you. He'll be in on the nine a.m. Meet him at the airport." It did cheer us a little, but it all seemed so hopeless.

The plane was close to on-time and we, erstwhile enemies of Ryan, greeted him like a long lost brother. He said to Father López. "Drive right to the embassy."

I said, "Tom, I hate to say it, but I'm afraid it's futile."

"We'll see," said Tom. I looked at Tom, the set of his jaw. Archbishop Thomas Ryan had come to rescue his priest from the torturers, and he was not about to lose. As pessimistic as I felt, and as I knew Bob felt, there was an air of confidence in that van as we drove to the embassy. It was Ryan at his best, the take charge man, the natural leader, the man who hated defeat, and who would somehow get his way. My heart sank as I saw that the same orderly was at the desk. He did not smile this time, but peered at us if we were unwelcome intruders.

"I want to see Colonel Pierce," said Tom.

"Sorry, he's busy."

"I am Archbishop Ryan and I was assured by President Carter that I could see him." Ryan said this with that show of easy confidence which had always marked him. The orderly left and a few moments later emerged with Colonel Pierce. The Colonel shook his hand cooly. "And I believe you've met Monsignors Foley and Schwartz."

"I've had the pleasure," said the good Colonel, putting a peculiar twist on the word "pleasure" which indicated that it was anything but. "What can I do for you?" Again, he managed to convey that he couldn't do anything for the Archbishop and, if he could, he wouldn't.

"I think you know my mission. It is to get Father Fox out of jail, and out of the country."

"Yes, we had this conversation yesterday. As I informed your—uh—assistants here, I am not in power to do that. We are guests in this country. I can no more release him from prison than the Salvadoran ambassador could release one of his people in jail in the U.S."

"Oh, come now, the Salvadoran government is a client state, not the other way around. But I'm not here to argue politics. I want, first, your cooperation in getting in to see Father Fox. And then, I want to get him out of the country."

The Colonel, who had seated himself at the orderly's desk without inviting us to sit, now exploded in anger.

"I am not used to taking orders from priests! When your priest disobeys the laws of this country, he must be prepared to pay the consequences."

"And your job here is to protect American interests. We have eyewitness accounts that Fox is being tortured and I'm not leaving here without your assistance, which you are well able to give. By the way," he continued, as he took a newspaper clipping from his pocket, "this is a story in the New York Times about my visit here. There'll be similar stories, perhaps each day that I'm here."

The Colonel's face was as set as Ryan's. "I'm not taking orders from a cleric, as I said a moment ago."

Ryan walked over to the phone on the orderly's desk.

"But you do take orders from your commander-in-chief."

"We have received no orders from the President."

"May I use your phone? I'll pay for the call, of course."

The Colonel nodded reluctantly. Ryan dialed a series of numbers.

An aide came into the room. He said, "Colonel, they are waiting."

"I'll be finished here momentarily." But he stayed sitting at the orderly's desk. He was riveted on Ryan's phone call.

In the silence of the room, we could here the click of the phone on the other end, and a muffled voice.

"This is Archbishop Thomas Ryan. President Carter is expecting my call. Would you connect us, please?" There was a long pause, perhaps no more than two minutes, but it seemed much longer. I looked at the faces in the room; Foley's strained, as I guessed mine appeared; the Colonel, finally reduced to uncertainty; the aide and the orderly, less haughty and apprehensive; and Ryan, as calm as if he was speaking to his secretary. Finally, I heard the welcome words.

"Fine, Mr. President. The trip was fine, thank you." There was a pause. Then Ryan said, "Yes, I'm in the embassy now. Did you wish to speak to Colonel Pierce? He's right here."

"Colonel, President Carter wishes to speak to you." A

subdued Colonel Pierce picked up the phone. We heard one part of the conversation. It went like this.

"Fine, Mr. President."

"Yes, Mr. President."

"Yes, Mr. President."

"I'll do everything I can."

"Thank you, Mr. President. Goodbye."

Well, the climate in the office had changed considerably. The Colonel said, "I'll see what I can do." And he departed into an inner room. He was back in less than an hour.

"I've talked to President Romero, and he has talked to Colonel Mendez. They will let you see Father Fox. Colonel Mendez insisted that you come alone, Archbishop."

"But I need Father, I mean. Monsignor Foley to interpret for me."

"I'll explain," said Colonel Pierce. He was back in a moment. "That'll be all right." Then he looked at me. "Sorry, they insisted that there only be the two. You can wait here in the embassy if you wish."

"No, I'll go over to the plaza. Tom, I'll be in that outdoor cafe, there." I pointed out of the window.

Father López had waited with the car all that time. After the two of them left, I wandered over to the cafe and sat under an umbrella. It was hot, but passable. The waiter came over and I was about to order coffee, but then decided on a cool drink. After I'd ordered it, I thought about the danger of polluted ice in the drink and I called the waiter back. "Una cerveza." I said, and the waiter laughed. I presumed that my accent was strange. I sat and sipped my beer, then, being hungry, I was about to order a salad, when, again, I thought of Montezuma's revenge. I ordered hot soup. It was past two when Ryan and Foley came back. The corners of Ryan's mouth were turned down, a bad sign.

"Well?" I said.

"Well, indeed," said Ryan. We got a snag. Jerry is free to

leave the prison, but only on condition that he leave the country."

"So?" I said.

"So, Jerry won't leave. He thinks it would be desertion."

"My God," I said. What are you going to do now?"

"Wrong! Big fella; not what I'm gonna do. This is what you are gonna do."

"What can I do?"

"I've arranged for you to see Jerry. This is your role in this little scenario. You're the only one that could persuade Foxie." Foley looked at me knowingly. That's what he'd meant when he asked, "Why you and I?" So that was my role. There was a lump in my throat that presaged failure.

"But how?" I asked plaintively.

Ryan growled, "Just get him to go. Lie, persuasion, anything, but I'm leaving Jerry's fate in your hands."

"Thank's a lot." I left them there, ordering lunch while Father López and I went to the jail. At least it was easier to get in this time. They sat me in a small, smelly room where the walls were a sick grey, and then they brought him in. He smiled a wan smile. He had been cleaned up, but there were bruises all over his face, and although tan, he was pale under the tan. Always thin, he was now emaciated. When he opened his mouth to speak, I saw that some teeth were missing, knocked out, I presumed. He said, "It was good of you all to come." We hugged and I said, "Jerry, will he let us alone?"

Jerry spoke to the guard and the man left.

Jerry had tears in his eyes, but underneath the frail body, I could sense the steel in his soul. And I was supposed to change this inflexible mind. I decided it was time to lie. I said,

"Jerry, we're trying to save your life. Ryan was to chair a committee meeting on the Bishop's letter on the economy. Did he tell you?"

"No."

"He's lost the chair coming down here, and it's going to make a pretty half-assed statement from the bishops.

"I'm really sorry, but I have to stay in El Salvador. I can't desert these people."

I changed tactics. "Jerry, what's the upshot? You will be one more fatal statistic here, and then what? Nothing. If you come back to the states..." Here, I hesitated. "Do you think this room is bugged?"

"Probably."

I got close to him and whispered, "You come back and share your—uh—experiences here, and you'll be doing more effective action than being down here. You can be my assistant, and tell the folks the realities."

He smiled his broken-toothed smile. "And you won't get mad at me for upsetting your parish?"

"Not at all. Besides, they're already upset."

He laughed, a painful chuckle. "I can't do it."

"Jerry, did Tom tell you how he got Carter involved in this?"

"Yes, I appreciate it, but what Carter should do is to quit sending arms to this government. That would be much more important."

"Exactly, and that's my point. The source of much trouble is up there, not here. You've got to see that."

"George, I know that you mean well, but I must stay here."

The tears were in his eyes again, but the jaw in that emaciated face was rock strong. We sat there silently and I prayed to the Holy Spirit. "I've done all I can. Help!"

Then it came to me, whether from the Spirit or my subconscious, I'm sure I don't know. I said, "Congress will be asked to vote more military aid in a couple of months. There are two undecided Minnesota representatives. Your story in Minnesota papers could swing the vote. I heard that it's very close." It stopped him. He sat quietly for a minute, two minutes, five. I said, "Have you fallen asleep?"

"No, I'm thinking about what you said. I can't decide."

"Jerry, for God's sake, we have no time. We're walking a very thin line. The offer of freedom could be withdrawn any time."

He continued to ponder. Later, I was to discover just how thin that line of escape was. Again, I said, "Jerry?"

At last he said, "I'll do it." I called the embassy and asked them to find Ryan at the cafe. He was already in the embassy, and said, "We're on the way."

It took a while. Fox had to sign a paper which said that he wouldn't return to El Salvador. Father López wanted us to spend a few days with them, so that Fox could get his strength up, but Ryan was adamant. We were driven to the airport by Father López. We thanked him effusively, and hoped there would be a plane. We learned that we were just in time for the five p.m. to Miami.

I was nervous waiting for the plane, and so was Bob. Even the normally imperturbable Ryan seemed taut. Jerry, worn and ill, seemed to be the only calm one.

Once in the air, I heaved a sigh of relief. The flight attendant came to see if we wanted drinks.

Ryan said, "Jerry, how about some wine?"

"Thanks, that would be nice. Do you have a Chardonay?"

"Si." But Jerry took the little bottle out of her hands.

"No, this won't do. Their grape pickers are treated terribly."

I said, "For God's sake, Jer, take some Scotch. I have it from the best authorities that their workers are very well-paid, and each one gets a free case of Scotch at the end of the year."

He smiled. "O.K." he said.

"Make it a double," said Ryan.

We drank our drinks; Jerry, very slowly. When the dinners came, he ate his salad and picked at his chicken. Then he was asleep. The plane was half empty and Ryan called me over to an empty seat. "We gotta talk. I shouldn't have pushed you to resign St. Dismas. It would have calmed down in time. One thing I want you to know is that I didn't lie at the trial."

"I never thought that you did."

"What happened is that when Father Walsh told me about the coach, what's his name?"

"Zarth."

"Yeah, Zarth. I just got the homosexual part. He probably told me that they were right out of highschool, but I'd fastened on the homosexual part. The age thing didn't come through to me. So, when I said that I'd told you everything, I really thought I had."

"That's a big relief, thanks. You'll probably get a lot of flack from St. Elizabeth. I just canned half the staff."

"Yeah, Muldoon filled me in. It'll blow over."

Later, he talked to Foley. I guess it was a full apology for putting him out of teaching. Jerry was still sleeping, and Ryan gestured for me to join him and Foley. We talked about Jerry in the sem days, and how he had the same determination. Ryan said,

"I don't know how to thank you guys. I was afraid we'd never get him out."

Foley said, "Hey, not us O Lord, you're the star. How'd you get President Carter to stand by for your call? That was the winning hand."

Ryan chuckled. "That wasn't Jimmy Carter."

"What?!" said both of us in chorus. I imagine my face looked as startled as Foley's.

"There's this young guy who works at the U.S. Bishop's Conference. He's a great mimic. Can do Cardinal O'Brien, Nixon, Ford, me, whomever. Carter was unavailable, so we did the next best thing; we got Frankie Baglio to do the President. We even rehearsed it; we had the group do background conversation; like one guy would say 'General, that just won't do' and 'Mr. Secretary, that's going back to the drawing board'; stuff like that in case Frankie's imitation wasn't perfect. One thing, Frank Baglio is absolutely unflappable. He was doing the Cardinal one time and the real Cardinal happened to pick up the phone. They got in a hot exchange over who was the real Cardinal, so I figured that he wouldn't choke in the clutch."

Foley looked dazed. "I don't believe it!"

I said, "You, Tom, were pretty calm in the clutch yourself. How do you do it?"

"Dealing yearly with 500 assholes like you two gives a guy nerves of steel."

"But you could have gotten yourself in a lot of trouble."

"Wrong tense, George, I still could." Then he used a quote from an old priest, Father Hugh, who, when questioned about his traffic mistakes would say, as Tom did now, "Hell, it's not a federal offense—come to think of it, I guess it is."

The wild absurdity of it hit all three of us then and we laughed until there were tears in our eyes. We woke up Jerry, who asked, "What's so funny?" Ryan put a finger to his mouth; Jerry was not to know this, at least not now.

Ryan said, "Foley's telling dirty jokes in Latin."

Jerry responded, "I could tell you some in Spanish from my fellow prisoners." Then, he fell back asleep. I wondered what would happen if the Colonel found out. Ryan said, "Maybe some trouble, maybe not. It may never be questioned. I think Fritz (Mondale) would cover for me with the president. When the ambassador comes back—well, I know Robert Alban and I don't see him throwing me to the dogs. In addition, who's gonna fault a guy for using a little fancy footwork to save his priest from the torturers?"

I said, "I wonder what the Colonel would have done to us if he'd caught on."

"I was sure the Colonel's political vision was exactly the opposite of mine, but the old military obedience is "not to ask why, but to do and to die." What the hell, I sort of enjoyed it."

Any animosity I ever felt toward Ryan melted away like snow in summer. I knew that I could never have done what Tom had done. We were bone tired when we got out of the plane and were totally unprepared for a large reception committee, including Jerry's mother and family. There were even folk from St. Elizabeth's. Apparently, Colonel Pierce, still under the belief that he was following the President's orders, decided to cash in on it, and had notified Bishop Muldoon. So Muldoon was there and the press as well. I groaned as did Foley; Ryan, however, was up to the occasion. Someone put a mike in front of his face and he praised the help of the administration in rescuing Fox. He said: "I am particularly grateful to Colonel Pierce and his staff without whom we could not have succeeded." I didn't dare look at Foley. Jerry was to go home with his mother, but I asked him, if, despite his fragile health, he could come to St. Elizabeth's on Sunday, not to say Mass, but just to be introduced to the congregation as the new associate. I was being self-serving, in that having seen Fox in his beaten condition, the folks would receive Foxie's fiery homilies, not as some amateur Latin American visitor, but as one who'd experienced the realities. Also, I might as well bask in the rescue role which might redeem me partially for sacking half the staff. Fox got standing ovations at all the weekend Masses.

When I came to the church-offices on Monday, Cynthia Ryan gave me a hug and a kiss. "Behold the conquering hero!" she said.

"How's damage control?" I asked.

"Where should we start? Let's see. Phone calls are running heavily in your favor. You'll have to read your own mail; both Jennifer and Merwin are seeking arbitration from the grievance board. Nothing from Sweeney, and I think you scared off Sam.

Printon quit the council, but not the parish. Some of the choir also quit. Uh—maybe a dozen otherwise. And, of course, your little caper of last week has put a minor halo on your head. So, enjoy! but don't let it go to your head." She laughed her delightful laugh. I sat down and read the letters and returned phone calls. Nothing I couldn't handle. One call was from Beth. I recognized it as a downtown St. Paul number. I dialed it with a slight tremor. "Hospitality House!" was the greeting.

"Beth, what gives?"

"Gotta talk to you. I can't explain all this in a few minutes, but basically I'm, uh—sublimating—I guess my love for a stubborn cleric by helping the poor. I've said that very badly. I can't explain it better on the phone. C'mon down here; I'm on Second, half block from St. Christopher's."

A few days later I did. I sat on a rickety chair in Beth's "office." She had just moved a pile of used clothing which someone had dropped off, from the chair, so I could sit down.

"So," I said, "Hospitality House. After Dorothy Day. How did you get into this business?"

"After we split, I went into a tizzy. I finally sought out a counsellor . . ."

"Beth, did I . . . ?"

"No, stop, please; I'll come to you in a minute. I found that I was unhappy with my life, my job, too. She, the counsellor, got me to see that I was unfulfilled. She got me to read various things and one was a life of Dorothy Day. I was forcing myself through the book, and, I don't know how or why, but I suddenly knew that Dorothy Day's work was what I wanted, no needed. I'll always love you, George, really love you, and this is no—uh—no substitute, but a kind of continuation of our love.

Does this make any sense to you at all?"

"Yeah, I guess so. I'll always love you too, but maybe we've found a way of coping . . ."

"I'm gonna hit you for a contribution before I let you go. I've worn out Ma and Bill asking for money, and Bill's mad at me for exhausting my inheritance on this."

"You say you find it fulfilling?"

"I love these people; I really do. And you are a part of this. You taught me how to love. When I am privileged to help someone here, I'm not doing it out of repentance, if that's what you're thinking; it's not some duty. Did you ever watch Mother Teresa? Look at her face. She's not carrying out some cold law; you can see the love in her face. Well, I'm no Mother Teresa, but this is love, not work."

The sight of Beth in that crummy old hall where she fed and clothed the poor stayed in my head, as did her words. A few weeks later, I was in my rectory counselling a man about to leave his wife. I had promised myself that I wouldn't use the rectory for work, but this man did not want to be seen at my office at church, and I could understand why. He was an usher on Sundays and well-known in the parish. I was counselling, despite Dr. Merwin's dismissal of my counselling background. I had learned to counsel, not professionally, but helpfully, or so I thought. For one thing, I had learned to listen, more than talk or give advice. I mirrored back what Lee Dotson had said to me.

"Now as I understand you, Lee, you truly love your wife, but you also love this new friend. Right?"

"That's why it's so hard to make up my mind. I love 'em both."

In the old days, I would have been giving him a lecture on faithfulness. Now I mostly listened. I was no Moses on a pedestal. I'd made my own mistakes; broke my vow. Who was I to judge? I wondered if I'd run off with Beth, whether I'd have tired of her. I didn't think so. I asked more questions; how long were they married? Did his wife have annoying habits? But mostly I listened, encouraging him especially when he told of his wife's virtues. When he left the rectory late that night, I thought it was all over. He was wrong, of course, but I had a certain sympathy for him. Was it hard to maintain a real love, a passion, through the years? How would I know? I knew the man's wife, too, and I liked her. What was to happen to her? I wished I could do something for them. I guess I really loved them. I had noticed that I had quit counting converts; thirty-four one year, fifty-six the next; how many fallen aways did I bring back this year? That part of my life was gone, thank God. No more quantifying my parochial successes. Maybe, just maybe, like Beth, I was learning to love my people. Maybe, maybe, at last.

Three weeks later, Lee was back to thank me. "Father, you showed me the way. I realized my selfishness. You taught me. Thanks!" I hadn't really. He'd found himself; his true self.

TWELVE

Pinecone Revisited

I never imagined that I'd ever get them all together again. When I invited Ryan, I said, "I suppose that if I invited Cody, you wouldn't come, so I won't."

"On the contrary, I'd love to see him. You don't know our subsequent history. About two years after the trial (and you recall that both you and I had, by then, more or less, won the appeals and had most of the punitive damages reduced) well, he wrote to me explaining that he really believed that the painful suits had forced dioceses to take a better stance on pedophilia.

He added that when he'd asked me about *'Sacerdos in Eternum,'* he was helping his own case, of course, but he was also establishing the dilemma faced by bishops. We have a lifelong responsibility for the priest, whether he messes up or not. To make a long story short, we write back and forth every few years."

And so we gathered at Pinecone Lake in July of 1991, a splendid summer. Fathers Bob and Clem; Archbishop Tom, and laymen now with wives, Bill and Mary Lou, Frank and Rosie, and I had invited Beth. It was a scenario impossible twenty years earlier.

"Oh sure," said Beth, when she heard the sleeping arrangements, "the clergy in the big house and the nuns crammed into the little house. Just like the old days!"

I said, "There is this difference; you're permitted to say that now. Remember, the Church moves slowly, especially in regard to the weaker sex." She hit me playfully. "Weaker sex, indeed, wait until I tell Margaret Thatcher."

"It has been decided by the Holy Spirit and us that you girls—oops—I mean, women prefer to be with your own kind. Therefore..." began Ryan.

Beth cut in, "Now this is the bishop who is going to write the first draft on 'The Place of Women in the Church'."

"As I was saying, from five until seven, we men will be in the main lodge, probing the fundamental issues of our time, while you people, by the lake, will discuss fashions or whatever."

"Two hours drinking time is too long for Frankie," said Rosie.

"At the end of that time, we invite you to join us," continued Ryan, "and George has promised to burn steaks at that hour."

"It is so ordered," finished Cody. And we did.

I began with, "Do you remember the retreat of 1947?"

"The one where you kept interrupting the retreat master?" asked Cody.

Clem said, "You mean the guy who began each conference with, "I knew a priest once...?"

"That was 1948," said Bill.

"'47" I insisted.

"Some of what he said happened," said Cody.

"Forty-two years and it's a whole era," said Foley, "and we've undergone culture-shock. It's amazing that we're all healthy."

Ryan said, "Who among us would have as much as guessed the enormous changes, in church—yes—but in society?"

Foley raised his hand. Ryan groaned. "I might have known."

"He's right, though; remember Cox coming in that night? And he made two predictions, one, that we'd forget that retreat master. He was wrong on that, but the other was that biblical studies, dogma, moral evaluations, etcetera would undergo change."

"And I agreed," said Foley.

Ryan said, "Yeah, and I argued with you."

"What d'ya mean 'that night'? You always argued with me."

"You guys are talking from a church point of view, but take an issue that is heavily church, but also with real consequences in the larger society," said Cody, "I refer to abortion. Who of us would have seen that one coming down the pike?"

"I'm almost afraid to ask your position, Cody," said Ryan.

"I always get the bad guy role," said Frank Cody, as he refilled his martini, "Yes, I would allow it after rape, etcetera, and maybe under some other circumstances. Who knows when there is a human being there?"

I said, "That's just it. Once you start making exceptions, the whole thing goes down the drain."

Clem said, "I think you chose an unfortunate metaphor."

"I think," said Frank, "you bishops are in an unwinnable war. Let's say Roe-Wade is reversed by the court. Then you've got to fight it out state-by-state. Then, if you win most of those, people will go to those remaining states where you lost. You've got to get into the hearts of people."

"I agree with you, Frank," said Foley, "get to the hearts of people, but the law is part of the problem. When the law says, 'it's O.K. to have an abortion,' it's like the whole community saying it's O.K. Sure, inside the Church community, we can try to form consciences against it, but we're waging an uphill battle, because the greater community has approved."

"Who would have thought, when we sat in the rec room at the seminary," began Clem, "what a windstorm of change would come into our seemingly predictable lives. As you guys know, I had trouble with Vatican II. Now it makes sense to me; gotta give credit to a couple of assistants—uh—associates who argued with me until I got it. I'm not as smart as the rest of you."

"Bullshit," said Bob, "you got brains that won't quit. It was an emotional issue with you. You got a military mind; like tell you to take that hill, and off you go. But once you saw that the military model didn't fit the Church, you had the guts to admit your error. Would that all the guys did the same."

"Vatican II was not the whole story," said Bill, "what was more compelling was a series of societal changes. Attitudes toward war, toward sex, toward authority, toward values . . . "

Bob cut in, "Amen. And inside the Church, biblical interpretation, a new moral theology, a new theology generally."

I said, "And a lot less fear!"

Ryan said, "I agree, but it's made my job a helluva lot harder. In the old days, Archbishop Dunn and I were the undisputed voice of God. We could move guys around with a letter. NOW!!"

"And that's not all bad," I said.

Ryan laughed. "If Clem had to change his ecclesiology, I had to revolutionize mine. Bob and George know what I mean." He nodded to the two of us. "I would never have taken Bob out of the seminary, if I wasn't working from a heavily authoritarian model of church. Nor would I have treated George as I did, but it's too late now . . . "

"Oh, we've been through all that long ago," I said. "But I was angry at you; somehow when you rescued Jerry Fox, all my anger just sort of dried up."

Cody said, "I've heard that story in part; tell me more."

So we told him. Cody said, "That's fabulous! but where is he tonight? He should be here; there's way too much sweetness and light around here. I'm sure ole Jer could liven up this entirely too agreeable bunch with some contrariness."

"I did invite him. But he's in some protest march in Washington."

Cody persisted, "Well, then let's invite the women into this discussion. All this saccharine nicety is making me ill."

But the women didn't need the invitation. Beth led the way. As she entered the room, she said, "It has seemed good to the Holy Spirit and her handmaidens that we come here ahead of schedule to enlighten you people of limited outlook on how the real world works."

Bill said, "Hang on to your billfolds. Sis will, at some time tonight, attempt to extract large sums for her work with the derelicts, the more or less willfully unemployed. She has already used up her patrimony on the idle poor, and now threatens to strip my mother and me from ours."

Beth mimicked her brother, "The idle poor! Huh, I'd make a guess, an educated guess, that most of the good people I serve, have done more real work than the rest of you. I mean not just telling other people how they ought to behave, but useful work like food gathering or building houses or factory work."

Cody grinned. "That's more like it. A little more acid in this sugary feast." Beth turned on him. "And as Jesus said, 'Woe to you lawyers!' You guys have already wrecked traffic safety by defending drunks. And have wrecked health care for the country by suing doctors for not being perfect diagnosticians. I won't even mention the Church."

"Sis, this not the right approach for extracting money from the clergy."

Beth went on. "Woe to you realtors who house the rich and ignore the unhoused."

"I wish," said Tom, "that you had listened to my Holy Spirit, who, after all, is ecclesiastically superior to yours, and stayed in the women's quarters until summoned by the proper authorities."

"I hope," said Bob, "that Frank is happy that we've abandoned sweetness and love. Fighting is much more fun. Let me add a little acid to this feast of love. Where do you women stand on your peace-loving sisters in the military who want the right to kill others just like men?"

Rosie spoke, "How many of you have read Penny Lernoux's book, *People of God*?" One hand went up, Foley's.

"Well, most of the feminist literature I've read, I agreed with, but they don't satisfy me with why the Church leaders resist the feminist movement. As I recall, her point was that they don't care how many women leave the Church, as long as some ancient system stays in place."

Ryan started turning red. "I haven't read that book, but I don't buy what you've said. Or what she may have said. Most women of the world aren't asking for change. I think it's an American thing."

"Is that so?" challenged Rosie, "have you interviewed many?"

"Touché!" from Ryan, "but you haven't either."

"Most of them," retorted Beth, "at least in the Third World, are too busy trying not to starve. So other rights are on the back burner." At last, Mary Lou entered the fray. "As, I think, most of you here know, I was sexually molested, so I speak with experience. It's only in the past few years that our complaints have drawn response, and that includes the clergy. George excepted."

"I suppose," began Bob, "that one of us ought to talk about how far we've come, but whether it's evolution or simply change for the worse, it'll go on. We, in the Church, however, have been pushed into the most change; 400 years of an institution frozen in time to a Church suddenly twentieth century."

"This is where I came in," said Cody, "the twentieth century."

"Maybe most of us will get out before it's over," from Bill.

"Except Frank," said Rosie, "only the good die young."

"Am I allowed to say something serious?" asked Cody.

I said, "No, it may be too much of a shock for us oldies."

"Here I am, ex-clergy, but I want to say how important you guys are, and I'll bet Bill agrees; there's a whole wide world out there of pain and sheer hunger, both the kind Beth ministers to, and the spiritual kind, and politicos and doctors and social workers and . . ."

Bill put in, "And lawyers."

"And lawyers," Frank agreed. "We might touch a bit of it, help a piece of it, but only you can give the vision, the overall foundation. Without it, the law, the educational system, yes, the doctors, the total scheme falls apart . . ."

Ryan teased, "You got a place even for bishops?"

"No, but Dante had some space left . . ."

"That's my husband. He couldn't sustain a whole serious paragraph."

I said, "Amen, Frank, but speaking of serious, how do you like your steaks?"

"Answer any way at all," put in Beth, "they'll all come out medium." Then to me, "I'll help."

"You always have." I said, "you always have."

Text design by Ellen Foos.
The Bembo type was set by The Typeworks,
and the book was manufactured by Thomson–Shore, Inc.